THE TEN BEST

How do you select the ten science fiction stories you would call the best of the year? Well, first of all you obtain all the magazines that specialize in fantastic fiction, all the anthologies in hard cover and soft, that contain new sf stories, and you keep an eye on the general magazines that are likely to include good sf occasionally. Then you scan them all—reading quickly—to eliminate the stories that do not quite stand out.

Then go to work and reread carefully each remaining tale. Ask yourself whether it was effective. Did it spark your imagination? Did it convey an original concept or a new twist? Would people remember it after they had forgotten the others?

When you've done this for as many years as Don Wollheim and Art Saha have, you get to know when a story has that special something. That's what it takes to put together this annual selection. *That's why it is the authentic leader.*

Anthologies from DAW

THE 1981 ANNUAL WORLD'S BEST SF

Edited by
DONALD A. WOLLHEIM
with Arthur W. Saha

DAW BOOKS, INC.
DONALD A. WOLLHEIM, PUBLISHER
1633 Broadway, New York, N.Y. 10019

FIRST PRINTING, MAY 1981

1 2 3 4 5 6 7 8 9

DAW TRADEMARK REGISTERED
U.S. PAT. OFF. MARCA
REGISTRADA. HECHO EN U.S.A.

PRINTED IN U.S.A.

Table of Contents

INTRODUCTION

The Chinese have an ancient curse which goes *May you live in interesting times*. Fortunately or unfortunately, depending on whether you are attuned to this century or long for the "good old days," we are living in the most "interesting" times of the whole of human existence. Perhaps this is a curse, perhaps not . . . but the acceleration of change in technology, living, health, and society has never been greater—and continues on its headlong pace.

But as with all such movements of human society there must be adjustments, slowdowns, even backward trends. People who are accustomed to the realization that changes are the order of the day confront the vertigo of swift turns, and the quakes of wondering whether this is all leading to catastrophe, or to some plateau of calm order—or if this acceleration is beyond anyone's control.

Science fiction is a central clearing house for consideration of these things. The imaginations of its writers and its readers extrapolate from the events of the present to speculate on their extensions into the future. There are whole cosmosgonies of those futures ranging through every manner of possibility, the indicators of which are recognizable not only by sf readers but by the general public which has been exposed to them via television and film.

Nevertheless science fiction has a way of reflecting immediate moods and times. In past volumes of these annuals I have noted trends to optimism, to utopianism, and to periods of cautious reflection. Gathering together the material in this volume, such a trend became apparent to me. I would name it terrestrialism. By which I mean that these stories tend to think about the crises and futures of Earth and humanity rather than to dwell on far-flung galactic concepts of colonized worlds and alien beings. In short, this last year writers and the editors of science fiction were more moved by stories that were more "down to earth" than in previous years.

Thus, of the ten stories selected for this annual of tales I regard as the most outstanding, eight take place in reasonably close terrestrial settings, and only two can be called stellar-locale stories. Of those two, the Bradley and the Martin, there also it is human terrestrial values that are basic.

Writers of science fiction still live day to day in today's 1980's world. They do not live in ivory towers nor Tibetan lamaseries. They are not immune to the moods and thoughts of the world around them. Indeed, they cannot help but reflect them.

Because of my role as editor of this annual anthology and because I am also a full-time editor-publisher of science fiction novels, these currents of thought come through perceptibly. I detect them in the year's novels. And last year I noticed a trend toward what I term morbid science fiction, exemplified by such acclaimed novels as *The Shadow of the Torturer, Timescape, On Wings of Song, Jem,* and away from what I would term vibrant science fiction such as *Serpent's Reach, Beyond the Blue Event Horizon, The Ringworld Engineers.*

These are reflections of the turn society is making today. The fact is, I hasten to add, that this morbid turn is still just a counter-current trickle. The bulk of science fiction continues to be socially optimistic.

1980 was a year of change in the publishing world of science fiction too. *Galaxy,* once a prime contender for sf's leader, finally died after a long terminal illness. *Galileo* died with it. *Analog* was finally pushed out of its Condé Nast home and was immediately purchased and continued by the publishers of the magazine that had already outdistanced it in sales and acclaim, *Isaac Asimov's Science Fiction Magazine. Amazing,* having swallowed its twin, *Fantastic,* staggers on. *Fantasy & Science Fiction* maintains its usual high standard of literature—consistently superior to all other periodicals.

Some of the sf book publishers indicated cutbacks in the quantity of sf/fantasy to be published, and at the same time other publishers announced new programs and extended lists, which would indicate some sort of crossed signals in that field! *Omni,* which in 1979 included several sf stories excellent enough to win awards and be anthologized, underwent a disturbing policy change resulting in a fiction list heavily into trivia and ephemera.

The British sf scene seems to be stagnant with no new periodicals raising their heads. In Europe, sf books are booming, especially in Germany, France and Holland, as well as in the Socialist countries. In Spain and Italy the prognosis is shaky, while in Japan sf goes on as strong as ever.

But all over the world, science fiction is thinking in terrestrial terms. There is change going on in economics, politics, social structures, and all speculation is on the meanings of these pressures. The American space program, while glorying in the spectacular results of its Saturn and Jupiter discoveries, is marking time pending the success of its space shuttle. The Soviets push ahead with efforts to keep a space laboratory in orbit and to extend the time its cosmonauts spend out there—as well as planning further Venus exploration probes.

Cautious conservatism seems to be the general order of the day. But watch your local science fiction writer for the first signs of a new spring. . . .

—DONALD A. WOLLHEIM

VARIATION ON A THEME FROM BEETHOVEN

by Sharon Webb

The conservation and development of genius is a prerequisite for human progress. As we go toward solving the problem of longevity, we try to progress in all other spheres as well. But suppose that triumph in one goal negates another equally desirable human aspiration? What if the cost of immortality is universal boredom or universal stagnation, as many philosophers claim. Can there be a way around this?

I.

They brought him before the Committee of Vesta when he was eleven years old. His bladder was tense with pressure and it hurt him. Sweat filmed his palms.

The night before, his name had lighted up on the big dormitory board: DAVID DEFOUR.

He'd never seen it there before.

"You're it," said one of the boys with a knowing look that made him feel childish and ignorant.

"I'm what?" His eyes flicked the question from one boy to another to another. "I'm *what?*"

"You're going to be the one."

"Yes," said another.

"You're going to be punished."

"Why?"

"Because."

"*Why?*"

"Not punished, stupid," said a new voice. "Picked." The new boy, an older boy from upper dorm, put a protective arm around David's shoulder. "They picked you," he said. "You must be special."

"Picked me for what?" But the fear was growing in him, pushing his heart upward to pound and flutter in his throat. He'd heard bits and snatches of gossip before, but he'd ignored it mostly. Now it was coming back to him, but his lips had to ask it—"*What?*"

"Why, you'll be fa-mous," drawled the new boy, clutching his shoulder. "You'll have everything you want. But later on—I guess you'll have to die." The boy's eyes sought his. "I wonder what it would be like—to die."

David thrust his small body away from the boy's restraining arm and ran on lean brown legs to the bathroom.

He wanted to empty his bladder. He wanted to cry.

It was like that now.

The Committee members, all three, wore their mole-gray robes because they were sitting in formal conclave. The tall square-faced woman who was the Chair touched a glass gavel to the soundpad before her. A tone sounded. "David Defour," said the woman, "approach the Chair."

Fear flickered across his thin face. Legs trembled. Knees wobbled.

"Don't be afraid," said the second woman, breaking protocol perhaps because she was kind and perhaps because she remembered what it was like to be eleven and frightened.

He stood before them, looking up at what seemed a great height to the seated members.

The Chair spoke again. "David Defour, do you know why you have been called before the Committee?"

He blinked, pulled in his chin, shook his head almost imperceptibly.

"Is your answer no?"

He summoned his voice, a soprano wavering. "It's no."

"Very well. Member Conway, read the Enlightenment."

Member Conway stared at David with gray steel eyes. Then he looked down and began to read:

"From the first shadows of time, humankind knew that it was mortal. For eons it strived to reach beyond itself. In one sense it failed; in another sense it succeeded magnificently. And always there was the quest.

"The quest led in many directions, meeting success and failure in each.

"Then humankind found ultimate success—and ultimate failure. Because, when humankind killed death in its laboratories, it killed the need for immortality. When death died, so did the Earth's poetry and its music. Philosophy was stilled; Art fell to dust; Science was stifled. Only the echoes remained.

"And so it was that humankind realized that great gains reflect great losses. And so it recognized the need to choose from among its members those few who, when denied their immortality, must create it for themselves to the benefit of all.

"It is for this purpose, David Defour, that you have been summoned here this day. . . ."

Member Conway pierced him with a stare. "Do you accept the responsibility with which humankind charges you?"

Cold winds blew through his small body, chilling his belly, creeping into his bones. He stood trembling, large eyes wide, trying to make sense of what he had heard.

The Chair said, "It is customary, David, to say 'I do'."

His mouth opened, closed, opened again. His voice vibrated in his throat, a captured bee flying out at last. "I do."

"David, I'm here to help ease the transition for you. Do you have any questions?"

He looked at the smooth bland face across the desk, trying to read it, failing—trying to make sense of the bewildering day, failing again.

After the Committee conclave, he had been taken to Medical Level, helpless, while his body was probed intimately until he felt his face grow hot with embarrassment. Sharp metal removed samples of his tissues, his blood. Then the pronouncement: *Decisional time, sixty lunar months.*

They fed him then, and gave him something to drink. He drank gratefully; the food he pushed around his bowl. Then he was brought here, to the bland-faced man with pink cheeks and skin as smooth as cream.

"You won't be staying on Vesta, David. Today you'll leave for Renascence. It's on Earth. You'll live there—" he consulted David's record, "—for sixty months—until Final Decision." The counselor absorbed the look that passed over

David's face. He smiled faintly; he had seen that look before. "You'll like it there, David. Everyone does. You'll prefer it after a time. And at Renascence you'll be with your own kind."

To leave Vesta? The dormitory? Everything he ever knew? He began to shiver. He'd never known another place. They were going to take him away from his home, from the boys he thought of as brothers, from his bed, from Mother Jacobs and Mother Chin. Hot tears pushed against his lashes, held back only by determined blinking.

And his music—Were they going to take that too? Would he be wrenched away from his flute? His cythar? "Please. Let me stay. I won't be in the way."

"We can't do that, David. Tomorrow, the boys you live with begin their treatments. The food you eat, the water you drink will be different from theirs. I'm sorry, but you leave today."

A small voice quivering with despair said, "May I take my things?"

"Mother Chin packed for you. Everything is on board the skiptor now." In answer to the dart of hope in the boy's eyes, the counselor added, "It's all there, David. Your musical instruments, too. Especially those. And you'll find more at Renascence. Much more." He rose abruptly. "Now I think we'd better get you aboard. It's a long trip."

"But I can't go yet. I have to say goodbye."

"No, David. We've found that it's better to make the break clean and quick."

He huddled alone in an enclosed compartment in the skiptor. When the door closed, he stared at it bleakly for a few minutes and then gave way to tears.

The flightman, watching his console, took note and wisely let him cry for a while before he pressed the tone button and activated the boy's viewer.

"Hello, David. I'm Heintz. I'll be here to help you through the trip," said the voice from the screen. "If you'll look to the right of your compartment, you'll see a button marked *water* and another marked *juice*. I recommend the juice. It's pretty good."

He *was* thirsty. He pressed the button and a drinking tube oozed out of the wall. It was good. It quenched his thirst.

Heintz waited until the mild sedative had taken effect. Then he said, "Ever ride a skiptor before?"

David shook his head.

"The captain has just come aboard, David. We'll be leaving in a few minutes. I'll tune your screen so you can see departure, but first I want you to engage the webbing. Press the lever in front of you."

A green light came on under his nose; below it, a small handle protruded. He pushed it and gossamer-light webbing emerged from the compartment walls and enfolded him gently but firmly, leaving only his arms free.

"Good. When we're underway, you can disengage on my signal. In the meantime, feel free to explore your compartment. If you want me, press the button over your head marked *Attendant*."

The screen went blank.

Just over his head, a bank of buttons gleamed silver. One said *Music*. He pressed it and a numbered selector presented itself. Indecisively, he pushed a random code and lay back, closing his eyes. The soft strains of a plucked cythar began, followed by the swelling of a senti'cello. An arrangement of a very old piano piece, he thought. What was it? He'd heard it before in his music history class, but the name, the composer, eluded him. The music, inexpressibly sad, seemed to enfold him. He burrowed two brown fists in his eyes to stop the flow of warm tears, but they ran through his curved fingers and traced their way to his chin, as Beethoven's Pathetique played through its silver tape.

A light voice shocked him. "Having a cry? So are all the rest." A sigh. "How boring." A girl about his age peered at him from the visiscreen. Her eyes were frank and blue and a nutmeg sprinkle of freckles dotted her nose. "I hoped you'd be different."

"I'm not crying." He rubbed his eyes vigorously in denial. "I was about to take a nap." He yawned elaborately, sneaking a look at the girl's face. "Who are you?"

"Liss. What's *your* name?"

"David. Where are you?"

"Compartment seventeen. You're in eight."

"I thought I was alone."

The girl giggled. "Do you have a vacuum between your ears?"

The giggle made him bridle. "What do you mean?"

"You didn't think the skiptor was making a trip just for you, did you?"

"Well, no—" His chin jutted out just a bit.

"You *did*." She giggled again.

Who did she think she was, anyway? "Why don't you flash off." He reached for the privacy button.

"Wait—Don't shut me out. Wait. Please?"

The touch of panic in her voice made him stop, hand on the button.

"Please," she said, "I want to talk awhile . . . I'm lonesome."

He looked at her for a long moment. "Where are *you* going?"

"Same place you are."

"How do you know where I'm going?"

"I have ways. Wait—Hear that? We're leaving."

The subliminal hum he'd heard since boarding gave way to a heavy vibration that he felt more than heard.

"The bays are opening," she said. "Look."

The girl's face on the visiscreen shrank to a ten centimeter oval in one corner. The rest of the screen filled with a view of the massive bays of Vesta jutting into hard vacuum. A million star points pierced the black of space.

A lump formed in his throat that wouldn't swallow away. He was really going. Leaving his home—perhaps forever.

"Are you going to cry again?"

He mustered up a scoop of righteous scorn. "No."

"Good. I don't think I could stand that. Watch—We're free."

The last vestige of the bay doors slipped away. Nothing but black and star fire now on his screen—and a ten-centimeter image of a freckle-faced girl.

"We'll be able to disengage webbing soon," she said.

"How come you know so much?" he demanded. He found her annoying and yet at the same time infinitely comforting to talk to, and he didn't quite know where to place his feelings.

"Experience," she said. "I've done all this before."

Skepticism rose. "When?"

"This morning. I was first aboard from Hoffmeir."

"Hoffmeir!"

"Yes. You didn't think they just picked from Vesta, did you?"

He shook his head. He hadn't thought about it at all.

"We stopped next at Hebe. Then we came to Vesta. This is my third departure," she said with the air of a seasoned belt-hopper.

"Oh. How many of us are there?"

"Nine, so far, in the aft compartments. Forward is full of grownups on business trips and vacations. I'm not interested in them. What's your talent?"

"Music."

"I'm going to be a writer. I read all the time. I've even read out of the archives. And I have an enormous vocabulary." She looked at him speculatively. "Most of the music people I've known are inordinately sensitive. Are you?"

He didn't know how to answer.

"I think you probably are, too. I expect you've been sheltered, so I'll try and take you in hand. You'll need somebody like me in Renascence."

"I don't *need* anybody."

She sighed. "I don't mean to be blunt. I just can't seem to help it. But you seem to be so helpless—"

He shut off the screen for a full five minutes until loneliness threatened to overwhelm him. He switched on the screen again, thumbing for compartment 17. "Liss?" he whispered. "Liss?"

Her face appeared—freckled, pink, and a little puffy around the eyes. Her cheeks showed tear tracks. "Are you going to talk to me, David?" she asked meekly.

"I guess so."

Her chin quivered slightly. "I'm sorry I made you mad."

"It's all right."

"I just say too much. I always have. I don't mean anything by it."

The steady, but almost imperceptible, acceleration suddenly gave way. "Freefall," said Liss.

The compartment light came on as Heintz's voice said, "Passengers may disengage webbing."

David pulled the lever in front of him. Most of the restraining webbing retracted, leaving him with a slightly elastic tether in its place. He found he could move around freely bounding gently off the padded walls of the little compartment. It quickly turned into a game. One, two (ceiling, wall), three, four (wall, wall) five, six (seat, wall).

He rolled himself into a ball, arms wrapped around his knees. If he pushed off the seat with his toes just so, his rump would impact on the ceiling, aiming him back to the seat. Ceiling, seat, ceiling. A little off center, he caromed toward the visiscreen. Stopped short of impact by the restraining

leash, he saw Liss on the screen rebounding too, like a bal-
loon in a wind shaft.

Heintz, watching from his console, chuckled, shaking his
head. He'd never encountered a kid who didn't discover that
game sooner or later. Natural-born trait he guessed. He'd
never failed to see the aftermath either.

In a few minutes, a slightly green David and a pale and
sweaty Liss clung to their seats with one trembling hand
while the other reached for the *Attendant* button.

"I'm way ahead of you, kids." Heintz pressed the lever for
cabins eight and seventeen, and a cloud of Neutravert
sprayed into the compartments. "Take slow, deep breaths."
Within thirty seconds, David's nausea was gone, and so was a
lot of his starch. "I think I'm going to take a nap now," he
said to the image on the screen.

"Me too." And in a moment, "Night, David."

"Night, Liss."

Hands stretching out toward visiscreens as if to touch each
other, they slept until time to engage the webbing for the
landing on Earth.

They debarked at Atlantic-Biscayne Terminal in the middle
of a hot blue morning. David's eyes, dazzled by the cut-glass
reflections of the ocean, narrowed to slits. Nearby waves
broke over the clear bubble-shields of the shopping centers
and the econdos that had sprung up in the wake of the man-
made island terminal. Miles away to the west, the skyline of
Miami Beach emerged like a steel oasis from the sea.

Though it was a hot day, he shivered at the sight of the
ocean. Nothing he had seen prepared him for it, nothing he
had smelled. . . . The odor of the sea clung to his nostrils.
The salt air pressed heavily on his body and seemed to resist
the movement in and out of his lungs. A fine film of sweat
beaded his forehead.

A woman in a blue uniform was saying something. ". . .
but you'll acclimate soon. We'll proceed at once to the hover.
We'll arrive at Renascence after lunch."

He saw Liss and moved toward her. She was taller than he
was, bigger than he thought she'd be. Stricken with sudden
shyness, he turned away and pretended to look at the ocean.
After a moment, her hand took his. It felt warm and friendly
to him.

On Earth-heavy legs that shook with effort after a few meters, they walked the short distance to the zontilator marked "Hover Boarding."

"This food is guckish," said Liss, wrinkling her nose in distaste.

He knew what she meant. So far, Earth food seemed wild and—well, *Earthish* compared to his diet on Vesta. And the water had a taste to it like metal.

"I guess we'll have to get used to it." Liss pushed her plate away and maneuvered herself into a more comfortable position in the hover seat next to him. Her arm pressed against his, plump and soft against his bony one. David tentatively decided that he liked it. He discovered that girls smelled different from boys, and he wondered why he'd never noticed it before. But then he hadn't paid much attention to girls up to now. He'd always found them exasperating and not worth bothering with. And Liss was certainly exasperating, but she was nice to be around too—in a way. He decided that Liss was all right. She probably wasn't a typical girl at all. He wondered if all the girls from Hoffmeir were like her.

"What was it like back home?" he asked.

"You mean compared to Vesta? Well, Hoffmeir is much smaller, of course, and newer, as you might expect of a man-made habitat, but we live inside just like you did on Vesta. And the people of Hoffmeir are ever so much more intelligent."

He faced her in surprise, pushing away her plump little arm in the process. "What are you talking about?"

"It's true. Everybody knows that Vestans are just technicians. There's variety on Hoffmeir. Why, the university alone is the best in the system. It says so in the archives. Besides, in a small select society like Hoffmeir, there's a premium on brains."

She'd almost had him fooled. She was a typical girl all right. In fact, she was so typical she was outstanding. He bet Hoffmeir was full of space-brained girls just like her. His voice dripped scorn. "I bet any *one* in my dorm is twice as smart as you."

"You lived in a dorm?" Her eyes widened, then crinkled at the corners. "Oh, of course."

"What do you mean, 'of course'? Where did *you* live?"

"With my parents."

He felt his mouth drop open. "Lie." She really must think he was stupid to believe a story like that. *Nobody* knew his parents until the day they welcomed him into the community of adults. A two-year-old would have better sense than to tell such a tale.

"It's not a lie. I knew Vestans weren't so intelligent, but you're proof that they're stupid."

"*I'm* stupid!"

"Yes, you are." She fumbled at her belt and drew out a little holo cube. "Look at it."

He thumbed the light on. A smiling man and woman sat at a table decorated with green Renewal Day light cubes. A girl—Liss—entered, carrying a ceremonial vinifountain. She set it down before them and the tall man drew three drinks from it. Their hands raised in a formal toast.

A three-dimensional greeting floated by:

> To our daughter on this day of rejoicing.
> May she find her way, and well.

David stared at the holo in disbelief.

"Now do you believe me?"

"I don't understand—" he began. "Why—How do you—" He stopped, not knowing how to phrase all the questions in his head. Only officials and a handful of others were allowed to reproduce themselves to begin with, but they never raised the child themselves. It just wasn't done. Finally, he said, "They must be very important."

"They are." She drew her shoulders back slightly. "My father painted the official portrait of Prime Minister Gerstein. And my mother is poet-laureate of the belt—including your precious Vesta."

One eyebrow rose, questioning. "Then, if they do that, that means—That means—"

"Yes," she said. "They're mortals."

The hover suddenly plunged below the cloud cover. "Look!" Liss's nose pressed against the curving window followed quickly by David's. A rumpled green rug of mountains stretched below them.

The hover swooped between two mountains, skimming through a narrow pass, dipping again, following a silver curving streak that plunged down a stony gorge, finally leveling in a wild wooded valley.

David felt giddy with the flight and slightly drunk with exhilaration. Nothing he'd ever experienced, not freefall in the skiptor, not anything, compared to it.

The hover dropped again, barely missing the tree tops. The silver streak became a river bounding over the rocks in its path. Ahead, the trees thinned to a small clearing. The forward rush of the hover ceased as it began its gentle vertical drop.

There were people waiting for them.

The man who had taken him in tow said, "We want you to rest today. Rather than gather you all together to listen to boring speeches, we've arranged private orientations."

They were walking along a winding gravel path through deep woods. Alongside, a bright stream jumped from stone to stone, gurgling and chuckling its way to the river. Here and there, small wooden buildings sprouted like brown mushrooms under the trees.

The effort of walking, of drawing breaths from the heavy air, was almost too much. He felt his knees buckle. A firm hand caught him, steadied him. "Here we are." The man pushed open the door to one of the little units.

The cabin was a single room with a tiny bath just off one end. A bed cylinder lay rolled against one wall. The man pushed a lever and it opened. "Rest awhile, David. Later—" he indicated the communications bank against the opposite wall "—you'll learn more about Renascence. After you've rested, someone will come to take you to dinner."

The man smiled and ran a large hand through the boy's hair. "I know how confusing it is, David. I know how you feel."

He looked up in surprise and disbelief. No one could *really* know how he felt.

The man looked at him, but it was as if David weren't there at all for a moment. Then he said, "This was my cabin, too. Twenty-two years ago."

He was too tired, too unsettled, to sleep. Like a wooden thing, he lay on the little bed and looked dully around him. The windows were open and the warm heavy air pressed into the room bringing strange smells and sounds. Once a bird called, and he started at the sound of it, trying to catalogue it in his mind. The only birds on Vesta were the chickens and ducks of Sustenance Level, and the empty holo images from Education.

The sun, coming through the window, laid a rectangle of light like dusty yellow chalk in the center of the room. In the rectangle stood a graceful music stand with manuscripts arranged on it. His own cythar and his flute sat next to the stand. He felt grateful for them, as if they represented a continuity in his life.

Across the room, attached to the communications bank, was a triple keyboard. Did it have amplifier bars? Curiosity propelled him to his feet and across the room. Amplifier bars. He couldn't believe it. There was only one symphosizer on Vesta that could compare with it. His own—the one they'd let him use—was like a toy compared to this one.

He stood before it, fingers poised, afraid to touch it, but tempted beyond redemption. He pressed the control marked "soloboe," and played a fragment of melody that had run through his head for a while. The symphosizer echoed in a plaintive reedy voice. "Remember," he said under his breath, pressing the "store" control. The bassoon was next, no—two bassoons—rollicking drolly in the lower registers. "Now. Together." The trio echoed in the little room. David, listening critically, pressed "delay," then the code for bassoon I and II. "Repeat," he said to himself. Better, he thought, dark eyes shining at the sound filling the cabin. Better. He stored it all, marveling at the intricacies of the symphosizer. It could cut out dozens of mechanical, uncreative steps. No more delays between the idea and the realization.

He activated the bassoon voices again, playing one against the other in an argument. The voices rose and he giggled at the strident duck squawks. Now a chase—A crash. A cartoon ending—two irate bassoons with duck mouths—tumbling over and over each other, protesting wildly until they were out of breath, their squawks subsiding to disgruntled, infrequent quacks.

An idea came. He held the sensor to his throat and sub-vocaled, "Duck-eater, duck-eater, duck-eater, duck-eater." He pressed an amplifier bar, sighing it . . . *d--u--c--k--e--a--t--e--r*. Now, chop it . . . *d'd'd'd'K--e--a--t--e--r*.

He played with the controls until he had his monster galumphing after the bassoon ducks. It started with a flat-footed walk in the lower registers: *D'D'Kuh*. Ominous. He keyed in the ducks in a low-pitched quack.

D'D'Kuh, D'D'Kuh.

Then a sighing, *e--a--t--t--t*.

Roll it down seventeen tones—*E--a--t--e--r-r-r!*

D'D'Kuh.

Nervous duck quacks, and then the chase: *D'D'Kuh. E--a--t-e-r-r-r-KUK---smeer-PING.*

It ended with a deliciously horrible duck scream and the monster's sighing, *E---a---t--t--t.*

Visions of swirling duck feathers floated in his head. Tickled at the image he'd evoked, he laughed out loud.

"Good afternoon, David," said a male voice from the communicator.

Startled, he looked up.

"We're going to begin your orientation now. Watch the viewer, please."

The image of a satellite map came on the viewer. "The skiptor landed here . . ." An enlargement of the map, then the scene at Biscayne-Atlantic. "You boarded the hover and arrived here." The green mountains appeared—pinpointed on the satmap. "You are in an area known as the Blood Mountain Wilderness, part of the North American continent once known as Georgia. The wilderness area is over 4000 square kilometers of which Renascence is allowed the use of 180 square kilometers." The image focused on a small area.

David recognized the brown cabins near the landing site.

"You are here, in dwelling six."

Actual images gave way to a stylized map showing study center, dining halls and a large recreational lake. At the edge of the lake, a series of performance halls were displayed.

"You'll soon learn your way around, David. Now, we want to tell you a little about Renascence. You were brought here, as were the others, with very little information about this operation. This is the way it was planned. We want each of you to discover for yourself what our life is like. Although your arrival was abrupt, and your discomfort acute, it has enabled you to look at your new life without preconceived attitudes and prejudices.

"We live a simple life here. Simple, but enriching. You will find complexity enough in your work and in the interactions with your teachers and your peers. This, too, is deliberate. We have sought to form an environment conducive to creativity and one which, we hope, simulates an earlier, simpler time when all humankind faced an abbreviated life span.

"While you are here, you will learn more than the discipline of your art. At Renascence, you will learn a reverence for the ideas and the cultures which humankind has pursued throughout its history.

"Each of you has received a Final Decision time. In your case, David, the time is sixty lunar months. In sixty months, if you decide not to remain with us, you may make your Final Decision for immortality treatments. Beyond that time, your body will have matured too much for treatments to begin.

"We, of course, hope that during your stay here you will choose to remain. However, if you decide to leave us, there will be no reproaches, and no disgrace whatsoever.

"You will be meeting your teachers soon, David. If you have questions, the communicator will answer them."

The voice fell silent.

A sharp tap on the door, and then it opened. "I'm exploring," said Liss closing the door behind her.

"How did you know where I was?"

"Easy. I asked the communicator. Come here and I'll show you where I'm staying." She pointed out the window to the creek, nearly hidden beyond a clump of dark graceful trees. "See those trees? The communicator says they're hemlocks. Anyway, just beyond, there's a little foot bridge. After you cross, there's a path right to my door." She giggled. "It's a little like the witch's house in Hansel and Gretel, don't you think?"

He looked at her blankly.

She searched his face and sighed. "Don't you know anything about mythology?" She shook her head. "Technicians. Well, I'll just have to take you in hand and—" She stopped. "I'm doing it again, aren't I? I'm sorry. Please don't squinch your face up at me like that. It gives me the wooly-woolies."

She seemed so distressed, and so sincere, he felt his face relax and a smile grow there. "All right."

"I really would like to tell you about Hansel and Gretel though. That is," she added quickly, "if you want to hear it."

"Well, go ahead then."

"Oh, not now. Tonight. It's a bedtime story. Show me your thngs," she said. She pointed to the symphosizer. "What's that?"

He told her how it worked.

"Interesting," she admitted. "Then you can work two ways just like I can."

"What do you mean?"

"Well, my cabin has a processor on the communicator. I can use that to write, but in the middle of the room, about where that music stand of yours is, sits the funniest thing. It's a tall piece of furniture with a slopey top. And it has a *stool* drawn up to sit on."

"What are you supposed to do *there*?" he asked.

"Write." She watched for his reaction, giggling when the puzzlement spread over his face. "There's a stack of paper and pens on the desk. Can you imagine something so primitive? I asked the communicator about it. Did you know that in the olden days lots of writers actually wrote that way?"

He shook his head.

"I think I might try it. It's rather romantic, don't you think? Anyway, I see that you have the same arrangement here." She walked up to the music stand. "What's this?"

David examined the sheets. Some were blank except for the musical staff printed on them. Others were compositions for cythar and for flute.

"How does this sound?" asked Liss, picking up a sheet at random.

He looked at it in surprise; it was titled, "David's Song." The composer was somebody called T. Rolfe. He fitted his flute together and began to play, slowly at first, for it was a difficult piece, then faster, more fluently as he began to feel the mood of the music.

"That's beautiful," said Liss as he finished.

"I agree," said the woman at the door who had entered unnoticed. "I can't imagine it played with more feeling."

David looked up with a flush of pleasure. The pleasure died when he saw her, and cold things crept on spider legs in his belly.

The woman was old. Old in a way that David had never seen. She was small and stooped. Wise dark eyes burned from a face encased in wrinkled, wilted flesh. Her hair fluttered in wild gray-white strands around her head. Sagging skin made jaw and throat a continuous webbed mass. He shuddered.

"I heard you playing the song I wrote for you," she said, "and so I stopped in. I'm going to be your teacher, David."

While he stood dumbly by, Liss said, "Oh, then you're T. Rolfe."

"Tanya."

"Will David learn to write music like you?"

The old woman smiled, increasing tenfold the wrinkles wreathing her face, cornering her mouth and her eyes. "We'll see."

When she'd gone, David still stood silent, contemplating the apparition of age.

"She's nice," said Liss. "Don't you think so?"

He looked at her, stricken. "She's—She's ugly."

"She's just old," said Liss. "She must be nearly a hundred."

Nearly a hundred! Smooth-faced Mother Chin at his dormitory was nearly two hundred. Mother Jacobs was older yet. He felt his jaw clench. "How can they do it? How can they?"

She touched his shoulder, patted it. "I'm sorry. I forgot. You've never seen mortals before, have you?"

He shook his head miserably. Then he looked at her for a long time. "You're not afraid of it, are you, Liss?"

Surprise flickered over her face. "Why, no. I guess I'm not. And now," she said briskly, "I suggest we investigate supper. I expect it will be guckish, but right now, I don't even care."

Later that night, he lay alone in his cabin, as miserable and skittish as a pup away from its litter mates for the first time. Far away, an owl called. Nearby, another answered. Startled, he sat up, looking through the window into deep shadows and moonlight. Nothing stirred.

Uneasily, he lay back. He wanted to be home, tucked into his bed in the middle row between Jeremy and Martin, lulled by soft snores and muffled sleep sounds. He wouldn't stay here. He wouldn't. Not even if they *tortured* him.

Slowly exhaustion and sleep overtook him.

He dreamed of walking alone in brooding woods. After a time, he knew that he was lost. He panicked and began to run until he came to a clump of trees and a foot bridge over the creek. His feet thrumming on the little path, he ran, calling "Liss. Liss." The door to the cabin—the wicked witch's house—fell open. Tanya Rolfe stood in the doorway beckoning with hands like claws.

He stirred and muttered in his sleep. Outside his window an owl swooped on silent wings, its talons pinioning a small gray mouse.

INTERLUDE

David stared at the corrections Tanya Rolfe had made on his composition. It wasn't any use. In the three years he'd been on the Earth, he'd never got back a score without those hated corrections. He crumpled the sheets in his hand and threw them to the floor.

The old woman shook her head slowly. "David, David. You are here to learn. You *are* learning, but you are like a young plant not yet grown. It's too soon to expect a harvest."

Too soon, always too soon. He waited for her next line.

"You must crawl before you can walk, David. Walk, before you can run." The old woman looked at him sharply, then she laughed. "You hate my platitudes nearly as much as my corrections."

His shin jutted defiantly.

"Oh, David. You're always so impatient. We can only lay a foundation here. Your music has to grow—to mature as you mature. It may take half a lifetime before you compose something of enduring value. Perhaps longer. Perhaps never." She touched the communicator controls and received another print-out of his piece. "Let's start again, David, from this measure. Now this is a good beginning, but you take it nowhere. . . ."

He heard her voice going over the piece, but her words didn't register. What she'd said before kept repeating itself in his brain:

Half a lifetime. Perhaps longer. Perhaps never.

II.

He tapped at the door of Tanya Rolfe's cottage. There was a sound of chair scraping against floor, then a voice, "Come in."

The wrinkled face moved in a smile. "Good morning, David. I've been expecting you to come by to see me."

"But how? Today isn't my lesson."

"No." The dark eyes looked at him keenly. "But most of my boys and girls come when they reach this point. Come and sit with me, David. Have a cup of tea." She took his firm hand in hers, drew him to a chair, and poured strong tea from a thin old china pot.

The odor of sassafras and lemon rose from the cup. It seemed to him as he sipped from it that Tanya Rolfe was like her teapot—crazed and fragile with age, but filled with good strong stuff that warmed him.

"Your Final Decision comes soon, doesn't it?"

He nodded. "Tomorrow."

"So soon?" She sighed deeply, her breath running out in

reedy tones. "I thought a month, perhaps, or two. So soon."
A veil seemed to come over her eyes for a moment, a fleeting
look of vulnerability.

He wondered that he'd missed it before. How had he
missed seeing how fragile she'd become the last few years?
Her hand on the cup was translucent porcelain, patterned
with thin blue veins. In dismay, he realized that he'd not really *seen* her before. He hadn't heard the faint rattle of air as it
moved in and out of her lungs. Hadn't noticed the swelling of
instep and ankle above her tiny feet. Hadn't seen the effort in
her movements. He clenched his fist, feeling nails bite into his
palm.

She set down the cup and took his hand in hers, opening it,
relaxing the curved fingers. "You want to know what will
happen to your music if you decide to leave us."

He nodded.

"You're a highly skilled musician, David. You have technique that can improve with time and maturity. You have
talent, too. You're musical. But you have something more—"
She paused, looking through the window at something that
lay far beyond the scope of her eyes. "It's something called
'The Divine Discontent.' *I* think of it as a yearning to move
outside of myself—to be a part of something more, something greater, and yet to still be uniquely Tanya Rolfe.

"It's the discontent of a sapient wave lapping on a beach,
shifting the sands, and knowing that when it is gone, another
will wipe out all traces of its path. And it feels rage—" A
touch of passion edged her voice. "Rage." Then she laughed
softly. "Some call it the thumb-scratch syndrome."

He looked at her, puzzled.

"We're transients too. Like the waves, our comings and go-
ings change the face of the earth. But it isn't enough. We feel
the need to personally scratch the face of eternity—deep
enough to leave a scar. Proof, you see, that we've been here."

"And if I'm *always* going to be here—"

"Then, there goes your motivation. Immortality is a sure
cure for the thumbscratch syndrome."

"But if I did—"

"You'd still be clever, David. And competent. But you'd
be striking a cooling iron. And after a while, it wouldn't matter to you."

He nodded, stood, walked to the door, then turned. "Has it
always happened like that? Is it for sure?"

"I can't say that the spark *must* go out. But it always has,

David." Her hand, gentle as a moth, touched his shoulder. "It always has."

He moved up the hill, feeling his leg muscles strain, feeling his breath come in short gasps. Sunlight, filtering the new leaves of May, dappled the spongy forest floor beneath his feet.

He sought a high crest, a place where he could overlook Renascence. He wanted to see it all, for once. If he could see it all, maybe he could make it fit together in his mind.

He stepped over a rotting tree trunk in his path and froze. Glittering death coiled by his foot. He heard the warning rattle with only part of his brain. Another part observed, actively orchestrating his fear . . . a rattling maraca; a tom-tom mimicking the beat of his heart. Accelerando. Silence. A silence whimpering in his mind at 440 cycles per second—increasing to a scream—ten thousand cycles, twenty, more. Pulsating beyond the audible range. Felt.

If it struck, if its fangs entered a vein, an artery, he was too far from help.

His muscles contracted. He sprang, running through the open woods to a raucous brass accompaniment in his head, running with a tom-tom throbbing against his chest, his throat.

Had it struck? Would he feel it, if it had?

Reason told him he was safe; fear thrust him ahead. His muscles propelled him on. He ran until his body rebelled and withdrew his strength and his breath. He fell in a heap at the foot of a wide oak, leaning his back against it for support.

"Coward," he said aloud to himself when he had breath. "Coward." But part of him rankled in defense. What else could he do? He didn't want to die.

He didn't want to die.

He made his way back down the mountain to the stream by the clearing. A tall reed-thin boy pressed wet clay in spiraling shapes on a flat stone emerging from the shallow water. He looked up. "Ah, David. Been up the mountain?"

It was more than a casual phrase. Sooner or later, nearly everyone made that trek, alone—as if it were a biological need like food or water, as if the mountain held answers that the valley couldn't. David nodded. "Been up the mountain, M'kumbe."

"Does the air breathe softer there?" The tension in the

question revealed itself in the long black fingers kneading the slick clay.

He didn't know how to answer.

The black eyes looked into his, the fingers moved. "I build my own—here." The lump of clay rose against the pressure of the boy's hands and grew ridged like a naked spine against the rock. "It rises, it falls. I can be a god to this little mountain. But in the end, it's only clay." He brought down his fist, smashing the earthen spine. Then he smoothed it into a flat cake, blending it with pale pink palms and long black fingers, bisecting it with a curving 'S.' "Up and down. Yin and Yang." The fingers stopped for a moment. "Liss is looking for you. She's looked all morning."

He found her in her cabin, sitting on the old tall stool in front of her desk, writing.

"A poem?" he asked.

"A letter. To myself." She wrote a few moments longer, then laid the pen down and looked up. "It's a thought-straightener."

"Three people told me you wanted to talk to me."

"I do. But right now, let's walk." She slipped off the stool and picked up a small split oak basket that sat in the corner of the room. "The blackberries are out." She swept out of the cabin and was halfway over the foot bridge before he caught up with her.

"What's wrong?"

"Nothing." She looked at a point just over his head, as if she found it of utmost importance.

He took her shoulders, turning her toward him. "What's wrong, Liss?"

She twisted the little basket from side to side in her hand. "Nothing. I've just developed a taste for blackberries." Her chin thrust defiantly, but she avoided his eyes. "I like them so well, in fact, that I've decided I want to eat them forever."

His hands slowly dropped to his sides. He leaned up against the railing of the little bridge, trying to think. Of all the people here, Liss had been the most sure.

Her lips turned up at the corners, but her eyes didn't match. "There's an old saying, David: 'It's a woman's prerogative to change her mind.' Ever heard it?"

He shook his head.

A slight crinkle grew around her eyes. "Technician." And then the old joke, "I'm going to have to take you in hand."

They began to walk. They walked for quite awhile before they came to the rambling patch of blackberry bushes, before he said, "Why, Liss?"

Her hands flew among the brambles, picking soft ripe berries, staining the basket and her fingers purple. Without answering, she reached for a cluster deep within a bush, and with a little cry, drew out her hand, empty. A deep scratch curved across the skin, and tiny drops of blood appeared here and there, merging into a red line. She began to cry, all out of proportion to the hurt, shoulders heaving, little snub nose turning red and snuffly.

He watched her, feeling utterly helpless.

The basket fell to the ground, spilling berries into the grass, and still she cried, curving her hands into fists. And then, between breathless racking sobs, she said, "Don't you know anything? Don't you know *anything*?"

He stood accused, not knowing of what.

"Technician." She drew in a huge snuffling breath. "You're supposed to comfort me. It says so in all the books."

Dismayed, he reached out awkwardly and patted her head, ruffling her soft hair under his fingers.

Unaccountably, she began to laugh. It started halfway between a giggle and a gasp. Then it grew to madhouse proportions, until she had to sit down in the warm new grass. It was infectious and he found himself on the ground beside her, laughing too. Hugging her, laughing, then kissing in a heap of scattered blackberries. And it seemed to him then that maybe they were both crazy, but it didn't matter.

Tossing their clothes in a purple-stained tangle, they clung together, rolling on the soft warm ground, pressing together with cool flesh and frantic need. Later, laughing at the purple stains on their bodies, they ran naked down the path to the lake and plunged into the frigid, heart-stopping water.

After they dressed, they walked in the sunlight, briskly at first, trying to warm up. They took the high path back along the broad back of a ridge. Below them, they could see the clearing.

In the sharp blue sky, a line grew to the shape of a disc. "Look," said Liss. "The hover. Let's watch."

The hover stopped its forward surge and dropped gently to the floor of the valley. The doors opened, disgorging a cargo of seven children.

"Do you remember the day we came, David?"

He nodded, watching the little group. One boy stood apart from the rest, shoulders back, legs slightly apart, looking braver than he could possibly feel. Another looked around with eyes as big as the landscape he tried to take in. They seemed so little.

She echoed his thoughts. "Were we ever that small?"

"I suppose we were."

"It must have been harder for you," she said. "You were plucked out of a dormitory and brought here. I never lived that way—there were just me and my parents. I was used to being alone back at home. But, you know, I think you did better than I did." She sat down, drawing her arms around her knees. "I've found out that I need people around me. You found out that you didn't."

He felt an eyebrow raise.

She laughed, crinkling her nose at him. "Well," she said coyly, "*sometimes* you need people. But most of the time you're buried in that cabin of yours like an ingrown nail in a toe."

"Is that your poetic opinion?"

"It may not be poetic, but it is decidedly my opinion. I don't think you know half of what goes on here."

"Such as what?"

Her eyes clouded. "Did you know Tanya Rolfe is dying?"

The words caught him like a fist in the stomach. "How do you know?" But he was remembering how frail she'd looked that morning, remembering the sound of her breath slipping from her lungs.

"I had to rewrite her obituary."

The word puzzled him.

"Her death-notice. It's an old custom in journalism—the writers still observe it here. When someone is important, we keep an obituary in the communicator in case they die suddenly. Hers was out of date. Her new conserere had to be added to it, and several sonatas.

"They told me to do it right away. Anyway, you know how I can't seem to keep from meddling—" She looked up at him. "One question seemed to bring up another, so I coded the communicator for her medical file."

"Is that why you decided to—eat blackberries forever?"

She shook her head. "Not really." She reached her hand up to him. "Help me up. Walk me back to my cabin and I'll show you."

He reached out a hand to her and pulled her to her feet.

They walked down the curving path, not talking, not feeling the need to talk, until they came to the old foot bridge that led to Liss's cabin.

"We didn't get any blackberries, did we?" she said at last, looking at the empty stained basket.

"You'll have a long time for that."

"Will you?"

He pushed open the door to the cabin, striding ahead of her. "I don't know."

She walked to the tall desk and rummaged through a stack of papers, drawing one out. "Read this."

"Your letter to yourself?"

She shook her head. "A poem."

He read, thrumming the cadences with fingers tapping against his knee.

"What do you think?" she asked when he finished. "Be honest."

"I'm always honest," he said.

"I know you are. That's why I wanted you to read it."

"But I'm not a poet."

She sank into a chair next to him and stared at the wide planked floor.

He looked at her for a moment, then he said, "It seems to be quite good. Technically, you've done well and your imagery is—"

"Pedestrian."

"I didn't say that."

"You didn't need to. I can see it in your face."

"I told you I'm not a poet."

"Neither am I." She took the paper from him and folded it in half, creasing the edges with a thumbnail. "I'm a little slow. It took me a long time to find out. But, now that I know, there's no point in drawing it out, is there?"

He considered his words carefully. Then he said, "You have to give yourself time, Liss. We all do. It doesn't come all at once."

"I *have* decided to give myself time. All the time in the world."

"Are you sure?"

"I've thought about it a lot. I'm glib. I'm clever. I have a knack with words. That doesn't make me a poet, David. Not even a fledgling poet. It just isn't there. If I could live forever and not lose whatever creative drive I have—it still wouldn't be enough. I could write until this cabin fell away to dust—"

She swept her arm toward the window, "—until these mountains crumbled. And it wouldn't matter." Her face twisted. "It's not easy to finally admit to yourself what should have been obvious."

He pulled her to him awkwardly, cradling her head against his shoulder. "What are you going to do now?"

After a few minutes, she sat up. "I have nearly a month to go before my Final Decision, but that won't change anything." She looked at him sharply. "I can still write, you know. Derivative stuff, non-fiction, so on. I suppose I'll do that. I'm basically a compiler anyway. I'm good at it. Not many people are."

She stood up, smoothing her clothes. Then she walked to the tiny dispenser, punched a lever, and extracted two containers of juice. "In a way, it's a relief. I don't have to prove myself anymore." She handed him one and drank deeply from the other. "I don't have to do anything, except *be*."

He fingered the juice container, wondering what to say to her, saying nothing.

She sat down beside him. "It's funny the way things work out, isn't it?" Her face moved in a wispy little smile. "I never thought it would turn out that *I'd* be the technician."

Liss ate with a good appetite, while David rearranged his food, absently pushing it into ridges and furrows, eating none.

She chided him. "You're as thin as a spar, now. If you fall away any more, the ants will carry you off."

His face quirked into a smile, but he couldn't eat.

After dinner as the evening sun slipped away in purple shadows, they walked to the open concert hall cantilevered over the lake shore.

"Have you heard any of it, yet?" she asked.

He shook his head. "She wouldn't let me see the score." He was going to hear Tanya Rolfe's "Summer Conserere" for the first time that night, and he was acutely aware that it was to be her last work.

They took seats near the rear. Beyond the stage, the last colors of evening blazed pink above the mountains at the far edge of the lake.

"That was planned, you know," said Liss admiring the sunset. "The visiographer is Lindner. I think he's a genius. Nobody else can combine nature and artifice like he can."

The stage rose silently before them, bearing the conductor

and the small orchestra. A hush—then a measured chorus of cicadas began, answered by the flickering lights of a hundred fireflies.

The chorus increased ten-fold, as the tiny fireflies became ten thousand points of light wheeling slowly across the darkening sky in constellations of cold fire.

A symphosizer sighed once, then a chorus of wind whispering through new leaves became a theme uttered by a single soloboe.

David felt himself swept away by the music and the subtle changing effects in the sky around him. In turn, he felt love, then grief and a heavy sense of loss, then hope. A throbbing of strings and colors began, so delicate he felt it as pain in the tightness of his throat. Then silence. Black. Night, until a single point of light—a shooting star—grew to a great ball of fire and a swelling chorus of exultation.

He felt tears rise in his eyes and blinked to keep them back. He felt vaguely ashamed of them, and yet they were echoed by bright eyes everywhere in the audience. He joined with the others in applause, rubbing his hands together slowly at first, then more briskly. The leathery rustle of appreciation grew in speed and then the ultimate compliment—spontaneously, the audience began the rhythmic, sighing breathing that symbolized an inspired performance. In . . . spired. Containing the breath of life.

A single light focused on the slight figure of Tanya Rolfe. She came onto the stage on the arm of Lindner, the visiographer, walking slowly with a halting step. She stood with her head flung back as if to take in more air.

The rhythmic breathing increased in tempo until David's fingers tingled and he felt quite giddy. Next to him, Liss sighed, fluttering on the edge of consciousness. Here and there, people in the audience toppled, overcome by the hyperventilation. And still it went on, until Tanya Rolfe signaled to Lindner and the two walked slowly off the stage.

He left Liss at the path near her cabin.

"You want to be alone?"

He nodded.

"I understand." She kissed him lightly and turned away, then stopped, saying, "David, we've been friends. That's important, isn't it?" She looked at him once again. "Will you tell a friend—when you decide?"

He kissed her then. They clung together like two lost things for a minute or two and then she gently pushed him away, and without saying goodbye, walked away toward the little foot bridge.

He wandered alone for a while, not noticing where he was going. He found himself near Tanya Rolfe's cabin. A light still shone through the window.

He tapped lightly on the door, got no answer, tapped again. The door was unlocked and he pushed it open.

Still dressed, she lay on her bed. Her eyes were closed. For a shattering moment, he thought she was dead. Then a thin whistling breath escaped from her lungs.

He stood watching her, wanting to wake her, not wanting to. She was like a candle, nearly spent, guttering out with a final glow—defying the night.

He stood for a long time, looking at the tracks of time on her face and body. The tears he'd kept back at the concert rolled down his face. "Was it worth it?" he whispered. "Was it worth it?"

He left her cabin, shutting the door softly behind him. He had until tomorrow morning, then Final Decision. Final. No turning back. No changing his mind from that point on.

He walked in the dark for an hour or two, trying to gather himself into one piece and failing. Moonlight glittered on the black lake and the trees cast shadows of ink. He felt tired and a little disoriented. There was a place up ahead where he could rest.

The path curved to the tiny wood building they called the chapel. He pushed the door open and went in. He'd never bothered with it before, but he knew that some of the others had.

He sat back in the dim room looking down on a small dark arena. The bench he sat on was made of wood with a hard curving back. In front of him lay a bank of controls. He pressed one at random.

The arena took on a pale blue cast and a three-dimensional hexagram formed. A soft, almost subliminal voice said, "The Star of David." A man with a long white flowing beard clutched two stone tablets. David watched awhile, not really listening as the voice purred on, ". . . Thou shalt not kill."

Thou shalt not kill.

If he stayed, wasn't what what he'd be doing? To himself? A shiver rippled down his back. He pressed the controls.

SHARON WEBB   37

A circle moved before him—yin and yang—as divided as his mind.

Another button. A cross—with a man pinioned to it. Helpless as a butterfly on a board. Suffering eyes.

Another button. A sunflower, yellow petals opening.

Another. A serpent coiled itself into a figure eight.

Confused, he pressed his hand over the controls to shut it off, but instead he disengaged the speed. Below him, the scenes changed like shifting crystals in a kaleidoscope. The sunflower melting into a crescent with a star . . . the star flowing into the hexagram . . . unfolding into a cross . . . melting serpent gliding across the face of a yellow flower. All the while, soft voices whispering, ". . . Allah . . . illusion . . . shalt not kill. . . ."

He ran. He ran until the cool night air swept away the shifting scenes in his head.

Back in his cabin with no hope of sleep, he dialed a communicator code. Prints began to tumble out of the machine— a dozen, two dozen, more. . . . The complete works of Tanya Rolfe.

He tuned his cythar and began to play what he could of her music. Sitting cross-legged on the floor, he played, his fingers moving from one set of strings to the other, leaping the ninety-degree angle easily.

Only as he played did his mind relax. No thoughts flickered consciously, but the undercurrent sang from the plucked strings. She wouldn't die, she couldn't die, as long as her music played.

She wouldn't die, she couldn't die. Only when he stopped did he think of his own body falling away in sagging ripples of flesh, falling away to nothing. Only when he stopped did he think of his music and how it would die while he lived on in smooth-muscled emptiness.

He played until his fingers bled, and then he set aside his cythar and fitted his flute together.

He fingered through the copies of her music, leaving little smears of blood on the pages. Then he came to the title-page of her last conserere.

He read:

SUMMER CONSERERE
by
Tanya Rolfe

And below that, the dedication:

To David Defour, who lives on.

Why hadn't she told him? Why hadn't she? He felt a lump grow in his throat that was too hard and dry for tears.

He looked at the inscription knowing that the meaning could be taken two ways, knowing also that it could have had only one meaning to Tanya Rolfe. And he knew, too, why she hadn't told him.

She knew he had to decide for himself.

When the night faded to shades of gray, he left the cabin carrying only a thin set of pan-pipes and a small recording device slung on his belt.

Exhaustion had brought its own kind of peace. Spent, he sank down at the foot of a wide beech tree near the clearing. The first glow of the new sun began to color the hills.

He crushed a blade of grass with his sore fingers, rolling it between them, inhaling its sharp sweet smell.

It was good to be alive. What would it be like to *not be*? To not find out what lay beyond the next day? To not see Thursday? To never slide down the hills of April?

A rabbit rustled at the edge of the blackberry patch, nibbled tentatively at a blade of grass, thrust cut-velvet ears in his direction. He felt pity for it. It was so small, so ephemeral. Its moments fleeted as he watched.

But it had to be what it was.

He reached for the pan-pipes and blew a melody in a minor key to the little creature. It was a theme, he remembered, from Beethoven. He didn't know just why the theme seemed important to him, but somehow it did. Somehow, it told him of the end of things—and of beginnings. The melody hung in the warm sweet air for a moment, and somehow that moment seemed a bit more alive to him.

Then the ideas, the variations, came tumbling out of his pan-pipes. He laughed and touched the tiny recorder slung from his hip. And in his mind he could hear the orchestration —swelling strings, then the theme whispered from a flute, answered by a kleidelphone, echoed by the dark double reeds.

Now a muttered tympani, a variation by Weidner horn. It was all there. It was all there because it was his lot to create.

And he realized suddenly that he was outrageously hungry. No wonder. It was getting late. It was time for him to tell them he was going to stay at Renascence—but only if they'd give him breakfast.

BEATNIK BAYOU

by John Varley

The author of Options, *a highly praised story about the option of changing sex, continues to explore options in the same environment—a sublunar society with remarkable advances in human manipulation. Some people like a stable life, sedate and comfortable. Others do not. Some even like things wild, messy, bohemian— and beatnik. Why should an advanced society deny anyone his heart's desire? Yet there must be some rules that cannot be transgressed.*

The pregnant woman had been following us for over an hour when Cathay did the unspeakable thing.

At first it had been fun. Me and Denver didn't know what it was about, just that she had some sort of beef with Cathay. She and Cathay had gone off together and talked. The woman started yelling, and it was not too long before Cathay was yelling, too. Finally Cathay said something I couldn't hear and came back to join the class. That was me, Denver, Trigger, and Cathay, the last two being the teachers, me and Denver being the students. I know, you're not supposed to be able to tell which is which, but believe me, you usually know.

That's when the chase started. This woman wouldn't take no for an answer, and she followed us wherever we went. She was about as awkward an animal as you could imagine, and I certainly wasn't feeling sorry for her after the way she had talked to Cathay, who is my friend. Every time she slipped and landed on her behind, we all had a good laugh.

For a while. After an hour, she started to seem a little frightening. I had never seen anyone so determined.

The reason she kept slipping was that she was chasing us through Beatnik Bayou, which is Trigger's home. Trigger herself describes it as "twelve acres of mud, mosquitoes, and moonshine." Some of her visitors had been less poetic but more colorful. I don't know what an acre is, but the bayou is fairly large. Trigger makes the moonshine in a copper and aluminum still in the middle of a canebrake. The mosquitoes don't bite, but they buzz a lot. The mud is just plain old mississippi mud, suitable for beating your feet. Most people see the place and hate it instantly, but it suits me fine.

Pretty soon the woman was covered in mud. She had three things working against her. One was her angle-length maternity gown, which covered all of her except her face, feet, and bulging belly and breasts. She kept stepping on the long skirt and going down. After a while, I winced every time she did that.

Another handicap was her tummy, which made her walk with her weight back on her heels. That's not the best way to go through mud, and every so often she sat down real hard, proving it.

Her third problem was the Birthgirdle pelvic bone, which must have just been installed. It was one of those which sets the legs far apart and is hinged in the middle so when the baby comes it opens out and gives more room. She needed it, because she was tall and thin, the sort of build that might have died in childbirth back when such things were a problem. But it made her waddle like a duck.

"Quack, quack," Denver said, with an attempt at a smile. We both looked back at the woman, still following, still waddling. She went down, and struggled to her feet. Denver wasn't smiling when she met my eyes. She muttered something.

"What's that?" I said.

"She's unnerving," Denver repeated. "I wonder what the hell she wants?"

"Something pretty powerful."

Cathay and Trigger were a few paces ahead of us, and I saw Trigger glance back. She spoke to Cathay. I don't think I was supposed to hear it, but I did. I've got good ears.

"This is starting to upset the kids."

"I know," he said, wiping his brow with the back of his hand. All four of us watched her as she toiled her way up the far side of the last rise. Only her head and shoulders were visible.

"Damn. I thought she'd give up pretty soon." He groaned, but then his face became expressionless. "There's no help for it. We'll have to have a confrontation."

"I thought you already did," Trigger said, lifting an eyebrow.

"Yeah. Well, it wasn't enough, apparently. Come on, people. This is part of your lives, too." He meant me and Denver, and when he said that we knew this was supposed to be a "learning experience." Cathay can turn the strangest things into learning experiences. He started back toward the shallow stream we had just waded across, and the three of us followed him.

If I sounded hard on Cathay, I really shouldn't have been. Actually, he was one damn fine teacher. He was able to take those old saws about learning by doing, seeing is believing, one-on-one instruction, integration of life experiences—all the conventional wisdom of the educational establishment—and make it work better than any teacher I'd ever seen. I knew he was a counterfeit child. I had known that since I first met him, when I was seven, but it hadn't started to matter until lately. And that was just the naural cynicism of my age-group, as Trigger kept pointing out in that smug way of hers.

Okay, so he was really forty-eight years old. Physically he was just my age, which was almost thirteen: a short, slightly chubby kid with curly blond hair and an androgenous face, just starting to grow a little fuzz around his balls. When he turned to face that huge, threatening woman and stood facing her calmly, I was moved.

I was also fascinated. Mentally, I settled back on my haunches to watch and wait and observe. I was sure I'd be learning something about "life" real soon now. Class was in session.

When she saw us coming back, the woman hesitated. She picked her footing carefully as she came down the slight rise to stand at the edge of the water, then waited for a moment to see if Cathay was going to join her. He wasn't. She made an awful face, lifted her skirt up around her waist, and waded in.

The water lapped around her thighs. She nearly fell over

when she tried to dodge some dangling Spanish moss. Her
lace dress was festooned with twigs and leaves and smeared
with mud.

"Why don't you turn around?" Trigger yelled, standing
beside me and Denver and shaking her fist. "It's not going to
do you any good."

"I'll be the judge of that," she yelled back. Her voice was
harsh and ugly and what had probably been a sweet face was
now set in a scowl. An alligator was swimming up to look
her over. She swung at it with her fist, nearly losing her balance. "Get out of here, you slimy lizard!" she screamed. The
reptile recalled urgent business on the other side of the
swamp, and hurried out of her way.

She clambered ashore and stood ankle-deep in ooze,
breathing hard. She was a mess, and beneath her anger I
could now see fear. Her lips trembled for a moment. I wished
she would sit down; just looking at her exhausted me.

"You've got to help me," she said, simply.

"Believe me, if I could, I would," Cathay said.

"Then tell me somebody who can."

"I told you, if the Educational Exchange can't help you, I
certainly can't. Those few people I know who are available
for a contract are listed on the exchange."

"But none of them are available any sooner than three
years."

"I know. It's the shortage."

"Then help me," she said, miserably. "Help me."

Cathay slowly rubbed his eyes with a thumb and forefin-
ger, then squared his shoulders and put his hands on his hips.

"I'll go over it once more. Somebody gave you my name
and said I was available for a primary stage teaching contract. I—"

"He did! He said you'd—"

"I never heard of this person," Cathay said, raising his
voice. "Judging from what you're putting me through, he
gave you my name from the Teacher's Association listings
just to get you off his back. I guess I could do something like
that, but frankly, I don't think I have the right to subject another teacher to the sort of abuse you've heaped on me." He
paused, and for once she didn't say anything.

"Right," he said, finally. "I'm truly sorry that the man you
contracted with for your child's education went to Pluto instead. From what you told me, what he did was legal, which
is not to say ethical." He grimaced at the thought of a

teacher who would run out on an ethical obligation. "All I can say is you should have had the contract analyzed, you should have had a standby contract drawn up *three years ago* . . . oh, hell. What's the use? That doesn't do you any good. You have my sympathy, I hope you believe that."

"Then help me," she whispered, and the last word turned into a sob. She began to cry quietly. Her shoulders shook and tears leaked from her eyes, but she never looked away from Cathay.

"There's nothing I can do."

"You have to."

"Once more. I have obligations of my own. In another month, when I've fulfilled my contract with Argus' mother," he gestured toward me, "I'll be regressing to seven again. Don't you understand? I've already got an intermediate contract. The child will be seven in a few months. I contracted for her education four years ago. There's no way I can back out of that, legally or morally."

Her face was twisting again, filling with hate.

"Why not?" she rasped. "Why the hell not? He ran out on *my* contract. Why the hell should I be the only one to suffer? Why me, huh? Listen to me, you shitsucking little son of a blowout. You're all I've got left. After you, there's nothing but the public educator. Or trying to raise him all by myself, all alone, with no guidance. You want to be responsible for that? What the hell kind of start in life does that give him?"

She went on like that for a good ten minutes, getting more illogical and abusive with every sentence. I'd vacillated between a sort of queasy sympathy for her—she *was* in a hell of a mess, even though she had no one to blame but herself—and outright hostility. Just then she scared me. I couldn't look into those tortured eyes without cringing. My gaze wandered down to her fat belly, and the glass eye of the wombscope set into her navel. I didn't need to look into it to know she was due, and overdue. She'd been having the labor postponed while she tried to line up a teacher. Not that it made much sense; the kid's education didn't start until his sixth month. But it was a measure of her desperation, and of her illogical thinking under stress.

Cathay stood there and took it until she broke into tears again. I saw her differently this time, maybe a little more like Cathay was seeing her. I was sorry for her, but the tears failed to move me. I saw that she could devour us all if we didn't harden ourselves to her. When it came right down to it, she was the one who had to pay for her carelessness. She was trying her best to get someone else to shoulder the blame, but Cathay wasn't going to do it.

"I didn't want to do this," Cathay said. He looked back at us. "Trigger?"

Trigger stepped forward and folded her arms across her chest.

"Okay," she said. "Listen, I didn't get your name, and I don't really want to know it. But whoever you are, you're on my property, in my house. I'm ordering you to leave here, and I further enjoin you never to come back."

"I won't go," she said, stubbornly, looking down at her feet. "I'm not leaving till he promises to help me."

"My next step is to call the police," Trigger reminded her.

"I'm not leaving."

Trigger looked at Cathay and shrugged helplessly. I think they were both realizing that this particular life experience was getting a little too raw.

Cathay thought it over for a moment, eye to eye with the pregnant woman. Then he reached down and scooped up a handful of mud. He looked at it, hefting it experimentally, then threw it at her. It struck her on the left shoulder with a wet plop, and began to ooze down.

"Go," he said. "Get out of here."

"I'm not leaving," she said.

He threw another handful. It hit her face, and she gasped and sputtered.

"Go," he said, reaching for more mud. This time he hit her on the leg, but by now Trigger had joined him, and the woman was being pelted.

Before I quite knew what was happening, I was scooping mud from the ground and throwing it. Denver was, too. I was breathing hard, and I wasn't sure why.

When she finally turned and fled from us, I noticed that my jaw muscles were tight as steel. It took me a long time to relax them, and when I did, my front teeth were sore.

There are two structures on Beatnik Bayou. One is an old, rotting bait shop and lunch counter called the Sugar Shack, complete with a rusty gas pump out front, a battered Grapette machine on the porch, and a sign advertising Rainbow Bread on the screen door. There's a gray Dodge pickup sitting on concrete blocks to one side of the building, near a pile of rusted auto parts overgrown with weeds. The truck has no wheels. Beside it is a Toyota sedan with no windows or engine. A dirt road runs in front of the shack, going down to the dock. In the other direction the road curves around a cypress tree laden with moss—

—and runs into the wall. A bit of a jolt. But though twelve acres is large for a privately owned disneyland, it's not big enough to sustain the illusion of really being there. "There," in this case, is supposed to be Louisiana in 1951, old style. Trigger is fascinated by the twentieth century, which she defines as 1903 to 1987.

But most of the time it works. You can seldom see the walls because trees are in the way. Anyhow, I soak up the atmosphere of the place not so much with my eyes but with my nose and ears and skin. Like the smell of rotting wood, the sound of a frog hitting the water or the hum of the compressor in the soft drink machine, the silver wiggle of a dozen minnows as I scoop them from the metal tanks in back of the shack, the feel of sun-heated wood as I sit on the pier fishing for alligator gar.

It takes a lot of power to operate the "sun," so we get a lot of foggy days, and long nights. That helps the illusion, too. I would challenge anyone to go for a walk in the bayou night with the crickets chirping and the bullfrogs booming and not think they were back on Old Earth. Except for the Lunar gravity, of course.

Trigger inherited money. Even with that and a teacher's salary, the bayou is an expensive place to maintain. It used to be a more conventional environment, but she discovered early that the swamp took less upkeep, and she likes the sleazy atmosphere, anyway. She put in the bait shop, bought the automotive mockups from artists, and got it listed with the Lunar Tourist Bureau as an authentic period reconstruction. They'd die if they knew the truth about the Toyota, but I certainly won't tell them.

The only other structure is definitely not from Louisiana of any year. It's a teepee sitting on a slight rise, just out of sight of the Sugar Shack. Cheyenne, I think. We spend most of our time there when we're on the bayou.

That's where we went after the episode with the pregnant woman. The floor is hard-packed clay and there's a fire always burning in the center. There's lots of pillows scattered around, and two big waterbeds.

We tried to talk about the incident. I think Denver was more upset than the rest of us, but from the tense way

Cathay sat while Trigger massaged his back I knew he was bothered, too. His voice was troubled.

I admitted I had been scared, but there was more to it than that, and I was far from ready to talk about it. Trigger and Cathay sensed it, and let it go for the time being. Trigger got the pipe and stuffed it with dexeplant leaves.

It's a long-stemmed pipe. She got it lit, then leaned back with the stem in her teeth and the bowl held between her toes. She exhaled sweet, honey-colored smoke. As the day ended outside, she passed the pipe around. It tasted good, and calmed me wonderfully. It made it easy to fall asleep.

But I didn't sleep. Not quite. Maybe I was too far into puberty for the drug in the plant to act as a tranquilizer anymore. Or maybe I was too emotionally stimulated. Denver fell asleep quickly enough.

Cathay and Trigger didn't. They made love on the other side of the teepee, did it in such a slow, dreamy way that I knew the drug was affecting them. Though Cathay is in his forties and Trigger is over a hundred, both have the bodies of thirteen-year-olds, and the metabolism that goes with the territory.

They didn't actually finish making love; they sort of tapered off, like we used to do before orgasms became a factor. I found that made me happy, lying on my side and watching them through slitted eyes.

They talked for a while. The harder I strained to hear them, the sleepier I got. Somewhere in there I lost the battle to stay awake.

I became aware of a warm body close to me. It was still dark, the only light coming from the embers of the fire.

"Sorry, Argus," Cathay said. "I didn't mean to wake you."

"It's okay. Put your arms around me?" He did, and I squirmed until my back fit snugly against him. For a long time I just enjoyed it. I didn't think about anything, unless it was his warm breath on my neck, or his penis slowly hardening against my back. If you can call that thinking.

How many nights had we slept like this in the last seven years? Too many to count. We knew each other every way possible. A year ago he had been female, and before that both of us had been. Now we were both male, and that was nice, too. One part of me thought it didn't really matter which sex we were, but another part was wondering what it

would be like to be female and know Cathay as a male. We
hadn't tried that yet.

The thought of it made me shiver with anticipation. It had
been too long since I'd had a vagina. I wanted Cathay between my legs, like Trigger had had him a short while before.

"I love you," I mumbled.

He kissed my ear. "I love you, too, silly. But how *much* do
you love me?"

"What do you mean?"

I felt him shift around to prop his head up on one hand.
His fingers unwound a tight curl in my hair.

"I mean, will you still love me when I'm no taller than
your knee?"

I shook my head, suddenly feeling cold. "I don't want to
talk about that."

"I know that very well," he said. "But I can't let you forget
it. It's not something that'll go away."

I turned onto my back and looked up at him. There was a
faint smile on his face as he toyed with my lips and hair with
his gentle fingertips, but his eyes were concerned. Cathay
can't hide much from me anymore.

"It has to happen," he emphasized, showing no mercy.
"For the reasons you heard me tell the woman. I'm commit-
ted to going back to age seven. There's another child waiting
for me. She's a lot like you."

"Don't do it," I said, feeling miserable. I felt a tear in the
corner of my eye, and Cathay brushed it away.

I was thankful that he didn't point out how unfair I was
being. We both knew it; he accepted that, and went on as
best he could.

"You remember our talk about sex? About two years ago,
I think it was. Not too long after you first told me you love
me."

"I remember. I remember it all."

He kissed me. "Still, I have to bring it up. Maybe it'll help.
You know we agreed that it didn't matter what sex either of
us was. Then I pointed out that you'd be growing up, while
I'd become a child again. That we'd grow further apart sexually."

I nodded, knowing that if I spoke I'd start to sob.

"And we agreed that our love was deeper than that. That
we didn't need sex to make it work. It *can* work."

This was true. Cathay was close to all his former students.
They were adults now, and came to see him often. It was just

to be close, to talk and hug. Lately sex had entered it again, but they all understood that would be over soon.

"I don't think I have that perspective," I said, carefully. "They know in a few years you'll mature again. I know it too, but it still feels like . . ."

"Like what?"

"Like you're abandoning me. I'm sorry, that's just how it feels."

He sighed, and pulled me close to him. He hugged me fiercely for a while, and it felt so good.

"Listen," he said, finally. "I guess there's no avoiding this. I could tell you that you'll get over it—you will—but it won't do any good. I had this same problem with every child I've taught."

"You did?" I hadn't known that, and it made me feel a little better.

"I did. I don't blame you for it. I feel it myself. I feel a pull to stay with you. But it wouldn't work, Argus. I love my work, or I wouldn't be doing it. There are hard times, like right now. But after a few months you'll feel better."

"Maybe I will." I was far from sure of it, but it seemed important to agree with him and get the conversation ended.

"In the meantime," he said, "we still have a few weeks together. I think we should make the most of them." And he did, his hands roaming over my body. He did all the work, letting me relax and try to get myself straightened out.

So I folded my arms under my head and reclined, trying to think of nothing but the warm circle of his mouth.

But eventually I began to feel I should be doing something for him, and knew what was wrong. He thought he was giving me what I wanted by making love to me in the way we had done since we grew older together. But there was another way, and I realized I didn't so much want him to stay thirteen. What I really wanted was to go back with him, to be seven again.

I touched his head and he looked up, then we embraced again face to face. We began to move against each other as we had done since we first met, the mindless, innocent friction from a time when it had less to do with sex than with simply feeling good.

But the body is insistent, and can't be fooled. Soon our movements were frantic, and then a feeling of wetness between us told me as surely as entropy that we could never go back.

On my way home the signs of change were all around me.

You grow a little, let out the arms and legs of your pressure suit until you finally have to get a new one. People stop thinking of you as a cute little kid and start talking about you being a fine young person. Always with that smile, like it's a joke that you're not supposed to get.

People treat you differently as you grow up. At first you hardly interact at all with adults, except your own mother and the mothers of your friends. You live in a kid's world, and adults are hardly even obstacles because they get out of your way when you run down the corridors. You go all sorts of places for free; people want you around to make them happy because there are so few kids and just about everybody would like to have more than just the one. You hardly even notice the people smiling at you all the time.

But it's not like that at all when you're thirteen. Now there was the hesitation, just a fraction of a second before they gave me a child's privileges. Not that I blamed anybody. I was nearly as tall as a lot of the adults I met.

But now I had begun to notice the adults, to watch them. Especially when they didn't know they were being watched. I saw that a lot of them spent a lot of time frowning. Occasionally, I would see real pain on a face. Then he or she would look at me, and smile. I could see that wouldn't be happening forever. Sooner or later I'd cross some invisible line, and the pain would stay in those faces, and I'd have to try to understand it. I'd be an adult, and I wasn't sure I wanted to be.

It was because of this new preoccupation with faces that I noticed the woman sitting across from me on the Archimedes train. I planned to be a writer, so I tended to see everything in terms of stories and characters. I watched her and tried to make a story about her.

She was attractive: physically mid-twenties, straight black hair and brownish skin, round face without elaborate surgery or startling features except her dark brown eyes. She wore a simple thigh-length robe of thin white material that flowed like water when she moved. She had one elbow on the back of her seat, absently chewing a knuckle as she looked out the window.

There didn't seem to be a story in her face. She was in an unguarded moment, but I saw no pain, no big concerns or fears. It's possible I just missed it. I was new at the game and

I didn't know much about what was important to adults. But I kept trying.

Then she turned to look at me, and she didn't smile.

I mean, she smiled, but it didn't say isn't-he-cute. It was the sort of smile that made me wish I'd worn some clothes. Since I'd learned what erections are for, I no longer wished to have them in public places.

I crossed my legs. She moved to sit beside me. She held up her palm and I touched it. She was facing me with one leg drawn up under her and her arm resting on the seat behind me.

"I'm Trilby," she said.

"Hi. I'm Argus." I found myself trying to lower my voice.

"I was sitting over there watching you watch me."

"You were?"

"In the glass," she explained.

"Oh." I looked, and sure enough, from where she had been sitting she could appear to be looking at the landscape while actually studying my reflection. "I didn't mean to be rude."

She laughed and put her hand on my shoulder, then moved it. "What about me?" she said. "I was being sneaky about it; you weren't. Anyhow, don't fret. I don't mind." I shifted again, and she glanced down. "And don't worry about that, either. It happens."

I still felt nervous but she was able to put me at ease. We talked for the rest of the ride, and I have no memory of what we talked about. The range of subjects must have been quite narrow, as I'm sure she never made reference to my age, my schooling, her profession—or just why she had started a conversation with a thirteen-year-old on a public train.

None of that mattered. I was willing to talk about anything. If I wondered about her reasons, I assumed she actually was in her twenties, and not that far from her own childhood.

"Are you in a hurry?" she asked at one point, giving her head a little toss.

"Me? No. I'm on my way to see—" No, no, not your mother. "—a friend. She can wait. She expects me when I get there." That sounded better.

"Can I buy you a drink?" One eyebrow raised, a small motion with the hand. Her gestures were economical, but seemed to say more than her words. I mentally revised her age upward a few years. Maybe quite a few.

This was timed to the train arriving at Archimedes; we got up and I quickly accepted.

"Good. I know a nice place."

The bartender gave me that smile and was about to give me the customary free one on the house toward my legal limit of two. But Trilby changed all that.

"Two Irish whiskeys, please. On the rocks." She said it firmly, raising her voice a little, and a complex thing happened between her and the bartender. She gave him a look, his eyebrow twitched and he glanced at me, seemed to understand something. His whole attitude toward me changed.

I had the feeling something had gone over my head, but didn't have time to worry about it. I never had time to worry when Trilby was around. The drinks arrived, and we sipped them.

"I wonder why they still call it Irish?" she said.

We launched into a discussion of the Invaders, or Ireland, or Occupied Earth. I'm not sure. It was inconsequential, and the real conversation was going on eye to eye. Mostly it was her saying wordless things to me, and me nodding agreement with my tongue hanging out.

We ended up at the public baths down the corridor. Her nipples were shaped like pink valentine hearts. Other than that, her body was unremarkable, though wonderfully firm beneath the softness. She was so unlike Trigger and Denver and Cathay. So unlike me. I catalogued the differences as I sat behind her in the big pool and massaged her soapy shoulders.

On the way to the tanning rooms she stopped beside one of the private alcoves and just stood there, waiting, looking at me. My legs walked me into the room and she followed me. My hands pressed against her back and my mouth opened when she kissed me. She lowered me to the soft floor and took me.

What was so different about it?

I pondered that during the long walk from the slide terminus to my home. Trilby and I had made love for the better part of an hour. It was nothing fancy, nothing I had not already tried with Trigger and Denver. I had thought she would have some fantastic new tricks to show me, but that had not been the case.

Yet she had not been like Trigger or Denver. Her body responded in a different way, moved in directions I was not used to. I did my best. When I left her, I knew she was happy, and yet felt she expected more.

I found that I was very interested in giving her more.

I was in love again.

With my hand on the doorplate, I suddenly knew that she had already forgotten me. It was silly to assume anything else. I had been a pleasant diversion, an interesting novelty.

I hadn't asked for her name, her address or call number. Why not? Maybe I already knew she would not care to hear from me again.

I hit the plate with the heel of my hand and brooded during the elevator ride to the surface.

My home is unusual. Of course, it belongs to Darcy, my mother. She was there now, putting the finishing touches on a diorama. She glanced up at me, smiled, and offered her cheek for a kiss.

"I'll be through in a moment," she said. "I want to finish this before the light fails."

We live in a large bubble on the surface. Part of it is partitioned into rooms without ceilings, but the bulk forms Darcy's studio. The bubble is transparent. It screens out the ultraviolet light so we don't get burned.

It's an uncommon way to live, but it suits us. From our vantage point at the south side of a small valley only three similar bubbles can be seen. It would be impossible for an outsider to guess that a city teemed just below the surface.

Growing up, I never gave a thought to agoraphobia, but it's common among Lunarians. I felt sorry for those not fortunate enough to grow up with a view.

Darcy likes it for the light. She's an artist, and particular about light. She works two weeks on and two off, resting during the night. I grew up to that schedule, leaving her alone while she put in marathon sessions with her airbrushes, coming home to spend two weeks with her when the sun didn't shine.

That had changed a bit when I reached my tenth birthday. We had lived alone before then, Darcy cutting her work schedule drastically until I was four, gradually picking it up as I attained more independence. She did it so she could devote all her time to me. Then one day she sat me down and told me two men were moving in. It was only later that I realized how Darcy had altered her lifestyle to raise me properly. She is a serial polyandrist, especially attracted to fierce-faced, uncompromising, maverick male artists whose work doesn't sell and who are usually a little hungry. She likes the hunger, and the determination they all have not to pander to public tastes. She usually keeps three or four of them around, feeding them and giving them a place to work. She demands little of them other than that they clean up after themselves.

I had to step around the latest of these household pets to get to the kitchen. He was sound asleep, snoring loudly, his hands stained yellow and red and green. I'd never seen him before.

Darcy came up behind me while I was making a snack, hugged me, then pulled up a chair and sat down. The sun would be out another half hour or so, but there wasn't time to start another painting.

"How have you been? You didn't call for three days."

"Didn't I? I'm sorry. We've been staying on the bayou."

She wrinkled her nose. Darcy had seen the bayou. Once.

"*That* place. I wish I knew why—"

"Darcy. Let's not get into that again. Okay?"

"Done." She spread her paint-stained hands and waved them in a circle, as if erasing something, and that was it. Darcy is good that way. "I've got a new roommate."

"I nearly stumbled over him."

She ran one hand through her hair and gave me a lopsided grin. "He'll shape up. His name's Thogra."

"Thogra," I said, making a face. "Listen, if he's housebroken, and stays out of my way, we'll—" But I couldn't go on. We were both laughing and I was about to choke on a bite that went down wrong. Darcy knows what I think of her choice in bedmates.

"What about . . . what's-his-name? The armpit man. The guy who kept getting arrested for body odor."

She stuck her tongue out at me.

"You know he cleaned up months ago."

"Hah! It's those months *before* he discovered water that I remember. All my friends wondering where we were raising sheep, the flowers losing petals when he walked by, the—"

"Abil didn't come back," Darcy said, quietly.

I stopped laughing. I'd known he'd been away a few weeks, but that happens. I raised one eyebrow.

"Yeah. Well, you know he sold a few things. And he had some offers. But I keep expecting him to at least stop by to pick up his bedroll."

I didn't say anything. Darcy's loves follow a pattern that she is quite aware of, but it's still tough when one breaks up. Her men would often speak with contempt of the sort of commercial art that kept me and Darcy eating and paying the oxygen bills. Then one of three things would happen. They would get nowhere, and leave as poor as they had arrived, contempt intact. A few made it on their own terms, forcing the art world to accept their peculiar visions. Often Darcy was able to stay on good terms with these; she was on a drop-in-and-make-love basis with half the artists in Luna.

But the most common departure was when the artist decided he was tired of poverty. With just a slight lowering of standards they were all quite capable of making a living. Then it became intolerable to live with the woman they had ridiculed. Darcy usually kicked them out quickly, with a minimum of pain. They were no longer hungry, no longer fierce enough to suit her. But it always hurt.

Darcy changed the subject.

"I made an appointment at the medico for your Change," she said. "You're to be there next Monday, in the morning."

A series of quick, vivid impressions raced through my mind. Trilby. Breasts tipped with hearts. The way it had felt when my penis entered her, and the warm exhaustion after the semen had left my body.

"I've changed my mind about that," I said, crossing my legs. "I'm not ready for another Change. Maybe in a few months."

She just sat there with her mouth open.

"Changed your *mind*? Last time I talked to you, you were all set to change your *sex*. In fact, you had to talk me into giving permission."

"I remember," I said, feeling uneasy about it. "I just changed my mind, that's all."

"But Argus. This just isn't fair. I sat up two nights convincing myself how nice it would be to have my daughter back again. It's been a long time. Don't you think you—"

"It's really not your decision, Mother."

She looked like she was going to get angry, then her eyes narrowed. "There must be a reason. You've met somebody. Right?"

But I didn't want to talk about that. I had told her the first time I made love, and about every new person I'd gone to bed with since. But I didn't want to share this with her.

So I told her about the incident earlier that day on the

bayou. I told her about the pregnant woman, and about the thing Cathay had done.

Darcy frowned more and more. When I got to the part about the mud, there were ridges all over her forehead.

"I don't like that," she said.

"I don't really like it, either. But I didn't see what else we could do."

"I just don't think it was handled well. I think I should call Cathay and talk to him about it."

"I wish you wouldn't." I didn't say anything more, and she studied my face for a long, uncomfortable time. She and Cathay had differed before about how I should be raised.

"This shouldn't be ignored."

"Please, Darcy. He'll only be my teacher for another month. Let it go, okay?"

After a while she nodded, and looked away from me.

"You're growing more every day," she said, sadly. I didn't know why she said that, but was glad she was dropping the subject. To tell the truth, I didn't want to think about the woman anymore. But I was going to have to think about her, and very soon.

I had intended to spend the week at home, but Trigger called the next morning to say that Mardi Gras '56 was being presented again, and it was starting in a few hours. She'd made reservations for the four of us.

Trigger had seen the presentation before, but I hadn't, and neither had Denver. I told her I'd come, went in to tell Darcy, found her still asleep. She often slept for two days after a Lunar Day of working. I left her a note and hurried to catch the train.

It's called the Cultural Heritage Museum, and though they pay for it with their taxes, most Lunarians never go there. They find the exhibits disturbing. I understand that lately, however, with the rise of the Free Earth Party, it's become more popular with people searching for their roots.

Once they presented London Town 1903, and I got to see what Earth museums had been like by touring the replica British Museum. The CHM isn't like that at all. Only a very few art treasures, artifacts, and historical curiosities were brought to Luna in the days before the Invasion. As a result, all the tangible relics of Earth's past were destroyed.

On the other hand, the Lunar computer system had a capacity that was virtually limitless even then; *everything* was recorded and stored. Every book, painting, tax receipt, statistic, photograph, government report, corporate record, film, and tape existed in the memory banks. Just as the disneylands are populated with animals cloned from cells stored in the Genetic Library, the CHM is filled with cunning copies made from the old records of the way things were.

I met the others at the Sugar Shack, where Denver was trying to talk Trigger into taking Tuesday along with us. Tuesday is the hippopotamus that lives on the bayou, in cheerful defiance of any sense of authenticity. Denver had her on a chain and she stood placidly watching us, blinking her piggy little eyes.

Denver was tickled at the idea of going to Mardi Gras with a hippo named Tuesday, but Trigger pointed out that the museum officials would never let us into New Orleans with the beast. Denver finally conceded, and shooed her back into the swamp. The four of us went down the road and out of the bayou, boarded the central slidewalk, and soon arrived in the city center.

There are twenty-five theaters in the CHM. Usually about half of them are operating while the others are being prepared for a showing. Mardi Gras '56 is a ten-year-old show, and generally opens twice a year for a two week run. It's one of the more popular environments.

We went to the orientation room and listened to the lecture on how to behave, then were given our costumes. That's the part I like the least. Up until about the beginning of the twenty-first century, clothing was designed with two main purposes in mind: modesty, and torture. If it didn't hurt, it needed redesigning. It's no wonder they killed each other all the time. Anybody would, with high gravity and hard shoes mutilating their feet.

"We'll be beatniks," Trigger said, looking over the racks of period clothing. "They were more informal, and it's accurate enough to get by. There were beatniks in the French Quarter."

Informality was fine with us. The girls didn't need bras, and we could choose between leather sandals or canvas sneakers for our feet. I can't say I cared much for something called Levis, though. They were scratchy, and pinched my balls. But after visiting Victorian England—I had been female at the time, and what those people made girls wear would shock most Lunarians silly—anything was an improvement.

Entry to the holotorium was through the restrooms at the back of a nightclub that fronted on Bourbon Street. Boys to the left, girls to the right. I think they did that to impress you right away that you were going back into the past, when people did things in strange ways. There was a third restroom, actually, but it was only a false door with the word "colored" on it. It was impossible to sort *that* out anymore.

I like the music of 1956 New Orleans. There are many varieties, all sounding similar for modern ears with their simple rhythms and blends of wind, string, and percussion. The generic term is jazz, and the particular kind of jazz that afternoon in the tiny, smoke-filled basement was called dixieland. It's dominated by two instruments called a clarinet and a trumpet, each improvising a simple melody while the rest of the band makes as much racket as it can.

We had a brief difference of opinion. Cathay and Trigger wanted me and Denver to stay with them, presumably so they could use any opportunity to show off their superior knowledge—translation: "educate" us. After all, they were teachers. Denver didn't seem to mind, but I wanted to be alone.

I solved the problem by walking out onto the street, reasoning that they could follow me if they wished. They didn't, and I was free to explore on my own.

Going to a holotorium show isn't like the sensies, where you sit in a chair and the action comes to you. And it's not like a disneyland, where everything is real and you just poke around. You have to be careful not to ruin the illusion.

The majority of the set, most of the props, and all of the actors are holograms. Any real people you meet are costumed visitors, like yourself. What they did in the case of New Orleans was to lay out a grid of streets and surface them as they had actually been. Then they put up two-meter walls where the buildings would be, and concealed them behind holos of old buildings. A few of the doors in these buildings were real, and if you went in you would find the interiors authentic down to the last detail. Most just concealed empty blocks.

You don't go there to play childish tricks with holos, that's contrary to the whole spirit of the place. You find yourself being careful not to shatter the illusion. You don't talk to people unless you're sure they're real, and you don't touch things until you've studied them carefully. No holo can stand up to a close scrutiny, so you can separate the real from the illusion if you try.

The stage was a large one. They had reproduced the French Quarter—or Vieux Carre—from the Mississippi River to the Rampart Street, and from Canal Street to a point about six blocks east. Standing on Canal and looking across, the city seemed to teem with life for many kilometers in the distance, though I knew there was a wall right down the yellow line in the middle.

New Orleans '56 begins at noon on Shrove Tuesday and carries on far into the night. We had arrived in late afternoon, with the sun starting to cast long shadows over the endless parades. I wanted to see the place before it got dark.

I went down Canal for a few blocks, looking into the "windows." There was an old flat movie theater with a marquee announcing *From Here to Eternity*, winner of something called an Oscar. I saw that it was a real place and thought about going in, but I'm afraid those old 2-D movies leave me flat, no matter how good Trigger says they are.

So instead I walked the streets, observing, thinking about writing a story set in old New Orleans.

That's why I hadn't wanted to stay and listen to the music with the others. Music is not something you can really put into a story, beyond a bare description of what it sounds like, who is playing it, and where it is being heard. In the same way, going to the flat movie would not have been very productive.

But the streets, the streets! There was something to study.

The pattern was the same as old London, but all the details had changed. The roads were filled with horseless carriages, great square metal boxes that must have been the most inefficient means of transport ever devised. Nothing was truly straight, nor very clean. To walk the streets was to risk broken toes or cuts on the soles of the feet. No wonder they wore thick shoes.

I knew what the red and green lights were for, and the lines painted on the road. But what about the rows of timing devices on each side of the street? What was the red metal object that a dog was urinating on? What did the honking of the car horns signify? Why were wires suspended overhead on wooden poles? I ignored the Mardi Gras festivities and spent a pleasant hour looking for the answers to these and many other questions.

What a challenge to write of this time, to make the story a slice of life, where these outlandish things seemed normal and reasonable. I visualized one of the inhabitants of New Orleans transplanted to Archimedes, and tried to picture her confusion.

Then I saw Trilby, and forgot about New Orleans.

She was behind the wheel of a 1955 Ford station wagon. I know this because when she motioned for me to join her, slid over on the seat, and let me drive, there was a gold plaque on the bulkhead just below the forward viewport.

"How do you run this thing?" I asked, flustered and trying not to show it. Something was wrong. Maybe I'd known it all along, and was only now admitting it.

"You press that pedal to go, and that one to stop. But mostly it controls itself." The car proved her right by accelerating into the stream of holographic traffic. I put my hands on the wheel, found that I could guide the car within limits. As long as I wasn't going to hit anything it let me be the boss.

"What brings you here?" I asked, trying for a light voice.

"I went by your home," she said. "Your mother told me where you were."

"I don't recall telling you where I live."

She shrugged, not seeming too happy. "It's not hard to find out."

"I . . . I mean, you didn't . . ." I wasn't sure if I wanted to say it, but decided I'd better go on. "We didn't meet by accident, did we?"

"No."

"And you're my new teacher."

She sighed. "That's an oversimplification. I *want* to be *one* of your new teachers. Cathay recommended me to your mother, and when I talked to her, she was interested. I was just going to get a look at you on the train, but when I saw you looking at me . . . well, I thought I'd give you something to remember me by."

"Thanks."

She looked away. "Darcy told me today that it might have been a mistake. I guess I judged you wrong."

"It's nice to hear that you can make a mistake."

"I guess I don't understand."

"I don't like to feel predictable. I don't like to be toyed with. Maybe it hurts my dignity. Maybe I get enough of that from Trigger and Cathay. All the lessons."

"I see it now," she sighed. "It's a common enough reaction, in bright children, they——"

"Don't say that."

"I'm sorry, but I must. There's no use hiding from you that my business is to know people, and especially children. That means the phases they go through, including the phase when they like to imagine they don't go through phases. I didn't recognize it in you, so I made a mistake."

I sighed. "What does it matter, anyway? Darcy likes you. That means you'll be my new teacher, doesn't it?"

"It does not. Not with me, anyway. I'm one of the first big choices you get to make with no adult interference."

"I don't get it."

"That's because you've never been interested enough to find out what's ahead of you in your education. At the risk of offending you again, I'll say it's a common response in people your age. You're only a month from graduating away from Cathay, ready to start more goal-oriented aspects of learning, and you haven't bothered to find what that will entail. Did you ever stop to think what's between you and becoming a writer?"

"I'm a writer, already," I said, getting angry for the first time. Before that, I'd been feeling hurt more than anything. "I can use the language, and I watch people. Maybe I don't have much experience yet, but I'll get it with or without you. I don't even *have* to have teachers at *all* anymore. At least I know that much."

"You're right, of course. But you've known your mother intended to pay for your advanced education. Didn't you ever wonder what it would be like?"

"Why should I? Did you ever think that I'm not interested because it just doesn't seem important? I mean, who's asked me what I felt about any of this up to now? What kind of stake do I have in it? Everyone seems to know what's best for me. Why should I be consulted?"

"Because you're nearly an adult now. My job, if you hire me, will be to ease the transition. When you've made it, you'll know, and you won't need me anymore. This isn't primary phase. Your teacher's job back then was to work with your mother to teach you the basic ways of getting along with people and society, and to cram your little head with all the skills a seven-year-old can learn. They taught you language, dexterity, reasoning, responsibility, hygiene, and not to go in an airlock without your suit. They took an ego-centered infant and turned him into a moral being. It's a tough job; so little, and you could have been a sociopath.

"Then they handed you to Cathay. You didn't mind. He showed up one day, just another playmate your own age. You were happy and trusting. He guided you very gently, letting your natural curiosity do most of the work. He discovered your creative abilities before you had any inkling of them, and he saw to it that you had interesting things to think about, to react to, to experience.

"But lately you've been a problem for him. Not your fault, nor his, but you no longer want anyone to guide you. You want to do it on your own. You have vague feelings of being manipulated."

"Which is not surprising," I put in. "I *am* being manipulated."

"That's true, so far as it goes. But what would you have Cathay do? Leave everything to chance?"

"That's beside the point. We're talking about my feelings now, and what I feel is you were dishonest with me. You made me feel like a fool. I thought what happens was . . . was spontaneous, you know? Like a fairy tale."

She gave me a funny smile. "What an odd way to put it. What I intended to do was allow you to live out a wet dream."

I guess the easy way she admitted that threw me off my stride. I should have told her there was no real difference. Both fairy tales and wet dreams were visions of impossibly convenient worlds, worlds where things go the way you want them to go. But I didn't say anything.

"I realize now that it was the wrong way to approach you. Frankly, I thought you'd enjoy it. Wait, let me change that. I thought you'd enjoy it even *after* you knew. I submit that you *did* enjoy it while it was happening."

I once again said nothing, because it was the simple truth. But it wasn't the point.

She waited, watching me as I steered the old car through traffic. Then she sighed, and looked out the viewport again.

"Well, it's up to you. As I said, things won't be planned for you anymore. You'll have to decide if you want me to be your teacher."

"Just what is it you teach?" I asked.

"Sex is part of it."

I started to say something, but was stopped by the novel

idea that someone thought she could—or *needed* to—teach me about sex. I mean, what was there to learn?

I hardly noticed it when the car stopped on its own, was shaken out of my musings only when a man in blue stuck his head in the window beside me. There was a woman behind him, dressed the same way. I realized they were wearing 1956 police uniforms.

"Are you Argus-Darcy-Meric?" the man asked.

"Yeah. Who are you?"

"My name is Jordan. I'm sorry, but you'll have to come with me. A complaint has been filed against you. You are under arrest."

Arrest. To take into custody by legal authority. Or, to stop suddenly.

Being arrested contains both meanings, it seems to me. You're in custody, and your life comes to a temporary halt. Whatever you were doing is interrupted, and suddenly only one thing is important.

I wasn't too worried until I realized what that one thing must be. After all, everyone gets arrested. You can't avoid it in a society of laws. Filing a complaint against someone is the best way of keeping a situation from turning violent. I had been arrested three times before, been found guilty twice. Once I had filed a complaint myself, and had it sustained.

But this time promised to be different. I doubted I was being hauled in for some petty violation I had not even been aware of. No, this had to be the pregnant woman, and the mud. I had a while to think about that as I sat in the bare-walled holding cell, time to get really worried. We had physically attacked her, there was no doubt about that.

I was finally summoned to the examination chamber. It was larger than the ones I had been in before. Those occasions had involved just two people. This room had five wedge-shaped glass booths, each with a chair inside, arranged so that we faced each other in a circle. I was shown into the only empty one and I looked around at Denver, Cathay, Trigger . . . and the woman.

It's quiet in the booths. You are very much alone.

I saw Denver's mother come in and sit behind her daughter, outside the booth. Turning around, I saw Darcy. To my surprise, Trilby was with her.

"Hello, Argus." The Central Computer's voice filled the

tiny booth, mellow as usual but without the reassuring resonance.

"Hello, CC," I tried to keep it light, but of course the CC was not fooled.

"I'm sorry to see you in so much trouble."

"Is it real bad?"

"The charge certainly is, there's no sense denying that. I can't comment on the testimony, or on your chances. But you know you're facing a possible mandatory death penalty, with automatic reprieve."

I was aware of it. I also knew it was rarely enforced against someone my age. But what about Cathay and Trigger?

I've never cared for that term "reprieve." It somehow sounds like they aren't going to kill you, but they are. Very, very dead. The catch is that they then grow a clone from a cell of your body, force it quickly to maturity, and play your recorded memories back into it. So someone very like you will go on, but *you* will be dead. In my case, the last recording had been taken three years ago. I was facing the loss of almost a quarter of my life. If it was found necessary to kill me, the new Argus—*not* me, but someone with my memories and my name—would start over at age ten. He would be watched closely, be given special guidance to insure he didn't grow into the sociopath I had become.

The CC launched into the legally required explanation of what was going on: my rights, the procedures, the charges, the possible penalties, what would happen if a determination led the CC to believe the offense might be a capital one.

"Whew!" the CC breathed, lapsing back into the informal speech it knew I preferred. "Now that we have that out of the way, I can tell you that, from the preliminary reports, I think you're going to be okay."

"You're not just saying that?" I was sincerely frightened. The enormity of it had now had time to sink in.

"You know me better than that."

The testimony began. The complainant went first, and I learned her name was Tiona. The first round was free-form; we could say anything we wanted to, and she had some pretty nasty things to say about all four of us.

The CC went around the circle asking each of us what had happened. I thought Cathay told it most accurately, except for myself. During the course of the statements both Cathay and Trigger filed counter-complaints. The CC noted them. They would be tried simultaneously.

There was a short pause, then the CC spoke in its "official" voice.

"In the matters of Argus and Denver: testimony fails to establish premeditation, but neither deny the physical description of the incident, and a finding of Assault is returned. Mitigating factors of age and consequent inability to combat the mob aspect of the situation are entered, with the following result: the charge is reduced to Willful Deprivation of Dignity.

"In the case of Tiona versus Argus: guilty.

"In the case of Tiona versus Denver: guilty.

"Do either of you have anything to say before sentence is entered?"

I thought about it. "I'm sorry," I said. "It upset me quite a bit, what happened. I won't do it again."

"I'm not sorry," Denver said. "She asked for it. I'm sorry for her, but I'm not sorry for what I did."

"Comments are noted," the CC said. "You are each fined the sum of three hundred Marks, collection deferred until you reach employable age, sum to be taken at the rate of ten percent of your earnings until paid, half going to Tiona, half to the State. Final entry of sentence shall be delayed until a further determination of matters still before the court is made."

"You got off easy," the CC said, speaking only to me. "But stick around. Things could still change, and you might not have to pay the fine after all."

It was a bit of a wrench, getting a sentence, then sympathy from the same machine. I had to guard against feeling that the CC was on my side. It wasn't, not really. It's absolutely impartial, so far as I can tell. Yet it is so vast an intelligence that it makes a different personality for each citizen it deals with. The part that had just talked to me was really on my side, but was powerless to affect what the judgmental part of it did.

"I don't get it," I said. "What happens now?"

"Well, I've been rashomoned again. That means you all told your stories from your own viewpoints. We haven't reached deeply enough into the truth. Now I'm going to have to wire you all, and take another round."

As it spoke, I saw the probes come up behind everyone's chairs: little golden snakes with plugs on the end. I felt one behind me search through my hair until it found the terminal. It plugged in.

There are two levels to wired testimony. Darcy and Trilby and Denver's mother had to leave the room for the first part, when we all told our stories without our censors working. The transcript bears me out when I say I didn't tell any lies in the first found, unlike Tiona, who told a lot of them. But it doesn't sound like the same story, nevertheless. I told all sorts of things I never would have said without being wired: fears, selfish, formless desires, infantile motivations. It's embarrassing, and I'm glad I don't recall any of it. I'm even happier that only Tiona and I, as interested parties, can see my testimony. I only wish I was the only one.

The second phase is the disconnection of the subconscious. I told the story a third time, in terms as bloodless as the stage directions of a holovision script.

Then the terminals withdrew from us and I suffered a moment of disorientation. I knew where I was, where I had been, and yet I felt like I had been told about it rather than lived it. But that passed quickly. I stretched.

"Is everyone ready to go on?" the CC asked, politely. We all said that we were.

"Very well. In the matters of Tiona versus Argus and Denver: the guilty judgments remain in force in both cases, but both fines are rescinded in view of provocation, lessened liability due to immaturity, and lack of signs of continuing sociopathic behavior. In place of the fines, Denver and Argus are to report weekly for evaluation and education in moral principles until such time as a determination can be made, duration of such sessions to be no less than four weeks.

"In the matter of Tiona versus Trigger: Trigger is guilty of an Assault. Tempering this judgment is her motive, which was the recognition of Cathay's strategy in dealing with Tiona, and her belief that he was doing the right thing. This court notes that he was doing the *merciful* thing; right is another matter. There can be no doubt that a physical assault occurred. It cannot be condoned, no matter what the motive. For bad judgment, then, this court fines Trigger ten percent of her earnings for a period of ten years, all of it to be paid to the injured party, Tiona."

Tiona did not look smug. She must have known by then that things were not going her way. I was beginning to understand it, too.

"In the matter of Tiona versus Cathay," the CC went on, "Cathay is guilty of an Assault. His motive has been determined to be the avoidance of just such a situation as he now finds himself in, and the knowledge that Tiona would suffer greatly if he brought her to court. He attempted to bring the confrontation to an end with a minimum of pain for Tiona, never dreaming that she would show the bad judgment to bring the matter to court. She did, and now he finds himself convicted of assault. In view of his motives, mercy will temper this court's decision. He is ordered to pay the same fine as his colleague, Trigger.

"Now to the central matter, that of Trigger and Cathay versus Tiona." I saw her sink a little lower in her chair.

"You are found to be guilty by reason of insanity of the following charges: harassment, trespassing, verbal assault, and four counts of infringement.

"Your offense was in attempting to make others shoulder the blame for your own misjudgments and misfortunes. The court is sympathetic to your plight, realizes that the fault for your situation was not entirely your own. This does not excuse your behavior, however.

"Cathay attempted to do you a favor, supposing that your aberrant state of mind would not last long enough for the filing of charges, that when you were alone and thought it over you would realize how badly you had wronged him and that a court would find in his favor.

"The State holds you responsible for the maintenance of your own mind, does not care what opinions you hold or what evaluations you make of reality so long as they do not infringe on the rights of other citizens. You are free to think Cathay responsible for your troubles, even if this opinion is irrational, but when you assault him with this opinion the State must take notice and make a judgment as to the worth of the opinion.

"This court is appointed to make that judgment of right and wrong, and finds no basis in fact for your contentions.

"This court finds you to be insane.

"Judgment is as follows:

"Subject to the approval of the wronged parties, you are given the choice of death with reprieve, or submission to a course of treatment to remove your sociopathic attitudes.

"Argus, do you demand her death?"

"Huh?" That was a big surprise to me, and not one that I liked. But the decision gave me no trouble.

"No, I don't demand anything. I thought I was out of this, and I feel just rotten about the whole thing. Would you really have killed her if I asked you to?"

"I can't answer that, because you didn't. It's not likely that I would have, mostly because of your age." It went on to ask the other four, and I suspect that Tiona would have been pushing up daisies if Cathay had wanted it that way, but he didn't. Neither did Trigger or Denver.

"Very well. How do you choose, Tiona?"

She answered in a very small voice that she would be grateful for the chance to go on living. Then she thanked each of us. It was excruciatingly painful for me; my empathy was working overtime, and I was trying to imagine what it would feel like to have society's appointed representative declare me insane.

The rest of it was clearing up details. Tiona was fined heavily, both in court costs and taxes, and in funds payable to Cathay and Trigger. Their fines were absorbed in her larger ones, with the result that she would be paying them for many years. Her child was in cold storage; the CC ruled that he should stay there until Tiona was declared sane, as she was now unfit to mother him. It occurred to me that if she had considered suspending his animation while she found a new primary teacher, we all could have avoided the trial.

Tiona hurried away when the doors came open behind us. Darcy hugged me while Trilby stayed in the background, then I went over to join the others, expecting a celebration.

But Trigger and Cathay were not elated. In fact, you would have thought they'd just lost the judgment. They congratulated me and Denver, then hurried away. I looked at Darcy, and she wasn't smiling, either.

"I don't get it," I confessed. "Why is everyone so glum?"

"They still have to face the Teacher's Association," Darcy said.

"I still don't get it. They won."

"It's not just a matter of winning or losing with the TA," Trilby said. "You forget, they were judged guilty of assault. To make it even worse, in fact as bad as it can be, you and Denver were there when it happened. They were the cause of you two joining in the assault. I'm afraid the TA will frown on that."

"But if the CC thought they shouldn't be punished, why should the TA think otherwise? Isn't the CC smarter than people?"

Trilby grimaced. "I wish I could answer that. I wish I was even sure how I feel about it."

She found me the next day, shortly after the Teacher's Association announced its decision. I didn't really want to be found, but the bayou is not so big that one can really hide there, so I hadn't tried. I was sitting on the grass on the highest hill in Beatnik Bayou, which was also the driest place.

She beached the canoe and came up the hill slowly, giving me plenty of time to warn her off if I really wanted to be alone. What the hell. I'd have to talk to her soon enough.

For a long time she just sat there. She rested her elbows on her knees and stared down at the quiet waters, just like I'd been doing all afternoon.

"How's he taking it?" I said, at last.

"I don't know. He's back there, if you want to talk to him. He'd probably like to talk to you."

"At least Trigger got off okay." As soon as I'd said it, it sounded hollow.

"Three years' probation isn't anything to laugh about. She'll have to close this place down for a while. Put it in mothballs."

"Mothballs." I saw Tuesday the hippo, wallowing in the deep mud across the water. Tuesday in suspended animation? I thought of Tiona's little baby, waiting in a bottle until his mother became sane again. I remembered the happy years slogging around in the bayou mud, and saw the waters frozen, icicles mixed with Spanish moss in the tree limbs. "I guess it'll cost quite a bit to start it up again in three years, won't it?" I had only hazy ideas of money. So far, it had never been important to me.

Trilby glanced at me, eyes narrowed. She shrugged.

"Most likely, Trigger will have to sell the place. There's a buyer who wants to expand it and turn it into a golf course."

"Golf course," I echoed, feeling numb. Manicured greens, pretty water hazards, sand traps, flags whipping in the breeze. Sterile. I suddenly felt like crying, but for some reason I didn't do it.

"You can't come back here, Argus. Nothing stays the same. Change is something you have to get used to."

"Cathay will, too." And just how much change should a person be expected to take? With a shock, I realized that now Cathay would be doing what I had wanted him to do. He'd be growing up with me, getting older instead of being regressed to grow up with another child. And it was suddenly just too much. It hadn't been my fault that this was happening to him, but having wished for it and having it come true made it feel like it was. The tears came, and they didn't stop for a long time.

Trilby left me alone, and I was grateful for that.

She was still there when I got myself under control. I didn't care one way or the other. I felt empty, with a burning in the back of my throat. Nobody had told me life was going to be like this.

"What . . . what about the child Cathay contracted to teach?" I asked, finally, feeling I should say something. "What happens to her?"

"The TA takes responsibility," Trilby said. "They'll find someone. For Trigger's child, too."

I looked at her. She was stretched out, both elbows behind her to prop her up. Her valentine nipples crinkled as I watched.

She glanced at me, smiled with one corner of her mouth. I felt a little better. She was awfully pretty.

"I guess he can . . . well, can't he still teach older kids?"

"I suppose he can," Trilby said, with a shrug. "I don't know if he'll want to. I know Cathay. He's not going to take this well."

"Is there anything I could do?"

"Not really. Talk to him. Show sympathy, but not too much. You'll have to figure it out. See if he wants to be with you."

It was too confusing. How was I supposed to know what he needed? He hadn't come to see me. But Trilby had.

So there was one uncomplicated thing in my life right then, one thing I could do where I wouldn't have to think. I rolled over and got on top of Trilby and started to kiss her. She responded with a lazy eroticism I found irresistible. She *did* know some tricks I'd never heard of.

"How was that?" I said, much later.

That smile again. I got the feeling that I constantly amused her, and somehow I didn't mind it. Maybe it was the fact that she made no bones about her being the adult and me being the child. That was the way it would be with us. I would have to grow up to her, she would not go back and imitate me.

"Are you looking for a grade?" she asked. "Like the twentieth century?" She got to her feet and stretched.

"All right. I'll be honest. You get an A for effort, but any thirteen-year-old would. You can't help it. In technique, maybe a low C. Not that I expected any more, for the same reason."

"So you want to teach me to do better? That's your job?"

"Only if you hire me. And sex is such a small part of it. Listen, Argus. I'm not going to be your mother. Darcy does that okay. I won't be your playmate, either, like Cathay was. I won't be teaching you moral lessons. You're getting tired of that, anyway."

It was true. Cathay had never really been my contemporary, though he tried his best to look it and act it. But the illusion had started to wear thin, and I guess it had to. I was no longer able to ignore the contradictions, I was too sophisticated and cynical for him to hide his lessons in everyday activities.

It bothered me in the same way the CC did. The CC could befriend me one minute and sentence me to death the next. I wanted more than that, and Trilby seemed to be offering it.

"I won't be teaching you science or skills, either," she was saying. "You'll have tutors for that, when you decide just what you want to do."

"Just what *is* it you do, then?"

"You know, I've never been able to find a good way of describing that. I won't be around all the time, like Cathay was. You'll come to me when you want to, maybe when you have a problem. I'll be sympathetic and do what I can, but mostly I'll just point out that you have to make all the hard choices. If you've been stupid I'll tell you so, but I won't be surprised or disappointed if you go on being stupid in the same way. You can use me as a role model if you want to, but I don't insist on it. But I promise I'll always tell you things straight, as I see them. I won't try to slip things in painlessly. It's time for pain. Think of Cathay as a professional child. I'm not putting him down. He turned you into a civilized being, and when he got you you were hardly that. It's because of him that you're capable of caring about his situation now, that you have loyalties to feel divided about. And he's good enough at it to know how you'll choose."

"Choose? What do you mean?"

"I can't tell you that." She spread her hands, and grinned. "See how helpful I can be?"

She was confusing me again. Why can't things be simpler?

"Then if Cathay's a professional child, you're a professional adult?"

"You could think of it like that. It's not really analogous."

"I guess I still don't know what Darcy would be paying you for."

"We'll make love a lot. How's that? Simple enough for you?" She brushed dirt from her back and frowned at the ground. "But not on dirt anymore. I don't care for dirt."

I looked around, too. The place *was* messy. Not pretty at all. I wondered how I could have liked it so much. Suddenly I wanted to get out, to go to a clean, dry place.

"Come on," I said, getting up. "I want to try some of those things again."

"Does this mean I have a job?"

"Yeah. I guess it does."

Cathay was sitting on the porch of the Sugar Shack, a line of brown beer bottles perched along the edge. He smiled at us as we approached him. He was stinking drunk.

It's strange. We'd been drunk many times together, the four of us. It's great fun. But when only one person is drunk, it's a little disgusting. Not that I blamed him. But when you're drinking together all the jokes make sense. When you drink alone, you just make a sloppy nuisance of yourself.

Trilby and I sat on either side of him. He wanted to sing. He pressed bottles on both of us, and I sipped mine and tried to get into the spirit of it. But pretty soon he was crying, and I felt awful. And I admit that it wasn't entirely in sympathy. I felt helpless because there was so little I could do, and a bit resentful of some of the promises he had me make. I would have come to see him anyway. He didn't have to blubber on my shoulder and beg me not to abandon him.

So he cried on me, and on Trilby, then just sat between us looking glum. I tried to console him.

"Cathay, it's not the end of the world. Trilby says you'll still be able to teach older kids. My age and up. The TA just said you couldn't handle younger ones."

He mumbled something.

"It shouldn't be that different," I said, not knowing when to shut up.

"Maybe you're right," he said.

"Sure I am." I was unconsciously falling into that false heartiness people use to cheer up drunks. He heard it immediately.

"What the hell do you know about it? You think you . . . damn it, what do you know? You know what kind of person it takes to do my job? A little bit of a misfit, that's what. Somebody who doesn't want to grow up any more than you do. We're *both* cowards, Argus. You don't know it, but *I* do. *I* do. So what the hell am I going to do? Huh? Why don't you go away? You got what you wanted, didn't you?"

"Take it easy, Cathay," Trilby soothed, hugging him close to her. "Take it easy."

He was immediately contrite, and began to cry quietly. He said how sorry he was, over and over, and he was sincere. He said, he hadn't meant it, it just came out, it was cruel.

And so forth.

I was cold all over.

We put him to bed in the shack, then started down the road.

"We'll have to watch him the next few days," Trilby said. "He'll get over this, but it'll be rough."

"Right," I said.

I took a look at the shack before we went around the false bend in the road. For one moment I saw Beatnik Bayou as a perfect illusion, a window through time. Then we went around the tree and it all fell apart. It had never mattered before.

But it was such a sloppy place. I'd never realized how ugly the Sugar Shack was.

I never saw it again. Cathay came to live with us for a few months, tried his hand at art. Darcy told me privately that he was hopeless. He moved out, and I saw him frequently after that, always saying hello.

But he was depressing to be around, and he knew it. Besides, he admitted that I represented things he was trying to forget. So we never really talked much.

Sometimes I play golf in the old bayou. It's only two holes, but there's talk of expanding it.

They did a good job on the renovation.

ELBOW ROOM

by Marion Zimmer Bradley

Successful lighthouse keepers are either natural hermits or learn to enjoy their own company in preference to the bustle of town or city. Marion Zimmer Bradley, famous for her Darkover novels, is not a loner as far as we know. However she is a professional writer, and there is one characteristic true of all writers—they spend long hours alone telling their thoughts to a machine— typewriter or tape recorder. So Ms. Bradley put two and two together and came up with this interplanetary necessity.

Sometimes I feel the need to go to confession on my way to work.

It's quiet at firstdawn, with Aleph Prime not above the horizon yet; there's always some cognitive dissonance because, with the antigravs turned up high enough for comfort, you feel that the "days" ought to reflect a planet of human mass, not a mini-planetoid space station. So at firstdawn you're set for an ordinary-sized day; twenty hours, or twenty-three, or something your circadian rhythms could compromise with. Thus when Prime sets again for firstdark you aren't prepared for it. With your mind, maybe, but not down where you need it, in your guts. By thirddawn you're

gearing up for a whole day on Checkout Station again, and
you can cope with thirddark and fifthdark and by twelfthdark
you're ready to put on your sleep mask and draw the curtains
and shut it all out again till firstdawn next day.

But at firstdawn you get that illusion, and I always enjoy it
for a little while. It's like being really alone on a silent world,
a real world. And even before I came here to Checkout I was
always a loner, preferring my own company to anyone else's.

That's the kind they always pick for the Vortex stations,
like Checkout. There isn't much company there. And we
learn to give each other elbow room.

You'd think, with only five of us here—or is it only four;
I've never been quite sure, for reasons I'll go into later—we'd
do a lot of socializing. You'd think we would huddle together
against the enormous agoraphobia of space. I really don't
know why we don't. I guess, though, the kind of person who
could really enjoy living on Checkout—and I do—would
have to be a loner. And I go squirrelly when there are too
many other people around.

Of course, I know I couldn't really live here alone, as
much as I'd like to. They tried that, early in the days of the
Vortex stations, sending one man or woman out alone. One
after another, with monotonous regularity, they suicided.
Then they tried sending well-adjusted couples, small groups,
sociable types who would huddle together and socialize, and
they all went nuts and did one another in. I know why, of
course; they saw too much of each other, and began to rely
on one another for their sanity and self-validation. And of
course that solution didn't work. You have to be the kind of
person who can be wholly self-reliant.

So now they do it this way. I always know I'm not alone.
But I never have to *see* too much of the other people here; I
never have to see them unless I *want* to. I don't know how
much socializing the others do, but I suspect they're as much
loners as I am. I don't really care, as long as they don't intrude on *my* privacy, and as long as they take orders the way
they're supposed to. I love them all, of course, all four or
maybe five of them. They told me, back at Psych Conditioning, that this would happen. But I don't remember how it
happened, whether it just happened or whether they *made* it
happen. I don't ask too many questions. I'm glad that I love
them; I'd hate to think that some Psych-tech *made* me love
them! Because they're sweet, dear, wonderful, lovable people.
All of them.

As long as I don't have to see them very often.

Because I'm the boss. I'm in control. It's *my* Station! Slight tendencies toward megalomania, they called it in Psych. It's good for a Station Programmer to have these mild megalomanic tendencies, they explained it all to me. If they put humble self-effacing types out here, they'd start thinking of themselves as wee little fleabites upon the vast face of the Universe, and sooner or later they'd be found with their throats cut, because they couldn't believe they were big enough to be in control of anything on the cosmic scale of the Vortex.

Lonely, yes. But I like it that way. I like being boss out here. And I like the way they've provided for my needs. I think I have the best chef in the galaxy. She cooks all my favorite foods—I suppose Psych gave her my profile. I wonder sometimes if the other people at the station have to eat what I like, or if they get to order their own favorites. I don't really care, as long as I get to order what I like. And then I have my own personal librarian, with all the music of the galaxy at her fingertips, the best sound-equipment known, state-of-the-art stuff I'd never be able to afford in any comparable job back Earthside. And my own gardener, and a technician to do the work I can't handle. And even my own personal priest. Can you imagine that? Sending a priest all the way out here, just to minister to my spiritual needs! Well, at least to a congregation of four. Or five.

Or is it six? I keep thinking I've forgotten somebody.

Firstdawn is rapidly giving way to firstnoon when I leave the garden and kneel in the little confessional booth. I whisper "Bless me, Father, for I have sinned."

"Bless you, my child." Father Nicholas is there, although his Mass must be long over. I sometimes wonder if this doesn't violate the sanctity of the confessional, that he cannot help knowing which of his congregation is kneeling there; I am the only one who ever gets up before seconddawn. And I don't really know whether I have sinned or not. How could I sin against God or my fellow man, when I am thousands of millions of miles away from all but five or six of them? And I so seldom see the others, I have no chance to sin with them or against them. Maybe I only need to hear his voice; a human voice, a light, not particularly masculine voice. Deeper than mine, though, *different* from mine. That's the important thing; to hear a voice which *isn't* mine.

"Father, I have entertained doubts about the nature of God."

"Continue, my child."

"When I was out in the Wheel the other day, watching the Vortex, I found myself wondering if the Vortex was God. After all, God is unknowable, and the Vortex is so totally alien from human experience. Isn't this the closest thing that the human race has ever found, to the traditional view of God? Something totally beyond matter, energy, space or time?"

There is a moment of silence. Have I shocked the priest? But after a long time his soft voice comes quietly into the little confessional. Outside the light is already dimming toward firstdark.

"There is no harm in regarding the Vortex as a symbol of God's relationship to man, my child. After all, the Vortexes are perhaps the most glorious of God's works. It is written in scripture that the Heavens declare the glory of God, and the firmament proclaims the wonder of His work."

"But does this mean, then, that God is distant, incapable of loving mankind? I can't imagine the Vortex loving anyone or being conscious of anyone. Not even me."

"Is that a defect in God, or a defect in your own imagination, my child, in ascribing limits to God's power?"

I persist. "But does it matter if I say my prayers to the Vortex and worship it?"

Behind the screen I hear a soft laugh. "God will hear your prayers wherever you say them, dear child, and whenever you find anything worthy of worship and admiration you are worshipping God, by whatever name you choose to call it. Is there anything else, my child?"

"I have been guilty of uncharitable thoughts about my cook, Father. Last night she didn't fix my dinner till late, and I wanted to tear her eyes out!"

"Did you harm her, child?"

"No. I just yelled through the screen that she was a lazy, selfish, stupid bitch. I wanted to go out and hit her, but I didn't."

"Then you exercised commendable self-restraint, did you not? What did she answer?"

"She didn't answer at all. And that made me madder than ever."

"You should love your neighbor—and I mean your chef, too—as yourself, child," he reproves, and I say, hanging my head, "I'm not loving myself very much these days, maybe that's the trouble."

Mind, now, I'm not sure there really is a Father Nicholas behind that screen. Maybe it's a relay system which puts me into touch with a priest Earthside. Or maybe Father Nicholas is only a special voice program on the main computer, which is why I sometimes ask the craziest questions, and play a game with myself to see how long it takes "Father Nicholas" to find the right program for an answer. As I said, it seems crazy to send a priest out here for five people. Or is it six?

But then, why not? We people at the Vortex stations keep the whole galaxy running. Nothing is too good for us, so why not my personal priest?

"Tell me what is troubling you, my child."

Always *my child*. Never by name. Does he even know it? He must. After all, I am in charge here, Checkout Programmer. The boss. Or is this just the manners of the confessional, a subtle way of reemphasizing that all of us are the same to him, equal in his sight and in the sight of God? I don't know if I like that. It's disquieting. Perhaps my chef runs to him and tells tales of me, how I shrieked foul names at her, and abused her through the kitchen hatch! I cover my face with my hands and sob, hearing him make soothing sounds.

I envy that priest, secure behind his curtain. Listening to the human faults of others, having none of his own. I almost became a priest myself. I tell him so.

"I know that, child, you told me. But I'm not clear in my mind why you chose not to be ordained."

I'm not clear either, and I tell him so, trying to remember. If I had been a man I would surely have gone through with it, but it is still not entirely easy to be ordained, for a woman, and the thought of seminary, with ninety or a hundred other priestlings and priestlets herded all together, even then the thought made me uneasy. I couldn't have endured the fight for a woman to be ordained. "I'm not a fighter, Father."

But I am disquieted when he agrees with me. "No. If you were, you wouldn't be out here, would you?" Again I feel uneasy; am I just running away? I choose to live here on the ragged rim of the Universe, tending the Vortex, literally at the back end of Beyond. I pour all this uncertainty out to him, knowing he will reassure me, understand me as always.

But his reassuring noises are too soothing, too calming, humoring me. Damn it, is there anyone *there* behind that curtain? I want to tear it down, to see the priest's face, his human face, or else to be sure that it is only a bland computer console programmed to reassure and thus to mock me. My hand already extended, I draw it back. I don't really want to know. Let them laugh at me, if there is really a *they*, a priest Earthside listening over this unthinkable extension of the kilometers and the megakilometers, let them laugh. They deserve it, if they are really such clever programmers, making it possible for me to draw endless sympathy and reassurance from the sound of an alien voice.

Whatever we do, we do to make it possible for you to live and keep your sanity . . . "I think, Father, that I am—am a little lonely. The dreams are building up again."

"Perfectly natural," he says soothingly, and I know that he will arrange one of Julian's rare visits. Even now I hang my head, blush, cannot face him, but it is less embarrassing this way than if I had to take the initiative alone, unaided. It's part of being the kind of loner I am, that I could never endure it, to call Julian direct, have to take—perhaps—a rebuff or a downright rejection. Well, I never claimed to be a well-adjusted personality. A well-adjusted personality could not survive out here, at the rim of nowhere. Back on Earthside I probably wouldn't even *have* a love life, I avoid people too much. But here they provide for all my needs. All. Even this one, which, left to myself, I would probably neglect.

Ego te absolvo.

I kneel briefly to say my penance, knowing that the ritual is foolish. Comforting; but foolish. He reminds me to turn on the monitor in my room and he will say Mass for me tomorrow. And again I am certain that there is nobody there, that it is a program in the computer; is there any other reason we do not all assemble for Christian fellowship? Or do we all share this inability to tolerate one another's company?

But I feel soothed and comforted as I go down between the automatic sprinklers through the little patch of garden tended so carefully by my own gardener. I catch a glimpse, a shimmer in the air, of someone in the garden, turned away like a distant reflection, but no one is supposed to be here at this hour and I quickly look away.

Still it is comforting not to be alone and I call out a cheery good-morning to the invisible image, wondering, with a strange little cramp of excitement low in my body; *is it Julian?* I see him so briefly, so seldom, except in the half-darkness of my room on those rare occasions he comes to me. I'm not even sure what he does here. We don't talk about his work. We have better things to do. Thinking of that makes me tremble, squeeze my legs tight, thinking that it may not be long till I see him again. But I have a day's work to do, and with seconddawn brightening the sky, glinting on reflections from which I glance away . . . *you never look in mirrors* . . . I climb up into the seat that will take me up to the Wheel, out by the Vortex.

There is an exhilaration to that, shooting up toward the strange seething no-color of it. There is a ship already waiting. Waiting for *me*, for the Vortex to open. All that power and burning and fusion and raw energy, all waiting for *me*, and I enjoy my daily dose of megalomania as I push the speech button.

"Checkout speaking. Register your name and business."

It is always a shock to hear a voice from outside, a really strange voice. But I register the captain's voice, the name and registry number so that later they can match programs with Checkin, my opposite number on the far side of the Vortex—in a manner of speaking. Where the Vortex is concerned, of course, Near and Far, or Here and There, or Before and After, have no more meaning than—oh, than I and Thou. In one of the mirrors on the wheel I catch a glimpse of my technician, waiting, and I sit back and listen as she rattles off the co-ordinates in a sharp staccato. She and I have nothing to say to each other. I don't really think that girl is interested in anything except mathematics. I drift, watching myself in the mirror, listening to the ship's captain arguing with the technician, and I am irritated. How dare he argue, her conduct reflects on me and I am enraged by any hint of rudeness to my staff. So I speak the code which starts the Vortex into its strange nonspace whorl, the colors and swirls.

This could all be done by computers, of course.

I am here, almost literally, to push a button by hand if one gets stuck. From the earliest days of telemetered equipment, machinery has tended to go flukey and sometimes jam; and during the two hundred years that the Vortex stations have been in operation, they've found out that it's easier and cheaper to maintain the stations with their little crews of agoraphobic and solitary loners. They even provide us with chefs and gardeners and all our mental and spiritual comforts. We humans are just software which doesn't—all things considered—get out of order quite as often as the elaborate self-maintaining machineries do. Furthermore, we can be serviced more cheaply when we *do* get out of order. So we're there to make sure that if any of the buttons stick, we can unstick them before they cost the galaxy more than the whole operating costs of Checkout for the next fifty years.

I watch the Vortex swirl, and my knowledge and judgment tell me the same thing as do my instruments. "Whenever you're ready," I say, receive their acknowledgment, and then the strange metal shape of the ship swirls with the Vortex, becomes nonshape, I almost see it vanish into amorphous nothingness, to come out—or so the theory is—at Checkin Station, several hundred light-years away. Do these ships go anywhere at all, I wonder? Do they ever return? They vanish when I push those buttons, and they never come back. Am I sending them into oblivion, or to their proper prearranged destination? I don't know. And, if the truth be told, I don't really care. For all the difference it makes to me they could be going into another dimension, or to the theological Hell.

But I like it out here on the Wheel. There is *real* solitude up here. Down there on Checkout there is solitude with other people around, though I seldom see them. I realize I am still twitching from a brief encounter with the gardener this morning. Don't they know, these people, that they aren't supposed to be around when I am walking in the gardens? But even that brief surge of adrenaline has been good for me, I suppose. Do they arrange for me to get a glimpse of one of my fellow humans only when I *need* that kind of stirring up?

Back at Checkout—there will not be another ship today—I walk again through the garden, putter a little, cherish with my eyes the choice melon I am growing under glass, warn the gardener through the intercom not to touch it until I myself order it served up for my supper. I remember the satisfaction of the cargo ship waiting, metal tentacles silent against the black of space, waiting. Waiting for me, waiting for my good pleasure, gatekeeper to the Void, Cerberus at a new kind of hell.

Rank has its privileges. While I am in the garden none of the others come near; but I am a little fatigued, I leave the garden to the others and go to my room for deep meditation. I can sense them all around me, the gardener working with the plants like an extension of my own consciousness, I sit like a small spider at the center of a web and watch the others working as I sit back to meditate. My mind floats free, my alpha rhythms take over, I disappear . . .

Later, waiting for my supper, I wonder what kind of woman would become chef on a Checkout station. I *can* cook, I *have* done my own cooking, I am a damn good cook, but I wouldn't have taken a job like that. Is she completely without ambition? I don't see her very often. We wouldn't have much in common; what could I possibly have to say to a woman like that? Waiting, floating, spider in my web, I find I can imagine her going carefully through the motions and little soothing rituals, chopping the fresh vegetables I fingered in the garden this morning, heating the trays, all the little soothing mindless things. But to spend her life like that? The woman must be a fool.

I come out of the meditative state to find my supper waiting for me. I call my thanks to her, eat. The food is good, it is always good, but the dishes are too hot, somehow I have burned my hand on them. But it doesn't matter, I have something more to look forward to, tonight. I delay, savoring the knowledge, listening to one of my operatic tapes, lost in a vague romantic reverie. Tonight, Julian is coming.

I wonder sometimes why we are not allowed to see one another more often. Surely, if he cares for me as much as he says, it would be proper to see each other casually now and then, to talk about our work. But I am sure Psych is right, that it is better for us not to see each other too often. On Earth, if we grew tired of one another, we could each find someone else. But here there *is* no one else—for either of us. A phrase floats through my mind from nowhere, *chains of mnemonic suggestion,* as I set the controls which will allow him to come, silent and alone, into my room after I have gone to bed.

He has come and gone.

I do not know why the rules are as they are. Perhaps to keep us from quarreling, to avoid the tragedies of the early days of the Vortex stations. Perhaps, simply, to avoid our growing bored with each other. As if I could ever be bored with Julian! To me, he is perfect, even his name. Julian has always seemed to me the most perfect name for a man, and Julian, *my* Julian, my lover, the perfect man to match the perfect name. So why is it we are not allowed to meet more often? Why can we meet like this, only in the silent dark?

Languorous, satisfied, exhausted, I muse drowsily, wondering if it is some obscure mystery of my inner Psych-profile, that one of us subconsciously desires the old myth of Psyche, who could retain her lover Eros only as long as she never saw his face? I see him only for a moment in the mirror, misty, never clearly perceived, over my shoulder; but I know he is handsome.

I am so sensitive to Julian's moods that I think sometimes I am developing special senses for my love; becoming a telepath, but only for him. When our bodies join it seems often as if I were one in mind with him, touching him, how else could I be so aware of his emotions, so completely secure of his tenderness and his concern? How else could he know so perfectly all my body's obscurer desires, when I myself can hardly bring myself to speak them, when I would be afraid or ashamed to voice them aloud? But he knows, he always knows, leaving me satisfied, worn, spent. I wish, with a longing so intense it is pain, that the regulations by which we live would let him lie here in my arms for the rest of the night, that I could feel myself held close and cherished, comforted against this vast, eternal loneliness; that he could cuddle me in his arms, that we could meet sometimes for a drink or share our dinner. Why not?

A terrible thought comes to me. They give me everything else. My own cook. My own gardener. My technician. My personal priest.

My very own male whore.

I cannot believe it. No, no. No. I do not believe it. Julian loves me, and I love him. Anyhow, it would not suit the Puritan consciences of our legislators. No, I can't see it; how would they justify it on the requisition forms? *Whore, male, one, Checkout Programmer, for the use of.* No, such a thing couldn't happen. Surely they just hired some male technician, determined by Psych-profile to have the maximum sexual compatibility with myself. That's bad enough, heaven knows.

Now an even more frightening thought surges up into my conscious mind. Can it be possible—oh, God, no!—that Julian, *my* Julian, is an android?

They have designed some of them, I know, with extremely sophisticated sex programs. I have seen them advertised in those catalogs we used to giggle over when we were little girls. I am sick with fear and dread at the thought that during those conditioning trances which I have been conditioned to forget, I gave up all that data about my secret dreams and desires and sexual fantasies, so that they might program them all into the computer of an android, and what emerged was . . . Julian.

Is he a multipurpose android, perhaps, then? Hardware, no more, both useful and economical; perhaps that gardener I see dimly sometimes, like a hologram, in the distance. He could, of course, be the gardener, though in the brief glimpses of the gardener I had the impression the gardener was a woman. Who can tell, with these coveralls we all wear, uniform, unisex? And it would look better on the congressional requisitions: *Android, one, multiprogrammed, Checkout Station, for the maintenance of.* And a special sexual program would only be a memo in the files of Psych. Nothing to embarrass anyone—anyone but me, that is, and I am not supposed to know. Just another piece of Station hardware. For maintenance of the Station. And of the Station Programmer. Hardware. Yes, very. Oh, God!

I have no time now for worrying about Julian, or what he is, or about my own dissatisfactions and fears. I cannot take any of these disquieting thoughts to that computerized priest, if he is indeed only a sophisticated computer, a mechanical priest-psychiatrist! Is he another android, perhaps? Or is he indeed the same android with still another program? Priest and male whore at the flip of a switch? Am I alone here with a multipurpose android serving all my functions? No time for that. A ship is out there, waiting for me; and my instruments tell me, as I ride out to the Wheel, even before I get the message; that ship is in trouble.

Perhaps all the signs, all my fears that I am going mad, are simply signs of developing telepathic potential; I never believed that I was even potentially an esper, yet somehow I am aware of nearly everything my technician said to the ship's captain. I did not understand it all, of course, I have no technical skill at all. My skills are all executive. I can barely manage to make my little pocket calculator figure out the tariffs for the ships I send into the Vortex; I joked with Central that they should allow me a bookkeeper, but they are too stingy. But even though I did not understand all of what the technician said, when I read the report she left for me, I know that if the ship went into the Vortex in this state, it might never emerge; worse, it might create spatial anomalies to disturb the fields for other ships and put the Vortex very badly out of commission. So I know that they dare not pass through that gate; I cannot follow the precise mathematics of the switch, though, and I feel like a fool. When I was in preparatory school I tested highest in all the groups, including mathematical ability. But I ended up with no technical skill. How, I wonder, did that happen?

Later I have leisure to visit the captain by screen. He is a big man, youthful, soft-spoken, his smile strangely stirring. And he asks me a strange question.

"You are the Programmer? Are you people a clone?"

"Why, no, nothing like that," I say to him, and ask why.

"The technician—she's very like you. Oh, of course, you are nothing alike otherwise, she's all business—a shame, in a lovely young woman! I could hardly get her to say a pleasant word to me!"

I tell him that I am an only child. Only children are best for work like this; the necessary isolation from peer groups. A child reared in a puppy-pack, under peer pressure from siblings and agemates, becomes other-directed; dependent upon the opinions and the approval of others, without the inner resources to tolerate the solitude which is the breath of life to me. I am even a little offended. "I can't see the slightest resemblance between us," I tell him, and he shakes his head and says diplomatically that perhaps it is a similarity of height and coloring which misled him.

"Anyway, I didn't like her much, she flayed me with her tongue, kept strictly to business—you'd think it was my *fault* the ship was out of commission! You're much, *much* pleasanter than she is!"

And that is as it should be, I am the one with leisure for reflection and conversation; it wouldn't be right for my technician to waste her time talking! So we talk, we even flirt a little. I am aware of it; I pose and preen a little for him, letting the animal woman surface from all the other faces I wear, and finally I agree to the hazardous step, to visit him on his ship.

So strange, so strange to think of being with one who is not carefully Psych-profiled to be agreeable to me. There is nothing in the regulations against it, of course, perhaps they believe our love of solitude will keep us away as it has always done before, for me. Even a little welcome, alien. But when I am actually through the airlock I am shocked into silence by the strange faces, the alien smells, the different body-chemistry of strange male life. They say that men give off hormones, analogous to pheromones in the lower kingdoms, which they cannot smell on one another; which only a woman is chemically able to smell. I believe it, it is true, the ship reeks of maleness. Ushered into a room where I may strip my suit I avoid the mirror. *Never look into a mirror, unless . . . unless . . .* why would Psych have imprinted that prohibition on me? I need to see that my hair is tidy, my coverall free of grease. Defiantly I look into it anyway, my head swims and I look away in haste.

Fear, fear of what I may see, my face dissolving, identity lost . . . stranger, not myself, unknown . . .

A drink in my hand, flattery and compliments; I find I am hungry for this after long isolation. Of course I am selfish and vain, it is a professional necessity, like my little touch of daily megalomania. I accept this, and revel in seeing others, interacting with strange faces—*really* strange, not programmed to my personal needs and wishes. Yes, I know I need to be alone, I remember all the reasons, but I know also, too well, the terrible face of loneliness. All my carefully chosen companions are so dovetailed to my personality that talking to them is like . . .

. . . like talking to myself, like looking in a mirror . . .

Two drinks help me unwind, relax. I know all the dangers of alcohol, but tonight I am defiant; we are off duty, both the captain and myself, we need not guard ourselves. Before too long I find the captain's hands on me, touching me, rousing me in a way Julian has not done since his first visits. I give myself over to his kisses, and when he asks the inevitable question I brace myself for a moment, then shrug and ask myself *Why not?* His touch on me is welcome, I brush aside thoughts of Julian, even Julian has been too carefully adjusted, dovetailed, programmed to my own personality; perhaps even a little abrasiveness helps to alter the far-too-even tenor of the days, to create something of the necessary *otherness* of lovemaking. That is what I have missed, the otherness; Julian being too carefully selected and Psych-profiled to me.

If a love-partner is too similar to the self there is not the needed, satisfying *merging.* Even the amoeba which splits itself, infinitely reduplicating perfect analogies of its own personality and awareness, feels now and then the need to merge, to exchange its very protoplasm and cell-stuff with the *other*; too much of even the most necessary similarity is deadly, and makes of lovemaking only a more elaborate and ritualized masturbation. It is good to be touched by *another.*

Together, then, into his room. And our bodies merge abruptly into an unlovely struggle at the height of which he blurts out, as if in shock, "But you couldn't *possibly* be that inexperienced . . ." and then, seeing and sensing my shock, he is all gentleness again, apologetic, saying he had forgotten how young I was. I am confused and distressed; *I* inexperi-

enced? Now I am on my mettle, to prove myself equal to
passion, sophisticated and knowledgeable, tolerating discomfort and strangeness, to think longingly of Julian. It serves me
right, to be unfaithful to him, Psych was right, Julian is exactly what I need; I know, even while the captain and I are
lying close, afterward, all tenderness, that I will not do this
again. The regulations are wise. Back to the Station, back to
my quarters, blur the experience all away in sleep, all of it
. . . *awkwardness, struggle that felt like rape* . . . no, I will
not do this again, I know now why it is forbidden. I do not
think I will confess it even to the priest, I have done penance
enough. Seal it all away in some inaccessible part of my
mind, the bruising and humiliation of the memory.

Flotsam in my mind from the vast amnesia of the training
program, as I seek to forget, that conditioning they will never
let us remember; that I am suitable for this work because I
dissociate with abnormal rapidity. . . .

And next morning at firstdawn I go up even before breakfast to the Wheel; their repairs are made and they do not
want to lose time. The captain wants to speak with me, but I
let him speak with the technician while I watch out of sight. I
do not want to look into his face again; I never want to see
again in any face that mixture of tenderness, pity—contempt.

I am glad to see their ship dissolve into the vast nonshape
of the Vortex. I do not care if their repairs have been made
properly or if they lose themselves somewhere inside the Vortex and never return. Watching their shape vanish I see a
face dissolving in a mirror and I am agitated and frightened,
frightened . . . they are not part of my world, I have seen
them go, I have perhaps destroyed them. I think of how easy
it would have been, how glad I would have been if my technician had given them the wrong program and they had vanished into the Vortex and come out . . . nowhere. As I have
destroyed everything not the self.

Julian has been destroyed for me too . . .

Maybe there is nothing out there, no ship, no Vortex, nothing. Everything comes into the human mind through the fil-
ters of self, my priest created to absolve a self which is not
there, or is it the priest who is not there at all? Maybe there
is nothing out there, maybe I created it all out of my own inner needs, priest, ship, Station, Vortex, perhaps I am still lying in the conditioning trances down there on Earth,
fantasizing people who would help me to survive the terrors
of loneliness, perhaps these people whom I see, but never

clearly, are all androids, or fantasies born of my own
madness and my inner needs . . . a random phrase floats
again through my mind, *always the danger of solipsism, in
the dissociator, the feeling that only the self exists . . . eternal preoccupation with internal states is morbid and we take
advantage . . .*

Was there ever a ship out there? Did my mind create it to
break the vast monotony of solitude, the loneliness I find I
cannot endure, did I even fantasize the captain's gross body
lying on my own?

*Or is it Julian that I created, my own hands on my body,
fantasy . . . a half-lighted image in a mirror . . .*

The terrible solitude, the solitude I need and yet cannot endure, the solitude that is madness. And yet I need the solitude, so that I will not kill them all, I could murder them as
all the earlier Vortex stations murdered another, or is it only
suicide when there is nothing but myself?

Is the whole cosmos out there—stars, galaxies, Vortex—
only an emanation of my own brain? If so, then I can un-
make it with a thought as I made it. I can snatch up my
cook's kitchen knife and plunge it into my throat and all the
stars will go away and all the universes. What am I doing in
the kitchen . . . the cook's knife in my hand . . . here where
I never go? She will be angry; I am supposed to give her the
same privacy I yield to myself, I call out an apology and
leave. Or is that pointless, am I crying out apology or abuse
to myself? I have had no breakfast, at this hour, near
thirddawn, the cook always prepares, I always prepare breakfast, I meditate while breakfast is prepared and served to me
on my tray, facing the mirror from which I emerge . . . I am
the other, the one with leisure for meditation and reflection—the executive, creative, I am God creating all these universes inside and outside of my mind . . . dizzied, I catch at
the mirror, the knife slips, my face dissolves, my hand bleeds
and all the universes wobble and spin on their cosmic axes,
the face in the mirror commands in the voice of Father Nicholas "Go, my child, and meditate."

"No! No!" I refuse to be tranquilized again, to be
deceived . . .

"Command over-ride!" A voice I do not remember. "Go
and meditate, meditate . . ." *meditate, meditate . . .*

Like the tolling of a great bell, commanding, rising out of
the deeps, the voice of God. I meditate, seeing my face dissolve and change . . .

No wonder I can read the technician's mind, I am the technician. . . .

There is no one here. There has never been anyone here.

Only myself, and I am all, I am the God, the maker and unmaker of all the universes, I am Brahma, I am the Cosmos and the Vortex, I am the slow unraveling . . .

. . . unraveling of the mind . . .

I stumble to the chapel, images dissolving in my mind like the cook's face with the knife, into the confessional, the confessional I have always known is empty, sob out a prayer to the empty shrine. *Oh, God, if there is a God, let there be a God, let there be somebody there. . . . or is God too only an emanation of my mind . . .*

And the slow dissolve into the mirror, the priest's voice saying soothing things which I do not really hear, the mirror as my mind dissolves, the priest's voice soothing and calm, my own voice weeping, pleading, sobbing, begging . . .

But his words mean nothing, a fragment of my own disintegration, I want to die, I want to die, I am dying, gone, nowhere . . .

The phenomenon of selective attention, what used to be called hypnosis, a self-induced dissociation or fugue state, dissociational hysteria sometimes regarded as multiple personality when the fragmented self-organized chains of memory and personality sets organize themselves into different consciousness. There is always the danger of solipsism, but the personality defends itself with enormously complex coping mechanisms. For instance, although we knew she had briefly attended a seminary, we had not expected the priest. . . .

"*Ego te absolvo.* Make a good act of contrition, my child."

I murmur the foolish, comforting, ritual words. He says, gently, "Go and meditate, child, you will feel better."

He is right. He is always right. I think sometimes that Father Nicholas is my conscience. That, of course, is the function of a priest. I meditate. All the terrors dissolve while I sit quietly in meditation, spinning the threads of this web where I sit, happy at the center, conscious of all the others moving around me. I must be developing esper powers, there is no other explanation, for while I sit quietly here meditating in the chapel the soothing vibrations of the garden come up through my fingers while my gardener works quietly, detached and calm, in my garden, growing delicious things for my supper. I love them all, all my friends around me here, they are all so kind to me, protecting my precious solitude, my privacy. I cannot cook the lovely things he grows, so I sit in my cherished solitude while my cook creates all manner of delicious things for my supper. How kind she is to me, a sweet woman really, though I know that I would have nothing to say to a woman like that. I waken out of meditation to see supper in my tray. How quickly the day has gone, seventhdawn brightening into seventhnoon, and darkness will be upon all of us again soon. How good it is, how sweet and fresh the food from my own garden; I call my thanks to her, this cook who spends all her time thinking up delightful things for me to eat. She must have esper powers too, my prize melon is on my tray, she knew exactly what I wanted after such a day as this.

"Good-night, dear cook, thank you, God bless you, goodnight."

She does not answer, I know she will not answer, she knows her place, but I know she hears and is pleased at my praise.

"Sleep well, my dear, good-night."

As I go to my room through the dimming of eighthdark, it crosses my mind that sometimes I am a little lonely here. But I am doing important work, and after all, the Psych people knew what they were doing. They knew that I need elbow room.

THE UGLY CHICKENS

by Howard Waldrop

Science fiction is subject to many definitions and there are some that are so specific that they might exclude this unusual story. But if science fiction deals with the probable that is just beyond the newspapers or with things that might have happened—even though they did not shake the world—then this is truly science fiction. Further, it's zoological science fiction—and you almost never get any of that!

My car was broken, and I had a class to teach at eleven. So I took the city bus, something I rarely do.

I spent last summer crawling through the Big Thicket with cameras and tape recorder, photographing and taping two of the last ivory-billed woodpeckers on the earth. You can see the films at your local Audubon Society showroom.

This year I wanted something just as flashy but a little less taxing. Perhaps a population study on the Bermuda cahow, or the New Zealand takahe. A month or so in the warm (not hot) sun would do me a world of good. To say nothing of the advancement of science.

I was idly leafing through Greenway's *Extinct and Vanishing Birds of the World*. The city bus was winding its way through the ritzy neighborhoods of Austin, stopping to let off the chicanas, black women, and Vietnamese who tended the kitchens and gardens of the rich.

"I haven't seen any of those ugly chickens in a long time," said a voice close by.

A gray-haired lady was leaning across the aisle toward me.

I looked at her, then around. Maybe she was a shopping-bag lady. Maybe she was just talking. I looked straight at her. No doubt about it, she was talking to me. She was waiting for an answer.

"I used to live near some folks who raised them when I was a girl," she said. She pointed.

I looked down at the page my book was open to.

What I should have said was: That is quite impossible, madam. This is a drawing of an extinct bird of the island of Mauritius. It is perhaps the most famous dead bird in the world. Maybe you are mistaking this drawing for that of some rare Asiatic turkey, peafowl, or pheasant. I am sorry, but you *are* mistaken.

I should have said all that.

What she said was, "Oops, this is my stop." And got up to go.

My name is Paul Lindberl. I am twenty-six years old, a graduate student in ornithology at the University of Texas, a teaching assistant. My name is not unknown in the field. I have several vices and follies, but I don't think foolishness is one of them.

The stupid thing for me to do would have been to follow her.

She stepped off the bus.

I followed her.

I came into the departmental office, trailing scattered papers in the whirlwind behind me. "Martha! Martha!" I yelled.

She was doing something in the supply cabinet.

"Jesus, Paul! What do you want?"

"Where's Courtney?"

"At the conference in Houston. You know that. You missed your class. What's the matter?"

"Petty cash. Let me at it!"

"Payday was only a week ago. If you can't—"

"It's business! It's fame and adventure and the chance of a lifetime! It's a long sea voyage that leaves . . . a plane ticket. To either Jackson, Mississippi, or Memphis. Make it Jackson, it's closer. I'll get receipts! I'll be famous. Courtney will be famous. *You'll* even be famous! This university will make even *more* money! I'll pay you back. Give me some paper. I gotta write Courtney a note. When's the next plane out? Could you get Marie and Chuck to take over my classes Tuesday and Wednesday? I'll try to be back Thursday unless something happens. Courtney'll be back tomorrow, right? I'll call him from, well, wherever. Do you have some coffee?"

And so on and so forth. Martha looked at me like I was crazy. But she filled out the requisition anyway.

"What do I tell Kemejian when I ask him to sign these?"

"Martha, babe, sweetheart. Tell him I'll get his picture in *Scientific American.*"

"He doesn't read it."

"*Nature*, then!"

"I'll see what I can do," she said.

The lady I had followed off the bus was named Jolyn (Smith) Jimson. The story she told me was so weird that it had to be true. She knew things only an expert, or someone with firsthand experience, could know. I got names from her, and addresses, and directions, and tidbits of information. Plus a year: 1927.

And a place. Northern Mississippi.

I gave her my copy of the Greenway book. I told her I'd call her as soon as I got back into town. I left her standing on the corner near the house of the lady she cleaned up for twice a week. Jolyn Jimson was in her sixties.

Think of the dodo as a baby harp seal with feathers. I know that's not even close, but it saves time.

In 1507 the Portuguese, on their way to India, found the (then unnamed) Mascarene Islands in the Indian Ocean—three of them a few hundred miles apart, all east of Madagascar.

It wasn't until 1598, when that old Dutch sea captain Cornelius van Neck bumped into them, that the islands received their names—names that changed several times through the centuries as the Dutch, French, and English changed them every war or so. They are now known as Rodriguez, Réunion, and Mauritius.

The major feature of these islands was large, flightless, stupid, ugly, bad-tasting birds. Van Neck and his men named them *dod-aarsen*, "stupid asses," or *dodars*, "silly birds," or solitaires.

There were three species: the dodo of Mauritius, the real gray-brown, hooked-beak, clumsy thing that weighed twenty kilos or more; the white, somewhat slimmer, dodo of Réunion; and the solitaires of Rodriguez and Réunion, which looked like very fat, very dumb light-colored geese.

The dodos all had thick legs, big squat bodies twice as large as a turkey's, naked faces, and big long downcurved beaks ending in a hook like a hollow linoleum knife. Long ago they had lost the ability to fly, and their wings had degenerated to flaps the size of a human hand with only three or four feathers in them. Their tails were curly and fluffy, like a child's afterthought at decoration. They had absolutely no natural enemies. They nested on the open ground. They probably hatched their eggs wherever they happened to lay them.

No natural enemies until van Neck and his kind showed up. The Dutch, French, and Portuguese sailors who stopped at the Mascarenes to replenish stores found that, besides looking stupid, dodos *were* stupid. The men walked right up to the dodos and hit them on the head with clubs. Better yet, dodos could be herded around like sheep. Ships' logs are full of things like: "Party of ten men ashore. Drove half a hundred of the big turkey-like birds into the boat. Brought to ship, where they are given the run of the decks. Three will feed a crew of 150."

Even so, most of the dodo, except for the breast, tasted bad. One of the Dutch words for them was *walghvogel*, "disgusting bird." But on a ship three months out on a return from Goa to Lisbon, well, food was where you found it. It was said, even so, that prolonged boiling did not improve the flavor.

Even so, the dodos might have lasted, except that the Dutch, and later the French, colonized the Mascarenes. The islands became plantations and dumping places for religious refugees. Sugarcane and other exotic crops were raised there.

With the colonists came cats, dogs, hogs, and the cunning *Rattus norvegicus* and the Rhesus monkey from Ceylon. What dodos the hungry sailors left were chased down (they were dumb and stupid, but they could run when they felt like it) by dogs in the open. They were killed by cats as they sat on their nests. Their eggs were stolen and eaten by monkeys, rats, and hogs. And they competed with the pigs for all the low-growing goodies of the islands.

The last Mauritius dodo was seen in 1681, less than a hundred years after humans first saw them. The last white dodo walked off the history books around 1720. The solitaires of Rodriguez and Réunion, last of the genus as well as the species, may have lasted until 1790. Nobody knows.

Scientists suddenly looked around and found no more of the Didine birds alive, anywhere.

This part of the country was degenerate before the first Snopes ever saw it. This road hadn't been paved until the late fifties, and it was a main road between two county seats. That didn't mean it went through civilized country. I'd traveled for miles and seen nothing but dirt banks red as Billy Carter's neck and an occasional church. I expected to see Burma Shave signs, but realized this road had probably never had them.

I almost missed the turnoff onto the dirt and gravel road the man back at the service station had marked. It led onto the highway from nowhere, a lane out of a field. I turned down it, and a rock the size of a golf ball flew up over the hood and put a crack three inches long in the windshield of the rental car I'd gotten in Grenada.

It was a hot, muggy day for this early. The view was obscured in a cloud of dust every time the gravel thinned. About a mile down the road, the gravel gave out completely. The roadway turned into a rutted dirt pathway, just wider than the car, hemmed in on both sides by a sagging three-strand barbed-wire fence.

In some places the fence posts were missing for a few meters. The wire lay on the ground and in some places disappeared under it for long stretches.

The only life I saw was a mockingbird raising hell with something under a thornbush the barbed wire had been nailed to in place of a post. To one side now was a grassy field that had gone wild, the way everywhere will look after we blow ourselves off the face of the planet. The other was fast becoming woods—pine, oak, some black gum and wild plum, fruit not out this time of the year.

I began to ask myself what I was doing here. What if Ms. Jimson were some imaginative old crank who—but no. Wrong, maybe, but even the wrong was worth checking. But I knew she hadn't lied to me. She had seemed incapable of lies—a good ol' girl, backbone of the South, of the earth. Not a mendacious gland in her being.

I couldn't doubt her, or my judgment either. Here I was, creeping and bouncing down a dirt path in Mississippi, after no sleep for a day, out on the thin ragged edge of a dream. I *had* to take it on faith.

The back of the car sometimes slid where the dirt had loosened and gave way to sand. The back tire stuck once, but I rocked out of it. Getting back out again, would be another matter. Didn't anyone ever use this road?

The woods closed in on both sides like the forest primeval, and the fence had long since disappeared. My odometer said ten kilometers, and it had been twenty minutes since I'd turned off the highway. In the rearview mirror, I saw beads of sweat and dirt in the wrinkles of my neck. A fine patina of dust covered everything inside the car. Clots of it came through the windows.

The woods reached out and swallowed the road. Branches scraped against the windows and the top. It was like falling down a long dark leafy tunnel. It was dark and green in there. I fought back an atavistic urge to turn on the headlights. The roadbed must be made of a few centuries of leaf mulch. I kept constant pressure on the accelerator and bulled my way through.

Half a log caught and banged and clanged against the car bottom. I saw light ahead. Fearing for the oil pan, I punched the pedal and sped out.

I almost ran through a house.

It was maybe ten meters from the trees. The road ended under one of the windows. I saw somebody waving from the corner of my eye.

I slammed on the brakes.

A whole family was on the porch, looking like a Walker Evans Depression photograph, or a fever dream from the mind of a "Hee Haw" producer. The house was old. Strips of peeling paint a meter long tapped against the eaves.

"Damned good thing you stopped," said a voice. I looked up. The biggest man I had ever seen in my life leaned down into the driver-side window.

"If we'd have heard you sooner, I'd've sent one of the kids down to the end of the driveway to warn you," he said.

Driveway?

His mouth was stained brown at the corners. I figured he chewed tobacco until I saw the sweet-gum snuff brush sticking from the pencil pocket in the bib of his coveralls. His hands were the size of catchers' mitts. They looked like they'd never held anything smaller than an ax handle.

"How y'all?" he said, by way of introduction.

"Just fine," I said. I got out of the car.

"My name's Lindberl," I said, extending my hand. He took it. For an instant, I thought of bear traps, sharks' mouths, closing elevator doors. The thought went back to wherever it is they stay.

"This the Gudger place?" I asked.

He looked at me blankly with his gray eyes. He wore a diesel truck cap and had on a checked lumberjack shirt beneath the coveralls. His rubber boots were the size of the ones Karloff wore in *Frankenstein*.

"Naw. I'm Jim Bob Krait. That's my wife, Jenny, and there's Luke and Skeeno and Shirl." He pointed to the porch.

The people on the porch nodded.

"Lessee. Gudger? No Gudgers round here I know of. I'm sorta new here." I took that to mean he hadn't lived here for more than twenty years or so.

"Jennifer!" he yelled. "You know of anybody named Gudger?" To me he said, "My wife's lived around here all her life."

His wife came down onto the second step of the porch landing. "I think they used to be the ones what lived on the Spradlin place before the Spradlins. But the Spradlins left around the Korean War. I didn't know any of the Gudgers myself. That's while we was living over to Water Valley."

"You an insurance man?" asked Mr. Krait.

"Uh . . . no," I said. I imagined the people on the porch leaning toward me, all ears. "I'm a . . . I teach college."

"Oxford?" asked Krait.

"Uh, no. University of Texas."

"Well, that's a damn long way off. You say you're looking for the Gudgers?"

"Just their house. The area. As your wife said, I understand they left. During the Depression, I believe."

"Well, they musta had money," said the gigantic Mr. Krait. "Nobody around here was rich enough to *leave* during the Depression."

"Luke!" he yelled. The oldest boy on the porch sauntered down. He looked anemic and wore a shirt in vogue with the Twist. He stood with his hands in his pockets.

"Luke, show Mr. Lindbergh—"

"Lindberl."

". . . Mr. Lindberl here the way up to the old Spradlin place. Take him as far as the old log bridge, he might get lost before then."

"Log bridge broke down, Daddy."

"When?"

"October, Daddy."

"Well, hell, somethin' else to fix! Anyway, to the creek."

He turned to me. "You want him to go along on up there, see you don't get snakebit?"

"No, I'm sure I'll be fine."

"Mind if I ask what you're going up there for?" he asked. He was looking away from me. I could see having to come right out and ask was bothering him. Such things usually came up in the course of conversation.

"I'm a—uh, bird scientist. I study birds. We had a sighting—someone told us the old Gudger place—the area around here—I'm looking for a rare bird. It's hard to explain."

I noticed I was sweating. It was hot.

"You mean like a good God? I saw a good God about twenty-five years ago, over next to Bruce," he said.

"Well, no." (A good God was one of the names for an ivory-billed woodpecker, one of the rarest in the world. Any other time I would have dropped my jaw. Because they were thought to have died out in Mississippi by the teens, and by the fact that Krait knew they *were* rare.)

I went to lock my car up, then thought of the protocol of the situation. "My car be in your way?" I asked.

"Naw. It'll be just fine," said Jim Bob Krait. "We'll look for you back by sundown, that be all right?"

For a minute, I didn't know whether that was a command or an expression of concern.

"Just in case I get snakebit," I said. "I'll try to be careful up there."

"Good luck on findin' them rare birds," he said. He walked up to the porch with his family.

"Les go," said Luke.

Behind the Krait house were a hen house and a pigsty where hogs lay after their morning slop like islands in a muddy bay, or some Zen pork sculpture. Next we passed broken farm machinery gone to rust, though there was nothing but uncultivated land as far as the eye could see. How the family made a living I don't know. I'm told you can find places just like this throughout the South.

We walked through woods and across fields, following a sort of path. I tried to memorize the turns I would have to take on my way back. Luke didn't say a word the whole twenty minutes he accompanied me, except to curse once when he stepped into a bull nettle with his tennis shoes.

We came to a creek that skirted the edge of a woodsy hill. There was a rotted log forming a small dam. Above it the water was nearly a meter deep; below it, half that much.

"See that path?" he asked.

"Yes."

"Follow it up around the hill, then across the next field. Then you cross the creek again on the rocks, and over the hill. Take the left hand path. What's left of the house is about three-quarters the way up the next hill. If you come to a big bare rock cliff, you've gone too far. You got that?"

I nodded.

He turned and left.

The house had once been a dog-run cabin, as Ms. Jimson had said. Now it was fallen in on one side, what they call sigoglin. (Or was it anti-sigoglin?) I once heard a hymn on the radio called "The Land Where No Cabins Fall." This was the country songs like that were written in.

Weeds grew everywhere. There were signs of fences, a flattened pile of wood that had once been a barn. Farther behind the house were the outhouse remains. Half a rusted pump stood in the backyard. A flatter spot showed where the vegetable garden had been; in it a single wild tomato, pecked by birds, lay rotting. I passed it. There was lumber from three outbuildings, mostly rotten and green with algae and moss. One had been a smokehouse and woodshed combination. Two had been chicken roosts. One was larger than the other. It was there I started to poke around and dig.

Where? Where? I wish I'd been on more archaeological digs, knew the places to look. Refuse piles, midden heaps, kitchen scrap piles, compost boxes. Why hadn't I been born on a farm so I'd know instinctively where to search?

I prodded around the grounds. I moved back and forth like a setter casting for the scent of quail. I wanted more, more. I still wasn't satisfied.

Dusk. Dark, in fact. I trudged into the Kraits' front yard. The tote sack I carried was full to bulging. I was hot, tired,

streaked with fifty years of chicken shit. The Kraits were on
their porch. Jim Bob lumbered down like a friendly mountain.

I asked him a few questions, gave them a Xerox of one of
the dodo pictures, left them addresses and phone numbers
where they could reach me.

Then into the rental car. Off to Water Valley, acting on information Jennifer Krait gave me. I went to the postmaster's
house at Water Valley. She was getting ready for bed. I asked
questions. She got on the phone. I bothered people until one
in the morning. Then back into the trusty rental car.

On to Memphis as the moon came up on my right. Inter-
state 55 was a glass ribbon before me. WLS from Chicago
was on the radio.

I hummed along with it, I sang at the top of my voice.

The sack full of dodo bones, beaks, feet, and eggshell fragments kept me company on the front seat.

Did you know a museum once traded an entire blue whale
skeleton for one of a dodo?

Driving, driving.

The Dance of the Dodos

I used to have a vision sometimes—I had it long before this
madness came up. I can close my eyes and see it by thinking
hard. But it comes to me most often, most vividly, when I am
reading and listening to classical music, especially Pachelbel's
Canon in D.

It is near dusk in The Hague, and the light is that of Frans
Hals, of Rembrandt. The Dutch royal family and their guests
eat and talk quietly in the great dining hall. Guards with hal-
berds and pikes stand in the corners of the room. The family
is arranged around the table: the King, Queen, some
princesses, a prince, a couple of other children, an invited
noble or two. Servants come out with plates and cups, but
they do not intrude.

On a raised platform at one end of the room an orchestra
plays dinner music—a harpsichord, viola, cello, three violins,
and woodwinds. One of the royal dwarfs sits on the edge of
the platform, his foot slowly rubbing the back of one of the
dogs sleeping near him.

As the music of Pachelbel's *Canon in D* swells and rolls

through the hall, one of the dodos walks in clumsily, stops, tilts its head, its eyes bright as a pool of tar. It sways a little, lifts its foot tentatively, one, then another, rocks back and forth in time to the cello.

The violins swirl. The dodo begins to dance, its great ungainly body now graceful. It is joined by the other two dodos who come into the hall, all three turning in a sort of circle.

The harpsichord begins its counterpoint. The fourth dodo, the white one from Réunion, comes from its place under the table and joins the circle with the others.

It is most graceful of all, making complete turns where the others only sway and dip on the edge of the circle they have formed.

The music rises in volume; the first violinist sees the dodos and nods to the King. But he and the others at the table have already seen. They are silent, transfixed—even the servants stand still, bowls, pots, and kettles in their hands, forgotten.

Around the dodos dance with bobs and weaves of their ugly heads. The white dodo dips, takes a half step, pirouettes on one foot, circles again.

Without a word the King of Holland takes the hand of the Queen, and they come around the table, children before the spectacle. They join in the dance, waltzing (anachronism) among the dodos while the family, the guests, the soldiers watch and nod in time with the music.

Then the vision fades, and the afterimage of a flickering fireplace and a dodo remains.

The dodo and its kindred came by ships to the ports of Europe. The first we have record of is that of Captain van Neck, who brought back two in 1599—one for the ruler of Holland, and one that found its way through Cologne to the menagerie of Emperor Rudolf II.

This royal aviary was at Schloss Negebau, near Vienna. It was here that the first paintings of the dumb old birds were done by Georg and his son Jacob Hoefnagel, between 1602 and 1610. They painted it among more than ninety species of birds that kept the Emperor amused.

Another Dutch artist named Roelandt Savery, as someone said, "made a career out of the dodo." He drew and painted the birds many times, and was no doubt personally fascinated by them. Obsessed, even. Early on, the paintings are consistent; the later ones have inaccuracies. This implies he worked from life first, then from memory as his model went to that place soon to be reserved for all its species. One of his drawings has two of the Raphidae scrambling for some goody on the ground. His works are not without charm.

Another Dutch artist (they seemed to sprout up like mushrooms after a spring rain) named Peter Withoos also stuck dodos in his paintings, sometimes in odd and exciting places—wandering around during their owner's music lessons, or stuck with Adam and Eve in some Edenic idyll.

The most accurate representation, we are assured, comes from half a world away from the religious and political turmoil of the seafaring Europeans. There is an Indian miniature painting of the dodo that now rests in a museum in Russia. The dodo could have been brought by the Dutch or Portuguese in their travels to Goa and the coasts of the Indian subcontinent. Or it could have been brought centuries before by the Arabs who plied the Indian Ocean in their triangular-sailed craft, and who may have discovered the Mascarenes before the Europeans cranked themselves up for the First Crusade.

At one time early in my bird-fascination days (after I stopped killing them with BB guns but before I began to work for a scholarship) I once sat down and figured out where all the dodos had been.

Two with van Neck in 1599, one to Holland, one to Austria. Another was in Count Solms's park in 1600. An account speaks of "one in Italy, one in Germany, several to England, eight or nine to Holland." William Boentekoe van Hoorn knew of "one shipped to Europe in 1640, another in 1685," which he said was "also painted by Dutch artists." Two were mentioned as "being kept in Surrat House in India as pets," perhaps one of which is the one in the painting. Being charitable, and considering "several" to mean at least three, that means twenty dodos in all.

There had to be more, when boatloads had been gathered at the time.

What do we know of the Didine birds? A few ships' logs, some accounts left by travelers and colonists. The English were fascinated by them. Sir Hamon Lestrange, a contemporary of Pepys, saw exhibited "a Dodar from the Island of Mauritius . . . it is not able to flie, being so bigge." One was stuffed when it died, and was put in the Museum Tradescantum in South Lambeth. It eventually found its way into the Ashmolean Museum. It grew ratty and was burned, all but a

leg and the head, in 1750. By then there were no more dodos, but nobody had realized that yet.

Francis Willughby got to describe it before its incineration.
Earlier, old Carolus Clusius in Holland studied the one in
Count Solms's park. He collected everything known about the
Raphidae, describing a dodo leg Pieter Pauw kept in his
natural-history cabinet, in *Exoticarium libri decem* in 1605,
seven years after their discovery.

François Leguat, a Huguenot who lived on Réunion for
some years, published an account of his travels in which he
mentioned the dodos. It was published in 1708 (after the
Mauritius dodo was extinct) and included the information
that "some of the males weigh forty-five pound. . . . One egg,
much bigger than that of a goos is laid by the female, and
takes seven weeks hatching time."

The Abbé Pingré visited the Mascarenes in 1761. He saw
the last of the Rodriguez solitaires and collected what information he could about the dead Mauritius and Réunion
members of the genus.

After that, only memories of the colonists, and some scientific debate as to *where* the Raphidae belonged in the great
taxonomic scheme of things—some said pigeons, some said
rails—were left. Even this nitpicking ended. The dodo was
forgotten.

When Lewis Carroll wrote *Alice in Wonderland* in 1865,
most people thought he had invented the dodo.

The service station I called from in Memphis was busier
than a one-legged man in an ass-kicking contest. Between
bings and dings of the bell, I finally realized the call had gone
through.

The guy who answered was named Selvedge. I got nowhere
with him. He mistook me for a real estate agent, then a law-
yer. Now he was beginning to think I was some sort of a con
man. I wasn't doing too well, either. I hadn't slept in two
days. I must have sounded like a speed freak. My only
progress was that I found that Ms. Annie Mae Gudger
(childhood playmate of Jolyn Jimson) was now, and had
been, the respected Ms. Annie Mae Radwin. This guy
Selvedge must have been a secretary or toady or something.

We were having a conversation comparable to that between a shrieking macaw and a pile of mammoth bones.
Then there was another click on the line.

"Young man?" said the other voice, an old woman's voice, southern, very refined but with a hint of the hills in it.

"Yes? Hello! Hello!"

"Young man, you say you talked to a Jolyn somebody? Do you mean Jolyn Smith?"

"Hello! Yes! Ms. Radwin, Ms. Annie Mae Radwin who used to be Gudger? She lives in Austin now. Texas. She used to live near Water Valley, Mississippi. Austin's where I'm from. I—"

"Young man," asked the voice again, "are you sure you haven't been put up to this by my hateful sister Alma?"

"Who? No, ma'am. I met a woman named Jolyn—"

"I'd like to talk to you, young man," said the voice. Then, offhandedly, "Give him directions to get here, Selvedge."

Click.

I cleaned out my mouth as best I could in the service station rest room, tried to shave with an old clogged Gillette disposable in my knapsack, and succeeded in gapping up my jawline. I changed into a clean pair of jeans and the only other shirt I had with me, and combed my hair. I stood in front of the mirror.

I still looked like the dog's lunch.

The house reminded me of Presley's mansion, which was somewhere in the neighborhood. From a shack on the side of a Mississippi hill to this, in forty years. There are all sorts of ways of making it. I wondered what Annie Mae Gudger's had been. Luck? Predation? Divine intervention? Hard work? Trover and replevin?

Selvedge led me toward the sun room. I felt like Philip Marlowe going to meet a rich client. The house was filled with that furniture built sometime between the turn of the century and the 1950s—the ageless kind. It never looks great, it never looks ratty, and every chair is comfortable.

I think I was expecting some formidable woman with sleeve blotters and a green eyeshade hunched over a rolltop desk with piles of paper whose acceptance or rejection meant life or death for thousands.

Who I met was a charming lady in a green pantsuit. She was in her sixties, her hair still a straw-wheat color. It didn't look dyed. Her eyes were blue as my first-grade teacher's had been. She was wiry and looked as if the word *fat* was not in her vocabulary.

"Good morning, Mr. Lindberl." She shook my hand. "Would you like some coffee? You look as if you could use it."

"Yes, thank you."

"Please sit down." She indicated a white wicker chair at a glass table. A serving tray with coffeepot, cups, tea bags, croissants, napkins, and plates lay on the tabletop.

After I swallowed half a cup of coffee at a gulp, she said, "What you wanted to see me about must be important."

"Sorry about my manners," I said. "I know I don't look it, but I'm a biology assistant at the University of Texas. An ornithologist. Working on my master's. I met Ms. Jolyn Jimson two days ago—"

"How is Jolyn? I haven't seen her in, oh, Lord, it must be on to fifty years. The time gets away."

"She seemed to be fine. I only talked to her half an hour or so. That was—"

"And you've come to see me about . . . ?"

"Uh. The . . . about some of the poultry your family used to raise, when they lived near Water Valley."

She looked at me a moment. Then she began to smile.

"Oh, you mean the ugly chickens?" she said.

I smiled. I almost laughed. I knew what Oedipus must have gone through.

It is now four-thirty in the afternoon. I am sitting in the downtown Motel 6 in Memphis. I have to make a phone call and get some sleep and catch a plane.

Annie Mae Gudger Radwin talked for four hours, answering my questions, setting me straight on family history, having Selvedge hold all her calls.

The main problem was that Annie Mae ran off in 1928, the year *before* her father got his big break. She went to Yazoo City, and by degrees and stages worked her way northward to Memphis and her destiny as the widow of a rich mercantile broker.

But I get ahead of myself.

Grandfather Gudger used to be the overseer for Colonel Crisby on the main plantation near McComb, Mississippi. There was a long story behind that. Bear with me.

Colonel Crisby himself was the scion of a seafaring family with interests in both the cedars of Lebanon (almost all cut down for masts for His Majesty's and others' navies) and Egyptian cotton. Also teas, spices, and any other salable commodity that came its way.

When Colonel Crisby's grandfather reached his majority in 1802, he waved good-bye to the Atlantic Ocean at Charleston, S.C., and stepped westward into the forest. When he stopped, he was in the middle of the Chickasaw Nation, where he opened a trading post and introduced slaves to the Indians.

And he prospered, and begat Colonel Crisby's father, who sent back to South Carolina for everything his father owned. Everything—slaves, wagons, horses, cattle, guinea fowl, peacocks, and dodos, which everybody thought of as atrociously ugly poultry of some kind, one of the seafaring uncles having bought them off a French merchant in 1721. (I surmised these were white dodos from Réunion, unless they had been from even earlier stock. The dodo of Mauritius was already extinct by then.)

All this stuff was herded out west to the trading post in the midst of the Chicksaw Nation. (The tribes around there were of the confederation of the Dancing Rabbits.)

And Colonel Crisby's father prospered, and so did the guinea fowl and the dodos. Then Andrew Jackson came along and marched the Dancing Rabbits off up the Trail of Tears to the heaven of Oklahoma. And Colonel Crisby's father begat Colonel Crisby, and put the trading post in the hands of others, and moved his plantation westward still to McComb.

Everything prospered but Colonel Crisby's father, who died. And the dodos, with occasional losses to the avengin' weasel and the egg-sucking dog, reproduced themselves also.

Then along came Granddaddy Gudger, a Simon Legree role model, who took care of the plantation while Colonel Crisby raised ten companies of men and marched off to fight the War for Southern Independence.

Colonel Crisby came back to the McComb plantation earlier than most, he having stopped much of the same volley of Minié balls that caught his commander, General Beauregard Hanlon, on a promontory bluff during the Siege of Vicksburg.

He wasn't dead, but death hung around the place like a gentlemanly bill collector for a month. The Colonel languished, went slapdab crazy, and freed all his slaves the week before he died (the war lasted another two years after that). Not now having any slaves, he didn't need an overseer.

Then comes the Faulkner part of the tale, straight out of *As I Lay Dying*, with the Gudger family returning to the area of Water Valley (before there was a Water Valley), moving through the demoralized and tattered displaced persons of the South, driving their dodos before them. For Colonel Crisby had given them to his former overseer for his faithful service. Also followed the story of the bloody murder of Granddaddy Gudger at the hands of the Freedman's militia during the rising of the first Klan, and of the trials and tribulations of Daddy Gudger in the years between 1880 and 1910, when he was between the ages of four and thirty-four.

Alma and Annie Mae were the second and fifth of Daddy Gudger's brood, born three years apart. They seem to have hated each other from the very first time Alma looked into little Annie Mae's crib. They were kids by Daddy Gudger's second wife (his desperation had killed the first) and their father was already on his sixth career. He had been a lumberman, a stump preacher, a plowman-for-hire (until his mules broke out in farcy buds and died of the glanders), a freight hauler (until his horses died of overwork and the hardware store repossessed the wagon), a politician's roadie (until the politician lost the election). When Alma and Annie Mae were born, he was failing as a sharecropper. Somehow Gudger had made it through the Depression of 1898 as a boy, and was too poor after that to notice more about economics than the price of Beech-Nut tobacco at the store.

Alma and Annie Mae fought, and it helped none at all that Alma, being the oldest daughter, was both her mother's and her father's darling. Annie Mae's life was the usual unwanted-poor-white-trash-child's hell. She vowed early to run away, and recognized her ambition at thirteen.

All this I learned this morning. Jolyn (Smith) Jimson was Annie Mae's only friend in those days—from a family even poorer than the Gudgers. But somehow there was food, and an occasional odd job. And the dodos.

"My father hated those old birds," said the cultured Annie Mae Radwin, née Gudger, in the solarium. "He always swore he was going to get rid of them someday, but just never seemed to get around to it. I think there was more to it than that. But they were so much *trouble*. We always had to keep them penned up at night, and go check for their eggs. They wandered off to lay them, and forgot where they were. Sometimes no new ones were born at all in a year.

"And they got so *ugly*. Once a year. I mean, terrible-looking, like they were going to die. All their feathers fell off, and they looked like they had mange or something. Then the whole front of their beaks fell off, or worse, hung halfway on for a week or two. They looked like big old naked pigeons. After that they'd lose weight, down to twenty or thirty pounds, before their new feathers grew back.

"We were always having to kill foxes that got after them in the turkey house. That's what we called their roost, the turkey house. And we found their eggs all sucked out by cats and dogs. They were so stupid we had to drive them into their roost at night. I don't think they could have found it standing ten feet from it."

She looked at me.

"I think much as my father hated them, they meant something to him. As long as he hung on to them, he knew he was as good as Granddaddy Gudger. You may not know it, but there was a certain amount of family pride about Granddaddy Gudger. At least in my father's eyes. His rapid fall in the world had a sort of grandeur to it. He'd gone from a relatively high position in the old order, and maintained some grace and stature after the Emancipation. And though he lost everything, he managed to keep those ugly old chickens the Colonel had given him as sort of a symbol.

"And as long as he had them, too, my daddy thought himself as good as his father. He kept his dignity, even when he didn't have anything else."

I asked what happened to them. She didn't know, but told me who did and where I could find her.

That's why I'm going to make a phone call.

"Hello. Dr. Courtney. Dr. Courtney? This is Paul. Memphis. Tennessee. It's too long to go into. No, of course not, not yet. But I've got evidence. What? Okay, how do trochanters, coracoids, tarsometatarsi and beak sheaths sound? From their hen house, where else? Where would you keep *your* dodos, then?

"Sorry. I haven't slept in a couple of days. I need some help. Yes, yes. Money. Lots of money.

"Cash. Three hundred dollars, maybe. Western Union, Memphis, Tennessee. Whichever one's closest to the airport. Airport. I need the department to set up reservations to Mauritius for me. . . .

"No. No. Not wild-goose chase, wild-*dodo* chase. Tame-dodo chase. I *know* there aren't any dodos on Mauritius! I know that. I could explain. I know it'll mean a couple of grand—if—but—

"Look, Dr. Courtney. Do you want *your* picture in *Scientific American*, or don't you?"

I am sitting in the airport café in Port Louis, Mauritius. It is now three days later, five days since that fateful morning my car wouldn't start. God bless the Sears Diehard people. I have slept sitting up in a plane seat, on and off, different planes, different seats, for twenty-four hours, Kennedy to Paris, Paris to Cairo, Cairo to Madagascar. I felt like a band-new man when I got here.

Now I feel like an infinitely sadder and wiser brand-new man. I have just returned from the hateful sister Alma's house in the exclusive section of Port Louis, where all the French and British officials used to live.

Courtney will get his picture in *Scientific American*, all right. Me too. There'll be newspaper stories and talk shows for a few weeks for me, and I'm sure Annie Mae Gudger Radwin on one side of the world and Alma Chandler Gudger Molière on the other will come in for their share of glory.

I am putting away cup after cup of coffee. The plane back to Tananarive leaves in an hour. I plan to sleep all the way back to Cairo, to Paris, to New York, pick up my bag of bones, sleep back to Austin.

Before me on the table is a packet of documents, clippings, and photographs. I have come across half the world for this. I gaze from the package, out the window across Port Louis to the bulk of Mont Pieter Both, which overshadows the city and its famous racecoruse.

Perhaps I should do something symbolic. Cancel my flight. Climb the mountain and look down on man and all his handi-works. Take a pitcher of martinis with me. Sit in the bright semitropical sunlight (it's early dry winter here). Drink the martinis slowly, toasting Snuffo, God of Extinction. Here's one for the great auk. This is for the Carolina parakeet. Mud in your eye, passenger pigeon. This one's for the heath hen. Most important, here's one each for the Mauritius dodo, the white dodo of Réunion, the Réunion solitaire, the Rodriguez solitaire. Here's to the Raphidae, great Didine birds that you were.

Maybe I'll do something just as productive, like climbing Mont Pieter Both and pissing into the wind.

How symbolic. The story of the dodo ends where it began, on this very island. Life imitates cheap art. Like the Xerox of the Xerox of a bad novel. I never expected to find dodos still alive here (this is the one place they would have been noticed). I still can't believe Alma Chandler Gudger Molière could have lived here twenty-five years and not *know* about the dodo, never set foot inside the Port Louis Museum, where they have skeletons and a stuffed replica the size of your little brother.

After Annie Mae ran off, the Gudger family found itself prospering in a time the rest of the country was going to hell. It was 1929. Gudger delved into politics again and backed a man who knew a man who worked for Theodore "Sure Two-Handed Sword of God" Bilbo, who had connections everywhere. Who introduced him to Huey "Kingfish" Long just after that gentleman lost the Louisiana governor's election one of the times. Gudger stumped around Mississippi, getting up steam for Long's Share the Wealth plan, even before it had a name.

The upshot was that the Long machine in Louisiana knew a rabble-rouser when it saw one, and invited Gudger to move to the Sportsman's Paradise, with his family, all expenses paid, and start working for the Kingfish at the unbelievable salary of $62.50 a week. Which prospect was like turning a hog loose under a persimmon tree, and before you could say Backwoods Messiah, the Gudger clan was on its way to the land of pelicans, graft, and Mardi Gras.

Almost. But I'll get to that.

Daddy Gudger prospered all out of proportion to his abilities, but many men did that during the Depression. First a little, thence to more, he rose in bureaucratic (and political) circles of the state, dying rich and well hated with his fingers in *all* the pies.

Alma Chandler Gudger became a debutante (she says Robert Penn Warren put her in his book) and met and married Jean Carl Molière, only heir to rice, indigo, and sugarcane growers. They had a happy wedded life, moving first to the West Indies, later to Mauritius, where the family sugarcane holdings were among the largest on the island. Jean Carl died in 1959. Alma was his only survivor.

So local family makes good. Poor sharecropping Mississippi people turn out to have a father dying with a smile on his face, and two daughters who between them own a large portion of the planet.

I open the envelope before me. Ms. Alma Molière had listened politely to my story (the university had called ahead and arranged an introduction through the director of the Port Louis Museum, who knew Ms. Molière socially) and told me what she could remember. Then she sent a servant out to one of the storehouses (large as a duplex) and he and two others came back with boxes of clippings, scrapbooks, and family photos.

"I haven't looked at any of this since we left St. Thomas," she said. "Let's go through it together."

Most of it was about the rise of Citizen Gudger.

"There's not many pictures of us before we came to Louisiana. We were so frightfully poor then, hardly anyone we knew had a camera. Oh, look. Here's one of Annie Mae. I thought I threw all those out after Momma died."

This is the photograph. It must have been taken about 1927. Annie Mae is wearing some unrecognizable piece of clothing that approximates a dress. She leans on a hoe, smiling a snaggle-toothed smile. She looks to be ten or eleven. Her eyes are half-hidden by the shadow of the brim of a gapped straw hat she wears. The earth she is standing in barefoot has been newly turned. Behind her is one corner of the house, and the barn beyond has its upper bay windows open. Out-of-focus people are at work there.

A few feet behind her, a huge male dodo is pecking at something on the ground. The front two thirds of it shows, back to the stupid wings and the edge of the upcurved tail feathers. One foot is in the photo, having just scratched at something, possibly an earthworm, in the new-plowed clods. Judging by its darkness, it is the gray, or Mauritius, dodo.

The photograph is not very good, one of those 3½ × 5 jobs box cameras used to take. Already I can see this one, and the blowup of the dodo, taking up a double-page spread in *S.A.* Alma told me that around then they were down to six or seven of the ugly chickens, two whites, the rest gray-brown.

Besides this photo, two clippings are in the package, one from the Bruce *Banner-Times*, the other from the Oxford newspaper; both are columns by the same woman dealing with "Doings in Water Valley." Both mention the Gudger family's moving from the area to seek its fortune in the swampy state to the west, and tell how they will be missed. Then there's a yellowed clipping from the front page of the Oxford paper with a small story about the Gudger Family Farewell Party in Water Valley the Sunday before (dated October 19, 1929).

There's a handbill in the package, advertising the Gudger Family Farewell Party, Sunday Oct. 15, 1929, Come One Come All. The people in Louisiana who sent expense money to move Daddy Gudger must have overestimated the costs by an exponential factor. I said as much.

"No," Alma Molière said. "There was a lot, but it wouldn't have made any difference. Daddy Gudger was like Thomas Wolfe and knew a shining golden opportunity when he saw one. Win, lose, or draw, he was never coming back *there* again. He would have thrown some kind of soiree whether there had been money for it or not. Besides, people were much more sociable then, you mustn't forget."

I asked her how many people came.

"Four or five hundred," she said. "There's some pictures here somewhere." We searched awhile, then we found them.

Another thirty minutes to my flight. I'm not worried sitting here. I'm the only passenger, and the pilot is sitting at the table next to mine talking to an RAF man. Life is much slower and nicer on these colonial islands. You mustn't forget.

I look at the other two photos in the package. One is of some men playing horseshoes and washer toss, while kids, dogs, and women look on. It was evidently taken from the east end of the house looking west. Everyone must have had to walk the last mile to the old Gudger place. Other groups of people stand talking. Some men, in shirt sleeves and suspenders, stand with their heads thrown back, a snappy story, no doubt, just told. One girl looks directly at the camera from close up, shyly, her finger in her mouth. She's about five. It looks like any snapshot of a family reunion which could have been taken anywhere, anytime. Only the clothing marks it as backwoods 1920s.

Courtney will get his money's worth. I'll write the article, make phone calls, plan the talk show tour to coincide with publication. Then I'll get some rest. I'll be a normal person

again—get a degree, spend my time wading through jungles
after animals that will all be dead in another twenty years,
anyway.

Who cares? The whole thing will be just another media
event, just this year's Big Deal. It'll be nice getting normal
again. I can read books, see movies, wash my clothes at the
laundromat, listen to Johnathan Richman on the stereo. I can
study and become an authority on some minor matter or
other.

I can go to museums and see all the wonderful dead things
there.

"That's the memory picture," said Alma. "They always
took them at big things like this, back in those days. Everybody who was there would line up and pose for the camera.
Only we couldn't fit everybody in. So we had two made. This
is the one with us in it."

The house is dwarfed by people. All sizes, shapes, dress,
and age. Kids and dogs in front, women next, then men at
the back. The only exceptions are the bearded patriarchs
seated toward the front with the children—men whose eyes
face the camera but whose heads are still ringing with something Nathan Bedford Forrest said to them one time on a
smoke-filled field. This photograph is from another age. You
can recognize Daddy and Mrs. Gudger if you've seen their
photographs before. Alma pointed herself out to me.

But the reason I took the photograph is in the foreground.
Tables have been built out of sawhorses, with doors and
boards nailed across them. They extend the entire width of
the photograph. They are covered with food, more food than
you can imagine.

"We started cooking three days before. So did the neighbors. Everybody brought something," said Alma.

It's like an entire Safeway had been cooked and set out to
cool. Hams, quarters of beef, chickens by the tubful, quail in
mounds, rabbit, butter beans by the bushel, yams, Irish potatoes, an acre of corn, eggplants, peas, turnip greens, butter in
five-pound molds, cornbread and biscuits, gallon cans of mo-
lasses, red-eye gravy by the pot.

And five huge birds—twice as big as turkeys, legs capped as
for Thanksgiving, drumsticks the size of Schwarzenegger's
biceps, whole-roasted, lying on their backs on platters large as
cocktail tables.

The people in the crowd sure look hungry.

"We ate for days," said Alma.

I already have the title for the *Scientific American* article. It's going to be called "The Dodo is *Still* Dead."

PRIME TIME

by Norman Spinrad

It seems that every ten years or so someone comes up with a new story based on this idea. We recall one way back in Science Wonder Stories that dealt with the future of total entertainment. As that industry has grown and applied new techniques year by year, a new story would appear. This is the latest, fit to our time, cut to the measure of the 1980's world, and written in the story of the time, too. Entertainment? Well, we wonder.

Edna chose to awake this morning to good old breakfast loop A. John was reading a newspaper over pancakes and sausages in the kitchen of their old home. The kids were gulping the last of their food and were anxious to be on their way to school.

After yesterday's real-time-shared breakfast with John, she really felt she needed the soothing old familiar tape from her files today. It might have been shot way back during the 1987–88 television season on a crude home deck, it might be snowy and shaky, but Edna still ran it three or four mornings a week in preference to the breakfast soaps or more updated domestic footage. Somehow it captured what prime breakfast time with John and the kids had really been like, and somehow that made it her prime breakfast programming choice.

Edna: Now, Sammy, you finish the rest of your milk before you run outdoors!
Sammy: (slugging down the rest of his milk) Aw, Ma, I'm gonna be late!
Edna: Not if you don't take your usual shortcut past the candy store.

Of course the old tape hadn't been shot from her stereo perspective, and there *was* something strange about seeing yourself in your own domestic programming, and it certainly wasn't as well written as a breakfast soap, but then none of the soaps were personalized and none of her other domestic tapes with John had footage of the kids at grade-school age.

John was always after her to share real-time programming with him. He'd voice her over on the communication channel and show her tapes he had made for himself with her in them, or he'd entice her with shared domestic tapes, or he'd bombard her with porn-channel footage.

But the domestic tapes he programmed for them to share all took place in exotic locales, and the story lines were strictly male-type fantasies—John's idea of suitable real-time programming for the two of them to share ran to camel caravans across the desert, spaceship journeys to strange planets full of weird creatures, sailing the South Seas, discovering lost cities, fighting in noble wars. And her viewpoint role was usually a cross between Wonder Woman and Slave Girl. Well, that might be how John wished to real-time-share with her, but Edna preferred her soaps and romantic historicals, which John categorically refused to real-time-share with her under any circumstances.

As for the porn channels that he wanted to real-time-share with her, the only word was *disgusting*.

Still, he *was* her husband, and she felt she had to fulfill her conjugal obligations from time to time; so five or ten times a season she gritted her teeth and real-time-shared one of his crude male porn channels in the sex-object role. Less frequently he consented to time-share a historical X with her, but only because of the implied threat she'd withhold her porn-channel favors from him if he didn't.

So by and large it was mealtime program sharing that was their least distasteful channel of contact and the one that saw most frequent use.

John: (wiping his lips with his napkin) Well, honey, it's off to the salt mines. Ready to go, Ellie?
Ellie: I got to make wee-wee first.

TOTAL TELEVISION HEAVEN 60-SECOND SPOT #12 FINALIZED BROADCAST VERSION HARD CUT FROM BACK

A series of low, pink buildings, emphasizing sunrise through the palm trees.

Announcer's voice-over: (medium hard sell) Total Television Heaven, the ultimate retirement community for Electronic Age seniors . . .

A rapidly cut montage from the adventure channels, the porn channels, the soaps, etc. Make it the most colorful and exciting footage we've got and emphasize expensive crowd scenes and special effects.

Announcer's voice-over: (orgasmic) Twenty full channels of pornography, thirty-five full channels of adventure, forty channels of continuing soaps—live, full-time, in over a hundred possible realities, produced by the finest talents in Hollywood . . .

CLOSE-UP ON A MAN'S HEAD

Intelligent, with neat, dignified, gray hair. As hands fit stereo TV goggles over his eyes. (Earphones already in place.)

Announcer's voice-over: (institutional) You live as the viewpoint character in a wonderland of sex and adventure through the electronic magic of total stereo TV!

MEDIUM SHOT ON A FAMOUS OLD ACTOR

Cast someone with recognition value who's willing to sign up for a two-hundred-year annuity.

Famous Old Actor: And that's not all! Tape your family! Tape your friends! Take your loved ones with you to Total Television Heaven and keep them with you forever!

CAMERA PULLS BACK FOR A FULL SHOT

We see that the Famous Old Actor is being helped into a glass amnion tank. He keeps talking and smiling as the attendants strap him to the couch, fit the earphones and stereo TV goggles, hook up his breathing mask and waste tube, and begin filling the tank with fluid.

Famous Old Actor: A vast tape library. Custom-cut programs to your order! I wish I'd signed up years ago!

The throat mike is attached, his hand is taped to the tuner knob, the nutrient tube is inserted in his arm (no on-camera needle penetration, please), the amnion tank is topped off and sealed. The camera moves in for a close-up on the face of the Famous Old Actor, seen floating blissfully in his second womb.

Famous Old Actor: (filtered) I'm never coming out—and I'm glad!

DISSOLVE TO: SUNSET OVER TOTAL TELEVISION HEAVEN

The sun sinks into the sea in speeded-up time over the pink pastel client-storage buildings, and a glorious, star-filled sky comes on like an electronic billboard.

Announcer's voice-over: (transcendent) No man knows God's intent for the hereafter, but at Total Television Heaven modern biological science *guarantees* you a full two hundred years of electronic paradise in the safety and comfort of your own private tank. And a full annuity costs less than you think!

FADE-OUT

John: Maybe we can make it out to the lake this weekend.
Edna: Supposed to be clear, in the seventies, I heard on the weather . . .

This season John had been acting stranger and stranger, even during their mealtime sharing. His conversation was becoming more and more foulmouthed and even incoherent. He had taken to appearing in elaborate character roles even over breakfast, and yesterday's real-time-shared breakfast had been just about more than Edna could take.

He'd voiced her over the night before and invited her to breakfast the next morning in Hawaii, where they had real-time-shared their honeymoon in the dim, distant past—so many seasons ago that no recording tape of it existed; none had been made way back then, before anyone had even dreamed of retiring to Total Television Heaven. It had been a very long time indeed since John had invited her to real-time-share their past at all, even in a reconstructed version, and so when he told her he had custom-programmed breakfast on the beach in Hawaii, Edna had been so thrilled that she agreed to time-share his breakfast program against what had lately been becoming her better judgment.

The program wakened her to sunrise on the beach, the great golden ball rising out of the dark sea in speeded-up stop-motion animation like a curtain going up, illumining the bright blue sky that suddenly flared into existence as she found herself lying on the sand beneath it.

This to the theme of an ancient prime-time show called *Hawaii Five-O*, as a majestic breaker rolled and broke, rolled and broke, again and again, in a closed loop beyond the shoreline foam.

John appeared in the role of a tanned, blond, muscled Adonis wearing a ludicrously short grass skirt. A breakfast table was set up at the edge of the sea itself, in the foot-high wash of foam kicked up by the eternal rolling wave that towered and broke, towered and broke, above them.

Naked, godlike Polynesians—a youth for her, a maiden for John—helped them to their feet and escorted them to the wicker peacock chairs on either side of the strange table. The table was a block of polished obsidian on Victorian-looking brass legs, there was a depression in the center, out of which a grooved channel ran to the seaside edge of the tabletop.

This was certainly not their Hawaiian honeymoon as Edna recollected it, and she didn't need a tape in order to be sure of that!

"Welcome, O love goddess of the north, to my groovy pad," John crooned in a strange, cracked voice. He clapped his hands. "An oblation in thine honor."

The naked maiden produced a squealing piglet, which she pressed into the pit in the center of the table. The naked youth handed John a huge machete. "Hai!" John screamed, hacking the piglet in half with a swipe of his blade. Blood pooled in the pit in the table, then ran down the groove to the edge and dripped off into the sea. As the first drops of blood touched the ocean, the water abruptly changed color, and for a few moments a towering wave of blood arched over them.

A few moments later, when the eternal wave was blue water again and Edna's viewpoint angle returned to a shot on the table, the gory mess had been replaced by a white tablecloth, two plates of ham and eggs, a pot of coffee, and a bottle of dark island rum.

"Oh, John," she said disgustedly, "it's all so . . . so—"

"Eldritch? Excessive? Demented?" John said petulantly, crotchety annoyance cracking his handsome, twenty-year-old features. "You're such a timid bird, Edna. No sense of fun. No imagination."

"Killing things is not my idea of either fun or imagination," Edna retorted indignantly.

John laughed a weird, nervous laugh. A whale breached not far offshore, and immediately a giant squid wrapped tentacles around it. A fight to the death began. "Killing things?" John said. "But there's nothing alive here to kill! This is Heaven, not Earth, and we can do anything we want without consequences. What else can we do?"

"We can have a normal, civilized breakfast like decent human beings."

"Normal, civilized breakfast!" John shouted. "Decent human beings!" A volcano erupted somewhere inland. Terrified natives fled before a wall of fiery lava. "Who cares about being decent human beings when we're not even alive, my princess?"

"I haven't the faintest idea what you're talking about," Edna said primly. But of course some small part of her did, and that part was chilled to the core.

"Sure and begorra, you do, Edna!" John said mockingly. "Avast, matey, what makes you so sure we're still alive? For lo, how many television seasons has it been since we retired? A hundred? Two hundred? Verily and forsooth, time out of mind. Can you even guess, my slave girl? I can't."

Edna blanched. She didn't like this kind of talk at all. It was worse than his machismo adventure programs, worse than the porno programming he enjoyed putting her through, worse on a whole other level she had trained herself not to contemplate.

"Of course we're alive," she said. "We're real-time-sharing now, aren't we?"

Bathing beauties water-skied in a chorus line through the curl of the wave. A flying saucer buzzed the beach. A giant crab seized their servants in its pincers. It whisked them away as they screamed.

"Ah, mine Aphrodite, how can we be sure of that? Thou couldst be croaked and I could be tuning in to an old tape where you still lived. Har-har, I could be dead except in this program of yours."

"This is certainly no program of mine, John Rogers!" Edna shouted. "Only *you* could have invited me to a breakfast program like this!"

"I stink, therefore I am," John cackled. Lightning rattled. Schools of porpoises leaped in and out of the great wave.

And so it had gone. Nubian slaves lighting cigarettes. Dancing gulls. An orgy sequence. And all throughout it, John babbling and ranting like a demented parrot in his beachboy body. Only one thing had kept Edna from tuning him out and tuning in a breakfast soap, and that was the dim, distant thought that to do so might precipitate the final break between them, the break between her and something that she could no longer conceptualize clearly.

John: (rising from the table) What's for dinner tonight, by the way?
Edna: Roast chicken with that corn bread stuffing you like.

He kisses her briefly on the lips.

John: Mmmmm . . . ! I'll try to pick up a bottle of that German wine on the way back from work if I'm not too late.

He opens the door, waves, and exits.

Edna: Have a good day.

But now, while she watched her image bid good-bye to John as he left for work on that dim, fuzzy old tape she found so soothing, Edna wondered how long it would be before she would consent to real-time-share a meal with the "real" John again, a John she no longer recognized as the husband in her domestic tapes, a John she was not sure she wanted to know about.

After all, she thought, tuning to *Elizabeth the Queen*, her favorite historical romance of this season, too much of that could ruin her domestic tapes with John for her, and then where would she be if she could no longer live comfortably in her past?

Right now she was seated on her throne in the early evening light, and Sir Walter Raleigh was bowing to her with a boyish twinkle in his eye that made her quiver.

Rolling among naked teen-aged girls in a great marbled Roman bath. Popping off Indians with his Remington repeater. Swinging on a vine through a jungleful of dinosaurs. Leading the pack around the last turn at the Grand Prix de Monaco.

Boring, boring, boring! Irritably John flipped through the broadcast channels, unable to find anything capable of holding his attention. What a lousy season this was, even worse than the last! There wasn't a single adventure program that had any originality to it; the porno channels made him think of Edna and her damned disapproval of anything still capable of turning him on; and old domestic tapes, he knew, would just make him furious.

Of course he had a big file of classic recordings and custom-programmed favorites to draw upon when real-time programming got boring, and so he started flipping through his videx, desperately looking for something to fill this time slot.

Flying his one-man space fighter low over an alien glass city, shattering the crystal towers with his shock wave as he rose to meet the bandits. Chasing a fat merchantman under a full head of sail. Avast, me hearties, prepare a broadside! Auctioned as a sex slave to a mob of horny women. Doing a smart left bank around a skyscraper, with Lois Lane in his arms.

He really had some choice footage in his tape library, but he had run all of it so often down through the long seasons that every bit of it seemed engraved in his real-time memory. He had lost the ability to surprise himself, even with how gross he could get, and he had to go further and further out to avert . . . to avert . . . to avert . . .

Onward, the Light Brigade! Thousands of screaming teen-aged groupies mobbed the stage, grabbed his guitar, tore off his clothes. "Frankly, Scarlett," he said, as she sank to her knees, "I don't give a damn."

If only Edna had the gumption to be a real wife to him!

Lord knew, he tried to be a real husband to her. Didn't he regularly invite her to real-time-share the porn channels with him, and didn't he take pains to choose the most far-out sex programming available? Didn't he invite her to all his best adventure programs? Didn't he invite her to the best meal-time custom programming instead of the same old domestic tapes?

He did his best to make her programming day interesting and surprising, and what did he get from her in return? A lot of whining about his dirty mind, a determination to get him caught in one of those saccharine historical X's with her, and a dreary desire to mealtime-share the same musty old domestic tapes over and over again. What was the purpose of retiring to Total Television Heaven in the first place if you were afraid of grossness, if you insisted on realism, if all you wanted was to watch endless reruns of the same old, boring past?

Striding through the jungle, a great, hairy gorilla beating his chest while the natives flee in terror. Executing a snappy Immelmann and coming up on the Red Baron's tail, machine guns blazing. Getting head from the legendary Marilyn Monroe.

Damn it, retiring to Total Television Heaven before either of them was sixty-five had been Edna's idea in the first place, John told himself, though a part of him knew that wasn't exactly totally true. With the kids at the other end of the continent and the economy in such bad shape and nothing interesting going on in their real-time lives, it was only his job that had kept them from trading in their Social Security equity for a two-hundred-year annuity to Total Television Heaven. He figured that if he could work another ten years and save at the same rate, it would enable them to buy an extra fifty years of Heaven. But when the cost of living rose to the point where he wasn't saving anything . . . well, at that point he hadn't really needed that much convincing, especially since there was a rumor that Social Security was about to go bust and the smart thing to do was get into Heaven while you could.

But what good was two hundred and ten years in Total Television Heaven if your wife insisted on living in her tape loops of the past? How much fun could you have if all you had to rely on was the broadcast programmers and your own imagination?

Making love to a fair rescued damsel on the steaming

corpse of a slain dragon. The image began to flicker. Diving out of an airplane, spreading his arms and flying like a bird, the air seemed to turn to a thick, choking fluid. Tarzan of the Apes, making love to an appreciative lioness, felt an uncomfortable pressure against his eyeballs.

Oh, God, it was happening again! For some time now something had been corroding John Rogers. He could feel it happening. He didn't know what it was, but he knew that he didn't want to know what it was.

I'm just sick and tired of having to fill every time slot in my programming day with something I have to choose myself, he told himself nervously. Sure, he could time-share with Edna and let her fill some time slots for him, but her idea of programming made him want to puke.

In fact, the lover of the insatiable Catherine the Great felt a bubble of nausea rising within him even as the beautiful czarina crawled all over him. Napoleon's mind felt a nameless dread even as he led the triumphal march through Paris. Because the thought that had intruded unbidden into his mind was, What would happen if he didn't choose anything to fill the time slot? Was it possible? Would he still be there? Where *was* there?

And questions like those brought on the leading edge of an immense, formless, shapeless, choking dread that took him out of the viewpoint character and made him see the whole thing as if through the eyes of a video camera: lines of dots, pressure against his eyeballs . . .

He shuddered inwardly. Convulsively he switched to a domestic porno tape of himself and Edna making love in the grass on the slope of a roaring volcano. She screamed and cursed and moaned as he stuck it to her, but . . . but . . .

Edna, I've got to get out of here!

But what can I possibly mean by that?

Frantically he voiced her over. "Edna, I've got to real-time-share with you," he said shrilly. "Now!"

"I'm tuned in to *China Clipper* now, and it's my favorite historical X," her voice-over whined as he continued to pound at her under the volcano.

"Please, Edna, porn channel Eight, real-time-share with me now, if you don't . . . if you don't . . ." A wave of molten lava roared and foamed down the mountain toward them as Edna moaned and swore toward climax beneath him.

"Not now, John, I'm enjoying my program," her distant voice-over said.

"Edna! Edna! Edna!" John shrieked, overcome with a terror he didn't understand, didn't want to understand.

"John!" There was finally concern in her voice, and it seemed to come from the Edna who thrashed and moaned beneath him in orgasm as the wave of lava enfolded them in painless fire.

"John, you're disgusting!" she said at the height of the moment. "If you want to time-share with me, we'll have to go to a domestic tape *now*. Loop E."

Raging with fear, anger, and self-loathing, he followed her to the domestic tape. They were sitting on the back porch of their summer cabin at the lake, overlooking the swimming raft, where the kids were playing a ragtag game of water polo. *Oh, Jesus . . .*

"Now what's got you all upset, John?" Edna said primly, pouring him a glass of lemonade.

John didn't know what to say. He didn't know how to deal with it. He didn't even want to know what he was dealing with. He was talking to a ghost. He was talking to his wife talking to a ghost. He . . . he . . .

"We've got to do more real-time-sharing, Edna," he finally said. "It's important. We shouldn't be alone in here all the time."

"I haven't the faintest idea what you're babbling about," Edna said nervously. "As for more real-time-sharing, I'm perfectly willing to share mealtimes with you on a regular basis if you behave yourself. Here. At the house. On our honeymoon. Even in a good restaurant. But not in any of your disgusting programming, John, and that goes double for the porn channels. I don't understand you, John. You've become some kind of pervert. Sometimes I think you're going crazy."

A burst of multicolored snow flickered the old tape. Edna sipped her lemonade. His eyes ached. He was choking.

"I'm going crazy?" John cried thickly. "What about you, Edna, living back here and trying to pretend we're really still alive back then, instead of here in . . . in—"

"In Total Television Heaven, John," Edna said sharply. "Where we're free to program all our time slots to suit ourselves. And if you don't like my programming, you don't have to time-share it. As for your programming, I don't know how you stand it."

"But I can't stand it!" John shouted as a water-skier was drawn by a roaring speed-boat past their porch. "That's

what's driving me crazy." From somewhere came the sounds
of a softball game. A 747 glided by overhead.

"Daddy! Daddy!" the kids waved at him.

"But this is worse!" he screamed at Edna, young and trim
in her two-piece bathing suit. A neighbor's dog came up,
wagging its tail, and she gave it her hand to lick. "This isn't
real, and it's not even an honest fantasy, you're dead inside
of here, Edna, living through your old tape loops, floating in
... floating in ..."

He gagged. An image of a fetus faded in, faded out, faded
in again. He felt something pressing against his face like an
ocean of time drowning him, pulling him under. Nothing was
real. Nothing but whatever Edna had become speaking
through her long-dead simulacrum near the lake.

"Stop it, John! I won't listen to such filth!"

"Oh, Jesus. Edna, we're dead, don't you see? We're dead
and drifting forever in our own tape loops, and only—"

"Good-bye, John," Edna said frostily, taking another sip of
lemonade. "I much prefer the way you were to this!"

"Edna! Edna! Don't break the time-share! You're all that's
left!"

Edna: Say, honey, why don't we go inside and make a little
love in the afternoon.

*A thunderclap rends the sky. It begins to rain. Edna laughs
and undoes the halter of her swimsuit.*

Edna: Oh, I'm getting wet. Why don't you grab a towel and
dry me off.

*She gets up, giggling, takes John's hand, and leads him
inside.*

"Oh, no, no!" John shouted as his viewpoint followed her.
For she was no longer there, and he remembered every scene,
every angle, every special effect of this program. Something
inside him snapped. He had to get out of here. He switched
his videx to rapid random scan, unable to think of choosing a
program to fill his time slot.

Getting head from Marilyn Monroe sailing the Spanish
Main—fetus floating in the eternal amnion—a giant gorilla
chasing dusky natives from dinner with Edna and the kids in
the dining room of their house—a million flickering elec-

tronic dots against his eyeballs—flying like a bird through the towers of New York around the Eiffel Tower—choking in the sea of time—leading the cavalry charge to plant the flag on Iwo Jima—lungs straining for a surface that wasn't there— stepping out of the air lock under triple suns—trapped in syrupy quicksand forever—arriving at the sultan's harem in King Arthur's squad car—

Awake, aware, alive for a long, horribly lucid moment— —floating and choking in the amniotic quicksand with meaningless images attacking his eyeballs—walking up from a long suffocation dream into a long suffocation dream that wouldn't go away, couldn't go away, or there'd be—

Dueling with the musketeers swinging on a vine through the jungle of the Great Barrier Reef with Edna in a hammock screaming orgasm in the harem with a dozen houris soaring through space screaming around great ringed Saturn screaming against the dead cold black phosphor-dotted everlasting void drowning choking screaming god oh god oh oh oh—

As she faded out of the viewpoint character of Elizabeth the Queen, Edna thought of John. How long ago had that terrible final real-time sharing taken place? Was it still the same television season?

It was time for dinner, and she programmed dinner loop C. She, John, and the kids were seated at Thanksgiving dinner. She was wearing her Sunday best, the kids were neat and combed, and John was wearing a suit.

John: This stuffing is delicious, honey!
Sammy: Can I have the other drumstick?
Ellie: Pass the cranberry sauce.
Edna: It's wonderful to have a quiet Thanksgiving dinner just for the four of us, isn't it, John?

Edna felt so contented, so at peace with herself and her family, so right with the world. *I really should invite John to real-time-share this wonderful Thanksgiving,* she thought maternally. *I really ought to give him one last chance to be a proper father to the kids and husband to me.*

Filled with Christian charity, she voiced over to his channel. "John?" she said, scooping up mashed yams with brown sugar and passing the salt to her beaming husband, who planted a little kiss on her wedding ring *en passant*. "I'm having Thanksgiving dinner with you and the kids, and I'd like you to be a good father and real-time-share with us."

There was nothing on the voice-over channel for a moment as John handed the drumstick to Sammy. Then, as Sammy took it from him and bit into it with boyish gusto, John screamed.

An endless, ghastly, blubbering shriek that rattled Edna's teeth and poisoned the moment with unremitting horror.

"John Rogers, you're an animal. I don't know you anymore, and I don't want to!" she shouted back at the horrid sound and broke the connection once and for all.

John: Don't gobble your food, Sammy, or you'll turn into a turkey.
Sammy: (turkey sound) Gobble, gobble!

All four of them laugh heartily.

John: Please pass me some more of the peas, honey. What do you say, kids, isn't your mother the best cook in the world?
Sammy and Ellie: Yay, Mom!

Edna beamed as she handed John the bowl of creamed peas. He smiled at her. Edna relaxed. How good it was to have a nice, civilized Thanksgiving dinner with your husband and your family just the way you liked it. Peaceful and loving and together forever.

She decided to play a romantic porn program after dinner. She would meet John in an elegant café in old Vienna, waltz in a grand ballroom, share a bottle of champagne on a barge in the Seine, and then make love on a bear rug in front of a roaring fireplace. She knew that everything would be just perfect.

NIGHTFLYERS

by George R. R. Martin

This one spans the galaxy. It concerns the quest for a cosmic mystery that began two thousand years ago and may never end. It took humanity thousands of years to develop interstellar travel sufficiently to go out there to the edge of the stars and crack this enigma. But this novella, in the hands of an award-winner, is not one you will easily forget after reading. There are indeed more things in heaven. . . .

When Jesus of Nazareth hung dying on his cross, the *volcryn* passed within a light-year of his agony, headed outward. When the Fire Wars raged on Earth, the *volcryn* sailed near Old Poseidon, where the seas were still unnamed and unfished. By the time the stardrive had transformed the Federated Nations of Earth into the Federal Empire, the *volcryn* had moved into the fringes of Hrangan space. The Hrangans never knew it. Like us they were children of the small bright worlds that circled their scattered suns, with little interest and less knowledge of the things that moved in the gulfs between.

War flamed for a thousand years and the *volcryn* passed through it, unknowing and untouched, safe in a place where no fires could ever burn. Afterwards the Federal Empire was shattered and gone, and the Hrangans vanished in the dark of the Collapse, but it was no darker for the *volcryn.*

When Kleronomas took his survey ship out from Avalon, the *volcryn* came within ten light-years of him. Kleronomas found many things, but he did not find the *volcryn.* Not then did he and not on his return to Avalon a lifetime later.

When I was a child of three Kleronomas was dust, as distant and dead as Jesus of Nazareth and the *volcryn* passed close to Daronne. That season all the Crey sensitives grew strange and sat staring at the stars with luminous, flickering eyes.

When I was grown, the *volcryn* had sailed beyond Tara, past the range of even the Crey, still heading outward.

And now I am old and the *volcryn* will soon pierce the Tempter's Veil where it hangs like a black mist between the stars. And we follow, we follow. Through the dark gulfs where no one goes, through the emptiness, through the silence that goes on and on, my *Nightflyer* and I give chase.

From the hour the *Nightflyer* slipped into stardrive, Royd Eris watched his passengers.

Nine riders had boarded at the orbital docks above Avalon; five women and four men, each an Academy scholar, their backgrounds as diverse as their fields of study. Yet, to Royd, they dressed alike, looked alike, even sounded alike. On Avalon, most cosmopolitan of worlds, they had become as one in their quest for knowledge.

The *Nightflyer* was a trader, not a passenger vessel. It offered one double cabin, one closet-sized single. The other academicians rigged sleepwebs in the four great cargo holds, some in close confinement with the instruments and computer systems they had packed on board. When restive, they could wander two short corridors, one leading from the driveroom and the main airlock up past the cabins to a well-appointed lounge-library-kitchen, the other looping down to the cargo holds. Ultimately it did not matter where they wandered. Even in the sanitary stations, Royd had eyes and ears.

And always and everywhere, Royd watched.

Concepts like a right of privacy did not concern him, but he knew they might concern his passengers, if they knew of his activities. He made certain that they did not.

Royd's own quarters, three spacious chambers forward of the passenger lounge, were sealed and inviolate; he never left them. To his riders, he was a disembodied voice over the communicators that sometimes called them for long conversations, and a holographic spectre that joined them for meals in the lounge. His ghost was a lithe, pale-eyed young man with white hair who dressed in filmy pastel clothing twenty years out of date, and it had the disconcerting habit of looking past the person Royd was addressing, or in the wrong direction altogether, but after a few days the academicians grew accustomed to it. The holograph walked only in the lounge, in any event.

But Royd, secretly, silently, lived everywhere, and ferreted out all of their little secrets.

The cyberneticist talked to her computers, and seemed to prefer their company to that of humans.

The xenobiologist was surly, argumentative, and a solitary drinker.

The two linguists, lovers in public, seldom had sex and snapped bitterly at each other in private.

The psipsych was a hypochondriac given to black depressions, which worsened in the close confines of the *Nightflyer*.

Royd watched them work, eat, sleep, copulate; he listened untiringly to their talk. Within a week, the nine of them no longer seemed the same to him at all. Each of them was strange and unique, he had concluded.

By the time the *Nightflyer* had been under drive for two weeks, two of the passengers had come to engage even more of his attention. He neglected none of them, watched all, but now, specially, he focused on Karoly d'Branin and Melantha Jhirl.

"Most of all, I want to know the *why* of them," Karoly d'Branin told him one false night the second week out from Avalon. Royd's luminescent ghost sat close to d'Branin in the darkened lounge, watching him drink bittersweet chocolate. The others were all asleep. Night and day are meaningless on a starship, but the *Nightflyer* kept the usual cycles, and most of the passengers followed them. Only Karoly d'Branin, administrator and generalist, kept his own solitary time.

"The *if* of them is important as well, Karoly," Royd replied, his soft voice coming from the communicator panels in the walls. "Can you be truly certain if these aliens of yours exist?"

"*I* can be certain," Karoly d'Branin replied. "That is enough. If everyone else were certain as well, we would have a fleet of research ships instead of your little *Nightflyer*." He sipped at his chocolate, and gave a satisfied sigh. "Do you know the Nor T'alush, Royd?"

The name was strange to him, but it took Royd only a moment to consult his library computer. "An alien race on the other side of human space, past the Fyndii worlds and the Damoosh. Possibly legendary."

D'Branin chuckled. "Your library is out-of-date. You must supplement it the next time you are on Avalon. Not legends, no, real enough, though far away. We have little information about the Nor T'alush, but we are sure they exist, though you and I may never meet one. They were the start of it all.

"I was coding some information into the computers, a packet newly arrived from Dam Tullian after twenty standard years in transit. Part of it was Nor T'alush folklore. I had no idea how long that had taken to get to Dam Tullian, or by what route it had come, but it was fascinating material. Did you know that my first degree was in xenomythology?"

"I did not," Royd said. "Please continue."

"The *volcryn* story was among the Nor T'alush myths. It awed me; a race of sentients moving out from some mysterious origin in the core of the galaxy, sailing towards the galactic edge and, it was alleged, eventually bound for intergalactic space itself, meanwhile keeping always to the interstellar depths, no planetfalls, seldom coming within a light-year of a star. And doing it all *without a stardrive*, in ships moving only a fraction of the speed of light! That was the detail that obsessed me! Think how *old* they must be, those ships!"

"Old," Royd agreed. "Karoly, you said *ships*. More than one?"

"Oh, yes, there are," d'Branin said. "According to the Nor T'alush, one or two appeared first, on the innermost edges of their trading sphere, but others followed. Hundreds of them, each solitary, moving by itself, bound outward, always outward. The direction was always the same. For fifteen thousand standard years they moved between the Nor T'alush stars, and then they began to pass out from among them. The myth said that the last *volcryn* ship was gone three thousand years ago."

"Eighteen thousand years," Royd said, adding, "are your Nor T'alush that old?"

D'Branin smiled. "Not as star-travellers, no. According to their own histories, the Nor T'alush have only been civilized for about half that long. That stopped me for a while. It seemed to make the *volcryn* story clearly a legend. A wonderful legend, true, but nothing more.

"Ultimately, however, I could not let it alone. In my spare time, I investigated, cross-checking with other alien cosmologies to see whether this particular myth was shared by any races other than the Nor T'alush. I thought perhaps I would get a thesis out of it. It was a fruitful line of inquiry.

"I was startled by what I found. Nothing from the Hrangans, or the Hrangan slaveraces, but that made sense, you see. They were *out* from human space, the *volcryn* would not reach them until after they had passed through our own sphere. When I looked *in*, however, the *volcryn* story was everywhere. The Fyndii had it, the Damoosh appeared to accept it as literal truth—and the Damoosh, you know, are the oldest race we have ever encountered—and there was a remarkably similar story told among the gethsoids of Aath. I checked what little was known about the races said to flourish further in still, beyond even the Nor T'alush, and they had the *volcryn* story too."

"The legend of the legends," Royd suggested. The spectre's wide mouth turned up in a smile.

"Exactly, exactly," d'Branin agreed. "At that point, I called in the experts, specialists from the Institute for the Study of Nonhuman Intelligence. We researched for two years. It was all there, in the files and the libraries at the Academy. No one had ever looked before, or bothered to put it together.

"The *volcryn* have been moving through the manrealm for most of human history, since before the dawn of spaceflight. While we twist the fabric of space itself to cheat relativity, they have been sailing their great ships right through the heart of our alleged civilization, past our most populous worlds, at stately slow sublight speeds, bound for the Fringe and the dark between the galaxies. Marvelous, Royd, marvelous!"

"Marvelous," Royd agreed.

Karoly d'Branin set down his chocolate cup and leaned forward eagerly towards Royd's projection, but his hand passed through empty light when he tried to grasp his companion by the forearm. He seemed disconcerted for a moment, before he began to laugh at himself. "Ah, my *volcryn*. I grow overenthused, Royd. I am so close now. They have preyed on my mind for a dozen years, and within a month I will have them. Then, *then*, if only I can open communication, if only my people can reach them, then at last I will know the *why* of it!"

The ghost of Royd Eris, master of the *Nightflyer*, smiled for him and looked on through calm unseeing eyes.

Passengers soon grow restless on a starship under drive, sooner on one as small and spare as the *Nightflyer*. Late in the second week, the speculation began. Royd heard it all.

"Who is this Royd Eris, really?" the xenobiologist complained one night when four of them were playing cards. "Why doesn't he come out? What's the purpose of keeping himself sealed off from the rest of us?"

"Ask him," the linguist suggested.

No one did.

When he was not talking to Karoly d'Branin, Royd watched Melantha Jhirl. She was good to watch. Young, healthy, active, Melantha Jhirl had a vibrancy about her that the others could not touch. She was big in every way; a head taller than anyone else on board, large-framed, large-breasted, long-legged, strong, muscles moving fluidly beneath shiny coal-black skin. Her appetites were big as well. She ate twice as much as any of her colleagues, drank heavily without ever seeming drunk, exercised for hours every day on equipment she had brought with her and set up in one of the cargo holds. By the third week out she had sexed with all four of the men on board and two of the other women. Even in bed she was always active, exhausting most of her partners. Royd watched her with consuming interest.

"I am an improved model," she told him once as she worked out on her parallel bars, sweat glistening on her bare skin, her long black hair confined in a net.

"Improved?" Royd said. He could not send his holographic ghost down to the holds, but Melantha had summoned him with the communicator to talk while she exercised, not knowing he would have been there anyway.

She paused in her routine, holding her body aloft with the strength of her arms. "Altered, Captain," she said. She had taken to calling him that. "Born on Prometheus among the elite, child of two genetic wizards. Improved, Captain. I require twice the energy you do, but I use it all. A more efficient metabolism, a stronger and more durable body, an expected lifespan half again the normal human's. My people have made some terrible mistakes when they try to radically redesign the lessers, but the small improvements they do well."

She resumed her exercises, moving quickly and easily, silent until she had finished. Then, breathing heavily, she crossed her arms and cocked her head and grinned. "Now you know my life story, Captain, unless you care to hear the part about my defection to Avalon, my extraordinary work in nonhuman anthropology, and my tumultuous and passionate lovelife. Do you?"

"Perhaps some other time," Royd said, politely.

"Good," Melantha Jhirl replied. She snatched up a towel and began to dry the sweat from her body. "I'd rather hear your life story, anyway. Among my modest attributes is an insatiable curiosity. Who are you, Captain? Really?"

"One as improved as you," Royd replied, "should certainly be able to guess."

Melantha laughed, and tossed her towel at the communicator grill.

By that time all of them were guessing, when they did not think Royd was listening. He enjoyed the rumors.

"He talks to us, but he can't be seen," the cyberneticist said. "This ship is uncrewed, seemingly all automated except for him. Why not entirely automated, then? I'd wager Royd Eris is a fairly sophisticated computer system, perhaps an Artificial Intelligence. Even a modest program can carry on a blind conversation indistinguishable from a human's."

The telepath was a frail young thing, nervous, sensitive, with limp flaxen hair and watery blue eyes. He sought out Karoly d'Branin in his cabin, the cramped single, for a private conversation. "I feel it," he said excitedly. "Something is wrong, Karoly, something is very wrong. I'm beginning to get frightened."

D'Branin was startled. "Frightened? I don't understand, my friend. What is there for you to fear?"

The young man shook his head. "I don't know, I don't know. Yet it's there, I feel it. Karoly, I'm picking up something. You know I'm good, I am, that's why you picked me. Class one, tested, and I tell you I'm afraid. I sense it. Something dangerous. Something volatile—and alien."

"My *volcryn*?" d'Branin said.

"No, no, impossible. We're in drive, they're light-years away." The telepath's laugh was desperate. "I'm not *that* good, Karoly. I've heard your Crey story, but I'm only a human. No, this is close. On the ship."

"One of us?"

"Maybe," the telepath said. "I can't sort it out."

D'Branin sighed and put a fatherly hand on the young man's shoulder. "I thank you for coming to me, but I cannot act unless you have something more definite. This feeling of yours—could it be that you are just tired? We have all of us been under strain. Inactivity can be taxing."

"This is real," the telepath insisted, but he left peacefully.

Afterwards d'Branin went to the psipsych, who was lying in her sleepweb surrounded by medicines, complaining bitterly of aches. "Interesting," she said when d'Branin told her. "I've felt something too, a sense of threat, very vague, diffuse. I thought it was me, the confinement, the boredom, the way I feel. My moods betray me at times. Did he say anything more specific?"

"No."

"I'll make an effort to move around, read him, read the others, see what I can pick up. Although, if this is real, he should know it first. He's a one, I'm only a three."

D'Branin nodded, reassured. Later, when the rest had gone to sleep, he made some chocolate and talked to Royd through the false night. But he never mentioned the telepath once.

"Have you noticed the clothes on that holograph he sends us?" the xenobiologist said to the others. "A decade out of style, at least. I don't think he really looks like that. What if he's deformed, sick, ashamed to be seen the way he really looks? Perhaps he has some disease. The Slow Plague can waste a person terribly, but it takes decades to kill, and there are other contagions, manthrax and new leprosy and Langamen's Disease. Could it be that Royd's self-imposed quarantine is just that. A quarantine. Think about it."

In the fifth week out, Melantha Jhirl pushed her pawn to the sixth rank and Royd saw it was unstoppable and resigned. It was his eighth straight defeat at her hands in as many days. She was sitting cross-legged on the floor of the lounge, the chessmen spread out before her on a viewscreen, its receiver dark. Laughing, she swept them away. "Don't feel bad, Royd," she told him. "I'm an improved model. Always three moves ahead."

"I should tie in my computer," he replied. "You'd never

know." His holographic ghost materialized suddenly, standing in front of the viewscreen, and smiled at her.

"I'd know within three moves," Melantha Jhirl said. "Try it." She stood up and walked right through his projection on her way to the kitchen, where she found herself a bulb of beer. "When are you going to break down and let me behind your wall for a visit, Captain?" she asked, talking up to a communicator grill. She refused to treat his ghost as real. "Don't you get lonely there? Sexually frustrated? Claustrophobic?"

"I've flown the *Nightflyer* all my life, Melantha," Royd said. His projection ignored, winked out. "If I were subject to claustrophobia, sexual frustration, or loneliness, such a life would have been impossible. Surely that should be obvious to you, being as improved a model as you are?"

She took a squeeze of her beer and laughed her mellow, musical laugh at him. "I'll solve you yet, Captain," she warned.

"Fine," he said. "Meanwhile, tell me some more lies about your life."

"Have you ever heard of Jupiter?" the xenotech demanded of the others. She was drunk, lolling in her sleepweb in the cargo hold.

"Something to do with Earth," one of the linguists said. "The same myth system originated both names, I believe."

"Jupiter," the xenotech announced loudly, "is a gas giant in the same solar system as Old Earth. Didn't know that, did you? They were on the verge of exploring it when the stardrive was discovered, oh, way back. After that, nobody bothered with gas giants. Just slip into drive and find the habitable worlds, settle them, ignore the comets and the rocks and the gas giants—there's another star just a few light-years away, and it has more habitable planets. But there were people who thought those Jupiters might have life, you know. Do you see?"

The xenobiologist looked annoyed. "If there is intelligent life on the gas giants, it shows no interest in leaving them," he snapped. "All of the sentient species we have met up to now have originated on worlds similar to Earth, and most of them are oxygen breathers. Unless you suggest that the *volcryn* are from a gas giant?"

The xenotech pushed herself up to a sitting position and smiled conspiratorially. "Not the *volcryn*," she said. "Royd

Eris. Crack that forward bulkhead in the lounge, and watch the methane and ammonia come smoking out." Her hand made a sensuous waving motion through the air, and she convulsed with giddy laughter.

"I dampened him," the psipsych reported to Karoly d'Branin during the sixth week. "Psionine-4. It will blunt his receptivity for several days, and I have more if he needs it."

D'Branin wore a stricken look. "We talked several times, he and I. I could see that he was becoming ever more fearful, but he could never tell me the why of it. Did you absolutely have to shut him off?"

The psipsych shrugged. "He was edging into the irrational. You should never have taken a class one telepath, d'Branin. Too unstable."

"We must communicate with an alien race. I remind you that is no easy task. The *volcryn* are perhaps more alien than any sentients we have yet encountered. Because of that we needed class one skills."

"Glib," she said, "but you might have no working skills at all, given the condition of your class one. Half the time he's catatonic and half the time crazy with fear. He insists that we're all in real physical danger, but he doesn't know why or from what. The worst of it is I can't tell if he's really sensing something or simply having an acute attack of paranoia. He certainly displays some classic paranoid symptoms. Among other things, he believes he's being watched. Perhaps his condition is completely unrelated to us, the *volcryn*, and his talent. I can't be sure at this point in time."

"What of your own talent?" d'Branin said. "You are an empath, are you not?"

"Don't tell me my job," she said sharply. "I sexed with him last week. You don't get more proximity or better rapport for esping than that. Even under those conditions, I couldn't be sure of anything. His mind is a chaos, and his fear is so rank it stank up the sheets. I don't read anything from the others either, besides the ordinary tensions and frustrations. But I'm only a three, so that doesn't mean much. My abilities are limited. You know I haven't been feeling well, d'Branin. I can barely breathe on this ship. My head throbs. Ought to stay in bed."

"Yes, of course," d'Branin said hastily. "I did not mean to criticize. You have been doing all you can under difficult circumstances. Yet, I must ask, is it vital he be dampened? Is there no other way? Royd will take us out of drive soon, and we will make contact with the *volcryn*. We will need him."

The psipsych rubbed her temple wearily. "My other option was an injection of esperon. It would have opened him up completely, tripled his psionic receptivity for a few hours. Then, hopefully, he could home in this danger he's feeling. Exorcise it if it's false, deal with it if it's real. But psionine-4 is a lot safer. The physical side effects of esperon are debilitating, and emotionally I don't think he's stable enough to deal with that kind of power. The psionine should tell us something. If his paranoia continues to persist, I'll know it has nothing to do with his telepathy."

"And if it does not persist?" Karoly d'Branin said.

She smiled wickedly. "Then we'll know that he really was picking up some sort of threat, won't we?"

False night came, and Royd's wraith materialized while Karoly d'Branin sat brooding over his chocolate. "Karoly," the apparition said, "would it be possible to tie in the computer your team brought on board with my shipboard system? Those *volcryn* stories fascinate me, and I'd like to be able to study them at my leisure."

"Certainly," d'Branin replied in an offhand, distracted manner. "It is time we got our system up and running in any case. Soon, now, we will be dropping out of drive."

"Soon," Royd agreed. "Approximately seventy hours from now."

At dinner the following day, Royd's projection did not appear. The academicians ate uneasily, expecting their host to materialize at any moment, take his accustomed place, and join in the mealtime conversation. Their expectations were still unfulfilled when the afterdinner pots of chocolate and spiced tea and coffee were set on the table before them.

"Our captain seems to be occupied," Melantha Jhirl observed, leaning back in her chair and swirling a snifter of brandy.

"We will be shifting out of drive soon," Karoly d'Branin said. "There are preparations to make."

Some of the others looked at one another. All nine of them were present, although the young telepath seemed lost in his own head. The xenobiologist broke the silence. "He doesn't eat. He's a damned holograph. What does it matter if he misses a meal? Maybe it's just as well. Karoly, a lot of us have been getting uneasy about Royd. What do you know about this mystery man anyway?"

D'Branin looked at him with wide, puzzled eyes. "Know, my friend?" he said, leaning forward to refill his cup with the thick, bittersweet chocolate. "What is there to know?"

"Surely you've noticed that he never comes out to play with us," the female linguist said drily. "Before you engaged his ship, did anyone remark on this quirk of his?"

"I'd like to know the answer to that too," her partner said. "A lot of traffic comes and goes through Avalon. How did you come to choose Eris? What were you told about him?"

D'Branin hesitated. "Told about him? Very little, I must admit. I spoke to a few port officials and charter companies, but none of them were acquainted with Royd. He had not traded out of Avalon originally, you see."

"Where *is* he from?" the linguists demanded in unison. They looked at each other, and the woman continued. "We've listened to him. He has no discernible accent, no idiosyncrasies of speech to betray his origins. Tell us, where did this *Nightflyer* come from?"

"I—I don't know, actually," d'Branin admitted, hesitating. "I never thought to ask him about it."

The members of his research team glanced at each other incredulously. "You never thought to *ask?*" the xenotech said. "How did you select this ship, then?"

"It was available. The administrative council approved my project and assigned me personnel, but they could not spare an Academy ship. There were budgetary constraints as well." All eyes were on him.

"What d'Branin is saying," the psipsych interrupted, "is that the Academy was pleased with his studies in xenomyth, with the discovery of the *volcryn* legend, but less than enthusiastic about his plan to prove the *volcryn* real. So they gave him a small budget to keep him happy and productive, assuming that this little mission would be fruitless, and they assigned him workers who wouldn't be missed back on Avalon." She looked around at each person. "Except for d'Branin," she said, "not a one of us is a first-rate scholar."

"Well, you can speak for yourself," Melantha Jhirl said. "I volunteered for this mission."

"I won't argue the point," the psipsych said. "The crux is that the choice of the *Nightflyer* is no large enigma. You engaged the cheapest charter you could find, didn't you, d'Branin?"

"Some of the available ships would not even consider my proposition," d'Branin said. "The sound of it is odd, we must admit. And many ship masters seemed to have a superstitious fear of dropping out of drive in interstellar space, without a planet near. Of those who agreed to the conditions, Royd Eris offered the best terms, and he was able to leave at once."

"And we *had* to leave at once," said the female linguist. "Otherwise the *volcryn* might get away. They've only been passing through this region for ten thousand years, give or take a few thousand," she said sarcastically.

Someone laughed. D'Branin was nonplussed. "Friends, no doubt I could have postponed departure. I admit I was eager to meet my *volcryn*, to ask them the questions that have haunted me, to discover the why of them, but I must also admit that a delay would have been no great hardship. But *why*? Royd is a gracious host, a skilled pilot, he has treated us well."

"He has made himself a cipher," someone said.

"What is he hiding?" another voice demanded.

Melantha Jhirl laughed. When all eyes had moved to her, she grinned and shook her head. "Captain Royd is perfect, a strange man for a strange mission. Don't any of you love a mystery? Here we are flying light-years to intercept a hypothetical alien starship from the core of the galaxy that has been outward bound for longer than humanity has been having wars, and all of you are upset because you can't count the warts of Royd's nose." She leaned across the table to refill her brandy snifter. "My mother was right," she said lightly. "Normals are subnormal."

"Melantha is correct," Karoly d'Branin said quietly. "Royd's foibles and neuroses are his business, if he does not impose them on us."

"It makes me uncomfortable," someone complained weakly.

"For all we know, Karoly," said the xenotech, "we might be travelling with a criminal or an alien."

"*Jupiter*," someone muttered. The xenotech flushed red, and there was sniggering around the long table.

But the young, pale-haired telepath looked up suddenly and stared at them all with wild, nervous eyes. "An *alien*," he said.

The psipsych swore. "The drug is wearing off," she said quickly to d'Branin. "I'll have to go back to my room to get some more."

All of the others looked baffled; d'Branin had kept his telepath's condition a careful secret. "What drug?" the xenotech demanded. "What's going on here?"

"Danger," the telepath muttered. He turned to the cyberneticist sitting next to him, and grasped her forearm in a trembling hand. "We're in danger, I tell you, I'm reading it. Something *alien*. And it means us ill."

The psipsych rose. "He's not well," she announced to the others. "I've been dampening him with psionine, trying to hold his delusions in check. I'll get some more." She started towards the door.

"Wait," Melantha Jhirl said. "Not psionine. Try esperon."

"Don't tell me my job, woman."

"Sorry," Melantha said. She gave a modest shrug. "I'm one step ahead of you, though. Esperon might exorcise his delusions, no?"

"Yes, but—"

"And it might let him focus on this threat he claims to detect, correct?"

"I know the characteristics of esperon," the psipsych said testily.

Melantha smiled over the rim of her brandy glass. "I'm sure you do," she said. "Now listen to me. All of you are anxious about Royd, it seems. You can't stand not knowing what he's concealing about himself. You suspect him of being a criminal. Fears like that won't help us work together as a team. Let's end them. Easy enough." She pointed. "Here sits a class one telepath. Boost his power with esperon and he'll be able to recite our captain's life history to us, until we're all suitably bored with it. Meanwhile he'll also be vanquishing his personal demons."

"*He's watching us,*" the telepath said in a low, urgent voice.

"Karoly," the xenobiologist said, "this has gone too far. Several of us are nervous, and this boy is terrified. I think we all need an end to the mystery of Royd Eris. Melantha is right."

D'Branin was troubled. "We have no right—"

"We have the *need*," the cyberneticist said.

D'Branin's eyes met those of the psipsych, and he sighed. "Do it," he said. "Get him the esperon."

"*He's going to kill me,*" the telepath screamed and leapt to his feet. When the cyberneticist tried to calm him with a hand on his arm, he seized a cup of coffee and threw it square in her face. It took three of them to hold him down. "Hurry," one commanded, as the youth struggled.

The psipsych shuddered and quickly left the lounge.

Royd was watching.

When the psipsych returned, they lifted the telepath to the table and forced him down, pulling aside his hair to bare the arteries in his neck.

Royd's ghost materialized in its empty chair at the foot of the long dinner table. "Stop that," it said calmly. "There is no need."

The psipsych froze in the act of slipping an ampule of esperon into her injection gun, and the xenotech startled visibly and released one of the telepath's arms. But the captive did not pull free. He lay on the table, breathing heavily, too frightened to move, his pale blue eyes fixed glassily on Royd's projection.

Melantha Jhirl lifted her brandy glass in salute. "Boo," she said. "You've missed dinner, Captain."

"Royd," said Karoly d'Branin, "I am sorry."

The ghost stared unseeing at the far wall. "Release him," said the voice from the communicators. "I will tell you my great secret, if my privacy intimidates you so."

"He *has* been watching us," the male linguist said.

"Tell, then," the xenotech said suspiciously. "What are you?"

"I liked your guess about the gas giants," Royd said. "Sadly, the truth is less dramatic. I am an ordinary *Homo sapien* in late middle-age. Sixty-eight standard, if you require precision. The holograph you see before you was the real Royd Eris, although some years ago. I am older now."

"Oh?" The cyberneticist's face was red where the coffee had scalded her. "Then why the secrecy?"

"I will begin with my mother," Royd replied. "The *Nightflyer* was her ship originally, custom-built to her design in the Newholme spaceyards. My mother was a freetrader, a notably successful one. She made a fortune through a willingness to accept the unusual consignment, fly off the major trade routes, take her cargo a month or a year or two years beyond where it was customarily transferred. Such practices are riskier but more profitable than flying the mail runs. My mother did not worry about how often she and her crews returned home. Her ships were her home. She seldom visited the same world twice if she could avoid it."

"Adventurous," Melantha said.

"No," said Royd. "Sociopathic. My mother did not like people, you see. Not at all. Her one great dream was to free herself from the necessity of crew. When she grew rich enough, she had it done. The *Nightflyer* was the result. After she boarded it at Newholme, she never touched a human being again, or walked a planet's surface. She did all her business from the compartments that are now mine. She was insane, but she did have an interesting life, even after that. The worlds she saw, Karoly! The things she might have told you! Your heart would break. She destroyed most of her records, however, for fear that other people might get some use or pleasure from her experience after her death. She was like that."

"And you?" the xenotech said.

"I should not call her my mother," Royd continued. "I am her cross-sex clone. After thirty years of flying this ship alone, she was bored. I was to be her companion and lover. She could shape me to be a perfect diversion. She had no patience with children, however, and no desire to raise me herself. As an embryo, I was placed in a nurturant tank. The computer was my teacher. I was to be released when I had attained the age of puberty, at which time she guessed I would be fit company.

"Her death, a few months after the cloning, ruined the plan. She had programmed the ship for such an eventuality, however. It dropped out of drive and shut down, drifted in interstellar space for eleven years while the computer made a human being out of me. That was how I inherited the *Nightflyer*. When I was freed, it took me some years to puzzle out the operation of the ship and my own origins."

"Fascinating," said d'Branin.

"Yes," said the female linguist, "but it doesn't explain why you keep yourself in isolation."

"Ah, but it does," Melantha Jhirl said. "Captain, perhaps you should explain further for the less improved models?"

"My mother hated planets," Royd said. "She hated stinks and dirt and bacteria, the irregularity of the weather, the sight of other people. She engineered for us a flawless environment, as sterile as she could possibly make it. She disliked gravity as well. She was accustomed to weightlessness, and preferred it. These were the conditions under which I was born and raised.

"My body has no natural immunities to anything. Contact

with any of you would probably kill me, and would certainly make me very sick. My muscles are feeble, atrophied. The gravity the *Nightflyer* is now generating is for your comfort, not mine. To me it is agony. At the moment I am seated in a floating chair that supports my weight. I still hurt, and my internal organs may be suffering damage. It is one reason why I do not often take on passengers."

"You share your mother's opinion of the run of humanity, then?" the psipsych said.

"I do not. I like people. I accept what I am, but I did not choose it. I experience human life in the only way I can, vicariously, through the infrequent passengers I dare to carry. At those times, I drink in as much of their lives as I can."

"If you kept your ship under weightlessness at all times, you could take on more riders, could you not?" suggested the xenobiologist.

"True," Royd said politely. "I have found, however, that most people choose not to travel with a captain who does not use his gravity grid. Prolonged free-fall makes them ill and uncomfortable. I could also mingle with my guests, I know, if I kept to my chair and wore a sealed environment suit. I have done so. I find it lessens my participation instead of increasing it. I become a freak, a maimed thing, one who must be treated differently and kept at a distance. I prefer isolation. As often as I dare, I study the aliens I take on as riders."

"Aliens?" the xenotech said, in a confused voice.

"You are all aliens to me," Royd answered.

Silence then filled the *Nightflyer's* lounge.

"I am sorry this had to happen, my friend," Karoly d'Branin said to the ghost.

"Sorry," the psipsych said. She frowned and pushed the ampule of esperon into the injection chamber. "Well, it's glib enough, but is it the truth? We still have no proof, just a new bedtime story. The holograph could have claimed it was a creature from Jupiter, a computer, or a diseased war criminal just as easily." She took two quick steps forward to where the young telepath still lay on the table. "He still needs treatment, and we still need confirmation. I don't care to live with all this anxiety, when we can end it all now." Her hand pushed the unresisting head to one side, she found the artery, and pressed the gun to it.

"No," the voice from the communicator said sternly. "Stop. I order it. This is my ship. Stop."

The gun hissed loudly, and there was a red mark when she lifted it from the telepath's neck.

He raised himself to a half-sitting position, supported by his elbows, and the psipsych moved close to him. "Now," she said in her best professional tones, "focus on Royd. You can do it, we all know how good you are. Wait just a moment, the esperon will open it all up for you."

His pale blue eyes were clouded. "Not close enough," he muttered. "One, I'm one, tested. Good, you know I'm good, but I got to be *close*." He trembled.

She put an arm around him, stroked him, coaxed him. "The esperon will give you range," she said. "Feel it, feel yourself grow stronger. Can you feel it? Everything's getting clear, isn't it?" Her voice was a reassuring drone. "Remember the danger now, remember, go find it. Look beyond the wall, tell us about it. Tell us about Royd. Was he telling the truth? Tell us. You're good, we all know that, you can tell us." The phrases were almost an incantation.

He shrugged off her support and sat upright by himself. "I can feel it," he said. His eyes were suddenly clearer. "Something—my head hurts—I'm *afraid*!"

"Don't be afraid," the psipsych said. "The esperon won't make your head hurt, it just makes you better. Nothing to fear." She stroked his brow. "Tell us what you see."

The telepath looked at Royd's ghost with terrified little-boy eyes, and his tongue flicked across his lower lip. "He's—"

Then his skull exploded.

It was three hours later when the survivors met again to talk.

In the hysteria and confusion of the aftermath, Melantha Jhirl had taken charge. She gave orders, pushing her brandy aside and snapping out commands with the ease of one born to it, and the others seemed to find a numbing solace in doing as they were told. Three of them fetched a sheet, and wrapped the headless body of the young telepath within, and shoved it through the driveroom airlock at the end of the ship. Two others, on Melantha's order, found water and cloth and began to clean up the lounge. They did not get far. Mopping the blood from the tabletop, the cyberneticist suddenly began to retch violently. Karoly d'Branin, who had sat still and shocked since it happened, woke and took the blood-soaked rag from her hand and led her away, back to his cabin.

Melantha Jhirl was helping the psipsych, who had been standing very close to the telepath when he died. A sliver of bone had penetrated her cheek just below her right eye, she was covered with blood and pieces of flesh and bone and brain, and she had gone into shock. Melantha removed the bone splinter, led her below, cleaned her, and put her to sleep with a shot of one of her own drugs.

And, at length, she got the rest of them together in the largest of the cargo holds, where three of them slept. Seven of the surviving eight attended. The psipsych was still asleep, but the cyberneticist seemed to have recovered. She sat cross-legged on the floor, her features pale and drawn, waiting for Melantha to begin.

It was Karoly d'Branin who spoke first, however. "I do not understand," he said. "I do not understand what has happened. What could . . ."

"Royd killed him, is all," the xenotech said bitterly. "His secret was endangered, so he just—just blew him apart."

"I cannot believe that," Karoly d'Branin said, anguished. "I cannot. Royd and I, we have talked, talked many a night when the rest of you were sleeping. He is gentle, inquisitive, sensitive. A dreamer. He understands about the *volcryn*. He would not do such a thing."

"His holograph certainly winked out quick enough when it happened," the female linguist said. "And you'll notice he hasn't had much to say since."

"The rest of you haven't been usually talkative either," Melantha Jhirl said. "I don't know what to think, but my impulse is to side with Karoly. We have no proof that the captain was responsible for what happened."

The xenotech make a loud rude noise. "Proof."

"In fact," Melantha continued unperturbed, "I'm not even sure anyone was responsible. Nothing happened until he was given the esperon. Could the drug be at fault?"

"Hell of a side effect," the female linguist muttered.

The xenobiologist frowned. "This is not my field, but I know esperon is an extremely potent drug, with severe physical effects as well as psionic. The instrument of death was probably his own talent, augmented by the drug. Besides boosting his principal power, his telepathic sensitivity, esperon would also tend to bring out other psi-talents that might have been latent in him."

"Such as?" someone demanded.

"Biocontrol. Telekinesis."

Melantha Jhirl was way ahead of him. "Increase the pressure inside his skull sharply, by rushing all the blood in his body to his brain. Decrease the air pressure around his head simultaneously, using teke to induce a short-lived vacuum. Think about it."

They thought about it, and none of them liked it.

"It could have been self-induced," Karoly d'Branin said.

"Or a stronger talent could have turned his power against him," the xenotech said stubbornly.

"No human telepath has talent on that order, to seize control of someone else, body and mind and soul, even for an instant."

"Exactly," the xenotech said. "No *human* telepath."

"Gas giant people?" The cyberneticist's tone was mocking.

The xenotech stared her down. "I could talk about Crey sensitives or *githyanki* soulsucks, name a half-dozen others off the top of my head, but I don't need to. I'll only name one. A Hrangan Mind."

That was a disquieting thought. All of them fell silent and moved uneasily, thinking of the vast, inimicable power of a Hrangan Mind hidden in the command chambers of the *Nightflyer*, until Melantha Jhirl broke the spell. "That is ridiculous," she said. "Think of what you're saying, if that isn't too much to ask. You're supposed to be xenologists, the lot of you, experts in alien languages, psychology, biology, technology. You don't act the part. We warred with Old Hranga for a thousand years, but we *never* communicated successfully with a Hrangan Mind. If Royd Eris is a Hrangan, they've certainly improved their conversational skills in the centuries since the Collapse."

The xenotech flushed. "You're right," she mumbled. "I'm jumpy."

"Friends," Karoly d'Branin said, "we must not panic or grow hysterical. A terrible thing has happened. One of our colleagues is dead, and we do not know why. Until we do, we can only go on. This is no time for rash actions against the innocent. Perhaps, when we return to Avalon, an investigation will tell us what happened. The body is safe, is it not?"

"We cycled it through the airlock into the driveroom," said the male linguist. "Vacuum in there. It'll keep."

"And it can be examined on our return," d'Branin said, satisfied.

"That return should be immediate," the xenotech said. "Tell Eris to turn this ship around."

D'Branin looked stricken. "But the *volcryn!* A week more, and we will know them, if my figures are correct. To return would take us six weeks. Surely it is worth one week additional to know that they exist?"

The xenotech was stubborn. "A man is dead. Before he died, he talked about aliens and danger. Maybe we're in danger too. Maybe these *volcryn* are the cause, maybe they're more potent than even a Hrangan Mind. Do you care to risk it? And for what? Your sources may be fictional or exaggerated or wrong, your interpretations and computations may be incorrect, or they may have changed course—the *volcryn* may not even be within light-years of where we'll drop out!"

"Ah," Melantha Jhirl said, "I understand. Then we shouldn't go on because they won't be there, and besides, they might be dangerous."

D'Branin smiled and the female linguist laughed. "Not funny," said the xenotech, but she argued no more.

"No," Melantha continued, "any danger we are in will not increase significantly in the time it will take us to drop out of drive and look about for *volcryn*. We would have to drop out anyway, to reprogram. Besides, we have come a long way for these *volcryn*, and I admit to being curious." She looked at each of them in turn, but none of them disagreed. "We continue, then."

"And what do we do with Royd?" D'Branin asked.

"Treat the captain as before, if we can," Melantha said decisively. "Open lines to him and talk. He's probably as shocked and dismayed by what happened as we are, and possibly fearful that we might blame him, try to hurt him, something like that. So we reassure him. I'll do it, if no one else wants to talk to him." There were no volunteers. "All right. But the rest of you had better try to act normally."

"Also," said d'Branin, "we must continue with our preparations. Our sensory instruments must be ready for deployment as soon as we shift out of drive and reenter normal space, our computer must be functioning."

"It's up and running," the cyberneticist said quietly. "I finished this morning, as you requested." She had a thoughtful look in her eyes, but d'Branin did not notice. He turned to the linguists and began discussing some of the preliminaries he expected from them, and in a short time the talk had turned to the *volcryn*, and little by little the fear drained out of the group.

Royd, listening, was glad.

She returned to the lounge alone.

Someone had turned out the lights. "Captain?" she said, and he appeared to her, pale, glowing softly, with eyes that did not really see. His clothes, filmy and out-of-date, were all shades of white and faded blue. "Did you hear, Captain?"

His voice over the communicator betrayed a faint hint of surprise. "Yes. I hear and I see everything on my *Nightflyer*, Melantha. Not only in the lounge. Not only when the communicators and viewscreens are on. How long have you known?"

"Known?" She laughed. "Since you praised the gas giant solution to the Roydian mystery."

"I was under stress. I have never made a mistake before."

"I believe you, Captain," she said. "No matter. I'm the improved model, remember? I'd guessed weeks ago."

For a time Royd said nothing. Then: "When do you begin to reassure me?"

"I'm doing so right now. Don't you feel reassured yet?"

The apparition gave a ghostly shrug. "I am pleased that you and Karoly do not think I murdered that man."

She smiled. Her eyes were growing accustomed to the room. By the faint light of the holograph, she could see the table where it had happened, dark stains across its top. Blood. She heard a faint dripping, and shivered. "I don't like it in here."

"If you would like to leave, I can be with you wherever you go."

"No," she said. "I'll stay. Royd, if I asked you to, would you shut off your eyes and ears throughout the ship? Except for the lounge? It would make the others feel better, I'm sure."

"They don't know."

"They will. You made that remark about gas giants in everyone's hearing. Some of them have probably figured it out by now."

"If I told you I had cut myself off, you would have no way of knowing whether it was the truth."

"I could trust you," Melantha said.

Silence. The spectre looked thoughtful. "As you wish," Royd's voice said finally. "Everything off. Now I see and hear only in here."

"I believe you."

"Did you believe my story?" Royd asked.

"Ah," she said. "A strange and wondrous story, Captain. If it's a lie, I'll swap lies with you any time. You do it well. If it's true, then you are a strange and wondrous man."

"It's true," the ghost said quietly. "Melantha——" His voice hesitated.

"Yes."

"I watched you copulating."

She smiled. "Ah," she said. "I'm good at it."

"I wouldn't know," Royd said. "You're good to watch."

Silence. She tried not to hear the dripping. "Yes," she said after a long hesitation.

"Yes? What?"

"Yes, Royd, I would probably sex with you if it were possible."

"How did you know what I was thinking?"

"I'm an improved model," she said. "And no, I'm not a telepath. It wasn't so difficult to figure out. I told you, I'm three moves ahead of you."

Royd considered that for a long time. "I believe I'm reassured," he said at last.

"Good," said Melantha Jhirl. "Now reassure me."

"Of what?"

"What happened in here? Really?"

Royd said nothing.

"I think you know something," Melantha said. "You gave up your secret to stop us from injecting him with esperon. Even after your secret was forfeit, you ordered us not to go ahead. Why?"

"Esperon is a dangerous drug," Royd said.

"More than that, Captain," Melantha said. "What killed him?"

"*I* didn't."

"One of us? The *volcryn*?"

Royd said nothing.

"Is there an alien aboard your ship, Captain?" she asked. "Is that it?"

Silence.

"Are we in danger? Am *I* in danger, Captain? I'm not afraid. Does that make me a fool?"

"I like people," Royd said at last. "When I can stand it, I like to have passengers. I watch them, yes. It's not so terrible. I like you and Karoly especially. You have nothing to fear. I won't let anything happen to you."

"What might happen?" she asked.

Royd said nothing.

"And what about the others, Royd? Are you taking care of them, too? Or only Karoly and me?"

No reply.

"You're not very talkative tonight," Melantha observed.

"I'm under strain," his voice replied. "Go to bed, Melantha Jhirl. We've talked long enough."

"All right, Captain," she said. She smiled at his ghost and lifted her hand. His own rose to meet it. Warm dark flesh and pale radiance brushed, melded, were one. Melantha Jhirl turned to go. It was not until she was out in the corridor, safe in the light once more, that she began to tremble.

False midnight. The talks had broken up, the nightmares had faded, and the academicians were lost in sleep. Even Karoly d'Branin slept, his appetite for chocolate quelled by his memories of the lounge.

In the darkness of the largest cargo hold, three sleepwebs hung, sleepers snoring softly in two. The cyberneticist lay awake, thinking, in the third. Finally she rose, dropped lightly to the floor, pulled on her jumpsuit and boots, and shook the xenotech from her slumber. "Come," she whispered, beckoning. They stole off into the corridor, leaving Melantha Jhirl to her dreams.

"What the hell," the xenotech muttered when they were safely beyond the door. She was half-dressed, disarrayed, unhappy.

"There's a way to find out if Royd's story was true," the cyberneticist said carefully. "Melantha won't like it, though. Are you game to try?"

"What?" the other asked. Her face betrayed her interest.

"Come," the cyberneticist said.

One of the three lesser cargo holds had been converted into a computer room. They entered quietly; all empty. The system was up, but dormant. Currents of light ran silkily down crystalline channels in the data grids, meeting, joining, splitting apart again; rivers of wan multihued radiance crisscrossing a black landscape. The chamber was dim, the only noise a low buzz at the edge of human hearing, until the cyberneticist moved through it, touching keys, tripping switches, directing the silent luminescent currents. Slowly the machine woke.

"What are you *doing*?" the xenotech said.

"Karoly told me to tie in our system with the ship," the cyberneticist replied as she worked. "I was told Royd wanted to study the *volcryn* data. Fine, I did it. Do you understand what that means?"

Now the xenotech was eager. "The two systems are tied together!"

"Exactly. So Royd can find out about the *volcryn*, and we can find out about Royd." She frowned. "I wish I knew more about the *Nightflyer's* hardware, but I think I can feel my way through. This is a pretty sophisticated system d'Branin requisitioned."

"Can you take over?" the xenotech asked excitedly.

"Take over?" The cyberneticist sounded puzzled. "You been drinking again?"

"No, I'm serious. Use your system to break into the ship's control, overwhelm Eris, countermand his orders, make the *Nightflyer* respond to us, down here."

"Maybe," the cyberneticist said doubtfully, slowly. "I could try, but why do that?"

"Just in case. We don't have to use the capacity. Just so we have it, if an emergency arises."

The cyberneticist shrugged. "Emergencies and gas giants. I only want to put my mind at rest about Royd." She moved over to a readout panel, where a half-dozen meter-square viewscreens curved around a console, and brought one of them to life. Long fingers brushed across the holographic keys that appeared and disappeared as she touched them, the keyboard changing shape even as she used it. Characters began to flow across the viewscreen, red flickerings encased in glassy black depths. The cyberneticist watched, and finally froze them. "Here," she said, "here's my answer about the hardware. You can dismiss your takeover idea, unless those gas giant people of yours are going to help. The *Nightflyer's* bigger and smarter than our little system here. Makes sense, when you stop to think about it. Ship's all automated, except for Royd." She whistled and coaxed her search program with soft words of encouragement. "It looks as though there *is* a Royd, though. Configurations are all wrong for a robot ship. Damn, I would have bet anything." The characters began to flow again, the cyberneticist watching the figures as they drifted by. "Here's life support specs, might tell us something." A finger jabbed, and the screen froze once more.

"Nothing unusual," the xenotech said in disappointment.

"Standard waste disposal. Water recycling. Food processor, with protein and vitamin supplements in stores." She began to whistle. "Tanks of Renny's moss and neograss to eat up the

CO_2. Oxygen cycle, then. No methane or ammonia. Sorry about that."

"Go sex with a computer."

The cyberneticist smiled. "Ever tried it?" Her fingers moved again. "What else should I look for? Give me some ideas."

"Check the specs for nurturant tanks, cloning equipment, that sort of thing. Find Royd's life history. His mother's. Get a readout on the business they've done, all this alleged trading." Her voice grew excited, and she took the cyberneticist by her shoulder. "A log, a ship's log! There's got to be a log. Find it! You must!"

"All right." She whistled, happy, one with her systems, riding the data winds, in control, curious. The readout screen turned a bright red and began to blink at her, but she only smiled. "Security," she said, her fingers a blur. As suddenly as it had come, the blinking red field was gone. "Nothing like slipping past another system's security. Like slipping onto a man."

Down the corridor, an alarm sounded a whooping call. "Damn," the cyberneticist said, "that'll wake everyone." She glanced up when the xenotech's fingers dug painfully into her shoulder, squeezing, hurting.

A grey steel panel slid almost silently across the access to the corridor. "Wha—?" the cyberneticist said.

"That's an emergency airseal," the xenotech said in a dead voice. She knew starships. "It closes when they're about to load or unload cargo in vacuum."

Their eyes went to the huge curving outer airlock above their heads. The inner lock was almost completely open, and as they watched it clicked into place, and the seal on the outer door cracked, and now it was open half a meter, sliding, and beyond was twisted nothingness so bright it burned the eyes.

"Oh," the cyberneticist said. She had stopped whistling.

Alarms were hooting everywhere. The passengers began to stir. Melantha Jhirl leapt from her sleepweb and darted into the corridor, nude, concerned, alert. Karoly d'Branin sat up drowsily. The psipsych muttered fitfully in her drug-induced sleep. The xenobiologist cried out in alarm.

Far away metal crunched and tore, and a violent shudder ran through the ship, throwing the linguists out of their sleepwebs, knocking Melantha from her feet.

In the command quarters of the *Nightflyer* was a spherical room with featureless white walls, a lesser sphere—a control console—suspended in its center. The walls were always blank when the ship was in drive; the warped and glaring underside of spacetime was painful to behold.

But now darkness woke in the room, a holoscape coming to life, cold black and stars everywhere, points of icy unwinking brilliance, no up and no down and no direction, the floating control sphere the only feature in the simulated sea of night.

The *Nightflyer* had shifted out of drive.

Melantha Jhirl found her feet again and thumbed on a communicator. The alarms were still hooting, and it was hard to hear. "Captain," she shouted, "what's happening?"

"I don't know," Royd's voice replied. "I'm trying to find out. Wait here. Gather the others to you."

She did as he had said, and only when they were all together in the corridor did she slip back to her web to don some clothing. She found only six of them. The psipsych was still unconscious and could not be roused, and they had to carry her. And the xenotech and cyberneticist were missing. The rest looked uneasily at the seal that blocked cargo hold three.

The communicator came back to life as the alarms died. "We have returned to normal space," Royd's voice said, "but the ship is damaged. Hold three, your computer room, was breached while we were under drive. It was ripped apart by the flux. The computer automatically dropped us out of drive, or the drive forces might have torn my entire ship apart."

"Royd," d'Branin said, "two of my team are . . ."

"It appears that your computer was in use when the hold was breached," Royd said carefully. "We can only assume that they are dead. I cannot be sure. At Melantha's request, I have deactivated most of my eyes and ears, retaining only the lounge inputs. I do not know what happened. But this is a small ship, Karoly, and if they are not with you, we must assume the worst." He paused briefly. "If it is any consolation, they died quickly and painlessly."

The two linguists exchanged a long, meaningful look. The xenobiologist's face was red and angry, and he started to say something. Melantha Jhirl slipped her hand over his mouth firmly. "Do we know how it happened, Captain?" she asked.

"Yes," he said, reluctantly.

The xenobiologist had taken the hint, and Melantha took away her hand to let him breathe. "Royd?" she prompted.

"It sounds insane, Melantha," his voice replied, "but it appears your colleagues opened the hold's loading lock. I doubt that they did so deliberately, of course. They were apparently using the system interface to gain entry to the *Nightflyer's* data storage and controls."

"I see," Melantha said. "A terrible tragedy."

"Yes," Royd agreed. "Perhaps more terrible than you think. I have yet to assess the damage to my ship."

"We should not keep you, Captain, if you have duties to perform," Melantha said. "All of us are shocked, and it is difficult to talk now. Investigate the condition of your ship, and we'll continue our discussion in the morning. All right?"

"Yes," Royd said.

Melantha thumbed the communicator plate. Now officially, the device was off. Royd could not hear them.

Karoly d'Branin shook his large, grizzled head. The linguists sat close to one another, hands touching. The psipsych slept. Only the xenobiologist met her gaze. "Do you believe him?" he snapped abruptly.

"I don't know," Melantha Jhirl said, "but I do know that the other three cargo holds can all be flushed just as hold three was. I'm moving my sleepweb into a cabin. I suggest those who are living in hold two do the same."

"Good idea," the female linguist said. "We can crowd in. It won't be comfortable, but I don't think I'd sleep the sleep of angels in the holds anymore."

"We should also take our suits out of storage in four and keep them close at hand," her partner suggested.

"If you wish," Melantha said. "It's possible that all the locks might pop open simultaneously. Royd can't fault us for taking precautions." She flashed a grim smile. "After today, we've earned the right to act irrationally."

"This is no time for your damned jokes, Melantha," the xenobiologist said, fury in his voice. "Three dead, a fourth maybe deranged or comatose, the rest of us endangered—"

"We still have no idea what is happening," she pointed out.

"Royd Eris is killing us!" he shouted, pounding his fist into an open palm to emphasize his point. "I don't know who or what he is and I don't know if that story he gave us is true, and I don't *care*. Maybe he's a Hrangan Mind or the avenging angel of the *volcryn* or the second coming of Jesus

Christ. What the hell difference does it make. *He's killing us!*"

"You realize," Melantha said gently, "that we cannot actually know whether the good captain has turned off his inputs down here. He could be watching and listening to us right now. He isn't, of course. He told me he wouldn't and I believe him. But we have only his word on that. Now, *you* don't appear to trust Royd. If that's so, you can hardly put any faith in his promises. It follows that from your point of view it might not be wise to say the things that you're saying." She smiled slyly.

The xenobiologist was silent.

"The computer is gone, then," Karoly d'Branin said in a low voice before Melantha could resume.

She nodded. "I'm afraid so."

He rose unsteadily to his feet. "I have a small unit in my cabin," he said. "A wrist model, perhaps it will suffice. I must get the figures from Royd, learn where we have dropped out. The *volcryn*—" He shuffled off down the corridor and disappeared into his cabin.

"Think how distraught he'd be if *all* of us were dead," the female linguist said bitterly. "Then he'd have no one to help him look for *volcryn*."

"Let him go," Melantha said. "He is as hurt as any of us, maybe more so. He wears it differently. His obsessions are his defense."

"What's *our* defense?"

"Ah," said Melantha. "Patience, maybe. All of the dead were trying to breach Royd's secret when they died. We haven't tried. Here we sit discussing their deaths."

"You don't find that suspicious?"

"Very," Melantha Jhirl said. "I even have a method of testing my suspicions. One of us can make yet another attempt to find out whether our captain told us the truth. If he or she dies, we'll know." She stood up abruptly. "Forgive me, however, if I'm not the one who tries. But don't let me stop you if you have the urge. I'll note the results with interest. Until then, I'm going to move out of the cargo area and get some sleep."

"Arrogant bitch," the male linguist observed almost conversationally after Melantha had left.

"Do you think he can hear us?" the xenobiologist whispered quietly.

"Every pithy word," the female linguist said, rising. They

all stood up. "Let's move our things and put her"—she jerked
a thumb at the psipsych—"back to bed." Her partner nodded.

"Aren't we going to *do* anything?" the xenobiologist said.
"Make plans. Defenses."

The linguist gave him a withering look, and pulled her
companion off in the other direction.

"Melantha? Karoly?"

She woke quickly, alert at the mere whisper of her name,
and sat up in the narrow bunk. Next to her, Karoly d'Branin
moaned softly and rolled over, yawning.

"Royd?" she asked. "Is it morning now?"

"Yes," replied the voice from the walls. "We are drifting in
interstellar space three light-years from the nearest star, however. In such a context, does morning have meaning?"

Melantha laughed. "Debate it with Karoly, when he wakes
up enough to listen. Royd, you said *drifting*? How bad . . .?"

"Serious," he said, "but not dangerous. Hold three is a
complete ruin, hanging from my ship like a broken metal
eggshell, but the damage was confined. The drives themselves
are intact, and the *Nightflyer's* computers did not seem to
suffer from your machine's destruction. I feared they might.
Electronic death trauma."

D'Branin said, "Eh? Royd?"

Melantha patted him. "I'll tell you later, Karoly," she said.
"Royd, you sound serious. Is there more?"

"I am worried about our return flight, Melantha," he said.
"When I take the *Nightflyer* back into drive, the flux will be
playing directly on portions of the ship that were never engineered to withstand it. The airseal across hold three is a
particular concern. I've run some projections, and I don't
know if it can take the stress. If it bursts, my whole ship will
split apart in the middle. My engines will go shunting off by
themselves, and the rest . . ."

"I see. Is there anything we can do?"

"Yes. The exposed areas would be easy enough to rein-
force. The outer hull is armored to withstand the warping
forces, of course. We could mount it in place, a crude shield,
but it would suffice. Large portions of the hull were torn
loose when the locks opened, but they are still out there,
floating within a kilometer or two, and could be used."

At some point, Karoly d'Branin had come awake. "My
team has four vacuum sleds. We can retrieve these pieces for
you."

"Fine, Karoly, but that is not my primary concern. My ship is self-repairing within certain limits, but this exceeds those limits. I will have to do this myself."

"You?" D'Branin said. "Friend, you said—that is, your muscles, your weakness—cannot we help with this?"

"I am only a cripple in a gravity field, Karoly," Royd said. "Weightless, I am in my element, and I will be killing our gravity grid momentarily, to try to gather my own strength for the repair work. No, you misunderstand. I am capable of the work. I have the tools, and my own heavy-duty sled."

"I think I know what you are concerned about," Melantha said.

"I'm glad," Royd said. "Perhaps, then, you can answer my question. If I emerge from the safety of my chambers, can you keep your friends from killing me?"

Karoly d'Branin was shocked. "Royd, Royd, we are scholars, we are not soldiers or criminals, we do not—we are human, how can you think that we would threaten you?"

"Human," Royd repeated, "but alien to me, suspicious of me. Give me no false assurances, Karoly."

The administrator sputtered. Melantha took his hand and bid him quiet. "Royd," she said, "I won't lie to you. You'd be in some danger. But I'd hope that, by coming out, you'd make the rest of them joyously happy. They'd be able to see that you told the truth, wouldn't they?"

"They would," Royd said, "but would it be enough to offset their suspicions? They believe I killed your friends, do they not?"

"Some, perhaps. Half believe it, half fear it. They are frightened, Captain. *I* am frightened."

"No more than I."

"I would be less frightened if I knew what *did* happen. Do you know?"

Silence.

"Royd, if . . ."

"I tried to stop the esperon injection," he said. "I might have saved the other two, if I had seen them, heard them, known what they were about. But you made me turn off my monitors, Melantha. I cannot help what I cannot see." Hesitation. "I would feel safer if I could turn them back on. I am blind and deaf. It is frustrating. I cannot help if I am blind and deaf."

"Turn them on, then," Melantha said suddenly. "I was wrong. I did not understand. Now I do, though."

"Understand what?" Karoly said.

"You do not understand," Royd said. "You do *not*. Don't pretend that you do, Melantha Jhirl. *Don't*!" The calm voice from the communicator was shrill with emotion.

"What?" Karoly said. "Melantha, I do not understand."

Her eyes were thoughtful. "Neither do I," she said. "Neither do I, Karoly." She kissed him lightly. "Royd," she resumed, "it seems to me you must make this repair, regardless of what promises we can give you. You won't risk your ship by slipping back into drive in your present condition. The only other option is to drift here until we all die. What choice do we have?"

"I have a choice," Royd said with deadly seriousness. "I could kill all of you, if that were the only way to save my ship."

"You could try," Melantha said.

"Let us have no more talk of death," d'Branin said.

"You are right, Karoly," Royd said. "I do not wish to kill any of you. But I must be protected."

"You will be," Melantha said. "Karoly can set the others to chasing your hull fragments. I'll never leave your side. I'll assist you; the work will be done three times as fast."

Royd was polite. "In my experience, most planet-bound are clumsy and easily tired in weightlessness. It would be more efficient if I worked alone."

"It would not," she replied. "I remind you that I'm the improved model, Captain. Good in free-fall as well as in bed. I'll help."

"As you will. In a few moments, I shall depower the gravity grid. Karoly, go and prepare your people. Unship your sled and suit up. I will exit *Nightflyer* in three hours, after I have recovered from the pains of your gravity. I want all of you outside the ship when I leave."

It was as though some vast animal had taken a bite out of the universe.

Melantha Jhirl waited on her sled close by the *Nightflyer*, and looked at stars. It was not so very different out here, in the depths of interstellar space. The stars were cold, frozen points of light; unwinking, austere, more chill and uncaring somehow than the same suns made to dance and twinkle by an atmosphere. Only the absence of a landmark primary reminded her of where she was: in the places between, where men do not stop, where the *volcryn* sail ships impossibly an-

cient. She tried to pick out Avalon's sun, but she did not
know where to search. The configurations were strange to
her, and she had no idea of how she was oriented. Behind
her, before her, above, all around, the starfields stretched
endlessly. She glanced down, beneath her sled and the
Nightflyer, expecting still more alien stars, and the bite hit
her with an almost physical force.

Melantha fought off a wave of vertigo. She was suspended
above a pit, a yawning chasm in the universe, black, starless,
vast.

Empty.

She remembered then: the Tempter's Veil. Just a cloud of
dark gas, nothing really, galactic pollution that obscured the
light from the stars of the Fringe. But this close at hand, it
looked immense, terrifying. She had to break her gaze when
she began to feel as if she were falling. It was a gulf beneath
her and the frail silver-white shell of the *Nightflyer*, a gulf
about to swallow them.

Melantha touched one of the controls on the sled's forked
handle, swinging around so the Veil was to her side instead
of beneath her. That seemed to help, somehow. She concentrated on the *Nightflyer*. It was the largest object in her universe, bright-lit, ungainly; three small eggs side-by-side, two
larger spheres beneath and at right angles, lengths of tube
connecting it all. One of the eggs was shattered now, giving
the craft an unbalanced cast.

She could see the other sleds as they angled through the
black, tracking the missing pieces of eggshell, grappling with
them, bringing them back. The linguistic team worked together, as always, sharing a sled. The xenobiologist was alone.
Karoly d'Branin had a silent passenger; the psipsych, freshly
drugged, asleep in the suit they had dressed her in. Royd had
insisted that the ship be cleared completely, and it would have
taken time and care to rouse the psipsych to consciousness;
this was the safer course.

While her colleagues labored, Melantha Jhirl waited for
Royd Eris, talking to the others occasionally over the comm
link. The two linguists, unaccustomed to weightlessness, were
complaining a lot. Karoly tried to soothe them. The xenobiologist worked in silence, argued out. He had been vehement
earlier in his opposition to going outside, but Melantha and
Karoly had finally worn him down and it seemed as if he had
nothing more to say. Melantha now watched him flit across

her field of vision, a stick figure in form-fitting black armor standing stiff and erect at the controls of his sled.

At last the circular airlock atop the foremost of the *Night-flyer's* major spheres dilated, and Royd Eris emerged. She watched him approach, wondering what he would look like. She had so many different pictures. His genteel, cultured, too-formal voice sometimes reminded her of the dark aristocrats of her native Pometheus, the wizards who toyed with human genes. At other times his naïveté made her think of him as an inexperienced youth. His ghost was a tired looking thin young man, and he was supposed to be considerably older than that pale shadow, but Melantha found it difficult to hear an old man talking when he spoke.

Royd's sled was larger than theirs and of a different design; a long oval plate with eight jointed grappling arms bristling from its underside like the legs of a metal spider, and the snout of a heavy-duty cutting laser mounted above. His suit was odd too, more massive than the Academy worksuits, with a bulge between its shoulder blades that was probably a powerpack, and rakish radiant fins atop shoulders and helmet.

But when he was finally near enough for Melantha to see his face, it was just a face. White, very white, that was the predominant impression she got; white hair cropped very short, a white stubble around the sharply-chiseled lines of his jaw, almost invisible eyebrows beneath which blue eyes moved restlessly. His skin was pale and unlined, scarcely touched by time.

He looked wary, she thought. And perhaps a bit frightened.

He stopped his sled close to hers, amid the twisted ruin that had been cargo hold three, and surveyed the damage, the pieces of floating wreckage that once had been flesh and blood, glass, metal, plastic. Hard to distinguish now, all of them fused and burned and frozen together. "We have a good deal of work to do, Melantha," he said.

"First let's talk," she replied. She shifted her sled closer and reached out to him, but the distance was still too great, the width of the two vacuum sleds keeping them apart. Melantha backed off, and turned herself over completely, so that Royd hung upside down in her world and she upside down in his. Then she moved towards him again, positioning her sled directly over/under his. Their gloved hands met, brushed, parted. Melantha adjusted her altitude. Their helmets touched.

"I don't—" Royd began to say uncertainly.

"Turn off your comm," she commanded. "The sound will carry through the helmets."

He blinked and used his tongue controls and it was done.

"Now we can talk," she said.

"I do not like this, Melantha," he said. "This is too obvious. This is dangerous."

"There's no other way," she said. "Royd, I *do* know."

"Yes," he said. "I knew you did. Three moves ahead, Melantha. I remember the way you play chess. You are safer if you feign ignorance, however."

"I understand that, Captain. Other things I'm less sure about. Can we talk about it?"

"No. Don't ask me to. Just do as I tell you. You are in danger, all of you, but I can protect you. The less you know, the better I can protect you." Through the transparent faceplates, his expression was grim.

She stared into his upside-down eyes. "Your ship is killing us, Captain. That's my suspicion, anyway. Not you. It. Only that doesn't make sense. You command the *Nightflyer*. How can it act independently? And why? What motive? How was that psionic murder accomplished? It can't be the ship. Yet it can't be anything else. Help me, Captain."

He blinked; there was anguish behind his eyes. "I should never have accepted Karoly's charter. Not with a telepath among you. It was risky. But I wanted to see the *volcryn*.

"You understand too much already, Melantha," Royd continued. "I can't tell you more. The ship is malfunctioning, that is all you need know. It is not safe to push too hard. As long as I am at the controls, however, you and your colleagues are in small danger. Trust me."

"Trust is a two-way bond," Melantha said steadily.

Royd lifted his hand and pushed her away, then tongued his comm back to life. "Enough gossip," he briskly announced. "We have repairs to make. Come. I want to see just how improved you are."

In the solitude of her helmet, Melantha Jhirl swore softly.

The xenobiologist watched Royd Eris emerge on his oversized work sled, watched Melantha Jhirl move to him, watched as she turned over and pressed her faceplate to his. He could scarcely contain his rage. Somehow they were all in it together, Royd and Melantha and possibly old d'Branin as well, he thought sourly. She had protected him from the first, when they might have taken action together, stopped him, found out who or what he was. And now three were dead, killed by the cipher in the misshapen spacesuit, and Melantha hung upside down, her face pressed to his like lovers kissing.

He tongued off his comm and cursed. The others were out of sight, off chasing spinning wedges of half-slagged metal. Royd and Melantha were engrossed in each other, the ship abandoned and vulnerable. This was his chance. No wonder Eris had insisted that all of them precede him into the void; outside, isolated from the controls of the *Nightflyer*, he was only a man. A weak one at that.

Smiling a thin hard smile, the xenobiologist brought his sled around in a wide circle and vanished into the gaping maw of the driveroom. HIs lights flickered past the ring of nukes and sent long bright streaks along the sides of the closed cylinders of the stardrives, the huge engines that bent the stuff of spacetime, encased in webs of metal and crystal. Everything was open to the vacuum. It was better that way; atmosphere corroded and destroyed.

He set the sled down, dismounted, moved to the airlock. This was the hardest part, he thought. The headless body of the young telepath was tethered loosely to a massive support strut, a grisly guardian by the door. The xenobiologist had to stare at it while he waited for the lock to cycle. Whenever he glanced away, somehow he would find his eyes creeping back to it. The body looked almost natural, as if it had never had a head. The xenobiologist tried to remember the young man's face, and failed, but then the lock door slid open and he gratefully pushed the thought away and entered.

He was alone in the *Nightflyer*.

A cautious man, he kept his suit on, though he collapsed the helmet and yanked loose the suddenly-limp metallic fabric so it fell behind his back like a hood. He could snap it in place quickly enough if the need arose. In cargo hold four, where they had stored their equipment, the xenobiologist found what he was looking for; a portable cutting laser, charged and ready. Low power, but it would do.

Slow and clumsy in weightlessness, he pulled himself through the corridor into the darkened lounge.

It was chilly inside, the air cold on his cheeks. He tried not to notice. He braced himself at the door and pushed off across the width of the room, sailing above the furniture, which was all safely bolted into place.

As he drifted toward his objective, something wet and cold

touched his face. It startled him, but it was gone before he could make out what it was.

When it happened again, he snatched at it, caught it, and felt briefly sick. He had forgotten. No one had cleaned the lounge yet. The—*remains* were still there, floating now, blood and flesh and bits of bone and brain. All around him.

He reached the far wall, stopped himself with his arms, pulled himself down to where he wanted to go. The bulkhead. The wall. No doorway was visible, but the metal couldn't be very thick. Beyond was the control room, the computer access, safety, power. The xenobiologist did not think of himself as a vindictive man. He did not intend to harm Royd Eris, that judgment was not his to make. He would take control of the *Nightflyer*, warn Eris away, make certain the man stayed sealed in his suit. He would take them all back without any more mysteries, any more killings. The Academy arbiters could listen to the story, and probe Eris, and decide the right and wrong of it, guilt and innocence, what should be done.

The cutting laser emitted a thin pencil of scarlet light. The xenobiologist smiled and applied it to the bulkhead. It was slow work, but he had patience. They would not have missed him, quiet as he'd been, and if they did they would assume he was off sledding after some hunk of salvage. Eris' repairs would take hours, maybe days, to finish. The bright blade of the laser smoked where it touched the metal. He applied himself diligently.

Something moved on the periphery of his vision, just a little flicker, barely seen. A floating bit of brain, he thought. A sliver of bone. A bloody piece of flesh, hair still hanging from it. Horrible things, but nothing to worry about. He was a biologist, he was used to blood and brains and flesh. And worse, and worse; he had dissected many an alien in his day.

Again the motion caught his eye, teased at it. Not wanting to, he found himself drawn to look. He could not *not* look, somehow, just as he had been unable to ignore the headless telepath in the airlock. He looked.

It was an eye.

The xenobiologist trembled and the laser slipped sharply off to one side, so he had to wrestle with it to bring it back to the channel he was cutting. His heart raced. He tried to calm himself. Nothing to be frightened of. No one was home, and if Royd should return, well, he had the laser as a weapon and he had his suit on if an airlock blew.

He looked at the eye again, willing away his fear. It was just an eye, the eye of the young telepath, intact, bloody but intact, the same watery blue eye the boy had when alive, nothing supernatural. A piece of dead flesh, floating in the lounge amid other pieces of dead flesh. Someone should have cleaned up the lounge, he thought angrily. It was indecent to leave it like this, it was uncivilized.

The eye did not move. The other grisly bits were drifting on the air currents that flowed across the room, but the eye was still. Fixed on him. Staring.

He cursed himself and concentrated on the laser, on his cutting. He had burned an almost straight line up the bulkhead for about a meter. He began another at right angles.

The eye watched dispassionately. The xenobiologist suddenly found he could not stand it. One hand released its grip on the laser, reached out, caught the eye, flung it across the room. The action made him lose balance. He tumbled backward, the laser slipping from his grasp, his arms flapping like the wings on some absurd heavy bird. Finally he caught an edge of the table and stopped himself.

The laser hung in the center of the room, still firing, turning slowly where it floated. That did not make sense. It should have ceased fire when he released it. A malfunction, he thought. Smoke rose from where the thin line of the laser traced a path across the carpet.

With a shiver of fear, the xenobiologist realized that the laser was turning towards him.

He raised himself, put both hands flat against the table, pushed off out of the way.

The laser was turning more swiftly now.

He slammed into a wall, grunted in pain, bounced off the floor, kicked. The laser was spinning quickly, chasing him. He soared, braced himself for a ricochet off the ceiling. The beam swung around, but not fast enough. He'd get it while it was still firing off in the other direction.

He moved close, reached, and saw the eye.

It hung just above the laser. Staring.

The xenobiologist made a small whimpering sound low in his throat, and his hand hesitated—not long, but long enough—and the scarlet beam came up and around.

Its touch was a light, hot caress across his neck.

It was more than an hour later before they missed him. Karoly d'Branin noticed his absence first, called for him over the comm net, and got no answer. He discussed it with the others.

Royd Eris moved his sled back from the armor plate he had just mounted, and through his helmet Melantha Jhirl could see the lines around his mouth grow hard. His eyes were sharply alert.

It was just then that the screaming began.

A shrill bleat of pain and fear, followed by choked, anguished sobbing. They all heard it. It came over the comm net and filled their helmets.

"It's him," a woman's voice said. The linguist.

"He's hurt," her partner added. "He's crying for help. Can't you hear it?"

"Where—?" someone started.

"The ship," the female linguist said. "He must have returned to the ship."

Royd Eris said, "No. I warned—"

"We're going to go check," the linguist said. Her partner cut free the hull fragment they had been towing, and it spun away, tumbling. Their sled angled down towards the *Nightflyer*.

"Stop," Royd said. "I'll return to my chambers and check from there, if you wish. Stay outside until I give you clearance."

"Go to hell," the linguist snapped at him over the open circuit.

"Royd, my friend, what can you mean?" Karoly d'Branin said. His sled was in motion too, hastening after the linguists, but he had been further out and it was a long way back to the ship. "He is hurt, perhaps seriously. We must help."

"No," Royd said. "Karoly, *stop*. If your colleague went back to the ship alone, he is dead."

"How do you know that?" the male linguist demanded. "Did you arrange it? Set traps?"

"Listen to me," Royd continued. "You can't help him now. Only I could have helped him, and he did not listen to me. Trust me. Stop."

In the distance, d'Branin's sled slowed. The linguists did not. "We've already listened to you too damn much, I'd say," the woman said. She almost had to shout to be heard above the sobs and whimpers, the agonized sounds that filled their universe. "Melantha," she said, "keep Eris right where he is. We'll go carefully, find out what is happening inside, but I don't want him getting back to his controls. Understood?"

Melantha Jhirl hesitated. Sounds of terror and agony beat against her ears; it was hard to think.

Royd swung his sled around to face her, and she could feel the weight of his stare. "Stop them," he said. "Melantha, Karoly, order it. They do not know what they are doing." His voice was edged with despair.

In his face, Melantha found decision. "Go back inside quickly, Royd. Do what you can. I'm going to try to intercept them."

He nodded to her across the gulf, but Melantha was already in motion. Her sled backed clear of the work area, congested with hull fragments and other debris, then accelerated briskly as she raced toward the rear of the *Nightflyer*.

But even as she approached, she knew it was too late. The linguists were too close, and already moving much faster than she was.

"*Don't*," she said, authority in her tone. "The ship isn't safe, damn it."

"Bitch," was all the answer she got.

Karoly's sled pursued vainly. "Friends, you must stop, please, I beg it of you, let us talk this out together."

The unending whimpers were his only reply.

"I am your superior," he said. "I order you to wait outside. Do you hear me? I order it, I invoke the authority of the Academy. Please, my friends, please listen to me."

Melantha watched as the linguists vanished down the long tunnel of the driveroom.

A moment later she halted her sled near the waiting black mouth, debating whether she should follow them into the *Nightflyer*. She might be able to catch them before the airlock opened.

Royd's voice, hoarse counterpoint to the crying, answered her unvoiced question. "Stay, Melantha. Proceed no further."

She looked behind her. Royd's sled was approaching.

"What are you doing?" she demanded. "Royd, use your own lock. You have to get back inside!"

"Melantha," he said calmly, "I cannot. The ship will not respond to me. The control lock will not dilate. I don't want you or Karoly inside the ship until I can return to my controls."

Melantha Jhirl looked down the shadowed barrel of the driveroom, where the linguists had vanished.

"What will—?"

"Beg them to come back, Melantha. Plead with them. Perhaps there is still time, if they will listen to you."

She tried, Karoly d'Branin tried too. The crying, the moaning, the twisted symphony went on and on. But they could not raise the two linguists at all.

"They've cut out their comm," Melantha said furiously. "They don't want to listen to us. Or that . . . that *sound*."

Royd's sled and Karoly d'Branin's reached her at the same time. "I do not understand," Karoly said. "What is happening?"

"It is simple, Karoly," Royd replied. "I am being kept outside until—until Mother is done with them."

The linguists left their vacuum sled next to the one the xenobiologist had abandoned and cycled through the airlock in unseemly haste, with hardly a glance for the grim headless doorman.

Inside they paused briefly to collapse their helmets. "I can still hear him," the man said.

The woman nodded. "The sound is coming from the lounge. Hurry."

They kicked and pulled their way down the corridor in less than a minute. The sounds grew steadily louder, nearer. "He's in there," the woman said when they reached the chamber door.

"Yes," her partner said, "but is he alone? We need a weapon. What if . . . Royd had to be lying. There *is* someone else on board. We need to defend ourselves."

The woman would not wait. "There are two of us," she said. "Come *on*!" With that she launched herself through the doorway and into the lounge.

It was dark inside. What little light there was spilled through the door from the corridor. Her eyes took a long moment to adjust. "Where are you?" she cried in confusion. The lounge seemed empty, but maybe it was only the light.

"Follow the sound," the man suggested. He stood in the door, glancing warily about for a minute, before he began to feel his way down a wall, groping with his hands.

The woman, impatient, propelled herself across the room, searching. She brushed against a wall in the kitchen area, and that made her think of weapons. She knew where the utensils were stored. "Here," she said. "Here, I've got a knife, that should thrill you." She waved it, and brushed against a floating bubble of blood as big as her fist. It burst and re-formed into a hundred smaller globules.

"Oh, merciful God," the man said in a voice thick with fear.

"What?" she demanded. "Did you find him? Is he—?"

He was fumbling his way back towards the door, creeping along the wall the way he had come. "Get out of here," he warned. "Oh, *hurry*."

"Why?" She trembled despite herself.

"I found the source," he said. "The screams, the crying. Come *on!*"

"Wha—"

He whimpered. "It was the grill. Oh, don't you see? It's coming from the communicator!" He reached the door, and sighed audibly, and he did not wait for her. He bolted down the corridor and was gone.

She braced herself and positioned herself in order to follow him.

The sounds stopped. Just like that: turned off.

She kicked, floated towards the door, knife in hand.

Something dark crawled from beneath the dinner table and rose to block her path. She saw it clearly for a moment, out-lined in the light from the corridor. The xenobiologist, still in his vacuum suit, but with his helmet pulled off. He had some-thing in his hands that he raised to point at her. It was a laser, she saw, a simple cutting laser.

She was moving straight towards him. She flailed and tried to stop herself, but she could not.

When she got quite close, she saw that he had a second mouth below his chin, and it was grinning at her, and little droplets of blood flew from it, wetly, as he moved.

The man rushed down the corridor in a frenzy of fear, bruising himself as he smashed into walls. Panic and weight-lessness made him clumsy. He kept glancing over his shoulder as he fled, hoping to see his lover coming after him, but terri-fied of what he might see in her stead.

It took a long, *long* time for the airlock to open. As he waited, trembling, his pulse began to slow. He steadied him-self with an effort. Once inside the chamber, with the inner door sealed between him and the lounge, he began to feel safe.

Suddenly he could barely remember why he had been so terrified.

And he was ashamed; he had run, abandoned her. And for what? What had frightened him so? An empty lounge? Noises from a communicator? Why, that only meant the xenobiologist was alive somewhere else in the ship, in pain, spilling his agony into a comm unit.

Resolute, he reached out and killed the cycle on the airlock, then reversed it. The air that had been partially sucked out came gusting back into the chamber.

The man shook his head ruefully. He'd hear no end of this, he knew. She would never let him forget it. But at least he would return, and apologize. That would count for something.

As the inner door rolled back, he felt a brief flash of fear again, an instant of stark terror when he wondered what might have emerged from the lounge to wait for him in the corridors of the *Nightflyer*. He willed it away.

When he stepped out, she was waiting for him.

He could see neither anger nor disdain in her curiously calm features, but he pushed himself towards her and tried to frame a plea for forgiveness anyway. "I don't know why I—"

With languid grace, her hand came out from behind her back. The knife was in it. That was when he finally noticed the hole burned in her suit, just between her breasts.

"Your *mother*?" Melantha Jhirl said incredulously as they hung helpless in the emptiness beyond the ship.

"She can hear everything we say," Royd replied. "But at this point, it no longer makes any difference. Your friend must have done something very foolish, very threatening. Now she is determined to kill you all."

"She, she, what do you mean?" D'Branin's voice was puzzled. "Royd, surely you do not tell us that your mother is still alive. You said she died even before you were born."

"She did, Karoly," Royd said. "I did not lie to you."

"No," Melantha said. "I didn't think so. But you did not tell us the whole truth, either."

Royd nodded. "Mother is dead, but her—ghost still lives, and animates my *Nightflyer*." He chuckled grimly. "Perhaps it would be more fitting to say her *Nightflyer*. My control is tenuous at best."

"Royd," d'Branin said, "my *volcryn* are more real than any ghosts." His voice chided gently.

"I don't believe in ghosts either," Melantha Jhirl said with a frown.

"Call it what you will, then," Royd said. "My term is as good as any. The reality is unchanged. My mother, or some part of my mother, lives in the *Nightflyer*, and she is killing you all as she has killed others before."

"Royd, you do not make sense," d'Branin said. "I—"

"Karoly, let the captain explain."

"Yes," Royd said. "The *Nightflyer* is very—very *advanced*, you know. Automated, self-repairing, large. It had to be, if Mother were to be freed from the necessity of crew. It was built on Newholme, you will recall. I have never been there, but I understand that Newholme's technology is quite sophisticated. Avalon could not duplicate this ship, I suspect. There are few worlds that could."

"The point, Captain?"

"The point—the point is the computers, Melantha. They had to be extraordinary. They are, believe me, they are. Crystal-matrix cores, lasergrid data retrieval, and other—other features."

"Are you telling us that the *Nightflyer* is an Artificial Intelligence?"

"No," Royd said, "not as I understand it. But it is something close. Mother had a capacity for personality impress built in. She filled the central crystal with her own memories, desires, quirks, her loves and her—hates. That was why she trusted the computer with my education, you see? She knew it would raise me as she herself would, had she the patience. She programmed it in certain other ways as well."

"And you cannot deprogram, my friend?" Karoly asked.

Royd's voice was despairing. "I have *tried*, Karoly. But I am a weak hand at systems work, and the programs are very complicated, the machines very sophisticated. At least three times I have eradicated her, only to have her surface once again. She is a phantom program, and I cannot track her. She comes and goes as she will. A ghost, do you see? Her memories and her personality are so intertwined with the programs that run the *Nightflyer* that I cannot get rid of her without wiping the entire system. But that would leave me helpless. I could never reprogram, and with the computers down the entire ship would fail, drives, life support, everything. I would have to leave the *Nightflyer*, and that would kill me."

"You should have told us, my friend," Karoly d'Branin said. "On Avalon, we have many cyberneticists, some very great minds. We might have aided you. We could have provided expert help."

"Karoly, I have *had* expert help. Twice I have brought systems specialists on board. The first one told me what I have just told you; that it was impossible without wiping the programs completely. The second had trained on Newholme. She thought she could help me. Mother killed her."

"You are still omitting something," Melantha Jhirl said. "I understand how your cybernetic ghost can open and close airlocks at will and arrange other accidents of that nature. But that first death, our telepath, how do you explain that?"

"Ultimately I must bear the guilt," Royd replied. "My loneliness led me to a grievous error. I thought I could safeguard you, even with a telepath among you. I have carried other riders safely. I watch them constantly, warn them away from dangerous acts. If Mother attempts to interfere, I countermand her directly from the control room. That usually works. Not always. Usually. Before you she had killed only five times, and the first three died when I was quite young. That was how I learned about her. That party included a telepath too.

"I should have known better, Karoly. My hunger for life has doomed you all to death. I overestimated my own abilities, and underestimated her fear of exposure. She strikes out when she is threatened, and telepaths are always a threat. They sense her, you see. A malign, looming presence, they tell me, something cool and hostile and inhuman."

"Yes," Karoly d'Branin said, "yes, that was what he said. An alien, he was certain of it."

"No doubt she feels alien to a telepath used to the familiar contours of organic minds. Hers is not a human brain, after all. What it is I cannot say—a complex of crystalline memories, a hellish network of interlocking programs, a meld of circuitry and spirit. Yes, I can understand why she might feel alien."

"You still haven't explained how a computer program could explode a man's skull," Melantha said patiently.

"Have you ever held a whisper-jewel?" Royd Eris asked her.

"Yes," she replied. She had even owned one once; a dark blue crystal, packed with the memories of a particularly satisfying bout of lovemaking. It had been esper-etched on Avalon, her feelings impressed onto the jewel, and for more than a year she had only to touch it to grow randy. It had finally faded, though, and afterwards she had lost it.

"Then you know that psionic power can be stored," Royd said. "The central core of my computer system is resonant crystal. I think Mother impressed it as she lay dying."

"Only an esper can etch a whisper-jewel," Melantha said.

"You never asked me the *why* of it, Karoly," Royd said. "Nor you, Melantha. You never asked why Mother hated people so. She was born gifted, you see. On Avalon, she might have been a class one, tested and trained and honored, her talent nurtured and rewarded. I think she might have been very famous. She might have been stronger than a class one, but perhaps it is only after death that she acquired such power, linked as she is to the *Nightflyer*.

"The point is moot. She was not born on Avalon. On her birth world, her ability was seen as a curse, something alien and fearful. So they cured her of it. They used drugs and electroshock and hypnotraining that made her violently ill whenever she tried to use her talent. She never lost her power, of course, only the ability to use it effectively, to control it with her conscious mind. It remained part of her, suppressed, erratic, a source of shame and pain. And half a decade of institutional cure almost drove her insane. No wonder she hated people."

"What was her talent? Telepathy?"

"No. Oh, some rudimentary ability perhaps. I have read that all psi talents have several latent abilities in addition to their one developed strength. But Mother could not read minds. She had some empathy, although her cure had twisted it curiously, so that the emotions she felt literally sickened her. But her major strength, the talent they took five years to shatter and destroy, was teke."

Melantha Jhirl swore. "No wonder she hated gravity. Telekinesis under weightlessness is—"

"Yes," Royd finished. "Keeping the *Nightflyer* under gravity tortures me, but it limits Mother."

In the silence that followed that comment, each of them looked down the dark cylinder of the driveroom. Karoly d'Branin moved awkwardly on his sled. "They have not returned," he said finally.

"They are probably dead," Royd said dispassionately.

"What will we do, friend Royd? We must plan. We cannot wait here indefinitely."

"The first question is what can *I* do," Royd Eris replied. "I have talked freely, you'll note. You deserved to know. We have passed the point where ignorance was a protection. Obviously things have gone too far. There have been too many deaths and you have been witness to all of them. Mother cannot allow you to return to Avalon alive."

"Ah," said Melantha, "true. But what shall she do with *you*? Is your own status in doubt, Captain?"

"The crux of the problem," Royd admitted. "You are still three moves ahead, Melantha. I wonder if it will suffice. Your opponent is four ahead this game, and most of your pawns are already captured. I fear checkmate is imminent."

"Unless I can persuade my opponent's king to desert, no?"

She could see Royd smile at her wanly. "She would probably kill me too if I choose to side with you."

Karoly d'Branin was slow to grasp the point. "But—but what else could you—"

"My sled has a laser. Yours do not. I could kill you both, right now, and thereby earn my way into the *Nightflyer's* good graces."

Across the three meters that lay between their sleds, Melantha's eyes met Royd's. Her hands rested easily on the thruster controls. "You could try, Captain. Remember, the improved model isn't easy to kill."

"I would not kill you, Melantha Jhirl," Royd said seriously. "I have lived sixty-eight standard years and I have never lived at all. I am tired, and you tell grand gorgeous lies. If we lose, we will all die together. If we win, well, I shall die anyway, when they destroy the *Nightflyer*—either that or live as a freak in an orbital hospital, and I would prefer death—"

"We will build you a new ship, Captain," Melantha said.

"Liar," Royd replied. But his tone was cheerful. "No matter. I have not had much a life anyway. Death does not frighten me. If we win, you must tell me about your *volcryn* once again, Karoly. And you, Melantha, you must play chess with me once more, and. . . ." His voice trailed off.

"And sex with you?" she finished, smiling.

"If you would," he said quietly. "I have never—*touched*, you know. Mother died before I was born." He shrugged. "Well, Mother has heard all of this. Doubtless she will listen carefully to any plans we might make, so there is no sense making them. There is no chance now that the control lock will admit me, since it is keyed directly into the ship's computer. So we must follow your colleagues through the driveroom, and enter through the manual lock, and take what chances we are given. If I can reach consoles and restore gravity, perhaps we—"

He was interrupted by a low groan.

For an instant Melantha thought the *Nightflyer* was wailing at them again, and she was surprised that it was so stupid as to try the same tactic twice. Then the groan sounded a second time, and in the back of Karoly d'Branin's sled the forgotten fourth survivor struggled against the bonds that held her down. D'Branin hastened to free her, and the psipsych tried to rise to her feet and almost floated off the sled, until he caught her hand and pulled her back. "Are you well?" he asked. "Can you hear me? Have you pain?"

Imprisoned beneath a transparent faceplate, wide frightened eyes flicked rapidly from Karoly to Melantha to Royd, and then to the broken *Nightflyer*. Melantha wondered whether the woman was insane, and started to caution d'Branin, when the psipsych spoke suddenly.

"The *volcryn*," was all she said, "the *volcryn*, Oh, oh, the *volcryn!*"

Around the mouth of the driveroom, the ring of nuclear engines took on a faint glow. Melantha Jhirl heard Royd suck in his breath sharply. She gave the thruster controls of her sled a violent twist. "Hurry," she said, "the *Nightflyer* is preparing to move."

A third of the way down the long barrel of the driveroom, Royd pulled abreast of her, stiff and menacing in his black, bulky armor. Side by side they sailed past the cylindrical stardrives and the cyberweds; ahead, dimly lit, was the main airlock and its ghastly sentinel.

"When we reach the lock, jump over to my sled," Royd said. "I want to stay armed and mounted, and the chamber is not large enough for two sleds."

Melantha Jhirl risked a quick glance behind her. "Karoly," she called. "Where are you?"

"I am outside, Melantha," the answer came. "I cannot come, my friend. Forgive me."

"But we have to stay together," she said.

"No," d'Branin's voice replied, "no, I could not risk it, not when we are so close. It would be so tragic, so futile, Melantha, to come so close and fail. Death I do not mind, but I must see them first, finally, after all these years." His voice was firm and calm.

Royd Eris cut in. "Karoly, my mother is going to move the ship. Don't you understand? You will be left behind, lost."

"I will wait," d'Branin replied. "My *volcryn* are coming, and I will wait for them."

Then there was no more time for conversation, for the airlock was almost upon them. Both sleds slowed and stopped, and Royd Eris reached out and began the cycle while Melantha moved to the rear of the huge oval worksled. When the outer door moved aside, they glided through into the lock chamber.

"When the inner door opens, it will begin," Royd told her evenly. "Most of the permanent furnishings are either built in or welded or bolted into place, but the things that your team brought on board are not. Mother will use those things as weapons. And beware of doors, airlocks, any equipment tied in to the *Nightflyer's* computer. Need I warn you not to unseal your suit?"

"Hardly," she replied.

Royd lowered the sled a little, and its grapplers made a metallic sound as they touched against the chamber floor.

The inner door opened, and Royd applied his thrusters.

Inside the linguists were waiting, swimming in a haze of blood. The man had been slit from crotch to throat and his intestines moved like a nest of pale, angry snakes. The woman still held the knife. They swam closer with a grace they had never possessed in life.

Royd lifted his foremost grapplers and smashed them to the side. The man caromed off a bulkhead, leaving a wide wet mark where he struck, and more of his guts came sliding out. The woman lost control of the knife. Royd accelerated past them, driving up the corridor, through the cloud of blood.

"I'll watch behind," Melantha said, and she turned and put her back to his. Already the two corpses were safely behind them. The knife was floating uselessly in the air. She started to tell Royd that they were all right when the blade abruptly shifted and came after them, as if some invisible force had taken hold of it.

"*Swerve!*" she shouted.

The sled shot wildly to one side. The knife missed by a full meter, and glanced ringingly off a bulkhead.

But it did not drop. It came at them again.

The lounge loomed ahead. Dark.

"The door is too narrow," Royd said. "We will have to abandon the sled, Melantha." Even as he spoke, they hit: he wedged the sled squarely into the doorframe, and the sudden impact jarred them loose.

For a moment Melantha floated clumsily in the corridor, trying to get her balance. The knife slashed at her, opening her suit and her shoulder. She felt sharp pain and the warm flush of bleeding. "*Damn*," she shrieked. The knife came around again, spraying droplets of blood.

Melantha's hand darted out and caught it.

She muttered something under her breath, and wrenched the blade free of the force that had been gripping it.

Royd had regained the controls of his sled and seemed intent on some manipulation. Beyond, in the dimness of the lounge, Melantha saw a dark semi-human shape float into view.

"*Royd!*" she warned, but as she did the thing activated its laser. The pencil beam caught Royd square in the chest.

He touched his own firing stud. The sled's heavy-duty laser cindered the xenobiologist's weapon and burned off his right arm and part of his chest. Its pulsing shaft hung in the air, and smoked against the bar bulkhead.

Royd made some adjustments and began cutting a hole. "We'll be through in five minutes or less," he said curtly, without stopping or looking up.

"Are you all right?" Melantha asked.

"I'm uninjured," he replied. "My suit is better armored than yours, and his laser was a low-powered toy."

Melantha turned her attention back to the corridor.

The linguists were pulling themselves toward her, one on each side of the passage, to come at her from two directions at once. She flexed her muscles. Her shoulder throbbed where she had been cut. Otherwise she felt strong, almost reckless. "The corpses are coming after us again," she told Royd. "I'm going to take them."

"Is that wise?" he asked. "There are two of them."

"I'm an improved model," Melantha said, "and they're dead." She kicked herself free of the sled and sailed toward the man. He raised his hands to block her. She slapped them aside, bent one arm back and heard it snap, and drove her knife deep into his throat before she realized what a useless gesture that was. The man continued to flail at her. His teeth snapped grotesquely.

Melantha withdrew her blade, seized him, and with all her considerable strength threw him bodily down the corridor. He tumbled, spinning wildly, and vanished into the haze of his own blood.

Melantha then flew in the opposite direction.

The woman's hands went around her from behind.

Nails scrabbled against her faceplate until they began to bleed, leaving red streaks on the plastic.

Melantha spun to face her attacker, grabbed a thrashing arm, and flung the woman down the passageway to crash into her struggling companion.

"I'm through," Royd announced.

She turned to see. A smoking meter-square opening had been cut through one wall of the lounge. Royd killed the laser, gripped both sides of the doorframe, and pushed himself towards it.

A piercing blast of sound drilled through her head. She doubled over in agony. Her tongue flicked out and clicked off the comm; then there was blessed silence.

In the lounge it was raining. Kitchen utensils, glasses and plates, pieces of human bodies all lashed violently across the room, and glanced harmlessly off Royd's armored form. Melantha—eager to follow—drew back helplessly. That rain of death would cut her up to pieces in her lighter, thinner vacuum suit. Royd reached the far wall and vanished into the secret control section of the ship. She was alone.

The *Nightflyer* lurched, and sudden acceleration provided a brief semblance of gravity. She was thrown to one side. Her injured shoulder smashed painfully against the sled.

All up and down the corridors doors were opening.

The linguists were moving toward her once again.

The *Nightflyer* was a distant star sparked by its nuclear engines. Blackness and cold enveloped them, and below was the unending emptiness of the Tempter's Veil, but Karoly d'Branin did not feel afraid. He felt strangely transformed.

The void was alive with promise.

"They *are* coming," he whispered. "Even I, who have no psi at all, even I can feel it. The Crey story must be so, even from light-years off they can be sensed. Marvelous!"

The psipsych seemed very small. "The *volcryn*," she muttered. "What good can they do us. I hurt. The ship is gone. D'Branin, my head aches." She made a small frightened noise. "The boy said that, just after I injected him, before ... before ... you know. He said that his head hurt."

"Quiet, my friend. Do not be afraid. I am here with you.

Wait. Think only of what we shall witness, think only of that!"

"I can sense them," the psipsych said.

D'Branin was eager. "Tell me, then. We have the sled. We shall go to them. Direct me."

"Yes," she agreed. "Yes. Oh, yes."

Gravity returned: in a flicker, the universe became almost normal.

Melantha fell to the deck, landed easily and rolled, and was on her feet cat-quick.

The objects that had been floating ominously through the open doors along the corridor all came clattering down.

The blood was transformed from a fine mist to a slick covering on the corridor floor.

The two corpses dropped heavily from the air, and lay still.

Royd spoke to her. His voice came from the communicator grills built into the walls, not over her suit comm. "I made it," he said.

"I noticed," she replied.

"I'm at the main control console," he continued. "I have restored the gravity with a manual override, and I'm cutting off as many computer functions as possible. We're still not safe, though. She will try to find a way around me. I'm countermanding her by sheer force, as it were. I cannot afford to overlook anything, and if my attention should lapse for even a moment . . . Melantha, was your suit breached?"

"Yes. Cut at the shoulder."

"Change into another one. *Immediately.* I think the counter programming I'm doing will keep the locks sealed, but I can't take any chances."

Melantha was already running down the corridor, towards the cargo hold where the suits and equipment were stored.

"When you have changed," Royd continued, "dump the corpses into the mass conversion unit. You'll find the appropriate hatch near the driveroom, just to the left of the main lock. Convert any other loose objects that are not indispensible as well; scientific instruments, books, tapes, tableware—"

"Knives," suggested Melantha.

"By all means."

"Is teke still a threat, Captain?"

"Mother is vastly weaker in a gravity field," Royd said. "She has to fight it. Even boosted by the *Nightflyer's* power, she can only move one object at a time, and she has only a fraction of the lifting force she wields under weightless conditions. But the power is still there, remember. Also, it is possible she will find a way to circumvent me and cut out the gravity again. From here I can restore it in an instant, but I don't want any weapons lying around even for that brief period of time."

Melantha had reached the cargo area. She stripped off her vacuum suit and slipped into another one in record time. Then she gathered up the discarded suit and a double armful of instruments and dumped them into the conversion chamber. Afterwards she turned her attention to the bodies. The man was no problem. The woman crawled down the hall after her as she pushed him through, and thrashed weakly when it was her own turn, a grim reminder that the *Nightflyer's* powers were not all gone. Melantha easily overcame her feeble struggles and forced her through.

The corpse of the xenobiologist was less trouble, but while she was cleaning out the lounge a kitchen knife came spinning at her head. It came slowly, though, and Melantha just batted it aside, then picked it up and added it to the pile for conversion.

She was working through the second cabin, carrying the psipsych's abandoned drugs and injection gun under her arm, when she heard Royd cry out.

A moment later, a force like a giant invisible hand wrapped itself around her chest and squeezed and pulled her, struggling, to the floor.

Something was moving across the stars.

Dimly and far off, d'Branin could see it, though he could not yet make out details. But it was there, that was unmistakable, some vast shape that blocked off a section of the starscape. It was coming at them dead on.

How he wished he had his team with him now, his telepath, his experts, his instruments.

He pressed harder on the thrusters.

Pinned to the floor, hurting, Melantha Jhirl risked opening her suit's comm. She had to talk to Royd. "Are you there?" she asked. "What's happening?" The pressure was awful, and it was growing steadily worse. She could barely move.

The answer was pained and slow in responding. ". . . outwitted . . . me," Royd's voice managed. ". . . hurts . . . to . . . talk."

"Royd—"

". . . she . . . teked . . . dial . . . up . . . two . . . gees . . . three . . . higher . . . right . . . here . . . on . . . the . . . board . . . all . . . I . . . have to . . . to do . . . turn it . . . back . . . back . . . let me . . ."

Silence. Then, finally, when Melantha was near despair, Royd's voice again. One word: ". . . can't . . ."

Melantha's chest felt as if it were supporting ten times her own weight. She could imagine the agony Royd must be in; Royd, for whom even one gravity was painful and dangerous. Even if the dial was an arm's length away, she knew his feeble musculature would never let him reach it. "Why," she started, having somewhat less trouble talking than Royd, "why would she turn *up* the . . . gravity . . . it . . . weakens her too, yes?"

". . . yes . . . but . . . in a . . . a time . . . hour . . . minute . . . my . . . my heart . . . will burst . . . and . . . then . . . you alone . . . she . . . will . . . kill gravity . . . kill you . . ."

Painfully, Melantha reached out her arm and dragged herself half a length down the corridor. "Royd . . . hold on . . . I'm coming . . ." She dragged herself forward again. The psipsych's drug kit was still under her arm, impossibly heavy. She eased it down and started to shove it aside, then reconsidered. Instead she opened its lid.

The ampules were all neatly labeled. She glanced over them quickly, searching for adrenaline or synthastim, anything that might give her the strength she needed to reach Royd. She found several stimulants, selected the strongest, and was loading it into the injection gun with awkward, agonized slowness when her eyes chanced on the supply of esperon.

Melantha did not know why she hesitated. Esperon was only one of a half-dozen psionic drugs in the kit, but something about seeing it bothered her, reminded her of something she could not quite lay her finger on. She was trying to sort it out when she heard the noise.

"Royd," she said, "your mother . . . could she move . . . she couldn't move anything . . . teke it . . . in this high a gravity . . . could she?"

"Maybe," he answered, ". . . if . . . concentrate . . . all her . . . power . . . hard . . . maybe possible . . . why?"

"Because," Melantha Jhirl said grimly, "because something . . . some*one* . . . is cycling through the airlock."

The *volcryn* ship filled the universe.

"It is not truly a ship, not as I thought it would be," Karoly d'Branin was saying. His suit, Academy-designed, had a built-in encoding device, and he was recording his comments for posterity, strangely secure in the certainty of his impending death. "The scale of it is difficult to imagine, difficult to estimate. Vast, vast. I have nothing but my wrist computer, no instruments, I cannot make accurate measurements, but I would say, oh, a hundred kilometers, perhaps as much as three hundred, across. Not solid mass, of course, not at all. It is delicate, airy, no ship as we know ships. It is—oh, beautiful—it is crystal and gossamer, alive with its own dim lights, a vast intricate kind of spiderwebby craft—it reminds me a bit of the old starsail ships they used once, in the days before drive, but this great construct, it is not solid, it cannot be driven by light. It is no ship at all, really. It is all open to vacuum, it has no sealed cabins or life-support spheres, none visible to me, unless blocked from my line of sight in some fashion, and no, I cannot believe that, it is too open, too fragile. It moves quite rapidly. I would wish for the instrumentation to measure its speed, but it is enough to be here. I am taking our sled at right angles to it, to get clear of its path, but I cannot say that I will make it. It moves so much faster than we. Not at light speed, no, far below it, but still faster than the *Nightflyer* and its nuclear engines, I would guess. Only a guess.

"The *volcryn* craft has no visible means of propulsion. In fact, I wonder how—perhaps it *is* a light-sail, laser-launched millennia ago, now torn and rotted by some unimaginable catastrophe—but no, it is too symmetrical, too beautiful, the webbings, the great shimmering veils near the nexus, the beauty of it.

"I must describe it, I must be more accurate, I know. It is difficult, I grow too excited. It is large, as I have said, kilometers across. Roughly—let me count—yes, roughly octagonal in shape. The nexus, the center, is a bright area, a small darkness surrounded by a much greater area of light, but only the dark portion seems entirely solid—the lighted areas are translucent, I can see stars through them, though discolored, shifted towards the purple. Veils, I call those the veils. From the nexus and the veils eight long—oh, vastly long—spurs project, not quite spaced evenly, so it is not a true geometric octagon—ah, I see better now, one of the spurs is shifted, oh, very slowly, the veils are rippling—they are mobile then, those projections, and the webbing runs from one spur to the next, around and around, but there are—patterns, odd patterns, it is not at all the simple webbing of a spider. I cannot quite see order in the patterns, in the traceries of the webs, but I feel sure that the order is there, the meaning is waiting to be found.

"There are lights. Have I mentioned the lights? The lights are brightest around the center nexus, but they are nowhere very bright, a dim violet. Some visible radiation, then, but not much. I would like to take an ultraviolet reading of this craft, but I do not have the instrumentation. The lights move. The veils seem to ripple, and lights run constantly up and down the length of the spurs, at differing rates of speed, and sometimes other lights can be seen traversing the webbing, moving across the patterns. I do not know what the lights are or whether they emanate from inside the craft or outside.

"The *volcryn* myths, this is really not much like the legends, not truly. Though, as I think, now I recall a Nor T'alush report that the *volcryn* ships were impossibly large, but I took that for exaggeration. And lights, the *volcryn* have often been linked to lights, but those reports were so vague, they might have meant anything, described anything from a laser propulsion system to simple exterior lighting, I could not know it meant this. Ah, what mysteries! The ship is still too far away for me to see the finer detail. I think perhaps the darker area in the center *is* a craft, a life capsule. The *volcryn* must be inside it. I wish my team was with me, my telepath. He was a class one, we might have made contact, might have communicated with them. The things we would learn! The things they have seen! To think how old this craft is, how ancient this race, how long they have been outbound! It fills me with awe. Communication would be such a gift, such an impossible gift, but they are so alien."

"*D'Branin*," the psipsych said in a low, urgent voice. "Can't you feel it?"

Karoly d'Branin looked at his companion as if seeing her for the first time. "Can *you* feel them? You are a three, can you sense them now, strongly?"

"Long ago," the psipsych said. "Long ago."

"Can you project? Talk to them. Where are they? In the center area?"

"Yes," she replied, and she laughed. Her laugh was shrill and hysterical, and d'Branin had to recall that she was a very sick woman. "Yes, in the center, d'Branin, that's where the pulses come from. Only you're wrong about them. It's not a *them* at all, your legends are all lies, lies, I wouldn't be surprised if we were the first to ever see your *volcryn*, to ever come this close. The others, those aliens of yours, they merely *felt*, deep and distantly, sensed a bit of the nature of the *volcryn* in their dreams and visions, and fashioned the rest to suit themselves. Ships, and wars, and a race of eternal travellers, it is all—all—"

"What do you mean, my friend?" Karoly said, baffled. "You do not make sense. I do not understand."

"No," the psipsych said, her voice suddenly gentle. "You do not, do you? You cannot feel it, as I can. So clear now. This must be how a one feels, all the time. A one full of esperon."

"*What* do you feel? *What?*"

"It's not a *them*, Karoly," the psipsych said. "It's an *it*. Alive, Karoly, and quite mindless, I assure you."

"Mindless?" d'Branin said. "No, you must be wrong, you are not reading correctly. I will accept that it is a single creature if you say so, a single great marvelous star-traveller, but how can it be mindless? You sensed it, its mind, its telepathic emanations. You and the whole of the Crey sensitives and all the others. Perhaps its thoughts are too alien for you to read."

"Perhaps," the psipsych admitted, "but what I do read is not so terribly alien at all. Only animal. Its thoughts are slow and dark and strange, hardly thoughts at all, faint. The brain must be huge, I grant you that, but it can't be devoted to conscious thought."

"What do you mean?"

"The propulsion system, d'Branin. Don't you *feel*? The pulses? They are threatening to rip off the top of my skull. Can't you guess what is driving your damned *volcryn* across the galaxy? Why they avoid gravity wells? Can't you guess how it is moving?"

"No," d'Branin said, but even as he denied it a dawn of comprehension broke across his face, and he looked away from his companion, back at the swelling immensity of the *volcryn*, its lights moving, its veils a-ripple, as it came on and on, across light-years, light-centuries, across eons.

When he looked back to her, he mouthed only a single word: "Teke," he said. Silence filled their world.

She nodded.

Melantha Jhirl struggled to lift the injection gun and press
it against an artery. It gave a single loud hiss, and the drug
flooded her system. She lay back and gathered her strength,
tried to think. Esperon, esperon, why was that important? It
had killed the telepath, made him a victim of his own abilities, tripled his power and his vulnerability. Psi. It all came
back to psi.

The inner door of the airlock opened. The headless corpse
came through...

It moved with jerks, unnatural shufflings, never lifting its
legs from the floor. It sagged as it moved, half-crushed by the
weight upon it. Each shuffle was crude and sudden; some
grim force was literally yanking one leg forward, then the
next. It moved in slow motion, arms stiff by its sides.

But it moved.

Melantha summoned her own reserves and began to crawl
away from it, never taking her eyes off its advance.

Her thoughts went round and round, searching for the
piece out of place, the solution to the chess problem, finding
nothing.

The corpse was moving faster than she was. Clearly, visibly, it was gaining.

Melantha tried to stand. She got to her knees, her heart
pounding. Then one knee. She tried to force herself up, to lift
the impossible burden on her shoulders. She was strong, she
told herself. She was the improved model.

But when she put all her weight on one leg, her muscles
would not hold her. She collapsed, awkwardly, and when she
smashed against the floor it was as if she had fallen from a
building. She heard a sharp *snap*, and a stab of agony flashed
up the arm she had tried to use to break her fall. She blinked
back tears and choked on her own scream.

The corpse was halfway up the corridor. It must be walking on two broken legs, she realized. It didn't care.

"Melantha . . . heard you . . . are . . . you . . . Melantha?"

"*Quiet*," she snapped at Royd. She had no breath to waste
on talk.

Now she had only one arm. She used the disciplines she
had taught herself, willed away the pain. She kicked feebly,
her boots scraping for purchase, and she pulled herself forward with her good arm.

The corpse came on and on.

She dragged herself across the threshold of the lounge,

worming her way under the crashed sled, hoping it would delay the cadaver.

It was a meter behind her.

In the darkness, in the lounge, there where it had all begun, Melantha Jhirl ran out of strength.

Her body shuddered, and she collapsed on the damp carpet, and she knew that she could go no further.

On the far side of the door, the corpse stood stiffly. The sled began to shake. Then, with the scrape of metal against metal, it slid backwards, moving in tiny sudden increments, jerking itself free and out of the way.

Psi. Melantha wanted to curse it, and cry. Vainly she wished for a psi power of her own, a weapon to blast apart the teke-driven corpse that stalked her. She was improved, she thought angrily, but not improved enough. Her parents had given her all the genetic gifts they could arrange, but psi was beyond them. The gene was astronomically rare, recessive, and—

—and suddenly it came to her.

"Royd!" she yelled, put all of her remaining will into her words. "The dial . . . *teke it*. Royd, teke it!"

His reply was very faint, troubled. ". . . can't . . . I don't . . . Mother . . . only . . . her . . . not me . . . no . . ."

"Not mother," she said, desperate. "You always . . . say . . . *mother*. I forgot . . . forgot. Not your mother . . . listen . . . you're a *clone* . . . same genes . . . you have it, too. The power."

"Don't," he said. "Never . . . must be . . . sex-linked."

"*No!* It *isn't*. I know . . . Promethean, Royd . . . don't tell a Promethean . . . about genes . . . turn it!"

The sled jumped a third of a meter, and listed to the side. A path was clear.

The corpse came forward.

". . . trying," Royd said. "Nothing . . . I *can't*!"

"She *cured* you," Melantha said bitterly. "Better than . . . she was . . . cured . . . pre-natal . . . but it's only . , . . suppressed . . . you *can*!"

"I . . . don't . . . know . . . how."

The corpse now stood above her. Stopped. Pale-fleshed hands trembled spasticly. Began to rise.

Melantha swore, and wept, and made a futile fist.

And all at once the gravity was gone. Far, far away, she heard Royd cry out and then fall silent.

The corpse bobbed awkwardly into the air, its hands hanging limply before it. Melantha, reeling in the weightlessness, tried to ready herself for its furious assault.

But the body did not move again. It floated dead and still. Melantha moved to it, pushed it, and it sailed across the room.

"Royd?" she said uncertainly.

There was no answer.

She pulled herself through the hole into the control chamber.

And found Royd Eris, master of the *Nightflyer*, prone on his back in his armored suit, dead. His heart had given out.

But the dial on the gravity grid was set at zero.

I have held the *Nightflyer's* crystalline soul within my hands.

It is deep and red and multifaceted, large as my head, and icy to the touch. In its scarlet depths, two small sparks of light burn fiercely and sometimes seem to whirl.

I have crawled through the consoles, wound my way carefully past safeguards and cybernets, taking care to damage nothing, and I have laid rough hands on that great crystal, knowing that it is where *she* lives.

And I cannot bring myself to wipe it.

Royd's ghost has asked me not to.

Last night we talked about it once again, over brandy and chess in the lounge. Royd cannot drink, of course, but he sends his spectre to smile at me, and he tells me where he wants his pieces moved.

For the thousandth time he offered to take me back to Avalon, or any world of my choice, if only I would go outside and complete the repairs we abandoned so many years ago, so that the *Nightflyer* might safely slip into stardrive.

For the thousandth time I refused.

He is stronger now, no doubt. Their genes are the same, after all. Their power is the same. Dying, he too found the strength to impress himself upon the great crystal. The ship is alive with both of them, and frequently they fight. Sometimes she outwits him for a moment, and the *Nightflyer* does odd, erratic things. The gravity goes up or down or off completely. Blankets wrap themselves around my throat when I sleep. Objects come hurtling out of dark corners.

Those times have come less frequently of late, though. When they do come, Royd stops her, or I do. Together, the *Nightflyer* is ours.

Royd claims he is strong enough alone, that he does not really need me, that he can keep her under check. I wonder. Over the chessboard, I still beat him nine games out of ten.

And there are other considerations. Our work, for one. Karoly would be proud of us.

The *volcryn* will soon enter the mists of the Tempter's Veil, and we follow close behind. Studying, recording, doing all that old d'Branin would have wanted us to do. It is all in the computer. It is also on tape and on paper, should the computer ever be wiped. It will be interesting to see how the *volcryn* thrives in the Veil. Matter is so thick there, compared to the thin diet of interstellar hydrogen on which the creature has fed for endless eons.

We have tried to communicate with it, with no success. I do not believe it is sentient at all.

And lately Royd has tried to imitate its ways, gathering all his energies in an attempt to move the *Nightflyer* by teke. Sometimes, oddly, his mother even joins him in those efforts. So far they have failed, but we will keep trying.

So the work goes on, and it *is* important work, though not the field I trained for, back on Avalon. We know that our results will reach humanity. Royd and I have discussed it. Before I die, I will destroy the central crystal and clear the computers, and afterwards I will set course manually for the close vicinity of an inhabited world. I know I can do it. I have all the time I need, and I am an improved model.

I will not consider the other option, though it means much to me that Royd suggests it again and again. No doubt I could finish the repairs. Perhaps Royd could control the ship without me, and continue the work. But that is not important.

When I finally touched him, for the first and last and only time, his body was still warm. But *he* was gone already. He never felt my touch. I could not keep that promise.

But I can keep my other.

I will not leave him alone with her.

Ever.

A SPACESHIP BUILT OF STONE

by Lisa Tuttle

Anyone who has wandered about the ruins of lost civilizations cannot help but be filled with the wonder and awe of time past. When the ruins are of peoples who have left no other trace—and of whom we may never learn anything more—we realize that peoples have been roving this world's surface long long before anyone started to write down history. But there's more to this story than an excursion to pre-Columbian ruins.

I came upon a vast and ruined city in the desert. Long ago, huge building blocks had been hewn from rock, cut to fit together so tightly that mortar was unnecessary. It was a city not of straight lines, but of rounded corners and circular enclosures, walls towering twice a man's height. It seemed immense and harshly white against the blue sky and emptiness of the desert.

I entered by an arching gateway and walked through narrow, winding streets, touching the sun-baked stone with my hands. Here and there signs had been incised in the rock. I traced one with my finger: a cup-shaped maze with a stylized symbol, a rising bird, at the center.

The city must have been abandoned centuries before. Everything was open to the sky, all roofs long since rotted away. The sand had drifted in to cover the cobblestone streets. But the emptiness of the city, although it seemed sad, was not oppressive. I felt comfortable there, at home, as if I had returned to a place familiar since childhood. I patiently followed the curving lanes and entered each abandoned building in turn, looking for something.

At last I found it. There was a large, semi-circular enclosure at the very center of the city. Inside, a hole cut into the earth. Without hesitation, I lowered myself into it, my dangling feet finding purchase on a stairway carved into the rock. The stairs were steep, forcing me into a rapid descent. It was more a ladder than a staircase.

I climbed for what seemed a very long time, the darkness growing deeper around me as I descended. But just as I was wondering how long I could continue to climb down to an unknown destination in total darkness, a dim light from some source further down began to reach me; and when I reached the bottom at last, I could see perfectly well. I was in a small stone alcove. Behind me were the stairs to the surface; ahead of me, three branching tunnels. I chose the well-lit central tunnel. As I walked, I looked around at the curving, featureless walls and ceiling, which apparently gave off light. After I had walked for a long time, I began to hear a sound ahead of me, a soft, irregular noise which I thought might be people talking.

At last I came to another branching, and an archway, which led into a room filled with people. They stopped talking when I entered, and looked at me with some apprehension.

They were familiar to me—I knew they were the people who had built the city above. They looked enough alike to be members of one family, with their unusual yellow-brown skin color, wide, round eyes, thin noses, and thick black hair.

A woman detached herself from the crowd and stepped forward, saying my name. Her eyes were intent upon my face; I had the idea that she knew me very well, was even perhaps in love with me.

"Rick!" she said. "You came back! Tell us, is it safe? Can we come out now? Will they let us live in peace?"

My earlier confusion dropped away. I had been here many times before, and knew these people well. They were not my own people; but I loved them and had agreed to help them. Why had I forgotten?

I opened my mouth to speak, to tell them that it was safe

now, and I would help them settle above ground; and then the alarm went off.

Groggy and fumbling in the dark, I stopped it, then sat up, switched on the light, and reached for my cigarettes. I felt disoriented and confused. Unlike most of my dreams, this one had the force of reality, of some remembered event. Had I dreamed of those people and those underground tunnels before, or had my memory in the dream been nothing more than a dream of a dream?

I found a notebook and pen and began to write down the details before they could slip away from me. I'd had bad luck with dreams, lately, waking every morning to find them gone, which was why I'd set my alarm to wake me up in the middle of the night. Describing the city in the desert, I wondered where I had seen it. I didn't usually dream about places I'd never been, and I wondered now if, perhaps, once as a child I had been taken to some stone ruins in a desert somewhere.

And the dream left me in an oddly vulnerable state. My last thoughts, as I settled down to sleep again, were that I would have to hurry back there, find the city again and the people who hid beneath it, and offer them my help.

But by morning I had nearly forgotten the dream—I remembered only waking and writing something down. I added the notebook to my stack of books and went outside to catch a university shuttle bus a little before noon. On the bus I saw a pretty, dark-haired girl I'd noticed before, and sat down next to her. She was an art student—her sketchpad open on her knee. On the paper, growing beneath her pencil, was a familiar design: a cup-shaped maze with a stylized bird rising from the center.

I stared at the drawing, aware only that it was a familiar symbol, when suddenly, with shocking vividness—as if it were a memory of something real and not just a dream—I saw again the white stone wall with the very same design incised on it. I had traced it with my finger in my dream.

"What are you drawing?" I asked.

She looked up, seemed to recognize me from other bus-rides, and smiled. "This? I'm just doodling."

"But what is that design? Where is it from?"

She laughed. "It's from my head! I just made it up."

I was startled. "Are you sure? Couldn't you have seen it somewhere before?"

"Yes, I suppose." She frowned, then her face cleared. "I

don't remember. But anyway, it was in a dream I had last night." She laughed again, a warm, delighted chuckle. "Don't look so amazed! Don't you ever get ideas from dreams?"

"All the time," I said dryly. "In fact, that's the reason I asked you about that design. It was in my dream last night." I tapped the notebook in my lap. "I wrote it down here. I woke myself up at 3:30, on purpose to catch a dream—part of an experiment for a class I teach."

Her brown eyes were very wide—she seemed to accept what I said without question. "How strange," she murmured. "Three-thirty . . ." She looked down at her sketch-pad and began to drawn an elaborate frame around the maze design. "You see, I probably wouldn't have remembered this dream at all; but Bogey—that's my dog—decided he had to go outside, and woke me up at about 3:30. So while I was up, waiting to let him back in, I sat and doodled in my sketch-book while I thought about my dream." She lifted the spiral-bound pad and flipped back a few pages, holding out one for my inspection.

A line of stone blocks, a wall. The maze-with-bird pattern again. A stone gateway. And faces—faces that I recognized. The people from my dream.

I felt strange, my pulse speeded up. "Looks like my dream," I said quietly.

"I was in the desert somewhere," she said. "And there was this ancient city there, which was supposed to have been abandoned; but the people who had built it had actually fled below ground and were hiding there. They were very gentle and peaceful and afraid that they would be killed if they came out. They were a wonderful people—I loved them, and was trying to help them. They kept asking me if it was really all right to come out, and I kept telling them that everyone would love them as I did. And then Bogey woke me."

I opened my notebook to the dream and handed it to her without a word. While she read I gazed past her, out the window at the sunny, familiar, neighborhood streets the bus was roaring through. The familiar had suddenly become strange, the strange familiar. The world was different—I couldn't tell if it was tinged with promise, or with menace.

"Telepathy," said a clear voice at my side.

I looked at her and shook my head. "But why? You and I don't even know each other—why should we be linked like that?"

She looked straight into my eyes. "Karma," she said. "We were meant to meet."

I laughed at her words, but I liked her look. I even liked the idea that we were somehow linked, that something had drawn us together, although it was a silly idea.

"A very scientific suggestion," I said, teasing her. "You want to have dinner with me tonight and talk about it some more?"

"Sure."

Through the window, I could see the tower lurching into view. I would have to get off at the next stop. "Meet me at Hansel and Gretel's at 6:30?" I suggested, gathering my books together.

She gave me another one of those high-voltage looks. "I'll be there."

It wasn't until I had gotten off the bus that I realized I didn't know her name.

But I didn't expect she would stand me up—not after such an opening. I walked up the grassy mall towards the building where I was teaching a workshop in journal writing. Most graduate assistants get saddled with the dullest of introductory courses, and I considered myself lucky this semester to have gotten something a little out of the ordinary—no matter that I thought it a self-indulgent and unnecessary course.

I paused on the steps outside to smoke a cigarette. I was really trying to get my mind on the class I had to teach, when all I wanted to think about was the dream—my dream, her dream—and what it meant. When I finally went inside, and down to the large, blank-walled basement classroom where we met, my class of ten had assembled.

I perched, as usual, on the old wooden desk at the front of the room, and looked at them. "Any of you have trouble catching a dream?" I asked.

Of the ten, it turned out, only five had dreams to report. One had slept through the alarm, another had simply forgotten the assignment; the other three were the most chagrined, however. They had ignored my suggestion of setting alarms for the middle of the night as unnecessary—they claimed to dream vividly and to remember what they had dreamed. But this morning had been unusual. They had remembered no dreams.

I nodded thoughtfully, feeling myself slip into the psychiatrist role this class seemed to reserve for me.

"Perhaps," I suggested, enjoying myself, "you dreamed of

things you would be too embarrassed to discuss before the whole class? So your unconscious thoughtfully censored them from your conscious? Well, try again tonight. We'll just move on to some of the dreams which were recalled. Anyone like to start by reading his or her dream?"

Eve Johnson flicked one impeccably manicured hand in the air and, at my nod, began to speak, referring only occasionally to her notebook.

"The dream began at a frat-party, which was pretty dull. But then some friends of mine started talking about driving to California, right then. This actually happened to me once—some friends decided to drive to California on the spur of the moment. Anyway, in the dream, all of a sudden it switched to us on the road, travelling through the desert someplace like New Mexico. We got off the highway onto a dirt road for some reason and drove through all this emptiness for awhile. Then, all of a sudden, right in front of us was this huge, stone city. It was built of big white stones, and we could see it clearly in the moonlight. But it was abandoned—and I found myself remembering, as I looked at it, that the people who had built it had been afraid that the government or somebody would kill them, so they had gone into hiding underground. Then—what's wrong?"

Only then did I realize that I had gotten off the desk and walked towards her.

"Uh, could I see the notebook, please?"

Eyebrows raised, she put the notebook into my hand. My eyes ran down the lines of neat, even handwriting, reading about her discovery of the tunnels, and meeting with the people who lived beneath the city-ruin.

I looked around at the others, some of whom looked puzzled, others of whom looked oddly excited. I said, "Something strange has happened. This dream of Eve's is remarkably similar to the dream I had last night...."

"Me too!"

"I dreamed the same thing!"

Pat Haggard and Bill Donaldson had spoken almost simultaneously. Now they looked from me to each other, their expressions mixtures of wonder, curiosity and suspicion.

"Anyone else?" I asked. I realized I was probably grinning foolishly. "Did anyone else have a dream with the same elements—the abandoned stone city in the desert, the tunnels underground, the people there afraid to come up?"

Slowly, Mary Crouch raised her hand. "I dreamed something like that, I think," she said. "I can't remember much about it. Just that I had been talking to these wonderful people, some sort of advanced, peaceful tribe, who seemed to live near some huge stone ruins."

I nodded slowly. "Bill, Pat . . . would each of you please read your dream reports?"

All the elements were there; all the inexplicable similarities. The same dream, dreamed by six different people. At least.

We spent the rest of class-time talking about the dreams and what this bizarre coincidence could mean. We discussed telepathy and precognition—one of the liveliest, most exciting, most wonder-filled classroom discussions I'd ever imagined. But of course we proved nothing and came up with no real answers. When the bell rang we were all frustratingly aware of how little we knew. My students all promised to continue recording their dreams and eagerly offered to do any other research I might suggest.

When they all left, I walked across campus to the library to start the research. I had decided first of all to try to find out if the place we had all been dreaming of had any objective reality.

I paged through volumes of anthropology, archeology and travel, but did not find the city I thought I knew in Anatolian ruins, nor in Greece, nor Peru, nor in the monolithic structures on Malta, nor in the Arabian desert. Because two dreamers had mentioned New Mexico, I turned next to books about the Southwest. There I found the stone and baked-earth structures of the Pueblo Indians, the hogans of the Navajo, and the legends of the Seven Cities of Cibola. The Pueblos believed their ancestors entered the present world from a hole in the ground, climbing up from a world below. I took notes, but I found no answers.

She was waiting at the restaurant when I arrived, even prettier and taller than I'd remembered, looking like a 1940s film star in a vintage black dress and lots of cheerfully fake diamonds, spike heels, and an upswept hairdo.

"I've got so much to tell you," she said at once, rushing to meet me.

I took her hand. "How about your name?"

We both laughed.

"I'm Judy Anderson."

"Rick Karp."

We shook hands, and that made us laugh again.

"You look great," I said. "I'm such a slob . . . I knew I should have rented a tux."

"No, no, that shirt is lovely." She reached out to pluck at the fabric. "In fact, I have one just like it at home, only the azaleas on it are a little smaller, and a brighter pink."

"It faded some between Hawaii and here," I said.

We took a booth near the back and I ordered a pitcher of dark beer and a plate of cheese and bread to start.

Judy leaned across the table. "In my design class this morning we were told to create a symbol for a made-up company. A pictograph, right? And one of the women in class drew a picture of a maze with a bird rising from the center, for a company she called 'Anasazi Airlines'."

I frowned in surprised recognition.

"So I asked her where she got the idea, and she said it had just come to her. Then the teacher overheard us and said, in his usual supercilious way, 'Give credit where credit is due, please. The Anasazi Indians came up with that design more than a thousand years ago.'"

"The Anasazi Indians," I said, remembering what I read about them that afternoon. "They were the ancestors of the present pueblo-dwelling Indians—the Hopis, the Zunis, the Pueblos. The Anasazi culture spread all across the Southwest. The word 'Anasazi' is Navajo, meaning 'ancient ones.'"

She pouted. "And I thought I'd surprise you by doing a lot of research! But you know, I went through practically the whole art library and couldn't find that bird-in-the-maze design. I figured if my teacher knew about it, it must be pretty common. Were we dreaming about the Anasazi, then?"

"Courtesy of the Anasazi Broadcasting Company?" I told her about what had happened in class that day and watched her eyes grow larger. I patted her hand. "So you see, it wasn't karma bringing us together, after all."

"Maybe it's *your* dream, and you're sending it to receptive people?"

I shook my head. "It sure doesn't feel like 'my' dream. But even if that explained the people in my class—why would you have picked it up?"

She looked at me through her lashes. "Maybe I noticed you on the bus before . . . maybe I was thinking about you . . . maybe I'm just very receptive to your thoughts."

I grinned. "And the woman in your design class?"

"Oh. Coincidence."

"I think coincidence is one thing it's *not*. There's something going on—"

"Rick. Maybe *everyone* had the dream. And only a few people remembered it—the people who woke up in the middle of it, like you and me."

For some reason that idea made my skin prickle. "We have no evidence for that."

"No, and if they've been made to forget it, we never will have."

I was silent, wild thoughts of a nation-wide—world-wide—survey on dreams racing through my head. "But what would that mean?" I asked. "Assuming that were true—*why* would everyone have the same dream? Is someone sending it? Why? And if there is some reason for everyone to dream the same thing—why would the majority forget it? What could that accomplish?"

"People are influenced by things they can't remember consciously," Judy reminded me.

"Yes, but . . . *why*? No, that world-wide theory doesn't make sense. It's more reasonable to assume that you and I and the woman in your design class and the people in my class are members of a group who are somehow telepathically linked, or receptive to . . . oh, each other, or one particular person. And this has happened before, and will surely happen again."

Judy grinned at me. "I try to tell you *we're* linked, and you sneer at me. Your theory is just karma under another name."

We talked of little else during dinner—our speculation ranged and soared—but there was more going on beneath the talk. She went home with me that night.

During the next two weeks Judy and I and the people in my class all kept dream-notebooks. But there were no further "coincidences"—all the dreams were idiosyncratic, personal, individual dreams. I began working on a report to send to the Maimonides dream laboratory in New York. Judy and I spent more and more time together.

One night, Judy and I lay cozily together in my bed, paying little attention to the newscast, carried on the little black and white set at the foot of the bed, when something alerted us.

Judy half sat up. "What was that—"

One word caught us from the televised babble: "Anasazi."

A well-dressed reporter was standing in a windy desert

with a man dressed in grimy jeans and a pith helmet. The camera panned back to reveal an excavation in progress.

"And who, exactly, were the Anasazi?" said the reporter.

The other man, identified in a title across the screen as **Dr. Reuben Collier, UCLA,** wiped his brow. "They were the precursors of today's Pueblo, Hopi, and Zuni tribes. We had never imagined that we would find anything as complex as this. We have right here in New Mexico uncovered an amazingly large, well-designed city built of stone and adobe. Many of the buildings are constructed with connecting underground tunnels. Hacking out those tunnels must have been a prodigious feat in itself. I'd say this rivals almost anything in the ancient world."

"Astonishing," said the reporter. "But you say this was unexpected? No one had any idea this city was here?"

"We didn't realize the Anasazi culture had ever attained such a height," the archeologist said. "Of course, this find raises the new question of what happened to that culture, how it fell. But by calling this the work of the 'Anasazi,' we are simplifying, you realize—"

"How did you find this site, Dr. Collier?"

He grimaced. "Most unscientifically, I'm afraid. I had a grant to do work in this area, of course, and was working on aerial photographs for some indications of what lay below the surface. But why we picked this particular spot to dig—well, quite truthfully, it came to me in a dream."

"Many archeologists dream of great finds; Reuben Collier's dream came true," said the reporter, turning his handsome visage back to the camera. "Steve Carpenter reporting."

My chest was tight. I realized I hadn't been breathing, and let out my breath with a sigh.

"Well, so that's it," Judy said. "*He* was the one the message was for." She sounded remarkably satisfied.

I stared at her. "What are you talking about?"

"The dreams. They didn't mean anything to us—but they did to him."

"Well, yes, but so what? What are you saying?"

"That getting someone to dig up the city was the *point* of the dream."

"And who was it who wanted that particular task done, may I ask? A bunch of dead Indians?"

She chewed her lower lip. "Well, I don't know. But now that the city has been discovered, the dreams seem to make a little more sense, don't they?"

"Not at all," I said. I was thinking about getting in touch with Collier and wondering if anyone else who'd had the dream might have seen him on television and decide to do the same.

"Look," said Judy. "If the dream had a *point*—if it was supposed to have an effect on someone—that could be it. Maybe it was beamed out; and a lot of people picked up on it, like us; but only a few would be in any position to do anything about it—like that anthropologist. The dream meant something to him, and he could do something about it."

I shook my head, annoyed because what she seemed to think was an answer was no answer at all. "Where did the dreams come from? *Who* beamed them out? Who could possibly want that city discovered yet have no way of ensuring that discovery except by giving people dreams?"

"Well *I* don't know," she said, sounding aggrieved. "I didn't ever say I had the answer—I was just making a suggestion."

So then, of course, I had to kiss her and tell her that her suggestion was a good one—as good as any other. And it probably was—but it still didn't make sense.

The discovery in the New Mexico desert had to be the biggest archeological find of all time. It caused more excitement than King Tut's tomb ever had, and suddenly the whole country was Anasazi-crazy. Everywhere you looked there were the headlines, the magazine articles and books, television specials, and commercials. Stores carried Anasazi toys, games, and postcards. One day Judy showed up in a sundress covered with the bird-in-a-maze design.

It was a flood, a bombardment. Everyone knew about and talked about the Anasazi. We all dreamed about them. It would have been odd, given the sea of information we all swam in, *not* to have dreamed about them. In the dreams—in my dreams and Judy's, at any rate—the Anasazi were always the gentle, wise, and peaceful people of that first dream, only emerged now from their tunnels. Even that original dream, shared by an unknown number, no longer seemed so odd to me. We were all so obsessed with the Anasazi now that it was as if the force of the present had been pressing against our unconscious minds then, demanding to be recognized: the Anasazi knocking to be let in, calling with ghostly voices for remembrance.

I had a recurring vision, during this time, of a crowd of

the Anasazi emerging from the earth. They climbed up narrow stone steps and emerged from the tunnels into the open air, one by one, in starlight and daylight, unending. One by one they come, the line behind them going back forever, and each, to my foreign eyes, looks like the other. Their faces are watchful, thankful, wary. Are we home yet? they seem to ask. Will we be safe here?

Not exactly a dream—not at all like my other dreams about the Anasazi—but just a fleeting thought, an image that recurred to me, disturbing me.

Because the Anasazi *had* suddenly emerged; had come out when no one was looking. And everyone—except me—seemed content to believe their eyes instead of their memories and accept the common knowledge that they had always been among us.

I saw them everywhere. A woman with that distinctively Anasazi face would be sitting quietly on a city bus, or pushing a cart through a grocery store. I would see an Anasazi man, holding two small Anasazi children by their hands, crossing at the light. Faces in crowds, on the evening news, passing in cars. They had arrived quietly, without fuss, and integrated themselves into society as if they had always been here.

Even to myself this seemed an odd obsession—where, then, had they come from if they had not always been among us?—and so I tried not to think about it, and did not discuss it. I was under a lot of strain, trying to get my dissertation written and adjusting to life with Judy—at the beginning of the summer we took a house together, and talked of marriage "eventually."

At the end of the summer I emerged from my stupor of research and writing to discover that the Anasazi had united to ask for their city (baptised, naturally, "Cibola," months before) and surrounding lands to be turned over to them. They asked to reclaim their homeland.

Indian groups had asked for Florida and New York, as well as other chunks of property, before, so there was nothing so unusual in the request. What *was* unusual was the response. Sentiment ran high in favor of giving the Indians their home back. Senators and representatives spoke in favor of it. Even the president . . .

It all seemed to happen with amazing speed as we read about it in the papers and watched it on our television screen. One hot day in September Judy and I were ensconced in the bedroom, the window-unit laboring mightily to cool the air, eating Chinese food from cardboard cartons and paying feeble attention to the images flickering across the screen at the foot of the bed when the president made his special appearance and deeded Cibola and surrounding lands to the Anasazi tribe. Just like that.

Judy gave a small cheer. I sat up, set my carton of food aside, and turned off the set.

"What's wrong?" she asked.

"Where did the Anasazi come from?" I asked. "Who are they? Two years ago, nobody but professors and archeologists had heard of them. Now they suddenly have not only a history, but a present and a future—and their own homeland."

She stared at me. "I thought you agreed that the Indians—"

I held up one hand, cutting her off. "I'm not talking about the Indians. I'm talking about . . . these people, who are called Anasazi. Where did they come from all of a sudden? Remember the research we did? The Anasazi culture died out long ago—their descendents are called the Pueblo, Zuni, and Hopi. Nowhere in any of those books was there a mention of a modern-day Anasazi tribe—yet there are suddenly thousands of them!"

"Oh, *books*," she said, with fine scorn. "What are you going to believe, Rick—what some old book tells you, or what you *know*, what your senses tell you?"

"What *do* I know? I know that since the dreams, and the discovery of Cibola, I've seen the Anasazi, and read about them, everywhere. Not before then—before, they weren't here."

"Of course they were here! We just weren't aware of them!"

"That's what they want us to think," I said. I paused, steeling myself to say aloud what I felt. It was a crazy idea—I knew that as well as anyone—but it haunted me nevertheless, unforgettable as a recurring dream; and I was tired of keeping it to myself.

"All right," I said after a few moments. "I'm not asking you to believe this, just to listen and consider it. Suppose that somewhere, maybe on another planet, was a race of beings who either looked like us; or could alter themselves to look like us. And something happens, maybe their planet is about to be destroyed, and they need a new place to live. A planet like this one." Plots of many old movies, comic books, and paperbacks avidly consumed in adolescence raced through my mind. "But they aren't aggressive—they're a peaceful people, unwilling to hurt or frighten the primitive earth-people. All they need, after all, is a base, room for a colony of maybe fifty or a hundred thousand people.

"They could be quite advanced, although they don't use their technology for war. They send advance propaganda in the form of dreams, so that we meet our new neighbors at night, in the most intimate circumstances, and absorb the lessons with no conscious memory later. Everyone loves them, without knowing why. Everyone is accustomed to the idea of them, sure they've always been around when they finally arrive, accepting them as the indigenous people whose name they use."

"You're saying that the Anasazi came here from outer space in UFOs?" Judy asked blandly.

"Maybe not in the way you think our popular culture has prepared us for," I said. "Instead of arriving here in bright silver ships with flashing lights, they came in the back way, climbing out of a hole in the ground. They stepped through some inter-dimensional doorway, bringing their city of underground tunnels and above-ground structures—they came in their spaceship made of stone, and no one noticed."

"Except you," said Judy. "Oh, Rick." Her face was distressed; she looked as if she was going to cry.

"You think I'm crazy," I said. "Just because I wonder where the Anasazi really come from."

"If I woke up some morning and began asking you, in a very worried way, where all those brown-skinned people with Spanish surnames came from all of a sudden, and wouldn't believe you when you told me that they hadn't suddenly invaded us, but had been around all the time—you'd think I was paranoid, wouldn't you?"

"I'd think you were putting me on," I said. I shrugged. "I don't begrudge them their desert city—they built it, after all, and nobody was using that land. But I don't like thinking that they've tampered with our memories, made us love them. Even while I'm saying this, Judy, part of me is protesting that this is crazy talk—that I *know* who the Anasazi are, as well as anyone! And I can't help feeling warmth for them. But I also know what I've read, and I think it's very suspicious that nothing written before the discovery of Cibola refers to Anasazi as if it were anything more than the name of a long-vanished culture. There is no reference to a present-day

tribe by that name. It's as if . . . when the Hittite civilization
was rediscovered by the archeologists and historians, suddenly
a group of people had appeared, calling themselves the Hit-
tites, saying they had been there all along, despite any refer-
ences to them in any book or—"

"Rick," said Judy, looking at me with tender sadness. "Oh,
Rick, and you think *my* theories are crazy!"

"It's not a theory," I said. "It's just a story." I was annoyed, at myself and at her. I didn't want to convert her or
even convince myself. I wanted to reconcile the two kinds of
"knowledge" I had about the Anasazi. I wanted to understand what had happened. "I didn't want to be right—but I
didn't want to be crazy, either.

"You think too much about books," Judy said. "After all
the work you've done on your dissertation, it's no wonder.
But plenty of things are real which aren't in books. I'm not in
any book, and neither are you—except the phone book—and
we're both real."

I didn't argue anymore. I didn't want to. We smoked and
talked about other things. I didn't forget my uneasiness about
the Anasazi, but I tried not to torment myself about it, either—there didn't seem to be anything I could do to prove
my fantasy had any foundation.

Two years later, we went to Cibola on our honeymoon.
Odd, to see a dream made solid.

This Cibola was different, of course. It had been fixed up,
repaired, and inhabited. There were domed roofs on the
round stone structures now, wooden doors, flowers and herbs
growing in window-boxes.

The stones were still brilliantly white against the blue sky,
just as they had been in my dream; but as we wandered
through the maze of cobbled streets the smells of people, animals, and frying food, and the sounds of tourists and Anasazi
bartering over jewelry and woven blankets added the hard,
undreamlike edge that was reality.

I reached out to touch the dressed stone blocks, so carefully fitted together. My fingers encountered the smoothly incised lines of a maze-design, and I traced it with a
finger—again? or for the first time?

There was a guide, pointing out sights of interest and ex-
plaining Anasazi customs. He led us with unerring instinct to
the shops and stalls where Judy was most likely to buy. While

she was comparing the merits of two silver bracelets I asked the guide about the tunnels.

"Tunnels?"

"Yes, when Cibola was discovered I remember it was mentioned that underground tunnels connected the buildings."

"Ah." His face told me nothing. "There isn't much to see. But of course it will be out of the sun, and perhaps you would like that?" He led us off in a new direction.

But this tunnel was nothing like the cool, wide, well-lit artery of my dream. It was narrow and dark, and we had to crouch slightly as we travelled along. My back soon began to hurt. After a few minutes of unrewarding exploration we climbed up a short wooden ladder and emerged in a candle-shop.

"Is that all?" I asked. "What about the other tunnels?"

"There are more," he nodded. "Cramped little passageways leading from one house to another—perhaps twenty of them in all, and none of them any bigger or longer than the one I just showed you."

I could feel Judy's eyes on me, and knew that she knew what I was thinking. I persisted. "Bigger tunnels," I said. "Wider, deeper below ground, well-lit. Underground chambers."

"Nothing like that here," he said, shaking his head.

I was suddenly impatient with him. "And if there were, and you didn't want us to see them, you'd say the same thing. Why do we need a guide at all here? What are you protecting?"

Judy took my arm. "Rick . . ."

"You are a guest here," the guide said, very quietly. "You must obey our rules, or leave. This is a reservation, which is to say a separate country."

"An alien outpost," I said. I was sweating, suddenly aware of how hot it was. "And we gave it to you. We accepted you, and gave you a place to live, just as you wanted. And it's too late to change our minds now. Come on, Judy, we're going."

It wasn't the greatest honeymoon in history. Judy's initial anger over my making a fool of myself and spoiling the trip soon turned to concern for my mental health when I began expressing the opinion that I would not be allowed to live very much longer, now that I had revealed my suspicions of the Anasazi.

But, of course, nothing happened. And eventually, to Judy's relief, I stopped talking about my paranoid fantasies.

They might be true, or they might be crazy—but in either case, they didn't do me, or anyone else, any good.

And so, for almost three years, I had no reason to remember my doubts. Until very recently.

Bogey woke us up in the middle of the night about two weeks ago, desperate to go outside. Judy went back to sleep after a sleepy argument over whose responsibility the dog was; and I got up to take him out, musing meanwhile on the dream he had interrupted. It had been an odd and vivid dream—and it reminded me of something I could not quite catch hold of. While waiting for Bogey to be ready to come back inside, I picked up one of Judy's sketchpads, and a pen, and began jotting down notes of what I remembered.

I was in the jungle, a tropical rain forest on the side of a mountain. I began to notice a faint trail that told me someone else had been here before me and, at the same time, became aware of an odd, soft, whispering sound. I stopped still and looked around carefully, and then I saw them.

People, their faces shy and frightened, peeking at me from hiding places among the trees and underbrush. I knew that it would require a great deal of care and patience on my part to get them to come out. And I wanted them to—I wanted them to trust me. I felt an overwhelming surge of affection for these people I could barely see—the urge to protect them, to offer them safety and shelter. As I tried to think how to let them know this, Bogey's cold, insistent nose in my ear woke me.

As I sat there, sleepily staring at what I had written, I suddenly knew what this dream reminded me of. Another dream. I hurried back to the bedroom and woke Judy.

"Judy," I said urgently, trying to break through her sleepy incomprehension. "What were you dreaming? Quick, tell me."

"Hmm? Tell them . . . tell them we love them. They're safe."

She was dropping off again. I shook her. "Judy! Please! Wake up."

She opened her eyes and sat up. "What's wrong?"

"What were you dreaming?"

"Huh?" She rubbed her eyes and yawned. "I don't know . . . something. I was in the forest. With friends. I don't know. What's the matter, honey?"

"Go back to sleep," I said. "I'll let Bogey back inside. We'll talk in the morning."

She made a face and grumbled at me, but was asleep again almost as soon as her head hit the pillow.

Since then, I have been waiting for the other shoe to drop. And today my waiting ended. It wasn't on the evening news. It was just a story on an inside page of the paper—so many other important things happened today, it seems. A report from the Philippines on the discovery of a group of people who may be a tribe previously unknown to civilization, living in mountain caves in an almost inaccessible rain forest. A shy and gentle people, who only want to live in peace. I know just what they look like.

WINDOW

by Bob Leman

*We like to speculate glibly about other dimensions, al-
ternate universes, parallel worlds. We think what fun it
would be to be able to explore such places—just like
Earth, in fact Earth itself, with different developments.
Different developments, however, bring about different
predators than those we know on this version of Terra.
We'd do well to be careful of opening windows on such
extended visions.*

"We don't know what the hell's going on out there," they
told Gilson in Washington. "It may be pretty big. The nut in
charge tried to keep it under wraps, but the army was fur-
nishing routine security, and the commanding officer tipped
us off. A screwball project. Apparently been funded for years
without anyone paying much attention. Extrasensory percep-
tion, for God's sake. And maybe they've found something.
The security colonel thinks so, anyway. Find out about it."

The Nut-in-Charge was a rumpled professor of psychology
named Krantz. He and the colonel met Gilson at the airport,
and they set off directly for the site in an army sedan. The
colonel began talking immediately.

"You've got something mighty queer here, Gilson," he said.
"I never saw anything like it, and neither did anybody else.

Krantz here is as mystified as anybody. And it's his baby. We're just security. Not that they've needed any, up to now. Not even any need for secrecy, except to keep the public from laughing its head off. The setup we've got here is—"

"Dr. Krantz," Gilson said, "you'd better give me a complete rundown on the situation here. So far, I haven't any information at all."

Krantz was occupied with the lighting of a cigar. He blew a cloud of foul smoke, and through it he said, "We're missing one prefab building, one POBEC computer, some medical machinery, and one, uh, researcher named Culvergast."

"Explain 'missing,'" Gilson said.

"Gone. Disappeared. A building and everything in it. Just not there any more. But we do have something in exchange."

"And what's that?"

"I think you'd better wait and see for yourself," Krantz said. "We'll be there in a few minutes." They were passing through the farther reaches of the metropolitan area, a series of decayed small towns. The highway wound down the valley beside the river, and the towns lay stretched along it, none of them more than a block or two wide, their side streets rising steeply toward the first ridge. In one of these moribund communities they left the highway and went bounding up the hillside on a crooked road whose surface changed from cobblestones to slag after the houses had been left behind. Beyond the crest of the ridge the road began to drop as steeply as it had risen, and after a quarter of a mile they turned into a lane whose entrance would have been missed by anyone not watching for it. They were in a forest now; it was second growth, but the logging had been done so long ago that it might almost have been a virgin stand, lofty, silent, and somewhat gloomy on this gray day.

"Pretty," Gilson said. "How does a project like this come to be way out here, anyhow?"

"The place was available," the colonel said. "Has been since World War Two. They set it up for some work on proximity fuzes. Shut it down in '48. Was vacant until the professor took it over."

"Culvergast is a little bit eccentric," Krantz said. "He wouldn't work at the university—too many people, he said. When I heard this place was available, I put in for it, and got it—along with the colonel, here. Culvergast has been happy with the setup, but I guess he bothers the colonel a little."

"He's a certifiable loony," the colonel said, "and his little helpers are worse."

"Well, what the devil was he doing?" Gilson asked.

Before Krantz could answer, the driver braked at a chain-link gate that stood across the lane. It was fastened with a loop of heavy logging chain and manned by armed soldiers. One of them, machine pistol in hand, peered into the car. "Everything O.K., sir?" he said.

"O.K. with waffles, Sergeant," the colonel said. It was evidently a password. The noncom unlocked the enormous padlock that secured the chain. "Pretty primitive," the colonel said as they bumped through the gateway, "but it'll do until we get proper stuff in. We've got men with dogs patrolling the fence." He looked at Gilson. "We're just about there. Get a load of this, now."

It was a house. It stood in the center of the clearing in an island of sunshine, white, gleaming, and incongruous. All around was the dark loom of the forest under a sunless sky, but somehow sunlight lay on the house, sparkling in its polished windows and making brilliant the colors of massed flowers in carefully tended beds, reflecting from the pristine whiteness of its siding out into the gray, littered clearing with its congeries of derelict buildings.

"You couldn't have picked a better time," the colonel said. "Shining there, cloudy here."

Gilson was not listening. He had climbed from the car and was staring in fascination. "Jesus," he said. "Like a goddamn Victorian postcard."

Lacy scrollwork foamed over the rambling wooden mansion, running riot at the eaves of the steep roof, climbing elaborately up towers and turrets, embellishing deep oriels and outlining a long, airy veranda. Tall windows showed by their spacing that the rooms were many and large. It seemed to be a new house, or perhaps just newly painted and supremely well-kept. A driveway of fine white gravel led under a high porte-cochère.

"How about that?" the colonel said. "Look like your grandpa's house?"

As a matter of fact, it did: like his grandfather's house enlarged and perfected and seen through a lens of romantic nostalgia, his grandfather's house groomed and pampered as the old farmhouse never had been. He said, "And you got this in exchange for a prefab, did you?"

"Just like that one," the colonel said, pointing to one of the seedy buildings. "Of course we could use the prefab."

"What does that mean?"

"Watch," the colonel said. He picked up a small rock and tossed it in the direction of the house. The rock rose, topped its arc, and began to fall. Suddenly it was not there.

"Here," Gilson said. "Let me try that."

He threw the rock like a baseball, a high, hard one. It disappeared about fifty feet from the house. As he stared at the point of its disappearance, Gilson became aware that the smooth green of the lawn ended exactly below. Where the grass ended, there began the weeds and rocks that made up the floor of the clearing. The line of separation was absolutely straight, running at an angle across the lawn. Near the driveway it turned ninety degrees, and sliced off lawn, driveway and shrubbery with the same precise straightness.

"It's perfectly square," Krantz said. "About a hundred feet to a side. Probably a cube, actually. We know the top's about ninety feet in the air. I'd guess there are about ten feet of it underground."

" 'It'?" Gilson said. " 'It'? What's 'it'?"

"Name it and you can have it," Krantz said. "A three-dimensional television receiver a hundred feet to a side, maybe. A cubical crystal ball. Who knows?"

"The rocks we threw. They didn't hit the house. Where did the rocks go?"

"Ah. Where, indeed? Answer that and perhaps you answer all."

Gilson took a deep breath. "All right. I've seen it. Now tell me about it. From the beginning."

Krantz was silent for a moment; then, in a dry lecturer's voice he said, "Five days ago, June thirteenth, at eleven thirty a.m., give or take three minutes, Private Ellis Mulvihill, on duty at the gate, heard what he later described as 'an explosion that was quiet, like.' He entered the enclosure, locked the gate behind him, and ran up here to the clearing. He was staggered—'shook-up' was his expression—to see, instead of Culvergast's broken-down prefab, that house, there. I gather that he stood gulping and blinking for a time, trying to come to terms with what his eyes told him. Then he ran over there to the guardhouse and called the colonel. Who called me. We came out here and found that a quarter of an acre of land and a building with a man in it had disappeared and been replaced by this, as neat as a peg in a pegboard."

"You think the prefab went where the rocks did," Gilson said. It was a statement.

"Why, we're not even asbolutely sure it's gone. What we're seeing can't actually be where we're seeing it. It rains on that house when it's sunny here, and right now you can see the sunlight on it, on a day like this. It's a window."

"A window on what?"

"Well—that looks like a new house, doesn't it? When were they building houses like that?"

"Eighteen seventy or eighty, something like—oh."

"Yes," Krantz said. "I think we're looking at the past."

"Oh, for God's sake," Gilson said.

"I know how you feel. And I may be wrong. But I have to say it looks very much that way. I want you to hear what Reeves says about it. He's been here from the beginning. A graduate student, assisting here. Reeves!"

A very tall, very thin young man unfolded himself from a crouched position over an odd-looking machine that stood near the line between grass and rubble and ambled over to the three men. Reeves was an enthusiast. "Oh, it's the past, all right," he said. "Sometime in the eighties. My girl got some books on costume from the library, and the clothes check out for that decade. And the decorations on the horses' harnesses are a clue, too. I got that from—"

"Wait a minute," Gilson said. "*Clothes?* You mean there are people in there?"

"Oh, sure," Reeves said. "A fine little family. Mamma, poppa, little girl, little boy, old granny or auntie. A dog. Good people."

"How can you tell that?"

"I've been watching them for five days, you know? They're having—*were* having—fine weather there—or then, or whatever you'd say. They're nice to each other, they *like* each other. Good people. You'll see."

"When?"

"Well, they'll be eating dinner now. They usually come out after dinner. In an hour, maybe."

"I'll wait," Gilson said. "And while we wait, you will please tell me some more."

Krantz assumed his lecturing voice again. "As to the nature of it, nothing. We have a window, which we believe to open into the past. We can see into it, so we know that light passes through; but it passes in only one direction, as evidenced by the fact that the people over there are wholly unaware of us. Nothing else goes through. You saw what happened to the rocks. We've shoved poles through the interface there—and there's no resistance at all—but anything that goes through is gone. God knows where. Whatever you put through stays there. Your pole is cut off clean. Fascinating. But wherever it is, it's not where the house is. That interface isn't between us and the past; it's between us and—someplace else. I think our window here is just an incidental side-effect, a—a twisting of time that resulted from whatever tensions exist along that interface."

Gilson sighed. "Krantz," he said, "what am I going to tell the secretary? You've lucked into what may be the biggest thing that ever happened, and you've kept it bottled up for five days. We wouldn't know about it now if it weren't for the colonel's report. Five days wasted. Who knows how long this thing will last? The whole goddamn scientific establishment ought to be here—should have been from day one. This needs the whole works. At this point the place should be a bee-hive. And what do I find? You and a graduate student throwing rocks and poking with sticks. And a girlfriend looking up the dates of costumes. It's damn near criminal."

Krantz did not look abashed. "I thought you'd say that," he said. "But look at it this way. Like it or not, this thing wasn't produced by technology or science. It was pure psi. If we can reconstruct Culvergast's work, we may be able to find out what happened; we may be able to repeat the phenomenon. But I don't like what's going to happen after you've called in your experimenters, Gilson. They'll measure and test and conjecture and theorize, and never once will they accept for a moment the real basis of what's happened. The day they arrive, I'll be out. And damnit, Gilson, this is *mine*."

"Not any more," Gilson said. "It's too big."

"It's not as though we weren't doing some hard experiments of our own," Krantz said. "Reeves, tell him about your batting machine."

"Yes, *sir*," Reeves said. "You see, Mr. Gilson, what the professor said wasn't absolutely the whole truth, you know? Sometimes something *can* get through the window. We saw it on the first day. There was a temperature inversion over in the valley, and the stink from the chemical plant had been accumulating for about a week. It broke up that day, and the wind blew the gunk through the notch and right over here. A really rotten stench. We were watching our people over there, and all of a sudden they began to sniff and wrinkle their noses and make disgusted faces. We figured it had to be the chemical stink. We pushed a pole out right away, but the end just disappeared, as usual. The professor suggested that maybe there was a pulse, or something of the sort, in the interface, that it exists only intermittently. We cobbled up a gadget to test the idea. Come and have a look at it."

It was a horizontal flywheel with a paddle attached to its rim, like an extended cleat. As the wheel spun, the paddle swept around a table. There was a hopper hanging above, and at intervals something dropped from the hopper onto the table, where it was immediately banged by the paddle and sent flying. Gilson peered into the hopper and raised an interrogatory eyebrow. "Ice cubes," Reeves said. "Colored orange for visibility. That thing shoots an ice cube at the interface once a second. Somebody is always on duty with a stopwatch. We've established that every fifteen hours and twenty minutes the thing is open for five seconds. Five ice cubes go through and drop on the lawn in there. The rest of the time they just vanish at the interface."

"Ice cubes. Why ice cubes?"

"They melt and disappear. We can't be littering up the past with artifacts from our day. God knows what the effect might be. Then, too, they're cheap, and we're shooting a lot of them."

"Science," Gilson said heavily. "I can't wait to hear what they're going to say in Washington."

"Sneer all you like," Krantz said. "The house is there, the interface is there. We've by God turned up some kind of time travel. And Culvergast the screwball did it, not a physicist or an engineer."

"Now that you bring it up," Gilson said, "just what *was* your man Culvergast up to?"

"Good question. What he was doing was—well, not to put too fine a point upon it, he was trying to discover spells."

"Spells?"

"The kind you cast. Magic words. Don't look disgusted yet. It makes sense, in a way. We were funded to look into telekinesis—the manipulation of matter by the mind. It's obvious that telekinesis, if it could be applied with precision, would be a marvelous weapon. Culvergast's hypothesis was that there are in fact people who perform feats of telekinesis, and although they never seem to know or be able to explain how they do it, they nevertheless perform a specific mental action that enables them to tap some source of energy that apparently exists all around us, and to some degree to focus and direct that energy. Culvergast proposed to discover the common factor in their mental processes.

"He ran a lot of putative telekinecists through here, and he reported that he had found a pattern, a sort of mnemonic device functioning at the very bottom of, or below, the verbal level. In one of his people he found it as a set of musical notes, in several as gibberish of various sorts, and in one, he said, as mathematics at the primary arithmetic level. He was feeding all this into the computer, trying to eliminate simple noise and the personal idiosyncrasies of the subjects, trying to lay bare the actual, effective essence. He then proposed to organize this essence into *words;* words that would so shape the mental currents of a speaker of standard American English that they would channel and manipulate the telekinetic power at the will of the speaker. Magic words, you might say. Spells.

"He was evidently further along than I suspected. I think he must have arrived at some words, tried them out, and made an attempt at telekinesis—some small thing, like causing an ashtray to rise off his desk and float in the air, perhaps. And it worked, but what he got wasn't a dainty little ashtray-lifting force; he had opened the gate wide, and some kind of terrible power came through. It's pure conjecture, of course, but it must have been something like that to have had an effect like *this.*"

Gilson had listened in silence. He said, "I won't say you're crazy, because I can see that house and I'm watching what's happening to those ice cubes. How it happened isn't my problem, anyhow. My problem is what I'll recommend to the secretary that we do with it now that we've got it. One thing's sure, Krantz: this isn't going to be your private playpen much longer."

There was a yelp of pure pain from Reeves. "They can't *do* that," he said. "This is ours, it's the professor's. Look at it, look at that house. Do you want a bunch of damn engineers messing around with *that?*"

Gilson could understand how Reeves felt. The house was drenched now with the light of a red sunset; it seemed to glow from within with a deep, rosy blush. But, Gilson reflected, the sunset wasn't really necessary; sentiment and the universal, unacknowledged yearning for a simpler, cleaner time would lend rosiness enough. He was quite aware that the

surge of longing and nostalgia he felt was nostalgia for something he had never actually experienced, that the way of life
the house epitomized for him was in fact his own creation,
built from patches of novels and films; nonetheless he found
himself hungry for that life, yearning for that time. It was a
gentle and secure time, he thought, a time when the pace was
unhurried and the air was clean; a time when there was grace
and style, when young men in striped blazers and boater hats
might pay decorous court to young ladies in long white
dresses, whiling away the long drowsy afternoons of summer
in peaceable conversations on shady porches. There would
be jolly bicycle tours over shade-dappled roads that twisted
among the hills to arrive at cool glens where swift little
streams ran; there would be long sweet buggy rides behind
somnolent patient horses under a great white moon, lover
whispering urgently to lover while nightbirds sang. There
would be excursions down the broad clean river, boats gentle
on the current, floating toward the sound from across the
water of a brass band playing at the landing.

Yes, thought Gilson, and there would probably be an old
geezer with a trunkful of adjectives around somewhere, carrying on about how much better things had been a hundred
years before. If he didn't watch himself he'd be helping
Krantz and Reeves try to keep things hidden. Young
Reeves—oddly, for someone his age—seemed to be
hopelessly mired in this bogus nostalgia. His description of
the family in the house had been simple doting. Oh, it was
definitely time that the cold-eyed boys were called in. High
time.

"They ought to be coming out any minute, now," Reeves
was saying. "Wait till you see Martha."

"Martha," Gilson said.

"The little girl. She's a doll."

Gilson looked at him. Reeves reddened and said, "Well, I
sort of gave them names. The children. Martha and Pete.
And the dog's Alfie. They kind of look like those names, you
know?" Gilson did not answer, and Reeves reddened further.
"Well, you can see for yourself. Here they come."

A fine little family, as Reeves had said. After watching
them for half an hour, Gilson was ready to concede that they
were indeed most engaging, as perfect in their way as their
house. They were just what it took to complete the picture, to
make an authentic Victorian genre painting. Mama and Papa
were good-looking and still in love, the children were healthy

and merry and content with their world. Or so it seemed to him as he watched them in the darkening evening, imagining the comfortable, affectionate conversation of the parents as they sat on the porch swing, almost hearing the squeals of the children and the barking of the dog as they raced about the lawn. It was almost dark now; a mellow light of oil lamps glowed in the windows, and fireflies winked over the lawn. There was an arc of fire as the father tossed his cigar butt over the railing and rose to his feet. Then there followed a pretty little pantomime, as he called the children, who duly protested, were duly permitted a few more minutes, and then were firmly commanded. They moved reluctantly to the porch and were shooed inside, and the dog, having delayed to give a shrub a final wetting, came scrambling up to join them. The children and the dog entered the house, then the mother and father. The door closed, and there was only the soft light from the windows.

Reeves exhaled a long breath. "Isn't that something," he said. "That's the way to live, you know? If a person could just say to hell with all this crap we live in today and go back there and live like that. . . . And Martha, you saw Martha. An angel, right? Man, what I'd give to—"

Gilson interrupted him: "When does the next batch of ice cubes go through?"

"—be able to—Uh, yeah. Let's see. The last penetration was at 3:15, just before you got here. Next one will be at 6:35 in the morning, if the pattern holds, and it has, so far."

"I want to see that. But right now I've got to do some telephoning. Colonel!"

Gilson did not sleep that night, nor, apparently, did Krantz and Reeves. When he arrived at the clearing at five a.m. they were still there, unshaven and red-eyed, drinking coffee from thermos bottles. It was cloudy again, and the clearing was in total darkness except for a pale light from beyond the interface, where a sunny day was on the verge of breaking.

"Anything new?" Gilson said.

"I think that's my question," Krantz said. "What's going to happen?"

"Just about what you expected, I'm afraid. I think that by evening this place is going to be a real hive. And by tomorrow night you'll be lucky if you can find a place to stand. I imagine Bannon's been on the phone since I called him at midnight, rounding up the scientists. And they'll round up the technicians. Who'll bring their machines. And the army's going to beef up the security. How about some of that coffee?"

"Help yourself. You bring bad news, Gilson."

"Sorry," Gilson said, "but there it is."

"Goddamn!" Reeves said loudly. "Oh, goddamn!" He seemed to be about to burst into tears. "That'll be the end for me, you know? They won't even let me in. A damn graduate student? In *psychology?* I won't get near the place. Oh, damn it to hell!" he glared at Gilson in rage and despair.

The sun had risen, bringing gray light to the clearing and brilliance to the house across the interface. There was no sound but the regular bang of the ice cube machine. The three men stared quietly at the house. Gilson drank his coffee.

"There's Martha," Reeves said. "Up there." A small face had appeared between the curtains of a second-floor window, and bright blue eyes were surveying the morning. "She does that every day," Reeves said. "Sits there and watches the birds and squirrels until I guess they call her for breakfast." They stood and watched the little girl, who was looking at something that lay beyond the scope of their window on her world, something that would have been to their rear had the worlds been the same. Gilson almost found himself turning around to see what it was that she stared at. Reeves apparently had the same impulse. "What's she looking at, do you think?" he said. "It's not necessarily forest, like now. I think this was logged out earlier. Maybe a meadow? Cattle or horses on it? Man, what I'd give to be there and see what it is."

Krantz looked at his watch and said, "We'd better go over there. Just a few minutes, now."

They moved to where the machine was monotonously batting ice cubes into the interface. A soldier with a stopwatch sat beside it, behind a table bearing a formidable chronometer and a sheaf of charts. He said, "Two minutes, Dr. Krantz."

Krantz said to Gilson, "Just keep your eye on the ice cubes. You can't miss it when it happens." Gilson watched the machine, mildly amused by the rhythm of its homely sounds: *plink*—a cube drops; *whuff*—the paddle sweeps around: *bang*—paddle strikes ice cube. And then a flat trajectory to the interface, where the small orange missile abruptly vanishes. A second later, another. Then another.

"Five seconds," the soldier called. "Four. Three. Two. One. *Now.*"

His timing was off by a second; the ice cube disappeared like its predecessors. But the next one continued its flight and dropped onto the lawn, where it lay glistening. It was really a fact, then, thought Gilson. Time travel for ice cubes.

Suddenly behind him there was an incomprehensible shout from Krantz and another from Reeves, and then a loud, clear, and anguished, "Reeves, *no!*" from Krantz. Gilson heard a thud of running feet and caught a flash of swift movement at the edge of his vision. He whirled in time to see Reeves' gangling figure hurtle past, plunge through the interface, and land sprawling on the lawn. Krantz said, violently, "Fool!" An ice cube shot through and landed near Reeves. The machine banged again; an ice cube flew out and vanished. The five seconds of accessibility were over.

Reeves raised his head and stared for a moment at the grass on which he lay. He shifted his gaze to the house. He rose slowly to his feet, wearing a bemused expression. A grin came slowly over his face, then, and the men watching from the other side could almost read his thoughts: Well, I'll be damned. I made it. I'm really here.

Krantz was babbling uncontrollably. "We're still here, Gilson, we're still here, we still exist, everything seems the same. Maybe he didn't change things much, maybe the future is fixed and he didn't change anything at all. I was afraid of this, of something like this. Ever since you came out here, he's been—"

Gilson did not hear him. He was staring with shock and disbelief at the child in the window, trying to comprehend what he saw and did not believe he was seeing. Her behavior was wrong, it was very, very wrong. A man had materialized on her lawn, suddenly, out of thin air, on a sunny morning, and she had evinced no surprise or amazement or fear. Instead she had smiled—instantly, spontaneously, a smile that broadened and broadened until it seemed to split the lower half of her face, a smile that showed too many teeth, a smile fixed and incongruous and terrible below her bright blue eyes. Gilson felt his stomach knot; he realized that he was dreadfully afraid.

The face abruptly disappeared from the window; a few seconds later the front door flew open and the little girl rushed through the doorway, making for Reeves with furious speed, moving in a curious, scuttling run. When she was a few feet away, she leaped at him, with the agility and eye-dazzling quickness of a flea. Reeves' eyes had just begun to take on a puzzled look when the powerful little teeth tore out his throat.

She dropped away from him and sprang back. A geyser of bright blood erupted from the ragged hole in his neck. He looked at it in stupefaction for a long moment, then brought up his hands to cover the wound; the blood boiled through his fingers and ran down his forearms. He sank gently to his knees, staring at the little girl with wide astonishment. He rocked, shivered, and pitched forward on his face.

She watched with eyes as cold as a reptile's, the terrible smile still on her face. She was naked, and it seemed to Gilson that there was something wrong with her torso, as well as with her mouth. She turned and appeared to shout toward the house.

In a moment they all came rushing out, mother, father, little boy, and granny, all naked, all undergoing that hideous transformation of the mouth. Without pause or diminution of speed they scuttled to the body, crouched around it, and frenziedly tore off its clothes. Then, squatting on the lawn in the morning sunshine, the fine little family began horribly to feed.

Krantz's babbling had changed its tenor: "Holy Mary, Mother of God, pray for us. . . ." The soldier with the stopwatch was noisily sick. Someone emptied a clip of a machine pistol into the interface, and the colonel cursed luridly. When Gilson could no longer bear to watch the grisly feast, he looked away and found himself staring at the dog, which sat happily on the porch, thumping its tail.

"By God, it just can't be!" Krantz burst out. "It would be in the histories, in the newspapers, if there'd been people like that here. My God, something like that couldn't be forgotten!"

"Oh, don't talk like a fool!" Gilson said angrily. "That's not the past. I don't know what it is, but it's not the past. Can't be. It's—I don't know—someplace else. Some other—dimension? Universe? One of those theories. Alternate worlds, worlds of If, probability worlds, whatever you call 'em. They're in the present time, all right, that filth over there. Culvergast's damn spell holed through to one of those parallels. Got to be something like that. And, my God, what the *hell* was its history to produce *those*? They're not human,

Krantz, no way human, whatever they look like. 'Jolly bicycle tours.' How wrong can you be?"

It ended at last. The family lay on the grass with distended bellies, covered with blood and grease, their eyelids heavy in repletion. The two little ones fell asleep. The large male appeared to be deep in thought. After a time he rose, gathered up Reeves' clothes, and examined them carefully. Then he woke the small female and apparently questioned her at some length. She gestured, pointed, and pantomimed Reeves' headlong arrival. He stared thoughtfully at the place where Reeves had materialized, and for a moment it seemed to Gilson that the pitiless eyes were glaring directly into his. He turned, walked slowly and reflectively to the house, and went inside.

It was silent in the clearing except for the thump of the machine. Krantz began to weep, and the colonel to swear in a monotone. The soldiers seemed dazed. And we're all afraid, Gilson thought. Scared to death.

On the lawn they were enacting a grotesque parody of making things tidy after a picnic. The small ones had brought a basket and, under the meticulous supervision of the adult females, went about gathering up the debris of their feeding. One of them tossed a bone to the dog, and the timekeeper vomited again. When the lawn was once again immaculate, they carried off the basket to the rear, and the adults returned to the house. A moment later the male emerged, now dressed in a white linen suit. He carried a book.

"A Bible," said Krantz in amazement. "It's a Bible."

"Not a Bible," Gilson said. "There's no way those—things could have Bibles. Something else. Got to be."

It looked like a Bible; its binding was limp black leather, and when the male began to leaf through it, evidently in search of a particular passage, they could see that the paper was the thin, tough paper Bibles are printed on. He found his page and began, as it appeared to Gilson, to read aloud in a declamatory manner, mouthing the words.

"What the hell do you suppose he's up to?" Gilson said. He was still speaking when the window ceased to exist.

House and lawn and white-suited declaimer vanished. Gilson caught a swift glimpse of trees across a broad pit between him and the trees. Then he was knocked off his feet by a blast of wind, and the air was full of dust and flying trash and the wind's howl. The wind stopped, as suddenly as it had come, and there was a patter of falling small objects that had momentarily been wind-borne. The site of the house was entirely obscured by an eddying cloud of dust.

The dust settled slowly. Where the window had been there was a great hole in the ground, a perfectly square hole a hundred feet across and perhaps ten feet deep, its bottom as flat as a table. Gilson's glimpse of it before the wind had rushed in to fill the vacuum had shown the sides to be as smooth and straight as if sliced through cheese with a sharp knife; but now small-landslides were occurring all around the perimeter, as topsoil and gravel caved and slid to the bottom, and the edges were becoming ragged and irregular.

Gilson and Krantz slowly rose to their feet. "And that seems to be that," Gilson said. "It was here and now it's gone. But where's the prefab? Where's Culvergast?"

"God knows," Krantz said. He was not being irreverent. "But I think he's gone for good. And at least he's not where those things are."

"What are they, do you think?"

"As you said, certainly not human. Less human than a spider or an oyster. But, Gilson, the way they look and dress, that house—"

"If there's an infinite number of possible worlds, then every possible sort of world will exist."

Krantz looked doubtful. "Yes, well, perhaps. We don't know anything, do we?" He was silent for a moment. "Those things were pretty frightening, Gilson. It didn't take even a fraction of a second for her to react to Reeves. She knew instantly that he was alien, and she moved instantly to destroy him. And that's a baby one. I think maybe we can feel safer with the window gone."

"Amen to that. What do you think happened to it?"

"It's obvious, isn't it? They know how to *use* the energies Culvergast was blundering around with. The book—it has to be a book of spells. They must have a science of it—tried-and-true stuff, part of their received wisdom. That thing used the book like a routine everyday tool. After it got over the excitement of its big feed, it didn't need more than twenty minutes to figure out how Reeves got there, and what to do about it. It just got its book of spells, picked the one it needed (I'd like to see the index of that book) and said the words. Poof! Window gone and Culvergast stranded, God knows where."

"It's possible, I guess. Hell, maybe even likely. You're right, we don't really know a thing about all this."

Krantz suddenly looked frightened. "Gilson, what if—look. If it was that easy for him to cancel out the window, if he has that kind of control of telekinetic power, what's to prevent him from getting a window on *us*? Maybe they're watching us now, the way we were watching them. They know we're here, now. What kind of ideas might they get? Maybe they need meat. Maybe they—my God."

"No," Gilson said. "Impossible. It was pure, blind chance that located the window in that world. Culvergast had no more idea what he was doing than a chimp at a computer console does. If the Possible-Worlds Theory is the explanation of this thing, then the world he hit is one of an infinite number. Even if the things over there do know how to make these windows, the odds are infinite against their finding us. That is to say, it's impossible."

"Yes, yes, of course," Krantz said, gratefully. "Of course. They could try forever and never find us. Even if they wanted to." He thought for a moment. "And I think they do want to. It was pure reflex, their destroying Reeves, as involuntary as a knee jerk, by the look of it. Now that they know we're here, they'll have to try to get at us; if I've sized them up right, it wouldn't be possible for them to do anything else."

Gilson remembered the eyes. "I wouldn't be a bit surprised," he said. "But now we both better—"

"Dr. Krantz!" someone screamed. *"Dr. Krantz!"* There was absolute terror in the voice.

The two men spun around. The soldier with the stopwatch was pointing with a trembling hand. As they looked, something white materialized in the air above the rim of the pit and sailed out and downward to land beside a similar object already lying on the ground. Another came; then another, and another. Five in all, scattered over an area perhaps a yard square.

"It's bones!" Krantz said. "Oh, my God, Gilson, it's bones!" His voice shuddered on the edge of hysteria. Gilson said, "Stop it, now. Stop it! Come on!" They ran to the spot. The soldier was already there, squatting, his face made strange by nausea and terror. "That one," he said, pointing. "That one there. That's the one they threw to the dog. You can see the teeth marks. Oh, Jesus. It's the one they threw to the dog."

They've already made a window, then, Gilson thought. They must know a lot about these matters, to have done it so quickly. And they're watching us now. But why the bones? To warn us off? Or just a test? But if a test, then still why the bones? Why not a pebble—or an ice cube? To gauge our reactions, perhaps. To see what we'll do.

And what *will* we do? How do we protect ourselves against *this?* If it is in the nature of these creatures to cooperate among themselves, the fine little family will no doubt lose no time in spreading the word over their whole world, so that one of these days we'll find that a million million of them have leaped simultaneously through such windows all over the earth, suddenly materializing like a cloud of huge, carnivorous locusts, swarming in to feed with that insensate voracity of theirs until they have left the planet a desert of bones. Is there any protection against that?

Krantz had been thinking along the same track. He said, shakily, "We're in a spot, Gilson, but we've got one little thing on our side. We know when the damn thing opens up, we've got it timed exactly. Washington will have to go all out, warn the whole world, do it through the U.N. or something. We know right down to the second when the window can be penetrated. We set up a warning system, every community on earth blows a whistle or rings a bell when it's time. Bell rings, everybody grabs a weapon and stands ready. If the things haven't come in five seconds, bell rings again, and everybody goes about his business until time for the next opening. It could work, Gilson, but we've got to work fast. In fifteen hours and, uh, a couple of minutes it'll be open again."

Fifteen hours and a couple of minutes, Gilson thought, then five seconds of awful vulnerability, and then fifteen hours and twenty minutes of safety before terror arrives again. And so on for—how long? Presumably until the things come, which might be never (who knew how their minds worked?), or until Culvergast's accident could be duplicated, which, again, might be never. He questioned whether human beings could exist under those conditions without going mad; it was doubtful if the psyche could cohere when its sole foreseeable future was an interminable roller coaster down into long valleys of terror and suspense and thence violently up to brief peaks of relief. Will a mind continue to function when its only alternatives are ghastly death or unbearable tension endlessly protracted? Is there any way, Gilson asked himself, that the race can live with the knowledge that it has no assured future beyond the next fifteen hours and twenty minutes?

And then he saw, hopelessly and with despair, that it was not fifteen hours and twenty minutes, that it was not even one hour, that it was no time at all. The window was not, it seemed, intermittent. Materializing out of the air was a confusion of bones and rent clothing, a flurry of contemptuously flung garbage that clattered to the ground and lay there in an untidy heap, noisome and foreboding.

THE SUMMER SWEET, THE WINTER WILD

by Michael G. Coney

Everyone claims to abhor violence, but nobody does anything about it. War departments announce that their business is peace. Revolutionaries extol the non-violent way to overturning governments, though no government in history was ever overturned without pain and injury. Poets extol the beauty of nature—while biologists conceal their smiles. So what if the non-violent way could be made to triumph? Peace and plenty? Think so?

All that summer We had travelled the barren ground and the eating had been good. By the time of the longest day the cows had begun to return, forming into groups and bringing their new calves with them. During this time We were always conscious of the growing entity—of bulls on the other side of low hills, of more cows down by the lakesides, all coming together, returning to the Oneness, the unity which is the Herd.

How many individuals comprise the Herd? It doesn't matter much, although a few individuals have a special importance because of one reason or another they had influence over the Whole. One group leader was a huge bull known as Basso for the timbre of his call—in fact, he still is a group leader. His queen at that time was Goldenfoot. Now, she is dead.

Basso and Goldenfoot met again by that place where the cold stream trickles down into the lake; by this time Goldenfoot's calf was strong, active and able to travel. It was suckling, butting upwards into Goldenfoot's underbelly in that frenzied manner of the very young while she gazed thoughtfully at the waters where a few dark char cruised. She scraped the ground with her broad hoof, dropped her head and nibbled succulent Arctic moss; then some instinct made her look up.

Basso stood against the sky.

Now Goldenfoot moved, ignoring the calf which stilted beside her, still considering the moist teat hopefully. As she reached Basso's side she experienced again that feeling that together they were greater than the sum of their parts—that incomprehensible, indescribable greatness which is the essence of Us, the Herd. Basso acknowledged her briefly, a touch of nose to nose, an inquisitive snuffle at the calf; then together the three animals ambled west.

Others joined them; cows with their calves, lone bulls, instinctively converging on the focal point of their group leader. Most of the familiar ones were there: Swayback, Splayfoot, Patch, rumps twitching and bobtails flicking against the everpresent clouds of mosquitoes. The insects plagued Us particularly that summer. Two strangers, contributing the sum of their knowledge to the Oneness, gave Us to understand that last winter had been exceptionally mild—they hadn't migrated south with the rest of their Herd the previous fall, but had wintered on the tundra with little discomfort. The mosquitoes had risen in spring in numbers far greater than usual, and had been troublesome ever since.

As We wandered the tundra that summer Basso observed the Herd members constantly, assessing the strengths and weaknesses. The strengths were no concern of Ours—the Herd is naturally strong—but they interested Basso because he would in due course be called upon to prove his right to lead and to mate. And as for the weaknesses, they would be eliminated, so We thought. . . .

The wolves were constantly with us, trotting along the skyline all through the endless day, circling, paying particular attention to the calves and the older animals. They could gauge a beast's age and condition by countless signs; the lift of the head, the placing of a hoof. They trotted white and smiling

among the flowers and low bush, weaving in and out of the
grazing animals, alert for horn and hoof, alert for weakness.
They were as much a part of the Arctic scene as the bright
pale sky, the low rolling hills and abrupt pingos, the lakes
and slow rivers—and the summer flowers, the patches of
purple saxifrage sucking unlikely nourishment from gravel,
the puffy cottongrass, soft pink willow pods, fleabane and
rhododendron. The flowers and the wolves, the Arctic.

A huge wolf had Paddler by the leg and was trying to pull
him down.

We felt Paddler's fear and pain; throughout the Herd We
felt it, and all animals turned to watch and suffer. The wolf
tugged and Paddler bellowed. Other wolves closed in, snapping at Paddler's hindquarters, leaping for his neck. Paddler
shook his head, lowered it and sent the first wolf rolling and
yelping.

Paddler was old and slow. We—the Herd—knew this; but
Paddler was only an individual, a scared animal. He'd lived a
long time and could not conceive that he shouldn't live forever. He roared with pain as a wolf bit into his haunches and
blood splashed to the ground. Excrement tumbled. Paddler
turned as quickly as he could, trying to reach the demons
who were tearing at his living flesh. The big male wolf
watched, seeking a route to the throat but deterred by the
lowered horns.

Then, suddenly, the wolf shook his head and shivered.

The other wolves let go, slunk away from Paddler and
joined their leader. They too shivered and one urinated, the
vapour rising in the keen air. They milled in an uncertain
group, watching the injured Paddler—then the leader yelped
as though himself maimed.

Immediately the pack broke into a united howling. Heads
raised and muzzles pointing to the sky they mourned—what?
Paddler didn't know or care. He thought only of escape and
began to limp away, his fear abating; so the communal fear
within Us abated too. The wolves stopped howling and
watched him go. One began to gnaw at a dwarf willow, seeking sustenance from the bitter wood. Others sniffed at the
spilled blood, and licked. Paddler reached the safety of the
Herd. By this time some of Us had drawn together, instinctively.

Briefly We wondered about the wolves. We had roamed
the Arctic for many summers, beyond the reach of Our
memory, and We were growing wise in proportion to Our

age. A Herd rarely dies, though its individual members may be replaced. At that time, that sweet summer when the wolves stopped attacking, We thought We would live forever.

Perhaps We weren't as wise as We thought.

Perhaps We should have remembered the apathy of recent rutting duels.

But the wolves slunk away, and only once bothered Us again. Later We moved to a place of thin snow and began to paw the ground for lichen, and then the mosquitoes didn't bother Us so much, either.

Later in the summer, a new restlessness began to possess Us. Goldenfoot faced her calf and bobbed her head, grunting. Then she turned and trotted away southwards, the calf following strongly. A few other females of similar age followed and soon a small group was moving away into the far distance where the trees stood. Basso watched them go, unconcerned. They would be back. It was, however, the first sign of approaching winter—that innate call felt all over the Herd, to move south, through the trees to the winter pasture.

It was too early yet, though. Basso stayed put, moving with the main body of the Herd as it grazed its way lazily westward. During this time other groups arrived from the north and east, familiar animals rejoining, their relationship with the Herd established before they'd even topped the last hill, so that the nearest animals turned and waited for them to appear. And there were other forays south too, little groups suddenly dashing off across the hills as though losing patience. Wolves loped by, interested but not attacking. There were fewer of them, that summer. They were gaunt, their coats untidy.

The warble flies disappeared, their eggs deposited under Our hides, the larvae already developing within Our very meat. There is a place for everyone in the scheme of things. Now the sun was dipping below the horizon and the first chills were in the air—and the Herd became cohesive again. Goldenfoot was back, the calf at her side. Others. Some calves were sickly; these the wolves would take—or so We thought. Fall was coming like it always did, and We were becoming set in Our ways, expecting despite hints to the contrary that because a thing had always happened, it would always happen This attitude had been the downfall of Herds before Us—increasing wisdom can be offset by increasing acceptance. Fall came. It always did.

Antlers clashed.

Basso's ears flicked. Two males faced each other, fencing. Strong and sleek, they were evenly matched and after a brief sparring session they broke off, turned away and resumed grazing. An observer, a wolf, might have thought that the Herd was behaving as usual, grazing quietly. He couldn't have sensed the undercurrent of excitement, of anticipation, which had touched every adult animal on the instant the tundra echoed to the rattle of horn on horn. The first sign had been given. The Herd knew.

The rut would soon be here.

Now We began to move with more purpose. The last of the stragglers arrived and We turned south, moving steadily, over a thousand animals heading for the sun. Behind Us, the long summer's day was darkening into winter's night. From time to time we saw others of Our species but they ignored Us, grazing among the lichens as they would continue to do all winter. They were the loners, the ones who refused to answer the call of the Herd for reasons known only to themselves.

It is the Herd who dictates the migration south each fall. Without the Herd—that cohesive entity—every one of these thousand beasts would have wandered the tundra all winter, scratching the snow for poor fodder, prey to wolf and bear, growing weaker. So, when We judged the time to be right, We simply uttered the command: *south*. The Herd now had no leaders; Basso and several other exceptionally dominant males became as the others, moving south almost without conscious volition.

Snow was falling lightly as We undertook what was to be the most uneventful migration in memory. We waded rivers; as they deepened, We swam. The calves were strong and there were few losses as We followed the regular trails which the Herd had known and used throughout its existence. If the winter went well, by the spring migration north We would be more numerous than ever before.

Somehow this thought was disturbing.

And then at last We arrived at the first winter pastures; the broad spreads of alpine meadow, the hillsides, the tall evergreen trees; all so familiar in the light dusting of snow—the grass so bland and succulent after the coarse tasty tundra fodder, the ground so soft—at last We arrived. . . .

And We found You there, Man.

There was a wisp of smoke trailing high above the trees

and a few of Us grunted alarmedly, carrying a Herd memory of a flight through blazing, toppling pines, across scorching scrub. We turned away from Our accustomed path, fording the creek at a different place, climbing an unfamiliar slope, then spreading out to browse on twigs of willow and aspen. Antlers rattled in more frequent combat while other bulls, hock-deep in the undergrowth, thrashed the stems of bushes with a side-to-side movement of their great heads calculated to attract the most frigid cow.

You heard Us because the rut is not a time for stealthy movement. We sensed a sudden awareness in Your tiny Herd, and We heard Your complex conversation. You sensed Us and felt something of the power of the rut, because that night You mated violently and with strange joy.

And afterwards came the voiced thought: "Tomorrow I'll go and kill us some meat."

And with that, the image—and We found Ourselves shifting nervously.

Now the nights were long and the days short; You were stirring long before the sun touched the treetops on the opposite mountain slope. We sensed the hunger still in Your bellies. You put Your feet on the cold floor of the cabin, feeling the dampness of Old Earth beneath. Lighting lamps, dressing, building fire in the cast stove; these were all familiar chores which You didn't have to think about, after many days of living in the mountains.

Like wolves, Your inner herd was two.

Your female voiced, "Yeah, well, get lucky, huh? This is the last can of beans."

"We said we'd give it a couple of months."

"We can starve in a couple of months."

"We agreed anything was better than Edmonton. Don't tell me you've forgotten what Edmonton was like already." Your male turned away, staring at the walls, through them. "Can't you feel them? The caribou—they've come back. We'll be O.K. now."

And Your female shivered. "Take care, love." She could sense Us, too. . . .

Now this strange thing happened. Your herd divided in a way quite unlike our separate wanderings on the tundra. You divided like the wolf pack, becoming individuals with a common purpose. Unlike the wolves, however, you undertook separate roles. You became Guardian, and Killer. . . . In each other's minds, if not in Ours.

Killer picked up his rifle and came. He hiked down the slope and across the creek, jumping from rock to rock, scared to get his feet wet. Then he climbed through dense trees and undergrowth, noisily, so that the animals knew he was coming by scent and sound, and the Herd knew he was coming by Our growing instinct—and he knew We knew. He climbed away, circling, and he was trying to remember not to get dirt packed up the muzzle of his rifle, because a guy he knew had got killed like that. Complex thoughts and strange concepts not always clear to Us.

But We, the Herd, were able to catch the images behind the thoughts. Year by year the powers of the Herd grow. We knew he had climbed above Us and was sitting on a rock overlooking the alpine meadow in which We grazed, browsed and mated. We knew—yet We were not alarmed, because killing was not in Killer's mind, not then.

Guardian was thinking of killing though, at that moment. She worked in the forest near the cabin, digging a pit in the middle of a trail leading from a small clearing. When the pit was finished she was going to lay branches over it, then twigs and finally moss. She was hoping that an animal would fall into the pit and be easily caught. Every animal in the valley could hear that hope in her mind. And perhaps she knew that too, but she had to try *something*. Anything, rather than go back to Edmonton. The pit was an open black scar in the soft snow.

Guardian heard a noise and crept to the edge of the clearing.

Basso stood in the low brush. Head down, he beat at the whippy saplings with his antlers, dislodging showers of fine snow. The noise was a continuous violent flailing; eerie, apparently meaningless yet with an underlying purpose. Guardian knew the purpose, and visions moved before her mind's eye, lent strength by her own hunger-weakness. She saw Killer, she saw other men. She moved into the clearing, drawn by Basso's thrashing, her hands plucking uncertainly at her clothing. Reality came and went, came and went. The forest seemed to be waiting and she thought of fish, big silver fish, the fish which Killer had promised her would be in the creek—but which were gone.

Her legs became weak and she fell to her knees, panting. It seemed there was a woodcutter who was laying aside his ax, surprised to see her—yet not surprised He regarded her without speaking and his strength, his maleness seemed to draw something from her, to make her feel something she hadn't felt since she was young: an urge to give, to take and to share. Smiling now, the figure drew near, standing over her as she lay. There was an intensity in those eyes, and a watchfulness; his gaze moved over her slowly and she felt it like heat wherever it lay.

Guardian sighed, a mind full of visions.

And Killer felt something too. He stood suddenly and carelessly against the skyline. We, the Herd, grazed on. He jumped down from the rock, scrambled down loose scree to the meadow and ran among Us, ran past Us as We moved aside, some individual animals panicking and bolting. He ran through the trees, waded across the creek, calling to Guardian. . . .

In the clearing she shivered suddenly and found herself lying on the ground. Her clothes were wet and crumpled about her. Shaking her head, she stood—and was in time to see Basso and Goldenfoot, having mated, walk away together into the forest.

"Are you all right?"

Your herd re-formed, re-united.

"I fainted from hunger, that's what happened. Listen, let's get back to Edmonton, huh? We were wrong. This is no place for us."

"It has to be here. Edmonton's dying. Everywhere's dying. This is the only place. Listen—I saw caribou today, dozens of them."

Sudden rage. "So did I! Right out there in the bush, and *you* had the gun! Now, listen to me. Tomorrow you forget all this crap about making like the great sportsman, and just get out back and *shoot something*. What in hell is the matter with you? The caribou have been around for days. Bear, too. Even squirrels, for God's sake."

"I've got them staked out. Tomorrow, honey."

"Not up that mountain. *Out back*. There's a big bastard with horns—I want *him*. Or better still, *the one with him* . . ."

You stared at each other, and the roles were not clear any more.

Yet the next day Killer crept up the mountain again, and sat on top where he could see the world and Us. His mind rested more easily, up there. His thoughts came to Us like drifting thistledown, thoughts of the place he called Edmonton where everyone lived in tunnels and ate canned food from looted stores. Thoughts of the rest of the world which—he felt—was exactly like Edmonton.

From these thoughts We understood You are very nearly an extinct species. Three generations of living off a civilization's stored food until the remaining cans must be fought for; three generations of unfavourable mutations until a sound child is also something to be fought for; three generations of such hunger that Your own very flesh is something to be fought for—this is the way you have gone, Man. You have lost art and science, you have lost culture and agriculture, until all you have is a gun, a small handcart of supplies, and each other, in that order of importance.

You didn't even have the skill to build the cabin in which You now live. You found it, left there a hundred years ago by some forgotten farmer, and You moved in. You feel You have accomplished something by the mere fact of taking a dead man's house. You feel things are moving ahead. We have come back to Our wintering grounds and—so you think—meat is here for the taking, for the pressing of a trigger.

Oh, Man, are you in for a disappointment!

Yet Killer pressed that trigger.

He screamed again! Again!

He dragged the carcass down the hill. Snow fell, and a solitary wolf skulked through the trees, watching him. Just one wolf, hungrily watching as Killer dragged meat home.

That winter the snow was light. Grass and lichen was available for the simple drawing of a hoof. The turmoil of the rut over, We ate peacefully, while the smoke rose in a slender column from Your ancient cabin. We let You be, never venturing nearer than earshot, never disturbing the snow from the queer plants near Your cabin because, that winter, there was enough food for all. . . .

We knew when the Man-calf was born, We shared Your joy.

Basso left Goldenfoot and wandered off with the other scrawny bulls, depleted by the demands of the rut, leaving the cows to browse on alder around the lower slopes. Soon the females too would be drifting further south. The bulls went first and Our entity diminished, spread out over long distances. As they went they sparred in desultory manner and shed their great antlers. They gnawed on the cast horn, replenishing the body's supply of vital salts, watched by wolves which became fewer day by day, observed by bears in passing but not molested.

Later We shared Your thoughts, Your anguish.

"Get on out there, you bum. If you won't provide for me, at least have some thought for the baby. The simple life, you said. Ha! At least there was food in Edmonton."

"They're moving south."

"Well, go kill a couple before they're all gone!"

"It's not that simple. They have a sort of sixth sense."

The fury in Your voiced thoughts burned Our mind. "Try. Just try. Just get up off your butt, get out there and try. You did it once, now do it again. Otherwise I move out tomorrow. Okay?"

Our nearest limb at that moment was Goldenfoot, browsing on willow twigs on the banks of a stream which, lower, flowed past the cottage. She received the hate and fear thoughts, became uneasy and grunted for Basso. But her mate was gone. Suddenly aware of her aloneness she thought of her calf. She sensed its presence further down the creek, near the cabin. Snuffling with alarm she broke into a trot, smashing through bushes.

Your herd divided. . . .

"Okay, okay! I said Okay!"

And We caught the image of the gun as Killer snatched it from the shelf, and We began to draw together, an instinctive gathering in the face of danger. Because he had killed before and he might kill again, against all that has become natural.

Goldenfoot, forgetting, fell.

The ground disappeared for an instant, then she felt something smash into her shoulder, and something else snapped underneath. . . .

We thought: *the pit!*

Goldenfoot screamed in pain and tried to move.

"Out back. Listen—do you hear that? The forest is alive with them." Then Guardian caught the echo of Goldenfoot's agony, and was silent.

Still Killer did not admit to Guardian why You were lost; there are some things about You We will never understand, Man. Killer took the rifle up the creekside and his brain screamed with Goldenfoot's pain, which he felt as though it were his own. So he walked on, weeping, his mind filled with the desolation which was filling Us too—which was filling the whole forest; the bears, the beavers, the wolves. . . . Killer came to Goldenfoot as she lay with her broken leg in that pit Guardian had dug, and he looked, weeping.

Guardian voiced the thought: "Put it out of its misery, love. I can't stand it."

Such agony, such sorrow. For a while You were of Us, as the forest mourned. Killer limped forward, feeling a phantom pain in his perfect leg, and raised the gun. He thought: *the head*.

He fired.

And yes, he missed. That bullet of heavy, smooth metal ripped into Goldenfoot just above the shoulder, bored through flesh in an instant—You felt it, We felt it!—struck bone with a jarring that shook every living thing in the forest, deflected and drove downwards through liver and lung, veins and arteries within the ribcage, tearing and destroying until finally, spent, it lodged in the intestine.

Killer dropped the gun, crying out, and fell to the ground.

We disassociated Ourself from the pain. We have that power. It is necessary—deaths within the Herd used to be frequent. We left the pain with the individuals in the forest, with Goldenfoot. . . . And with You, Man.

Killer crawled on the ground. "Oh, Christ. Oh, Christ."

"Please, love. Give me the gun."

And in the cabin the Man-calf was screaming.

Killer watched her standing there with her hand outstretched for the gun, his face wet with tears, the pain burning in his gut—and he knew the same pain burned in her gut too, but she was a female and more used to bearing such pain. . . .

Your herd united. Killer, Guardian, the distinction was lost to Us. It didn't matter anymore. You kneeled, then stood, clutching Yourself, lifting the rifle, weeping, flinching away as You pointed it at the head of Goldenfoot and pulled the trigger. . . .

Then You screamed once, short and sharp, and dropped.

We passed Your way in the spring during Our long trek north to the tundra. As We neared the valley there was some uncertainty in Our mind because We remembered the killing of winter. But We reached out and felt no menace so We passed through, grazing and browsing on Our accustomed grounds.

Basso was fleshing out well again and Goldenfoot was forgotten—as is the fate of individuals. Basso returned to the small clearing near the cabin more by instinct than any conscious remembrance and, while grazing, observed an interesting thing.

The snow had melted some time previously, and all over that area surrounding the cabin strange plants were sprouting—plants which We had seen before but never *considered*. Now We considered them briefly and as Basso moved forward to nibble at the nearest We warned him: *leave them alone. They are Man-plants.* They had been planted a hundred years ago by the last Man, and they had grown and multiplied each succeeding year, waiting for Man to return. Basso moved away and as he did Your female came out of the cabin and saw him. She smiled. . . .

And now Basso saw Your male.

He was wielding an implement on the other side of the cabin, turning the dark soil. He bent, and began to insert plants into a shallow trench, when Your female called:

"The caribou are back!"

He looked up, caught sight of Basso moving back into the trees, and greeted him, "Hi there, old fellow!" There was nothing but pleasure in Your thoughts. The sun was warm and the Man-calf lay gurgling in a rough crib. Fat birds strutted around an enclosed area—they had no thought in *their* minds, but We caught a glimpse of eggs from Your female's mind as she walked towards them.

Your male was still watching Basso, and now We caught the image of the rifle—and he grimaced, grinned, and returned to his work.

Man, You will never kill again.

You will live and prosper, because You have the capability to work with Your hands, to till the ground, to create food from dirt. Unlike the wolf, who must die because he is carnivorous. For how can any flesh-eating creature survive, when he must share the agony of his victim?

Seasons ago just a few calves were born with this new power—and they survived, because their fear and pain caused any wolf, any bear to draw back. They survived and bred, while Our more normal animals died out. Soon We all had this new power—and We were glad at first, because it is in Our nature to want to survive as individuals and as the Herd.

Yet We are doomed.

We were doomed from the first moment a wolf slunk away, unable to press home his kill because of the terror and pain of his victim burning in his mind. We are doomed because Paddler is still alive, and Swayback, and many others who ought to be dead because they are slightly *wrong* and weak, but who breed on year after year because *that* is an instinct. We all have. Individuals wouldn't know this. They struggle to survive; but We, the Herd, know. We know what is best for Us—and it is best that all the weak calves and all the queer calves die in the first season. But We can't make a calf die.

Only the wolves can do that. And soon there will be no more wolves.

The Arctic night is long.

ACHRONOS

by Lee Killough

A visit to the end of the world seems to be a good way to end this anthology. By the end of the world, humanity should have achieved every wonderful goal, have worked all the marvels dreamed by science fiction writers and social utopians, should be just about godlike in their being. Come along then with Lee Killough to the place where time has lapsed and meet our magnificent descendants.

The beach was a Tanguy landscape. Its grass-whiskered dunes, cast-up shells, and driftwood lay sharply etched in light and shadow before a background of fine mist that obscured the sea and distant arms of the cove and cast a glowing blue twilight over the beach even now in early afternoon. At least, Neil Dorn thought it should be early afternoon, though he could not swear to it. The past few days were a blur. He had driven blindly, following one highway after another down the coast, the roads growing increasingly narrower and less used, until he ended up on a sandy track and ran out of road here.

The smell of brine and seaweed was sharp in his nose, the seabreeze cool as it brushed his face and lifted his hair. Neil picked his way through the broken shells along the sea's edge, feeling the surf suck the sand from under his bare toes. This was the right place to come, he felt. He could be alone here. In the misty twilight, he could forget everything but the moment.

He could forget shrugging art dealers and paintings that no longer sold. He could shut out Connie, grown from the da Vinci beauty he had married to Reubens obesity, and her voice, shrill from disappointment and the strain of obsessive dieting.

"No wonder nothing sells. You paint the same things over and over. You need new vision."

As though vision could be ordered from a supply house, he thought bitterly. Well, to hell with her. To hell with everyone.

It was then, looking down, that he found the trilobite. Neil was no paleontologist, but he remembered enough from biology in high school and college to recognize that shape among the clamshells and sand dollars around it. He bent to pick it up. It was a moderate size, about six inches long. How had it come to be there? Trilobites did not ordinarily wash up out of the Paleozoic Era onto Twentieth Century beaches. It was in perfect condition, too. It looked as fresh as the sand dollar next to it, not at all like a fossil.

He put the shell in his shirt pocket and continued along the beach, feeling like the last man in the world. It would be easy to believe nothing existed beyond what he saw, that the universe consisted of nothing more than a misty cove and surf hissing over sand. He reveled in the feeling.

His satisfaction shattered in a bitter stab of anger at the sound of voices ahead of him. So he was not alone after all. Damn. Was there nowhere in the world uncontaminated by people?

The intruders appeared out of the mist a moment later. There were three, all children, slim and sexless, playing in near nudity on the sand. Neil was torn between his anger and a rush of pleasure. Against the glowing blue twilight, the children looked like a Maxfield Parrish illustration.

He called to them.

They stopped the intricate design they were building with shells and looked around. Two were fair, one with a short cap of curls, the other with hair reaching nearly to her buttocks. Both their eyes were blue as the twilight. The third had waist-length black hair and intense black eyes. They stared at him. The dark one nudged the long-haired fair one and whispered something. The fair one laughed.

Neil felt shock. The laugh was low and throaty, not a child's laugh at all.

The dark one said something that sounded like, "Gret."

They circled him, looking at him with curious eyes. He stared back. He had been wrong. They were not children, though they were still very young, hardly past adolescence. They were as tall as he and slender as willows, with skin tight and smooth. Clear, lively eyes watched him from unlined faces. And they were completely nude, he discovered with a start. What he had taken to be scraps of bathing suit were only designs painted on their skin.

The girl with short curls spoke. Neil could not understand a word. The girl frowned and scratched absently at the shell painted on one nipple. She spoke to her companions.

The dark one said something rapidly, then planting herself in front of Neil, began speaking in a loud, slow voice.

He wondered how treating him like he was deaf or retarded would help him understand her, but to his surprise, it did. What she said was distorted and oddly accented to his ears, but somewhere inside him he recognized enough of the words to grasp the sense of what she said. She was asking who he was.

He replied, "Neil Dorn."

Her smile was one of triumph. She pointed to herself. "Electra." Her finger turned to the long-haired fair girl. "Ivrian." Finally she pointed at the curly-haired girl. "Hero. When are you from?"

That was what it sounded like, anyway. Neil was sure she could not mean that. She must mean either *where* was he from or *when* had he *come* here. Since he did not know which she intended, he shook his head. "I don't understand." He decided to ask a question of his own. "Are you vacationing around here with your parents?"

That appeared to amuse them. Electra and Ivrian caught at his arms. "No parents." Laughing, they pulled him with them toward the dunes. "We'll introduce you to our companions."

They were camped in the dunes just off the beach. Like some Renoir painting, tents in gay circus colors clustered on the sand: red and white, green and yellow, blue and gold. Between the bright splashes moved several dozen people, all tall, slim, and laughing, like the three girls. Some wore nothing, or nothing but body paints, while others seemed to have wrapped themselves in fringe from hips to shoulders or been draped in abbreviated togas and sarongs. Whatever the covering, it was clearly for adornment rather than modesty or protection, and all of it was in colors that glowed in the mist.

The girls called to their companions, talking so fast Neil could not follow. The others raced to meet them. Neil found himself the center of an excited, chattering crowd, with fingers plucking at his clothing and touching the stubble of beard on his face. Electra pointed and called names that for the most part went by in a blur: Clell, Garold, Byron, Capricorn, Aries, Gemini, Pilar, Vesta. No one appeared to have a last name. Neil wondered if any were real names. Surely the zodiac names were assumed.

The swirl around him was exhausting. He started looking for a way out.

Hero caught his eye and smiled. "Here." Tugging at his arm, she pulled him through the crowd to a stool under the awning of a blue and silver tent.

"Thank you." It had never been a thanks more heartfelt. He looked up at them standing around him. "Who are you people?"

Several of them chuckled.

Electra sat down on a stool beside him. "We're . . . trippers . . . on a party."

"You mean on vacation, on holiday?"

She licked her lips. For a moment her black eyes flicked away. "Yes, on holiday."

Before he could wonder at the edge in her voice, she jumped up, laughing. "You must join us."

"I'd like that." Every one of them was so exquisitely beautiful they made his fingers itch for the sketch pad and charcoal he had left in his Scout up the beach. "Just let me go bring something from my own camp." He stood.

Electra wrapped her arm around his. "Let me come with you to get it."

She walked back up the beach with him. The Scout seemed to astonish her. She stared at it for several long minutes, then insisted he bring it and his supplies back to their camp. "You can stay in my tent."

The look in her eyes as she said it sent warmth through him. At the same time, he could hardly believe it. This child was offering herself to him? How could she know what she was doing?

As though reading his mind, Electra licked her lips, tracing her mouth slowly with the sharp pink tip of her tongue. She smiled.

Neil felt his pulse pound. She did know what she was doing. There was experience in that smile and in the gesture of her tongue. He felt a little breathless. He had had no woman but Connie for a long time, and Electra—he let his eyes wander down her sleek body, lingering on the painted stars covering her nipples and pubic area—Electra was nothing like Connie.

The—what should he call them? Electra's word would do, he supposed—the trippers were making a meal when the two of them came back in the Scout. He was no sooner out of the vehicle than they were pulling him to a stool and handing him a plate of food.

He did not know what it was. He had never had anything like it before. There seemed to be half a dozen different meats and vegetables, and something like rice. There were potatoes fixed as he had never eaten them before. The meal ended in a choice of desserts that would have shamed a gourmet restaurant.

"Do you eat like this all the time?"

Electra looked surprised. "If a meal isn't a banquet, what's the point of eating?"

She did not say exactly that. He could still not understand much of what she said, but that was the general meaning. He filled the blanks with what he hoped were appropriate words.

"How do you stay so thin, then?"

That surprised her even more. "It's only a matter of adjusting the metabolism."

She must go to a diet doctor Connie had never tried.

"Are you from around here?"

Electra sampled from a tray of fruits. "I suppose we are now."

"You mean you're recent arrivals in the area?"

Several of the trippers looked around. Electra considered. She smiled. "Yes . . . and no."

The amused note in her answer disturbed him. Something was more than strange here; something was wrong. They could not be just an ethnic group with a strange accent.

Out of thinking about their strangeness came fear. His food settled into a hard lump in his stomach. The hair on his neck began twitching. He had to get away.

He stood. "I need something from my car."

They made no attempt to stop him from walking away, but

Electra followed. She was just a girl, he reassured himself, forcing himself not to run. He could easily break away from her if he needed to. In any case, none of the trippers had shown any signs of hostility . . . yet.

"What's wrong, Neil?"

He rummaged through his gear, hoping she would leave. "Nothing."

She smiled. "You're a poor liar. Are you afraid of us?"

"Certainly not."

Her smile broadened. "A very poor liar. There's no reason to be afraid. We won't hurt you. We're fascinated by you. We've never seen anyone like you before. Twentieth Century people and vehicles like this are just museum pictures to us."

His head snapped toward her. "Museum pictures!"

She picked up his sketch pad. "What's this?" She opened it. Her black eyes widened. "Drawings." She looked up. "Do you really draw? By hand? Yourself?"

He resisted the desire to snatch the sketchbook away. "I'm an artist, yes."

Her face went incandescent with delight. "Oh, bring this back and draw me. I've never seen anyone draw by hand before."

"But the light won't be any good before long. Tomorrow, perhaps."

She laughed at him again. "The light won't change."

It was only then he realized that it had not changed since he arrived on the beach. He had been there for hours, yet the twilight was exactly the same.

Suddenly he was very frightened indeed. There was more strangeness here than just the trippers. He thought of the legends of fairy hills. They were just stories, of course, but what was around him was real. What *was* around him?

He was barely aware of being pulled back to the group, of his charcoal and sketchbook being thrust into his hands by an impatient, demanding Electra. "Draw me, Neil."

He sat with charcoal in his hand but made no move toward the sketchbook.

"He draws by hand," Electra told them. "Neil, show them."

He looked around at the beautiful, strange people. "Why doesn't the light change? Who are you? What's going on?"

A ripple of amusement ran through the group.

Only Hero did not smile. She frowned at her companions.

"How is he supposed to know?" She squatted before him. "This is an achronos point, a place where time is frozen."

Neil blinked. "What?"

A dark-skinned boy wearing a bright gold and green sarong—Neil thought the boy was named Clell—said, "Time is like a stream, but as it flows through the universe and eternity, it hits occasional snags. That makes currents and eddies and, sometimes, quiet pools where time doesn't flow at all. This beach is one of those pools. We think perhaps it's because of the timelessness of the sea and sand."

Hero said, "So there's always twilight and there are no tides. Nothing changes here."

Neil's head rang. He felt like he was about to faint. "But I walked onto it like any other beach."

"So did we," Clell said. "We don't quite understand why, but because an achron is timeless, it touches all times. It's simultaneously accessible to anyone from any time."

Neil remembered the trilobite in his pocket. He took it out and stared at it. "You mean this actually washed up out of the Paleozoic?"

They nodded.

"And I come from the Twentieth Century. You—" He looked around at them. *When are you from?* Electra had asked when they met. "You're from the future." He said it in awe.

They nodded.

It took his breath away. "When?"

Hero shrugged. "The dating system is different for us. It wouldn't mean anything to you. It's a very long time from your century to ours, though."

"Have people flown to the stars? Have they met alien intelligences?"

There was a ripple through them, a shifting and turning away. Hero bit her lip.

It occurred to Neil they might have rules about what they could tell people from the past. "I'm sorry," he apologized. He changed the subject. "What happens when I want to leave?"

"You just walk away." Hero resumed her smile. "You re-enter time at the same moment you left it. You'll begin to age again and time will go on for you as before."

"Begin to age again? You mean right now I'm not—"

"Nothing changes here."

He drew a breath. "What did you call this place?"

"An achronos point, an achron."

"And people of your time know about them? They're probably popular vacation places, aren't they?" Imagine being able to spend a year on vacation and come back into time without losing a day of work or a single paycheck. "So you're all on vacation here?"

Again there was a ripple of uneasiness, almost embarassment. Electra scowled at him. "Enough talk. Draw me, Neil. I want to see someone draw by hand."

It was like a signal. The next moment they were closing in on him, laughing and animated, all demanding to be drawn. As fast as he worked, charcoal flying over the pages, sketching one after the other, they wanted him to draw faster. Each sketch was greeted with a chorus of exclamations.

Their admiration buoyed him up and carried him forward on a crest of elation he had not felt in a long time. He made sketch after sketch, of Electra, of Ivrian, Hero, of Clell, Aries, Capricorn, Vesta . . . of all of them. The torn-out pages drifted to the sand around him, filled by their bright faces. Only when the sketchbook was used up would they let him alone.

He sagged on his stool, mind still churning but body exhausted. "Do people sleep in an achron?" he asked wearily.

"Of course." Electra caught him by the hand. "This way." She led him toward a black and gold tent.

He looked back. "My sketches."

"I'll look after them." Hero began gathering them, laying one on top of the next in a neat, precise stack.

Electra pulled him into the tent and dropped the flap.

Neil soon discovered he was not so tired after all. Electra had an entire encyclopedia of sexual tricks and took pride in demonstrating them all. His eventual protests that now he really *was* worn out just pushed her to greater efforts.

"Please. Enough," he begged. "Go play with one of your companions. They're younger and stronger than I am."

She frowned. "But I've done it all with all of them. There's nothing novel in putting them on. You're new. Here, let me try this and see if we can't go round one more time."

Eventually not even her enthusiasm and vigor could rouse him any longer. As he dropped into sleep, it occurred to Neil that if no one aged in an achron, one could gain a great deal of experience, of subjective age, without showing physical signs of it. How old might these young people really be?

By the time he woke Neil had forgotten that question. Opening his eyes to find Electra nestled under his arm left him marveling at her childlike beauty. He remembered, too, the adulation of the trippers while he sketched. The memory sent pleasure through him and helped beat back the stiffness caused by the acrobatics with Electra. His oils were in the Scout. If they had liked sketching so much, how might they react to seeing him paint?

He slid off the sleeping mat without waking Electra and pulled on his jeans and shirt.

It was a shock at first not to see a dawn outside, only the same glowing twilight that had seen him into the tent. He had always liked dawns. He missed the one that should have been here.

A number of trippers were up and about, looking as though they had been awake for some time. A couple were muttering about going to bed. That surprised him until he thought about it. Without the normal rhythm of night and day, each person would live on a personal cycle.

Clell and Capricorn were awake, involved in some complex game requiring shells to be moved across the sand in intricate patterns. They were so engrossed they just nodded to him as he passed. Clell made what must have been a good move. He chuckled. Capricorn cursed long and with a viciousness that startled Neil. As a final gesture, Capricorn kicked Clell's shell pattern apart and stalked off among the tents. Clell called something after him in an insulting tone. Despite the frowns and angry voices, though, Neil saw a certain satisfaction in the two trippers. It gave him the distinct impression that they were enjoying the quarrel, relishing their anger.

Neil shook his head. They were odd people.

At the Scout he found Hero sitting on the hood. Her body was painted with a blue lace design. She sat with face intense, studying last night's sketches.

She looked up as he approached. "Can you teach me to do this?"

"I can try," he smiled. "It interests you?"

She shrugged. "It's something different to do."

He raised his brows. "Something different? You sound bored."

"I am."

"Would you like to sit for a portrait?"

Her eyes snapped into focus on him. "You mean a real

painting? Like in a museum?" Sitting up straight, she raked her fingers through her curls. "What do I do?"

He pulled his oils and a canvas out of the back of the Scout. "First wash off that lace design. Can you find one of those toga-tunic things to wear?"

"Of course." She ran toward the tents.

Neil set up his easel near the water's edge. He would paint her in the style of Maxfield Parrish, he decided. Leaning over some shells, silhouetted against the glowing blue of the mist, she would be perfectly suited to it.

He was mixing paints, struggling for the right shade of blue, when Hero came back. She had most of the other trippers with her. In a toga that bared one small breast and draped low on her slim hips, she did indeed look like a Parrish subject. Now if he could only get the blue right.

"Everyone else is going to watch," she said. "Is that all right with you?"

"I'd be a better subject." It was Electra, of course, with a pout. "Why didn't you ask me?"

"You were asleep. I'll do one of you, too." He sighed. "I wish I had enough canvases to make portraits of you all to take back with me."

"Back with you?" A murmur of dismay went through them. "You're not going to leave?"

"I can't stay here forever."

Electra looked at him. "Why not?"

He stopped and considered. No one would miss him. Time outside was stopped for him, and he could leave whenever he wanted. Meanwhile, he had the company and adoration of these charming people. So why not stay? To hell with Connie and the dealers and finding new vision. This was vision enough.

"I won't leave right away."

He showed Hero how he wanted her to stand. "When you get tired, tell me and I'll let you rest a while." He dipped a brush into the blue. "How long are you people going to be here?"

Electra leaned over his shoulder as he began brushing on the first color areas. "That's just a blob of color. Does it really become a picture?"

"Watch."

They did, for a while, but he soon saw that painting was not going to fascinate them as much as sketching did. It went too slowly. One by one they became bored and wandered away until only he and Hero were left. Even Hero complained of being tired, though she did not want to stop posing. He heard the voices of the others off around the cove, shouting and laughing.

Hero was beginning to emerge from the canvas. She looked different than he intended. Instead of a Parrish subject, she looked more like something created by Toulouse-Lautrec, bright and gay on the surface but hard and sad beneath. He peered at her. To his surprise, he found the painting correct. His eyes had seen and his hands transmitted what his mind did not notice. He remembered her remark about boredom.

"Where would you rather be than here?" he asked.

Her sigh came from her soul. "Just about anywhere. I want to see different faces, experience new weather. I'd like to see the night sky again. I've always wanted to go to the stars. I was going to go to Zulac after school, but of course that trip was ruined along with the laser cannon on Pluto." Her voice grew wistful. "I was just two years late to ever visit the stars. I'm trapped here instead."

He looked at her around the easel. "Trapped? You can leave when you want, can't you?"

She looked up. Her eyes swam with despair. "No, I can't. This isn't a holiday; it's sanctuary. We left time in the last safe moments."

Cold washed through him in an icy wave. The brush felt stiff in his hand. "Last safe moments before what?"

Hero straightened and stretched, shaking her head. "It doesn't matter. Nothing can change the fact that this is a party at the end of the world, and no matter how monotonous, the party has to go on, because we're all too cowardly to end it." Her mouth twisted in a sardonic grimace that looked grotesque on her child's face. "Welcome to eternity . . . if you can stand the tedium."

"Hero!" It was Electra's voice, calling from up the beach. "Neil!"

She came out of the mist at them, running hard, black hair flying. Her face was alight and her eyes brilliant. "There's a dinosaur in the dunes on the other side of the cove. Clell is baiting it. Come and see."

A dinosaur? That sounded incredible, but if he and the trippers could wander in here and a trilobite wash up on the beach, why not expect a dinosaur to come walking through? "What kind of dinosaur?"

Electra tossed her head. "How should I know? It looks vicious is all I know. Hurry before it's all over."

She was off again. Hero was right behind her. Neil stared after them a minute with visions of a tyrannosaurus rex raging in the dunes, then he followed, too.

He heard the noise long before the dinosaur was visible. The reptilian hissing and roaring was overlaid by human voices shrill with excitement. Neil came out of the mist behind Hero and Electra to look down into a natural bowl formed by the depression between three dunes. In the bottom, twenty feet of prehistoric saurian stood high on long, muscular hind legs, bracing on its tail like a kangaroo. Tiny forelegs were folded against its chest. Its neck swiveled as it hissed and clashed a frightening set of teeth at Clell, who was running in mad circles around it, waving a driftwood club. The creature did not look to Neil like drawings purporting to show how the tyrannosaurus had looked. That was some relief, but the beast was still one of the predatory species. It started crouching, tail trembling a bit.

"For god's sake, Clell, stop that," Neil shouted. "You'll be killed!"

Clell laughed. "I'm faster than it is."

The saurian sprang. Three-clawed hind feet slashed for Clell. The tripper dodged sideways. The saurian followed with murderous speed, but Clell was even faster. The claws missed him by a wide margin.

Clell laughed up at Neil. "See?"

His companions yelled encouragement from where they stood on the dunes ringing the bowl. They waved driftwood and stones.

The saurian leaped again and again Clell was out of the way before it landed. The saurian hissed. Its lashing tail flung sand at the ring of watchers.

"You're too cautious, Clell," Electra yelled. "Move close."

Neil glared at her. "No! Stay back!"

Clell closed in on the saurian. He rapped it on the back with his club. The saurian came around just a moment too late to catch the tripper with its teeth. The spectators cheered in delight.

"Clell," Neil pleaded.

But grinning, Clell went back in again. This time, however, what Neil feared happened. The saurian anticipated him. A front claw raked down the tripper's arm. Blood spurted.

As though it were a signal, the trippers shrieked with a

single voice and charged down into the bowl. The saurian disappeared under a wave of human bodies. Even Electra and Hero joined. Neil was left alone on the side of the dune. He was horrified by what was happening, yet the excitement caught at him, too. Never before had humans hunted a dinosaur. Perhaps none ever would again, and he was here to see when puny humans challenged a thunder lizard.

The saurian was screaming. Human voices were screaming, too, though whether in agony, ecstasy, or anger was impossible to determine. The pile of saurian and humans twisted and heaved. The great tail lashed, churning up the sand. Human arms rose and fell, pounding wrinkled hide with clubs and stones and daggershards of shell. The air sharpened with the smell of blood.

Then all at once it was over. The saurian lay silent and unmoving on the sand. The victors backed off, yelling in triumph. Some dipped fingers in the saurian's blood and began painting each other.

Electra raced up the dune toward Neil, face ablaze. She threw her arms around him. "Wasn't it *exciting!* Put me on, right here, right now." She began pulling at his shirt. "It was so glorious. You should have joined. You should—"

Neil was distracted. Someone, somewhere, was still screaming. Only now it had the note of pain, not triumph. He looked down the dune to see Hero sprawled beside the saurian, clutching at her stomach. Blood poured between her fingers. "My god." Neil stumbled down the dune toward her.

When he reached her he wanted to cry. The saurian had opened her from shoulders to thighs with one rake of a hind foot. He started to kneel beside her.

Electra caught at his arm. "Neil, forget her. Put me on."

He turned on her incredulously. "How can you think of that *now?* We have to help Hero."

Electra scowled. "She's dying. Forget her."

Hero stared up at him with pain-glazed eyes. Her mouth worked. A hoarse whisper emerged. "I wanted to leave the party, but, god, this hurts so—" She went slack.

Neil felt a chill. No one aged here, but they could still die.

"You see," Electra said, "she's dead. Now, take off your clothes. Let me paint you with blood."

Neil slapped away her hands. "Hero is supposed to be your friend," he shouted. "Don't you care about her?"

She licked her lips. "What I care about is that I feel passion now I haven't felt in a very, very long time. I want to make the most of it."

Neil looked around. "Do *any* of you care?"

No one answered him. They were too busy starting an orgy. They were no Renoir painting now, no Maxfield Parrish. Neil was reminded of the hell panel from Hieronymus Bosch's "Garden of Earthly Delights."

Electra snapped, "If you're not interested, I'll find someone who is."

She flung away in disgust and hurled herself at Capricorn, who was carving a piece of hide from the saurian's flank. He caught her and bent her backwards over the huge carcass.

"No," Neil said, "I guess none of you do."

All they cared about was finding some new excitement to alleviate their boredom: a stranger, an old art form, a little blood and mayhem. What would be next? What would happen, he began to wonder, when they tired of their Twentieth Century pet? The possibilities sent cold through his bones.

He found himself running back around the beach toward the Scout. He was almost to the car before he remembered the rough painting of Hero, still by the water. He went after it and picked up the pile of sketches where Hero had left them on the hood.

So he needed a new vision. Well, by god, he had one now. He wished to god he did not have it . . . a Tanguy beach and a Bosch orgy, and dozens of desperately bright faces from the end of the world. They would probably haunt him the rest of his life. He hoped Connie was prepared to cope with his nightmares, and the public with what he put on canvas.

He gunned the motor into life and kicked in the four-wheel drive. With the visions burning from his head to his fingertips, he headed the Scout back across the dunes into time.

DAW BOOKS

Presenting JACK VANCE in DAW editions:

The "Demon Princes" Novels

☐ **STAR KING**   #UE1402—$1.75
☐ **THE KILLING MACHINE**   #UE1409—$1.75
☐ **THE PALACE OF LOVE**   #UE1442—$1.75
☐ **THE FACE**   #UJ1498J—$1.95
☐ **THE BOOK OF DREAMS**   #UE1587—$2.25

The "Tschai" Novels

☐ **CITY OF THE CHASCH**   #UE1461—$1.75
☐ **SERVANTS OF THE WANKH**   #UE1467—$1.75
☐ **THE DIRDIR**   #UE1478—$1.75
☐ **THE PNUME**   #UE1484—$1.75

The "Alastor" Trilogy

☐ **TRULLION: ALASTOR 2262**   #UE1590—$2.25
☐ **MARUNE: ALASTOR 933**   #UE1591—$2.25
☐ **WYST: ALASTOR 1716**   #UE1593—$2.25

Others

☐ **EMPHYRIO**   #UE1504—$2.25
☐ **THE FIVE GOLD BANDS**   #UJ1518—$1.95
☐ **THE MANY WORLDS OF MAGNUS RIDOLPH**   #UE1531—$1.75
☐ **THE LANGUAGES OF PAO**   #UE1541—$1.75
☐ **NOPALGARTH**   #UE1563—$2.25
☐ **DUST OF FAR SUNS**   #UE1588—$1.75

If you wish to order these titles,

please see the coupon in

the back of this book.

DAW presents TANITH LEE

"A brilliant supernova in the firmament of SF"—Progressef

To order these titles,
use coupon on the
last page of this book.

10th Year as the SF Leader!

Outstanding science fiction and fantasy

By Brian Stableford

- [ ] **OPTIMAN** (#UJ1571—$1.95)
- [ ] **THE CITY OF THE SUN** (#UW1377—$1.50)
- [ ] **CRITICAL THRESHOLD** (#UY1282—$1.25)

By John Brunner

- [ ] **THE WRONG END OF TIME** (#UE1598—$1.75)
- [ ] **THE AVENGERS OF CARRIG** (#UE1509—$1.75)
- [ ] **TO CONQUER CHAOS** (#UJ1596—$1.95)
- [ ] **TOTAL ECLIPSE** (#UW1398—$1.50)

By Gordon R. Dickson

- [ ] **THE STAR ROAD** (#UJ1526—$1.95)
- [ ] **ANCIENT, MY ENEMY** (#UE1552—$1.75)
- [ ] **NONE BUT MAN** (#UE1621—$2.25)
- [ ] **HOUR OF THE HORDE** (#UE1514—$1.75)

By M. A. Foster

- [ ] **THE GAMEPLAYERS OF ZAN** (#UE1497—$2.25)
- [ ] **THE DAY OF THE KLESH** (#UE1514—$2.25)
- [ ] **WAVES** (#UE1569—$2.25)
- [ ] **THE WARRIORS OF DAWN** (#UJ1573—$1.95)

By Ian Wallace

- [ ] **THE WORLD ASUNDER** (#UW1262—$1.50)
- [ ] **HELLER'S LEAP** (#UE1475—$2.25)
- [ ] **THE LUCIFER COMET** (#UE1581—$2.25)

To order these books,
use coupon on last page.

Presenting C. J. CHERRYH